TO KNOW MISS MAY

Printed in the United States of America

Published by Draft Horse Publishing

First Printed Edition, April 2023

ISBN: 978-1-956091-07-6

Deborah M. Hathaway

BOOKS BY DEBORAH M. HATHAWAY

A Cornish Romance Series

On the Shores of Tregalwen, a Prequel Novella

Behind the Light of Golowduyn, Book One

For the Lady of Lowena, Book Two

Near the Ruins of Penharrow, Book Three

In the Waves of Tristwick, Book Four

From the Fields of Porthlenn, Book Five

Belles of Christmas Multi-Author Series

Nine Ladies Dancing, Book Four

On the Second Day of Christmas, Book Four

Seasons of Change Multi-Author Series

The Cottage by Coniston, Book Five

Sons of Somerset Multi-Author Series

Carving for Miss Coventry, Book One

Christmas Escape Multi-Author Series (Contemporary)

Christmas Baggage

Castles & Courtship Multi-Author Series

To Know Miss May, Book Two

For John and Hayley,

Thank you for your love, for your support, and
for letting me take you on a tour around Cornwall!

Best trip ever.

PRONUNCIATION GUIDE

Marazion - ma-ruh-ZAI-uhn
Nanstallon - NAN-STAL-in
Cormoran - COR-mor-in
ye – ee

CHAPTER ONE

"I declare after all there is no enjoyment like reading!"
Pride & Prejudice, Jane Austen

Cornwall, April 1815

Lowering a book when one had just delved deep into the small, black-printed words of an engaging drama was a magnanimous feat for any literate individual.

For Miss Lavinia May, however, such a task was nearly impossible—nay, *unheard* of. Yet thrice she'd peered beyond the words of *The Life and Strange Surprising Adventures of Robinson Crusoe,* and, dare she say, she would do so again.

There was nothing she could find wrong with the novel. In truth, this story was shaping up to be her sixth favorite tale ever. But her lack of attention to Daniel Defoe's marooned sailor merely proved how desperately she loved the captivating view before her.

The view of St. Michael's Mount.

Karrek Loos yn Koos.

In the Cornish tongue, it meant *the grey rock in the woods,* as the Mount had once been surrounded by woodland.

Now, however, to an ordinary eye—an outsider's eye—the Mount was but a bit of land resting in the midst of the sea, connected to mainland Cornwall via a thin, cobblestoned causeway. But to those who inhabited the small tidal island, St Michael's was a place of wonder and beauty, of pilgrimages and faith, of legends and history.

The large mound burgeoned up from the water like a mighty sea creature, strong and sturdy and powerful, formed to take on any foe foolish enough to fight. And yet, with large, billowing trees situated between the terraced houses lining the bottom of the Mount and the mighty castle perched at the top, the island emanated a degree of gentility and ethereal beauty.

Was there anywhere so enchanting on this earth? She proclaimed that there was not. Never mind that she'd seen nothing of the world beyond Bodmin. Was it her fault that she only ever wished to leave the Mount to *look* at the Mount? No, it was not. Because when one lived in Heaven, why would one ever venture away from it?

Unless, of course, she was speaking of reading. Then, and only then, did she partake in adventures, as reading was always the safest, fastest, most convenient, and most comfortable way to travel.

Lavinia looked back down to *Robinson Crusoe*, but the words did not linger in her mind long before her eyes found their way back to the water sparkling beyond the Mount's causeway.

Heaven, indeed. How she loved it there.

That morning, just like every Tuesday morning—fine weather permitting—she had filled her basket with cherry tarts and sandwiches, a thick, woolen throw, two books, and a small jug filled with her now swiftly depleting reservoir of drinking chocolate. With her stash in hand, she'd ventured across the water on the boat at high tide, then made her way to her secret spot on the mainland. There, she'd plunked herself down and had a most wonderful time in peace and solitude.

And what a day she'd had, finishing for the fourth time the masterpiece that was *Hamlet* before settling down with *Robinson Crusoe*. Sadly, however, her time of reading was coming to an end. She had to be getting back. Father didn't like her reading the day away. Even though he understood her love of a good novel, he far preferred her to socialize.

She laughed to herself. As if she'd ever choose that over reading.

She peered up at the sun hanging just to the right of the Mount. Father wouldn't be heading back from the castle's gardens for at least three quarters of an hour.

With an excited smile, she lay back on her throw she'd fashioned as a pillow and settled her back against the thick grass. Now that she'd seen enough of her Mount, she could get back to Mr. Crusoe's harrowing adventure.

As she read more about his fishing attempts, the man snagging a dolphin instead of a fish, she imagined such a thing happening to herself, then she realized her eyebrows had raised again.

She chidingly put them back in their rightful positions. Her lips and brow were unruly playactors each time she read—raising, wriggling, frowning, smiling—without any say from herself.

Fortunately, no one could see her facial reactions from where she was in her hidden location. She was guarded by thick grass on either side of her and nearly impenetrable trees behind her—all with an unmarred view of the ocean before her. The location was only accessible by traversing through rather bothersome bushes...and then walking through just a touch of private land.

But that was neither here nor there. If she could scale the fifteen-foot stone wall that held Marazion higher than the tide, she wouldn't have to go traipsing through people's gardens now, would she?

Lavinia, or Livvy, as her friends knew her...

Rather, as her friends *would* know her, if she had anyone to call a friend.

Her brow crinkled, and she pulled in her lips, forgetting once again about Crusoe's daily log. Where the devil had that intrusive thought come from? She would allow no place for such a thing in her mind. At least not while she was in her second favorite spot, reading her possibly sixth favorite novel, in her third favorite weather.

Apart from being a little short on food and drink now, she had everything she could ever want.

Except a friend or two.

She groaned. Pesky little thoughts. Had a blasted pisky slipped into her brain overnight with these ridiculous notions? She'd been without friends since she was ten years old. It wasn't like she couldn't live without them for the rest of her days.

Besides, who needed friends with real flesh and blood when she had friends fashioned from fiction? Katherina Minola. Elizabeth Bennet. Evelina Anville. Of course, these friends didn't know she existed. In truth, none of *them* existed.

She clapped her book closed and sat straight up. It was time to leave. She could always tell home was calling when her thoughts began to stray too far into forbidden territory. Going back to the Mount would be just the reset her mind needed.

As she gathered her belongings, she heard it. His laughter. Excitement raced through her limbs. Swiftly, she glanced over her shoulder, facing the causeway in time to see a small group making their way to Marazion. As usual, he was surrounded by his friends.

Everyone always wanted to be around August Moon.

Livvy allowed a sigh to slip past her parted lips. Even his name elicited the ridiculous reaction. She prided herself on not being a silly female. Who would wish to be one after reading about Lydia Bennett? But truly, if the fictional Mr. Wickham boasted as gorgeous a face as the very-real, very-alluring August Moon, it was no wonder women fawned over him. He was so charming, so conversational. So...normal. Everything Livvy wasn't. And Society made sure she knew as much.

Her attention returned to the causeway. Rather, to August. Livvy really ought to be calling the man Mr. Moon now, but with their tightknit community having always referred to him by his given name, the thought of calling him by his father's name would feel far too strange. At least in the privacy of her own thoughts, where she would continue to give herself certain liberties.

August said something she couldn't hear, and the group around him laughed again. As if she cared a lick about what the group was doing. Her eyes focused solely on August's charming dimples, on the way his thick, wavy hair tossed about in the wind. His smile had always been her favorite thing about him. It brightened his whole face, caused his eyes to nearly disappear with glee, and spread joy to all who saw him.

She used to watch him like this when she was a child. Always from a distance, never brave enough to actually speak with him. He was seven years her senior, and she was...well, not the most sociable of creatures. She had been once. But that had all changed after Mother's death.

For a moment, she allowed her mind to stray. What would

her life be like, following August around like one of his friends? She'd obviously love that close connection, the opportunity to watch him unabashedly. But then, if she *was* friends with him and others, she'd have to start answering questions.

"Why do ye read so often?"

"Why do ye only speak when spoken to?"

"What really *'appened to your mother?"*

She pulled a face. The *idea* of being close to August was far more appealing than reality, she supposed.

Livvy craned her neck to see the last of him as he and his party took their final steps across the causeway, then she leaned back with a sigh and continued to load her basket.

When she'd first learned that August would be returning to the Mount after a two-year apprenticeship in Bath, then four years as head gardener somewhere up in Cumbria—not somewhere, it was Coniston. She knew exactly where he'd been—she could only imagine his return was due to the fact that he'd missed his home. There was no other explanation as to why he would accept a lower position and obviously lower pay at the castle.

But that was yet another reason she admired him—because he seemed to love St. Michael's Mount as much as she did. She could never see herself living anywhere but the island.

His contagious grin flashed in her mind's eye once again, but she didn't bother pushing it away. She'd told herself that her childhood feelings for August would be gone after all these years. Apparently, however, her stubborn heart was still grasping onto the hopeless fantasy she'd concocted as a ten-year-old. This was most unfortunate, seeing as how she was fairly certain the man didn't know she existed. How could he? They had lived next door to each other for her entire life, and she had yet to speak more than a handful of sentences to him, having always run away whenever he was nearby for fear of speaking and making a fool of herself.

Of course, she was ten years older now. She was certain she could prove that she was not so afraid of him, especially now that he worked as a castle undergardener with Father as his supervisor.

But as much as she dreamt of one day being noticed by August—perhaps even speaking to him like a normal person—life was easier without having to justify her strange behavior to anyone or explain what *really* happened to Mother. So her childhood infatuation with August Moon would remain that and solely that.

With her belongings piled neatly in her basket, she heaved it up, tucked it in the crook of her arm, and began the walk back to the causeway, thankful that she had missed August and his party along the way.

Because the last thing she wished to do was collide with a group of individuals who knew how odd she was—and a man whom she wished, despite her best efforts, would very much *not* share in that same opinion.

CHAPTER TWO

"Man was born for society. However little he may be attached to the world, he never can wholly forget it."
The Monk, Mathew Lewis

"Brother, come, ye must see the window display at Braddock's. It be simply stunnin'."

August Moon smiled in amusement as he followed the party consisting of his sisters and friends to the next shop. The window display at the milliners appeared quite like the last one they saw, and the last one, and the one before that, but his sisters wished to view them all, so he would gladly acquiesce.

After finishing work unexpectedly early that day, August had been asked by his younger sisters, identical twins Ophelia and Portia, to accompany them to Marazion. Obviously, he'd agreed with very little persuasion. After living off the mount for five years on account of his employment, he was going to do everything he could to make up for his absence. So he'd ignored the aches in his back and exhaustion in his limbs and traveled to the mainland with them by walking across the causeway that connected the Mount to Marazion.

"They be so beautiful," Portia said, leaning as close to the shop's glass as she could without touching it with the tip of her nose.

Standing back near a thick bramble of bushes tangled beside the shop, August watched his sisters and his two friends—Emma Pengelly and Nicholas Cuff—as they continued to peer through the windows.

Ophelia breathed out a sigh, her eyes fairly stroking the blue silk parasols through the glass. "There be no equal to their *beautiness*."

August's lips twitched. *Beautiness.* That was a new one. He'd thought after reaching the age of twenty, his sister might have learned the correct usage of words—or rather the correct words at all—but he could see now she had not changed in that regard.

Funnily enough, he took comfort in the knowledge. In seemingly every other way, Ophelia and Portia had grown beyond the young girls they *had* been, into the charming women they were today. He was glad to have been with them until they were nearly sixteen, but knowing he'd missed five years of his family's growing up stung. That was five years he would never get back.

He'd written frequent letters and had visited for holidays and other social events, but that was only two or three times a year. He was only grateful he'd taken the time to forge relationships with his sisters and parents before he'd left. Fortunately, that had provided a strong enough foundation for their friendships to remain the same.

Shaking the heaviness of the past off his shoulders, August peered beyond the thick shrubs to where the causeway curved across the land to meet with the Mount. At the sight, everything settled. His concerns, his regrets, all of them faded away as he peered at his home.

Yes, he'd missed much. But he was back, and there he would remain. With his new work as undergardener for the castle—a job he'd prayed to open for years—he would never leave again.

"I would choose the white ones," Portia said as August emerged from his thoughts. "They be so elegant."

"Oh, absolutely," Ophelia carried on. "Imagine 'ow they'd look on ye at a ball. Portia, we must convince Mother to purchase 'em."

A rustling occurred in the bushes beside him. August turned, peering at the nearly shoulder-height brambles. Just as soon as he did, however, the branches grew still.

Must have been a stray cat.

"Are ye not goin' to choose your own favorite gloves, August?"

August pulled his attention from the shrubbery as Emma stepped away from the others and stood beside him.

"Apparently," she continued in hushed tones, "it be of utmost importance."

August smiled. He had missed his friend these last few years. As a thirteen-year-old, he'd fancied himself attached to her, but he had swiftly realized they were better suited as friends. Fortunately so, or her request for help upon his return to the Mount would have come as quite a blow otherwise. To Nicholas, as well.

August glanced ahead to his friend. For the first time that morning, Nicholas was not staring at Emma. That would only prove to help all parties involved. August had advised Nicholas to not join them that afternoon, what with Emma being brought along by Ophelia and Portia. If their families knew they were together...

But Nicholas had insisted that he join them.

"No one on the mainland knows Emma or meself," he'd said. *"We'll be perfectly fine, especially with ye there as a diversion."*

Only time would tell if Nicholas had been too optimistic.

A movement in the corner of August's eye drew his attention once more to the bushes, and he frowned. That must be a ridiculously large cat to have swayed the shrubs that much.

"What be the matter?" Emma asked, following his gaze to the bushes.

"I thought I 'eard somethin'." He turned to face the shrubbery more directly, ducking his head lower to peer deeper into the nearly impenetrable branches. "No doubt an animal o' some sort."

A flash of white caught his eye—a tail, perhaps?—but it was gone in an instant.

"It might only be a bird," Emma offered.

But August shook his head. Too much movement to be a bird.

He peered deeper into the darkness, the branches so thick, no light from the bright sun could penetrate the shadows.

That is, until the bushes twitched again, and two eyes peered right back at him.

August flinched in surprise, rearing slightly back.

"'Eavens, what be it?" Emma breathed out.

"I..." He frowned. "I believe it be a person."

The eyes disappeared, but there was no hiding from him any longer as the distinct outline of a head and shoulders appeared in the darkness.

"Be that..." Emma tipped her head to the side, a soft smile touching her lips as she seemed to be speaking to herself. "I believe so, yes." She took a step toward the bushes. "Miss May, be that ye?"

Miss May? The Miss May who had grown up in the house

next to his? The Miss May he was fairly certain he'd never spoken more than a few greetings to?

They waited in silence, both of them watching the bushes remain still before another rustling shifted the leaves and a soft voice spoke from within.

"Yes?"

Had that been a question? Did Miss May not know she was, indeed, Miss May? A smile tugged at his lips.

"What..." Emma began. "What ye be doin' in the bushes?"

More silence. "I..." The voice paused as she cleared her throat. "I fear I be quite fixed to these brambles."

August exchanged glances with Emma, confusion shifting quickly to amusement. She was stuck?

He cleared his own throat then to rid himself of any humor he should not be feeling in this situation and drew closer to the bushes, knowing the task fell upon him. Should Emma attempt to help, her dress would become as snagged in the branches as Miss May's dress apparently was. He, on the other hand, had no skirts to hinder him.

"Allow me to 'elp ye, Miss May."

Looking closer, he tried to catch sight of a hand to grasp onto, but Miss May remained in the darkness. He was fairly certain he hadn't managed a single sighting of the woman in more than two years. She was never at any social gathering on the Mount or off, and when he *had* thought he'd seen her, her head had been more often than not lowered into the pages of an open book.

"Oh, I be quite all right," Miss May said, her voice taking on a higher pitch. "I be certain I can free meself on me own."

August held back, the bush shivering as if caught in a gale off the coast. Grunting sounded within, then the bush stopped and sighed. Or rather, Miss May stopped and sighed.

Would she accept his help now?

"Miss May?"

Silence.

"Miss May, be ye still there?"

Whispers sounded behind him, and he glanced back to find the rest of the party converging nearby, curiosity in each of their gazes.

"Do ye suppose I vanished into the air or somethin', sir? 'Course I be 'ere."

His smile grew. For someone stuck in a bush, she certainly maintained a sense of humor and pride through it all.

"Come," he said, pushing aside the branches with his gloved hands.

More rustling occurred as he drew farther into the bushes. How the devil had the woman become entangled so far into these branches? And *what* the devil was she doing there in the first place?

Another muted grunt occurred, closer this time, and he moved the branches aside farther and farther until finally, he came face-to-face with Miss May.

And what a sight she was. He'd thought he'd be observing the young Miss May from before—the one with ruddy cheeks and a rounded face.

But *this* Miss May, well, he'd never seen anyone so stunning. Her black hair had been tugged out by the branches, but that did nothing but add to her strikingness. Or, as Ophelia put it, her *beautiness.*

A soft breeze blew the leaves of the branches above them, allowing the sun to peek through and land squarely on Miss May's face. Soft curls fell down around her elegant features in waves—high cheekbones, curved lips, almond-shaped eyes. Those eyes. How had he never noticed how blue they were? Then again, she *had* only been fifteen or sixteen when he'd left the Mount. Before that, he'd been so wrapped up in his own life and his own interests, why would he have ever paid attention to a girl who was the same age as his younger sisters?

Another moment passed by before he realized he was still staring at her in silence. He pulled on a half-smile. “Miss May, I presume?”

CHAPTER THREE

"...nothing is so delicate as the reputation of a woman: it is, at once, the most beautiful and most brittle of all human things."
Evelina, Frances Burney

Miss May's crystal blue eyes stared at August with such an intensity, he almost had to look away for a moment, but she averted her gaze first.

"Yes. Yes, I be Miss May."

Her voice was soft and smooth, like water slipping back into the sea at low tide.

"Ye've grown," he said, though his words came out in a murmur.

Had he meant to speak them aloud? He seemed to have fallen into a sort of daze. Whether that was due to the surprise of finding a woman this beautiful hiding in the bushes or the surprise that Miss May had grown into such a stunning individual, he couldn't be sure.

"I suppose that be what time does to a person," she responded.

"Just so."

Still, he stared. Why did he say nothing more?

"Ye've grown yourself," she said.

Had he? He wasn't aware that he'd changed at all. Except, perhaps, in maturity. He was no longer chasing after girls on the Mount, trying to untie their bonnet ribbons. Although, he'd be half-tempted to do the same again if Miss May was one of those girls.

He cast his eyes about her face again, still reeling that this was the same girl he'd always seen hiding behind her books or her father.

Her father. The man who just so happened to be August's superior at the castle gardens. What would Mr. May think of his newly hired member of staff remaining in a secluded bramble of shrubbery with his only daughter?

August cleared his throat. That straightened his mind out. "Although I do 'ave a number o' questions as to 'ow ye've become tangled up in this mess, I assume ye would appreciate escapin' first from the culprit who 'as managed to capture ye in its grasp?"

Her smooth cheeks tinted pink, and she ducked her head, but not before he caught sight of a small smile. "I'd 'ppreciate it very much, thank ye."

Together they worked to break off the branches that had hooked onto the hem of her soft purple skirt and edges of her white spencer—what he'd thought had been a cat's tail had apparently been her arm flailing about—until finally, they fought their way through the branches and into the sunshine.

Somehow he'd managed to forget about the audience of his friends and sisters awaiting them until that moment.

Emma looked on with mild amusement. Nicholas, too. But Ophelia and Portia—who'd left the window displays to observe their brother's actions—stared at Miss May with widened eyes.

He glanced down at the woman as she pulled a few branches and leaves from her sleeves and skirt, averting her gaze from the others. Only then did he notice the basket hanging from her left arm, two books poking out of the top of it.

He narrowed his eyes. "Were ye...readin' in the bushes?"

A noise sounding suspiciously like a laugh came from the group, and he glanced to see Ophelia holding a gloved hand to her mouth, no doubt to stifle her amusement.

August cringed. He hadn't meant his comment to be taken as teasing or cruelty. He'd meant it in earnest. Had Miss May taken offense?

Unfortunately, she appeared as much, her blush growing a deeper red. She looked back at him—those eyes even bluer in the bright sunshine—then to the crowd gathered.

"No," she said. The word sounded clipped at the end, as if she wished to say more but couldn't.

The group waited, Ophelia and Portia exchanging glances with smiles—rather, smirks.

August's stomach tightened. Why were they behaving in such a way? Could they not see Miss May was uncomfortable? Should they not attempt to help her?

"I be so very glad to see ye out and about, Miss May," Emma said, stepping forward so the attention shifted to her—blessed woman that she was. "It be a fine day to be doin' so. We came to the mainland to admire the window displays in such fine weather. Would ye care to join us?"

August didn't miss Ophelia's stifled sigh, nor Portia's lips pulled downward with disappointment. They clearly did not wish for Miss May to join them. But, why?

More importantly, had Miss May noticed their rude behavior?

"Thank ye," she responded. "But I must be gettin' back to Father."

Emma nodded understandingly. "Per'aps next time."

Miss May nodded, backing away after a furtive glance toward August.

"Oh, Miss May," Ophelia called out.

August breathed a sigh of relief. Finally. His sister must have remembered her manners. She would no doubt ask Miss May to reconsider or invite her to another activity.

"Ye've still a few leaves in your 'air," she said, motioning to Miss May's head with a gloved finger. "There and there. And there. Also there."

Those hadn't been the words of kindness for which August had been hoping.

Miss May's blush increased. She attempted to pull them out, though four or five remained. "I s'pose they wished to hitch a ride," she mumbled.

August smiled at her joke, but his sisters didn't respond.

"'Ave I managed to find 'em all?" Miss May asked.

"Oh, indeed," Ophelia lied.

Portia stifled a laugh, and August frowned. Was this typical behavior from his sisters, teasing and laughing at other people's expenses? Or was it just to Miss May? Obviously, they had adopted this poor conduct in the years he'd been absent. There was no possible way Mother and Father were aware of it. They would not allow it to continue if they were.

"Well, we shan't keep ye from returnin' to your father any longer, Miss May," Ophelia said.

Emma averted her gaze as Ophelia latched onto Nicholas, who had remained silent through the ordeal. Such was typical for him, though. He'd always been the most soft-spoken of

August's friends. The last to wed, as well. Excepting August, of course.

"Come, Mr. Cuff," Ophelia continued. "We must be on our way to see more windows. Good day, Miss May."

Then she and Portia turned on their heels, not waiting for Miss May to respond.

"Readin' in the bushes," Portia said in tones she clearly did not intend to hush. She attached herself to Nicholas's other arm. "Can ye imagine such a thing?"

Ophelia laughed. "She reads everywhere else, why not in bushes, too?"

Nicholas did not respond, clearly unamused with the comments, though caught in the middle with no way of escaping. Emma watched them walk away before turning an apologetic gaze at Miss May.

August's stomach pinched. He looked to Miss May, as well, attempting to soften what had just occurred, but she was already backing away. "Thank ye again for your service, Au— Mr. Moon," she said, stumbling over her words. "Good day."

August opened his mouth, attempting to stop her, but her footing was quick.

"Miss May," he called out.

She stopped, turning to face him, though she remained a few feet away. "Yes?"

He scrambled for something to say. An apology? Not with the streets filled—that would surely add to her embarrassment. Should he tell her she still had leaves in her hair?

But as he noted how charming she looked with those leaves bespeckling her locks as enticing as any emerald jewels, how innocent she appeared with those stunning eyes and bedraggled hair, he simply didn't have the heart.

"I...I believe me family 'as invited your father to dine with us this evenin'," he said instead. "I 'ope ye will join us, as well."

He hoped his parents wouldn't mind. He hadn't even thought it was strange until that point that Miss May *hadn't* been invited to come along with her father, but they had clearly stated that morning that Mr. May would be joining them, not Mr. May and his very attractive daughter. But, why?

Miss May's brow rose in surprise at his invitation. "Oh, I...yes."

What exactly she was saying yes to was a mystery to him, but he nodded all the same, smiling as he bowed. "It be wonderful to see ye again after so long. Good day, Miss May."

She curtsied in silence, then scurried off in the direction of the causeway, leaving August to watch her until she disappeared from his view.

"She be a peculiar girl."

August looked over his shoulder, surprised to see Emma still standing there. He thought she would have gone with the others by now. He came to stand beside her, looking back at the causeway, though Miss May was no longer in sight.

August wasn't sure if Emma meant 'peculiar' in a negative way, but if she was referring to how different she seemed than others, he couldn't deny it. "Indeed."

"Did ye speak with 'er much 'fore ye left the Mount?"

"No," he responded. "Our interaction be limited. Nonexistent, e'en. Our conversation in 'em bushes be longer than all the times we've spoken combined."

Emma nodded, accepting his offered arm as they walked slowly toward the others who had stopped at another shop across the road.

She said nothing further, seemingly done with the conversation, but August wasn't. "Tell me, the way me sisters behaved...be that a normal occurrence?"

Emma gave him a sidelong glance. "I wouldn't wish to speak out o' turn."

"By all means, that be precisely what I wish for ye to do. I trust your words more than most on the Mount."

Still, Emma hesitated, continuing in a manner that showed how greatly she considered her words before voicing them. "Miss May be a kind woman. But she don't conform to Society's standards. She reads too much and speaks too little. As a result, I fear she 'as become the brunt o' much gossip and tongue waggin'. From your sisters, in particular."

"Me sisters?" he asked, shaking his head in dismay.

He could not abide cruelty of any form. To know that his sisters treated someone as seemingly innocuous as Lavinia May in such a way, he couldn't bear it.

"Be they cruel to others?" he asked.

Emma winced. "I fear they've adopted a newfound propensity to gossip about anyone and everyone."

He stared up ahead, seeing his sisters laughing boisterously at something Nicholas said, and he grimaced. Now he truly would need to speak with Mother and Father. This sort of behavior was unacceptable—especially for a Moon.

"Do not be too 'ard on 'em," Emma said, apparently reading his thoughts. "They still be young in the ways o' the world. They've not experienced much 'eartache or trials to mature 'em, I fear. But I be certain, with time, they shall grow kinder."

August was not so certain. Miss May had clearly been negatively affected by their teasing, and he would not allow it to continue.

He wasn't aware of Emma's continued silence for a moment until he glanced down at her, seeing her staring off at his sisters, or rather, at Nicholas. He didn't have to guess where her thoughts had strayed.

He thought back to her words—about maturing after trials

and heartache, and he couldn't help but think she was speaking of herself.

He placed a comforting hand over hers on his arm, and she looked up before releasing a heavy sigh. "Forgive me. I do not mean to sulk."

"If there be anyone who 'as earned the right to sulk, it is ye, Emma."

She gave him a warm smile, then faced the others again, her voice in a low whisper as she continued. "It be difficult, seein' 'im, but not bein' able to be near 'im."

He patted her hand again. "Keep up your spirits. In time, I be sure the two of ye will be allowed to be together."

She peered up at him with a smile. "Thank ye again for all your 'elp, August. We couldn't 'ave made it this far without ye."

He nodded, giving her another encouraging smile before they reached the others, even though he did not believe the words he said to her. He was *not* certain at all that things would work out for the best, especially because he was doing very little to help.

And honestly, how could everything work out, how could Nicholas and Emma marry, when both of their parents forbade it?

Still, he would keep his faith at the forefront of his mind, because if his best friends in the world had difficulty being with the person they loved, what hope did he have when he found someone to love, as well?

CHAPTER FOUR

She wanted to complain, not to be consoled; and it was by exclamations of complaint only, [she] learned the particular circumstances of her affliction."
The Mysteries of Udolpho, Ann Radcliffe

Of all the people to see—in all the places to see them.

Livvy marched across the causeway, her cheeks still aflame due to her stupidity. She should have waited longer before attempting to leave the bushes. She knew that. But then her blasted skirts had become all tangled up and the thickness of the shrubbery prevented her from seeing clearly and...

She blew out a sigh, peering up at the Mount as she neared it. Her skirts had become tangled up in those wretched branches many times before. Why had she not had the foresight that such a thing might occur again?

Honestly, this was the worst thing that could have happened to her. Being spotted by August Moon when she was stuck in the bushes, being *helped* by August Moon to emerge from said bushes, and then being *asked* by August Moon if she was, in actuality, reading in the bushes.

Reading in the bushes.

She pressed a hand to her brow, as if hiding her face could somehow diminish her mortification. Of course it didn't. Nothing could. She hadn't even had the courage to explain what she *had* been doing. Her words had come out in a squeak, then they'd simply...stopped.

That shouldn't surprise her. Such a thing was commonplace for her when an audience larger than one or two persons stared at her, as if expecting her to fail.

And Miss Ophelia and Miss Portia Moon were definitely expecting her to fail.

She groaned under her breath. Those girls. They always seemed to appear when Livvy was at her worst. Emerging from bushes with books in hand. Laughing to herself aloud when she thought of something funny. Falling flat onto her face in the mud after running during a storm.

When it all came down to it, Livvy was the one to be blamed for putting herself in such awkward situations. But those girls always knew what to say to annoy her, just as they had when they were children. That was one reason they'd never been friends, despite living next door to one another for the entirety of their lives.

That didn't explain her reasoning for not being friends with Miss Emma Pengelly, though. The blonde-haired, hazel-eyed beauty appeared in Livvy's mind as the specter who always haunted her dreams.

Very well, she was feeding into her inner Catherine Morland with that comment. In all honesty, Livvy was simply and monumentally envious of Miss Pengelly for no other reason other than the woman's friendship with August.

How Livvy wished to hate her, but Miss Pengelly had to be

the kindest woman on the Mount. Despite being nearly seven years Livvy's senior, the woman had never treated her with an ounce of disdain or condescension. Even today, when Livvy had made quite the spectacle of herself, Miss Pengelly had still invited her to join their party—which was more than could be said of the Moon sisters' poking fun at the leaves in Livvy's hair.

A couple walked by on the causeway, drawing Livvy's attention to the present. She delivered a brief smile in greeting, then dipped her head to avoid any chance of the couple stopping to speak with her. As if anyone ever would know. They all knew she liked to keep to herself.

She feared she may have ruined her reputation forever, and yet, somehow, she couldn't bring herself to mind. She didn't care for trivial conversations with strangers, nor did she wish for deep discussions about her own past. She was therefore caught in the middle of her desires, the simplest solution being that of speaking with others about books—or not speaking to anyone at all.

Just like a hermit.

She puffed out her cheeks with another sigh. She did not like to berate herself like she had done today. The truth of the matter was that she quite liked who she was. She wasn't ever rude to anyone—as far as she was aware—but she also would not conform to how Society wished her to behave. She had her mother to thank for that.

And while she occasionally wondered what life would be like if she simply chose to change who she fundamentally was—to be normal just like everyone else—she knew, deep down, she could never be happy being a ghost of her former self.

Which meant she would simply have to accept the fact that her first meeting with August upon his return to the Mount had been a disaster instead of the stirring moment she'd concocted in her addled brain that apparently was filled with nothing but literary romance and adventure.

She glanced across the sand and stones that had been revealed at the low tide—a few petrified remains of ancient trees sticking out and boasting of their dark wood. She needed to take a step back, to breathe and relax. There was nothing to be done now about the issue. August would simply think her as odd as everyone else did, and she was...mostly fine with that.

Her stomach tied in knots. That was a heinous lie. She was not fine with it at all. She couldn't bear the thought of August thinking she was strange, peculiar, odd, difficult, and every other word they used to describe her. But what could be done? Short of trying to prove that everyone was wrong about her strangeness—even though they were right—or perhaps explaining to August herself what she had been doing...

Her eyes flew open, an idea sparking in her mind. He'd invited her to dinner that evening. Could she...No, that would be preposterous. Hardly worth the sacrifice of socializing.

But then, to have the chance to salvage her reputation in regard to August was certainly tempting.

She used to dream of his return to the Mount, that she would make such a charming impression that he would drop everything and marry her in a matter of days. But such a dream had obviously been born during her obsession with unrealistic romance novels. Her life was far better suited to Shakespeare's tragedies now. Or his comedies. She knew if the impossible happened and she did draw closer to August, she would have to reveal the secrets she had bottled up inside her heart for years—but that was something she had promised herself she'd never do.

And yet, the mere thought of having another moment of

August's attention as she'd enjoyed in the bushes was enough to make her pause.

Her blush picked up despite the cool wind on her cheeks, though this blush wasn't caused by the embarrassment she'd felt earlier, merely by the memory of August's eyes exploring her face. He'd appeared amused by the whole situation, but there had been something else written across his expression as he'd perused her features. Almost as if he had been *admiring* her features.

She knew she was not the most attractive of creatures on the Mount, but she did not believe herself to be unattractive, either. To think that August Moon, Charmer of St. Michael's Mount, could find her pleasant to look at was beyond anything she could ever hope for.

Of course, any admiration on his part would have faded once he'd seen the books in her hands.

Her embarrassment returned. She obviously had a choice to make. Allow August to continue thinking she was as strange as everyone said she was—rather than just the small amount of strange that she actually was—thereby ending all future hope she might have of him looking at her the same way he had a few moments ago...or she had to find the courage she wasn't sure she had to explain her behavior to the man she'd never been able to speak with before that afternoon.

She arrived home before she could decide.

Reaching forward, she opened the door to her small, two-story, blue-colored house soundlessly. Over the years, she had discovered all that was needed was slight pressure on the handle to keep the top hinge from creaking—a handy trick whenever she came home far too late after getting carried away with her reading.

Closing the door behind her, she faced the corridor without a whisper of a sound.

Father would be smoking his pipe in the front sitting room, as he did every evening when he came home. Then he would encourage her not to read all day, as he did every evening, too. His advice always went in one of Livvy's ears and out the other, though. Reading was like eating for her soul. Avoiding that conversation would be best for them both.

Sure enough, as she listened, she heard the sucking in of his pipe and the creaking of wood as he adjusted in his chair in the sitting room.

It was now or never. Treating this circumstance as if she was Mr. Crusoe fleeing from pirates, she drew a deep breath, focused on being as light and quick as a swallow, then darted past the doorway.

"Liv? Be that ye?"

Her footsteps stopped just before she reached the stairs. Blast. She'd been so close.

She walked back to the sitting room, poking her head around the door frame but keeping her basket of books and goods out of sight. "Evenin', Father," she said with an innocent smile.

"What 'ave ye been doin'?" His words were muffled as he kept the pipe in his mouth, sucking in a deep breath.

Livvy lowered her basket to the floor out of sight in the corridor, then ventured into the sitting room. "I decided to take advantage o' the warm weather and walk to Marazion."

Truth.

"Lovely," Father murmured.

He blew out a puff of smoke, the white clouds pluming about the small room before disappearing. The walls were bare and wooden, just like the furnishings—two small chairs, a waist-height bookshelf, and a round table with a simple lace cloth over the top of it. Beside Father, a small fire crackled in the hearth.

"Did ye enjoy yourself?" he asked.

"I did, thank ye."

Half-truth.

Her boots clicked across the wooden flooring as she stepped toward the window. Peering beyond the warped glass, she viewed the harbor—empty at low tide—that was visible just past the small road and footpath in front of their home.

"And 'ow be your readin'?"

Her heart dropped. "I wasn't readin'."

Far-fetched, absurd, outright lie.

And Father would know it was, too.

CHAPTER FIVE

"It is never too late to be wise."
Robinson Crusoe, Daniel Defoe

Livvy sighed, turning to see, sure enough, a knowing smile on Father's face. "Very well. I *was* readin'."

He nodded. "As if I could e'er believe ye were out conversin' with people 'stead o' readin'."

Ah, now there he was wrong. She *had* been conversing with people. Just not a conversation she'd tell Father about. He somehow still maintained a preposterous hope that his daughter would one day be seen as normal. If today had taught her one thing, it was that she was proving to be anything but.

"Did ye start your new book?" came his next question.

She smiled, somewhat relieved she didn't have to hide any longer. The most difficult issue that came with reading was the necessity of discussing with others what she had read. When one had friends, such a task was not difficult. For Livvy, that was another story. Father did not have the attention span to listen to all she had to say about her books.

"I did," she said. "I be enjoyin' it so far."

"I be glad to 'ear it," Father responded, staring into the fire as he puffed out more smoke.

He had never been overly fond of Livvy's reading habits, but she was grateful to no end that he allowed her to read as much—or nearly as much—as she wished to. He often borrowed new books for her from his friends or purchased inexpensive, secondhand copies of her favorites.

Still, he often lectured her on how much more she would be accepted by others if she didn't read so often. Hence why she now tried to hide how much she truly did read.

She always expressed her gratitude for his half-hearted support, but she knew there was more that Father wanted—a daughter who was comfortable in Society, a daughter who could find a good match and make him proud. Unfortunately, he was not so blessed.

Biting her lower lip, she pressed the thoughts from her mind before finally making her decision about that evening, though Heaven knew she would come to regret it.

She stared hard out the window again. The pathway between her home and the harbor was virtually empty, most folks having already returned home from work and shopping and socializing. Now was when she enjoyed being out of doors most—when there were fewer eyes to pry on her and her reading.

But she had a task to see to, and a delicate one, at that. For she did not wish to reveal her secret feelings for August Moon to anyone, especially her own father.

"Do ye know what Cook be makin' for dinner this evenin'?" she asked.

"I believe she be makin' lamb loaf," Father replied. He made a popping sound with his lips as he inhaled the tobacco.

"Ye be eatin' alone tonight, though, as I be dinin' with the Moons."

"Oh?" Livvy could certainly be proud of that response. How amazingly unaffected had her voice sounded? She had almost managed to convince *herself* of her indifference.

"I be sorry to be leavin' ye alone again," Father replied. "Ye were invited too, 'course, but the Moons know ye don't take well to attendin' parties and such."

And well they should know it, just like everyone on the Mount did. Every dinner invitation she'd received, every request to attend an assembly, had sent Livvy into a panic, pushing her to make feeble excuses to remain at home as she professed headache after headache or excessive fatigue. Father would always attend alone.

It was not that she didn't like people. Quite the contrary, actually. She used to enjoy socializing as a young girl and had countless friends. But after Mother died...

Livvy shook her head. She'd attempted to enter Society at the age of sixteen—as per Father's request—but being in Society and not being *like* Society had simply brought forth one disaster after another. She'd been so anxious under Father's pressure that she'd made herself sick right before she would have begun her first dance.

After that, no man wished to stand up with her again, so she'd remained half-hidden behind curtains the rest of the evening, further solidifying her strange behavior to those on the Mount.

It was better to hide away, though, if only to avoid the need to exchange forced false pleasantries and hear questions about her past that she refused to answer—and questions about herself that she didn't feel like she was *required* to answer.

Fortunately, when she passed the age of seventeen three

years ago, the invitations stopped, Father's pressure lessened, and Livvy was granted relief.

That is, until last year when things had begun to...change. *She* had begun to change. She still did not wish for invitations to be extended to her, but then, she was so lonely at times. Perhaps receiving—

"Livvy?"

She withdrew from her reverie, grateful she hadn't followed that line of thought any further. She knew what would occur if she returned to Society, and she was not yet ready to share her secrets with the world.

"Yes, Father?"

"I asked ye a question," he repeated, giving her the same chiding look he always did when her mind wandered. "Are ye upset that I be goin'?"

"Oh, not at all. I be 'appy ye get to attend. Only..."

She paused. By attending this party, more invitations would follow, and she would inevitably reject them all to avoid more questions and more meaningless chatter.

If only those in Society did not take offense at a simple and polite rejection. If only people would see her for what she was—a woman without the strength to socialize. But misunderstandings would always occur when others were unwilling to accept someone different from themselves.

"Liv?"

She cleared her throat, straightening her mind in the process. There was one thing that would push her to follow through with her plan. For years, she'd dreamt of mingling with August Moon, and now was her chance. There was no turning back. She simply needed to take courage for one evening, then life would go back to normal. Would it not?

"Would ye like me company?" she blurted out before she could stop herself again.

Father removed the pipe from his mouth, his lips parted in surprise. "Ye wish to come? To a dinner party? At the Moons'?"

She shrugged, hoping to maintain her apathetic façade. She wouldn't wish for him to think she was attending for any other reason other than to help him. "I don't particularly wish to come," she clarified, and that was the whole truth. "But it 'as been quite some time, and I...Well, I figured ye allow me to read all day, so I ought to give ye a bit more effort on me part. Unless ye don't want me to come."

Father stood, placed his pipe on the table, then crossed the room toward Livvy. A small smile curved his lips as he gently held her upper arms in his hands.

"I would absolutely enjoy your company, daugh'er." His smile faltered. "So long as ye promise to keep your conversations 'bout books to a minimum. Ye know 'ow carried away ye can get when they be mentioned, and we don't want others thinkin'..."

He trailed off, and Livvy struggled to keep her spirits up. This was yet another reason she despised socializing. Following the rules of conversation—don't speak solely of books, engage in all topics, even if they're boring, keep subjects simple and surface-level. It was more exhausting than it was enjoyable.

Father was simply attempting to shelter them both from embarrassment, of course, because, unfortunately, Livvy was no stranger to embarrassing him. After all, she was the odd one on the Mount. She was the one who did not wish to conform. She was the one unwilling to speak beyond books for fear of releasing one of her many secrets.

Truth be told, she felt sorry for Father. Not just because he was dealing with a silly daughter, but because he'd had difficulties with his wife, too. More than he would ever know.

Livvy drew a deep breath. She would do her best not to

cause embarrassment to him that evening. Which meant she needed to ensure she spoke with August without Father overhearing about her little escapade in the bushes.

"Livvy, do try to stay present." Father's perturbed voice echoed in her thoughts, and she shook her head to focus.

She always had a difficult time not being entirely distracted with her own thoughts.

"Forgive me," she said. "I promise to be on me best behavior tonight. I'll remain present. I'll speak o' bonnets and bows. And I'll not mention a single book."

He nodded, crossing the room again to return to his pipe. "That be the Livvy I know and love."

Yes, the Livvy who hid away at the request of her own father.

"I'm certain ye will 'ave a grand time," he continued. "And August will add fine conversation. Did ye know 'e returned?"

She tipped her head to the side in feigned surprise, but fortunately, Father continued so she didn't have to respond.

"I be certain 'e don't need to work," Father continued as if speaking to himself, "what with the inheritance 'e's sure to receive from 'is father, but I s'pose gardenin' be in 'is blood." He paused, rubbing his chin, then glanced back to Livvy. "I do think it'll be fine for ye to be closer to the Moon daugh-'ers, too. They be fine girls who be well-loved across the Mount."

Livvy cringed. Little did he know how those "fine girls" treated her today. But knowing Father, he might be more on their side than her own.

"Yes, Father."

She glanced at the doorway. The edge of her basket poked out from the door frame, luring her closer with the promise of numbing her feelings in the pages of her books.

But Father continued. "Per'aps this'll be just the thing for ye to finally love socializin' again. There be much to experience, 'specially off the Mount."

Her chest tightened. So they would not escape this part of their daily conversation after all. "Father..."

"I only be sayin' that it might be time for ye to consider such a possibility."

She looked away. "Movin' away from me 'ome ain't a guarantee of a better life."

Nor was it what she wanted. But she didn't need to go through this all again. Father knew all too well her desire was to remain on the Mount.

"But it could be better," Father pressed. "Ye know me cousins in Nanstallon. They'd take ye in, watch o'er ye. They'd do a fine job of it, too. Ye'd no doubt love it once ye experienced it. After all, ye be more like your mother than ye think. Gettin' off this island might be just the thing to 'elp ye be 'appy."

Livvy looked away with a grimace. She hated it when he compared her to her mother, saying how similar they were, when frankly, Livvy could not think of another person she had less in common with—a person she strived less to be like.

She also couldn't abide the fact that Father seemed to think that the only way for her to be happy was to find a spouse off the Mount. As if she could not find one *on* the Mount. That wasn't like Mother, now, was it?

But perhaps he had a point. After all, Livvy was not yet married, was she? Nor did she have any prospects.

She pushed aside the image of August, as well as the thought that always accompanied her father attempting to push her off the Mount—because he didn't want her on the Mount.

Livvy was finished with the conversation. Walking to the doorway, she spoke over her shoulder. "Yes, Father. That would be a fine option. I'll take it into consideration, but I fear we must be gettin' ready for the party."

He drew in another long breath from his pipe. "Yes, ye be right. 'Ave Sarah do somethin' with that 'air o' yours. Ye've got leaves stuck in it again."

She pressed a hand to her head, feeling a leaf instantly. Blast. Ophelia had said she'd got them all. Wretched girl.

"Yes, Father," she mumbled, then she walked away.

"Leaves," Father mumbled to himself as she departed. "'Eaven knows where a girl must choose to read if she 'as leaves in 'er 'air."

Livvy ignored Father's words and worked to remove the leaves herself as she climbed the stairs, all the while trying to remember why the devil she'd agreed to go to the Moons' in the first place.

Ah, that was right. She was determined that August would finally know that she was not just a girl who read in bushes.

She was odd, but she was not *that* odd.

CHAPTER SIX

"I would challenge you to a battle of wits, but I see you are unarmed."
Taming of the Shrew, William Shakespeare

Dinner was an awkward affair. The only thing that pulled Livvy from dwelling on her misery were the subtle glances she was able to steal toward August and, of course, the fact that she hardly had to speak a word throughout the entire meal. The Moon sisters' continuous chatter about Mrs. Dunstone doing this and Mr. Clemow doing that while Miss Galty had this happen to her and Miss Prisk had that happen to her filled up most of the time.

Livvy had been concerned that they were going to spill the fact that they'd found her in the bushes that afternoon, but fortunately, Father wouldn't have heard if they'd tried. He was far too busy speaking over the girls and monopolizing August's attention by rambling on about Sir John—the baronet whose family had inherited the castle many years before—and the botanical collections the man obsessed over.

Livvy had a mind to tell her father that what he was doing was hardly socially appropriate, but then, what did she know? Besides, this only meant that August didn't attempt to speak with her the entirety of the meal, much to her relief. Obviously she wanted to speak with him, but in front of everyone, she would only be able to muster up one-word responses.

When the meal ended, the women went through to the sitting room, and Livvy glanced over her shoulder, stealing another look at August. He just so happened to look at her in the same moment. He delivered a nod and a kind smile before turning to Father, who stopped speaking for a feat of almost ten seconds.

Livvy did her best to quell her heart's flipping, but she was as successful as Mr. Crusoe and his fishing attempts.

She had to keep her wits about her that evening if she was going to defend her actions to August. She would not leave until she had, so the Moons had better prepare themselves for a possibly very long night, indeed.

She smiled at her own joke as she followed the women through the short corridor of the Moons' home. She was not looking forward to sitting with only the women to distract her, but she was willing to do so for her own sake.

Or rather, for the sake of August's opinion about her. She knew she shouldn't care so greatly about such a thing, especially when nothing would ever occur between them, but for one reason or another, she could not let this go.

Attempting to distract herself from leaving right that moment for home, she glanced around her. It had been at least two years since Livvy had been within the Moons' home, and she still could not overcome her surprise at how it had changed.

The family had become one of the foremost of the Mount after Mr. Piran Moon was left a decent-sized inheritance from a long-lost uncle more than five years before. He made a few lucrative investments in multiple copper mines in the west of Cornwall and had only grown in wealth and popularity. The Moons had adopted a few upper-class traditions, including the women leaving the men to their drinks after dinner and the family obtaining more servants. They had also purchased the house connected to theirs, tearing down the walls to increase the size of their lodging and redecorating each room in the newest styles.

Through it all, however, Mr. and Mrs. Moon had remained humble and inviting to their original friends and neighbors. Instead of leaving the Mount to purchase a large estate elsewhere, they chose to stay where they loved to live, and Livvy couldn't help but admire that.

She only wished Ophelia and Portia had maintained their humility, as well, as they seemed far changed from how they were as children. They'd always elevated themselves above Livvy, but now more than ever, they focused more on their appearances and how the upper-class functioned than on anything else.

Would August have become puffed up in his pride had he remained with his family instead of moving off the Mount for his employment?

Instantly, she pressed down the notion. August could never be prideful. He was too wise and kind.

"We be so pleased ye've come, Miss May," Mrs. Moon said as they sat down across from each other, her daughters' mouths closed for the first time that evening. "I know I keep sayin' so, but we really couldn't be 'appier."

Livvy smiled. The woman had said so at least twice during dinner, and once when Livvy and Father had first come. Father had sent word earlier to the Moons that Livvy would be joining them that evening, but when she'd first arrived, the shock on each of their faces—apart from August's—revealed that none of them had actually expected her to make good on her word.

"Thank ye," Livvy said.

Portia's and Ophelia's eyes shifted to her, and Livvy regretted saying a word. Somehow, she'd remained veritably unnoticed by the girls until that point. Surely they wouldn't say anything unnecessarily harsh with their mother seated beside them.

"Yes, Miss May," Ophelia piped up. "We be 'appy to see ye."

Miss May. She and the girls had grown up together. Using such names between each other sounded odd, but Livvy supposed that was merely due to the fact that she had always called the girls by their Christian names in her thoughts because she could never remember who was the elder of the two. Was it Miss Moon and Miss Portia? Or Miss Moon and Miss Ophelia?

"Surprised, but 'appy," Portia added.

Her accent, like all the Moons, held a slightly finer note to it, no doubt due to the fact that they mingled with the upper class more than most folks.

Livvy wasn't one to judge, of course, as her words had changed throughout her life due to her extensive reading. Father had taken issue with it many times over the years—"Why ye be speakin' all fancy-like?"—but Livvy couldn't help it when she 'heard' fine characters speaking more than her own father.

At any rate, her vocabulary had improved, but her accent remained the same. At least, according to her own ears. The Moon sisters sounded as if they didn't know *how* they wished to speak.

"Indeed," Ophelia added. "And we be 'appy to see ye were able to remove the rest o' the leaves from your 'air," Ophelia continued.

There it was. Livvy knew it was only a matter of time before the girls couldn't help but mention Livvy's odd behavior. At least August wasn't there. Or Father.

Mrs. Moon tipped her head to the side in question as she peered at her daughter. "Leaves, what do ye mean, Ophelia?"

Ophelia exchanged glances with Portia. "Oh, it be just a little joke 'tween us and Miss May. We found the poor dear stuck in a thicket o' bushes today." She leaned close to her mother. "We believe she was readin' in 'em."

Mrs. Moon looked to Livvy, confusion in her eyes before she blinked it away. Clearly, she was doing her best not to pry. Livvy appreciated the attempt, and while everything within her told her to keep the woman guessing—that she would not satisfy Ophelia with a victory of speaking of her behavior—she supposed practicing now on Mrs. Moon would help her be more eloquent with August.

With a stifled sigh, she opened her mouth, ready to explain, but Portia spoke instead. "I don't understand those who 'ave the desire to read."

Livvy clamped her mouth shut. This was not a conversation in which she would linger. Father had sworn her off from speaking of reading, and Livvy would receive no joy in speaking of books with girls who did not appreciate them.

She glanced about the room to distract herself, trying not to admire the fine décor but unable to keep from doing so. The room was painted in a light blue that brightened the space far more than her own little sitting room. The furnishings were much softer, cushioned with deep blue pillows, and the walls held a few paintings of Cornish landscapes.

Her attention was pulled first and foremost, however, to the large bookshelf at the front of the room, holding over a hundred books, if not two hundred. Livvy's mouth watered over the sight far more than the lemon and tarragon whitefish they'd served for dinner.

If she were to have an excess of money—not that she and Father were lacking in any degree—she would have bookshelves like that throughout her entire home.

"Ye must forgive me daugh'ers," Mrs. Moon said, drawing Livvy's attention away from the books. Mrs. Moon smiled in Ophelia's direction, though there was a hint of chiding in her tone. "I fear they ain't great readers." She turned to Livvy with sparkling eyes. "We 'aven't spoken in some time, but I trust ye remember me own fondness o' readin'?"

Livvy nodded. Mrs. Moon was whom Father borrowed most of the new books from. She'd sent a note or two to the woman—and always told Father to thank her—but she now heartily regretted her lack of spoken gratitude for Mrs. Moon's generosity.

"I do remember," she said. "I've been meanin' to thank ye for the books ye've allowed me to borrow. I've enjoyed each of 'em greatly."

Mrs. Moon hardly looked upset that Livvy had yet to thank her face-to-face, much to Livvy's relief. "Oh, I be that glad to 'ear it. 'Ave ye a favorite, per'aps?"

Ophelia and Portia exchanged glances of boredom. How someone as delightful as Mrs. Moon could have such daughters as tiresome as these was beyond Livvy.

She ought to have cringed at her own judgments. Instead, she decided to simply pray extra hard for forgiveness tonight.

"I be partial to many of 'em," Livvy said. "Though I especially liked..." She paused. She was speaking of reading. But then, surely she would be rude not to answer the question, wouldn't she? She would simply finish the conversation before Father came through. "I especially liked *Tales of the Dead*."

Mrs. Moon's eyes brightened. "Oh, a chillin' collection. One o' me personal favorites, too."

Laughter from the men in the dining room nearby rumbled toward them like a distant summer thunderstorm, a promise of moisture to ease a sweltering day, but Livvy didn't mind being away from them as much now. As their conversation continued with Mrs. Moon describing her plans to soon refurbish one of their rooms into a library to showcase even more of the books she possessed, Livvy also found her eyes darting less longingly to the door.

"And what 'ave ye been readin' lately?" Mrs. Moon asked next. "Anythin' to recommend?"

Livvy shifted her head back and forth as she thought. "I've read a few, yes. I only just started *Robinson Crusoe*. I be enjoyin' most of it, though there be moments with which I do not connect."

"Such as?" Ophelia asked, as if desperate to involve herself in the conversation somehow. She must have realized the two of them were going to continue speaking of books.

Livvy hesitated. "Oh, I'd never dream o' taintin' someone's opinion on a book they 'aven't read yet by sharin' moments I didn't enjoy—or issues I disagree with. 'Sides, every author be a product o' their own time, and every author, I believe, does 'is or 'er best to tell the tale they wish to. Who be I to judge what one chooses to write about?"

Ophelia sniffed. "Well, I for one take no issue in *judgmentin'* a book I do not like."

Livvy stifled the response she longed to give. Perhaps if Ophelia spent less time *'judgmenting'* books, she'd find more time learning to use proper words.

But that would hardly be the kind thing to say. Honestly, Ophelia was a clever girl. She knew how to converse and how to work a crowd, things Livvy would never be able to do. She shouldn't judge the girl for her lack of reading or proper speech simply because her strengths lied elsewhere.

"I can see your understandin'," Livvy said instead. "But so much of 'ow we judge a book is based off our moods, our education, our beliefs, our temperaments, e'en our very souls. What connects with one reader might not connect with another—but does that make it the author's fault...or the readers'?"

CHAPTER SEVEN

"Look like the innocent flower / But be the serpent under it."
Macbeth, William Shakespeare

Silence met the group. Ophelia and Portia looked hardly impressed with Livvy's speech, though Mrs. Moon smiled with an agreeing nod.

This was precisely the reason why Father told Livvy not to speak about books. Because she always seemed to get carried away. She hoped she hadn't offended the girls, though. She wouldn't wish to do the same thing they'd done to her earlier—even if the Lady Macbeth version of Livvy wished to do the same.

"An excellent viewpoint," Mrs. Moon said, leaning forward, "and one I wholeheartedly agree with."

Movement occurred near the doorway—a footman waiting for his mistress's attention.

"Oh, do excuse me," Mrs. Moon said, standing to join the young man. "I'll be just a moment."

Mrs. Moon hadn't left the room, but she may as well have,

what with how uncomfortable the air between the Moon sisters and Livvy became.

She looked between them both, noting their boredom. Ophelia's curls were tighter than Portia's, and her eyes were slightly rounder when she smiled than her sister's. In every other way, however, the girls were identical—nearly indistinguishable.

"'Ow fortunate ye enjoy readin', Miss May," Portia said, adjusting the lace on her collar. "I know our mother enjoys speakin' with ye. It be a shame none of 'er children be as voracious readers as ye."

The slight edge to her voice made Livvy pause. They didn't think she believed she was above them, did they? "'Tisn't a pastime for everyone. But that be fine. We've all our own likes and dislikes."

"Indeed," Ophelia said. "It be fortunate. Though I've 'eard people who read do so 'cause their lives lack excitement."

Livvy pressed her lips together. When she couldn't tell the sisters apart based on looks, she only had to hear them speak. Ophelia was always more biting.

Besides, Livvy did not read to give her life more excitement. She read to give her life *meaning*. But these girls would never understand it.

"I daresay Miss Pengelly doesn't read," Ophelia said, turning to face her body directly toward her sister.

Portia did the same. Clearly, they were finished speaking with Livvy and wished to carry on the conversation by themselves, which Livvy was more than fine to allow.

Unfortunately, she could still hear every word of it.

"No, I daresay she does not," Portia returned.

"I daresay she 'as far too wonderful a life to 'ave time to. Especially now August 'as returned."

Livvy ignored the repeat of the word 'daresay,' listening far more devotedly now August was mentioned.

"I do wish she could 'ave come this evenin'," Ophelia continued. "She be such a joyous person to 'ave near."

"We shan't 'ave to wait long to 'ave her join us permanently, though," Portia said with a small smile.

Livvy's heart thudded dully against her chest. Did that mean...Were the two attached? Livvy thought they were simply friends.

"Yes." Ophelia sighed. "If our foolish brother would simply request 'er 'and, we'd all be 'appier."

Livvy glanced over her shoulder. Were the men through yet? She needed to speak with August so she could leave once and for all. It was fortunate she was only a four-second walk from home. That possibility of a quick escape was the only thing giving her comfort now.

Then again, if August was set on marrying Miss Pengelly, did Livvy have any reason to clarify that she wasn't as odd as he may have thought when he clearly would not care?

Shaking her head, she determined to be rid of the girls' words until they could be proven. After all, she of all people knew how important it was to allow people to tell their own stories.

"So, Miss May."

Livvy pulled her gaze away from the doorway where Mrs. Moon and the footman were still speaking.

"Yes?" she questioned, facing Ophelia again.

Ophelia put on a sweet smile that seemed far too forced. "Do tell us why ye chose to come tonight of all nights."

Livvy froze. This was what she hated about gatherings—questions. Questions she didn't wish to answer. "I merely thought it be time for me to accompany Father."

Ophelia hardly looked convinced. "We were surprised ye could tear yourself away from your books long enough."

"Yes, quite surprised," Portia added.

Livvy only nodded. She felt herself sealing closed, like the barrels of pressed pilchards at the side of the Mount. This always happened when people tried to pry her open.

"Yes," Ophelia mused. "'Ow coincidental that ye decided to come the very week our brother 'as returned."

Livvy's mouth dried. Perhaps she hadn't been as vague as she'd hoped. Before she could think of anything to say to defend herself—which would have ultimately ended in a lie—Ophelia continued.

"Do tell us what ye've been doin' lately," she said. "We 'aven't seen ye in quite some time. Truly, we've all wondered what could've 'appened to make ye stay away for so long."

Her words were left hanging heavily open, which only proved to seal Livvy's lips instead. This was why people thought her odd and rude and rigid—because she would not divulge the most private happenings she held in her heart.

The girls waited, but Livvy refused to abide. "Nothin' happened," Livvy responded. "Aside from learnin' that I prefer the company o' fictional people to real ones."

Ophelia's eyes narrowed, but Livvy was finished. Dinner party be hanged. Her reputation be hanged. There was no possible way August would see the true Livvy when his sisters—indeed, even her own father—could not see past her foibles.

She shifted to stand, ready to leave for good when footsteps sounded behind her. The footman left just as the men joined them, and Mrs. Moon returned to her seat, followed closely by the others.

Livvy gritted her teeth. Perfect. Now she had to stay. Before, she would have only been embarrassing herself by leaving. Now, she would be humiliating her father. Again. She couldn't do it, not after all he'd done for her.

He'd stayed with her. Mother couldn't have said the same.

"Papa, thank goodness," Ophelia said, moving to stand beside him and kiss him on the cheek. "We were in want o' your intellectual conversation, as it 'as become so very drab without ye."

No one seemed to catch the slight but Father, who looked at Livvy with a condemning expression, as if to say, "What 'ave ye done, Lavinia?"

She longed to scoff. Of course he would blame her. She looked away, frankly done with this whole affair.

"Oh, I doubt your conversation could be very dull with Miss May 'ere."

Livvy glanced up at August, his charming smile directed at her from where he stood near the hearth.

Hmm. Well perhaps she could stay for a minute or more.

For Father.

The next half hour or so, the conversation shifted to August and his time at the estate in Coniston, where he'd served as head gardener. Livvy did her best not to seem too interested, though she clung to his every word as if they expelled the very air she needed to breathe.

"We be quite proud of our son," his father said, "bein' so young as head gardener for such an estate."

"'Tain't un'eard of, havin' a gentleman hire someone as young as I," August defended, as if he didn't deserve the praise.

"'Ow *did* ye get the position?" Father asked next.

August glanced to Livvy as he replied. "Mr. Eastwood, the gentleman o' the estate, 'eard o' me through me apprenticeship in Bath. 'E wished to change up the rigid gardens of 'is grandfather's estate to 'ave more life in it, so I agreed to do the best that I could. I'll always be grateful for what I learned there."

As he continued, Livvy was enraptured.

His anecdotes were simply delightful. His facial expressions, a pleasure to observe. And the deep, lulling quality to his voice mesmerized her from start to finish.

She'd heard the man talk before, but only ever from afar when she happened to overhear him...Very well, she had been eavesdropping, plain and simple. But now, having the opportunity to listen to him without the fear of being caught staring, she was certain this was what being in Heaven felt like.

That is, until Ophelia slipped in and began an in-depth description as to a person's choice of buttons and why choosing them was integral to an individual's sanity.

Before long, Livvy's lack of attention must have been revealed on her face, as Mrs. Moon leaned forward to face her more directly.

"My dear," she said softly as Ophelia and Portia continued their talk of buttons, "I was goin' to say this 'fore, but with the issue the footman brought to me about the tea and..." She shook her head, beginning again. "At any rate, would ye care to explore me new collection o' books? You're welcome to bring a few 'ome with ye for when ye finish what ye be readin' now."

Livvy's heart lifted at the mere thought, but with a quick glance at Father, whose stern eyes met hers, Livvy hesitated. "Oh, I...I wouldn't wish to disrupt the party."

But Mrs. Moon insisted. "Ye won't, I assure ye." Then, to Livvy's surprise, Mrs. Moon turned to August. "Will ye show Miss May the new collection your father 'as purchased for me, son?"

August nodded at once, but Livvy's cheeks instantly pinked as all eyes fell upon her. "I be sure I can find 'em on me own."

"No, no," Mrs. Moon continued. "Ye must choose at least

three books to take with ye, as I know 'ow fast ye read. August can be there to 'old 'em as ye make your decisions."

Before Livvy could protest further, August was at her side. "Allow me to show ye, Miss May," he said, then he bestowed on her yet another one of his warm smiles that stretched far into his eyes and reached far into the depths of her soul.

She swallowed hard, then moved toward the bookcase with August right behind her. Father gave her a warning look as she passed by, and she nodded subtly. He needn't worry. She wouldn't be speaking about books with August.

She would be speaking about reading in the bushes instead.

CHAPTER EIGHT

"Her next solicitude was to furnish herself with a well-chosen collection of books."
Cecilia; Memoirs of an Heiress, Frances Burney

Livvy stood before the towering bookshelves, eying the beautiful spines and leather bindings of Mrs. Moon's vast collection.

"As ye can see," August said, coming up behind her, "me mother 'as a bit of an obsession."

She smiled, though she was unsure how to respond. Did he disapprove of such an obsession? Should she reveal that she had just as much of one?

Laughter sounded at the other side of the room where their families still mingled, and August stared after them. He must be upset at having been dragged away from the rest of the party.

"Ye can return to your family if ye wish," she said. "I can set the books on the table just there 'stead of ye havin' to carry 'em."

As much as she had been hoping for the opportunity to speak with him this evening, she would hate to think that she was upsetting him in any way.

"If ye don't mind," August whispered for only her ears to hear, "I think I'd far prefer lookin' at these books with ye than 'ear another word 'bout gossip or ribbons from me sisters."

Livvy smiled. Charmer of the Mount, indeed. Nodding, she redirected her attention to the books, peering closer at the spines to distract herself from the smell of his sandalwood soap that continued to slip beneath her nose in pleasant waves.

"I take it ye 'ave a fair love o' books like me mother?" he asked next.

Livvy's stomach dropped like the tip of an oar plunging into a stormy sea. He had either gathered this knowledge from Mrs. Moon sending Livvy to choose a few books, or from seeing her that afternoon in the bushes.

Either way, it was the perfect shift into the conversation she had been hoping to start naturally.

It was time.

Drawing a deep breath, she brought the words to the forefront of her mind that she'd been rehearsing for hours. In a soft but firm whisper, she turned to him with her response. "I do 'ave an obsession with books. But I was not readin' in the bushes this afternoon."

August's eyebrows lifted in surprise. She could not be certain if he was doing so due to her seemingly random explanation or because she was denying reading in the bushes altogether.

"All right, then," he stated simply.

Livvy frowned. That was it? "Ye just...believe me?"

He tipped his head to the side. "Do ye take fault with my believin' ye?"

Livvy hesitated, glancing to Father. His eyes were focused on her in a way that made her think that he knew exactly what she was speaking of, though she was fairly certain he could not hear them from the far side of the room.

Her chest tightened, as if Sarah had too fiercely cinched her stays. Father was expecting her to not embarrass him, just like always.

Do not be odd. Do not be odd.

"No," she responded.

"Now *that* I don't believe," August said.

She bit the inside of her lip. August had believed her before. She didn't need to explain more. And yet...

"I just...." No. She shouldn't be speaking of this any further. She would simply be digging a deeper hole from which she would not be able to scramble out. And Father would be even more embarrassed.

"Yes?" August urged, obviously sensing her hesitance.

She glanced again to Father, and when she discovered him now speaking with the elder Mr. Moon, the tightness around her chest eased. If she could simply explain a bit more to August before Father looked back at her, she was certain she would feel far better.

"It be only that..." she paused, then finally released her pent-up words. "I spent a good deal o' time rehearsin' what I'd say to ye to convince ye that I wasn't readin' in the bushes, so havin' ye just believe me seems like a waste o' me time."

August's lip twitched. People typically laughed at her expense, making fun of her for her strange behavior, but with August, she wasn't so certain he was doing the same. Perhaps it was simply her fanciful state of mind that evening, but she felt as if he found her words humorous, not ridiculous.

His dark eyes sparkled like stars in the night's sky as he

smiled down at her. "Forgive me, Miss May. Allow me to start again."

He closed his eyes, straightened his back, then released a breath. When he looked at her again, he wrinkled his brow and delivered an exaggerated expression of dubiousness. "Ye claim ye weren't readin' in the bushes?" He let out a sniff. "As if I could believe that. Why don't ye try to defend yourself, then we'll see if I can trust ye."

Despite his quite admirable performance, his eyes still twinkled, and at the sight, every last thought of her father departed. Livvy was living an utter dream right now. She knew she ought not draw near to him. She knew any time spent with August would make her wish for more—which would inevitably lead to disappointment. But nothing was going to drag her back down to reality. She was an unfettered leaf drifting about on the winds of August's charisma.

"Very well, sir," she said, playing along as if she was as confident as the man standing before her. "I was not readin' in the bushes, though it appeared so. I was merely readin' beyond the bushes."

He waited for her to say more, then laughed when she didn't. His sisters' heads turned toward them, but he didn't seem to notice.

"Is that all ye 'ave to say?" he asked.

She nodded in silence.

"And 'ere I be waitin' for a grand explanation."

She couldn't help but meet that ever-contagious grin of his. "I suppose it sounded better in me 'ead than it did aloud."

He waved a hand in the air. "No, no. It was quite the succinct explanation. But now I can only wonder why ye 'ad to go *beyond* the bushes to read."

"Oh, that be 'cause I 'ave—" She stopped abruptly. She couldn't be telling August about her secret spot. Suppose he went there himself? Of course, that wouldn't be terrible. But he was almost always surrounded by his friends and sisters. She couldn't bear to have it overrun with folks.

"Because ye..." he pressed.

She pulled in her lips. "If I tell ye, ye 'ave to promise to keep it to yourself."

Intrigue lit his eyes. "Your secret will be safe with me, Miss May. Ye can trust me."

As if she had any choice but to tell him now. The man had captured her completely. She was fairly certain if he asked her to pretend to be a chicken on a boat in the middle of the sea, she would do so without hesitation.

"There be a location beyond the bushes," she began. "It be quite secluded and always quiet with a wonderful view o' the Mount. I enjoy readin' there, as I can do so uninterrupted." She pictured the spot, and she couldn't help the smile that tugged at her lips. "In the summer, there be a lovely little breeze that blows by, and when the sun shines, it warms me fingers as I turn the pages o' me books. I've yet to find a better spot on the mainland for readin'."

August's lips pressed together as he smiled, as if he were attempting to hide his full grin.

She looked away, her cheeks warming at his reaction. She'd gotten carried away, clearly. She'd revealed her strange behavior all while trying to *explain* her strange behavior.

"Or," she began, "perhaps I really am just as odd as everyone says, and I was truly readin' in the bushes."

August sniffed out a quiet laugh. "'Tisn't odd to wish to read without interruption. I can assure ye, if I told me mother 'bout such a spot, ye'd ne'er be alone there again." He smiled, and she was once more set to drifting on that airy, dream-induced wind.

"But worry not," he continued. "I shan't share your secret

with a soul. Though, it does make me wonder what a man must do to 'ave the privilege of knowing just 'ow far one must travel beyond the bushes to discover such a special location."

All August would have to do is smile at Livvy again and she'd share the deepest secrets of her heart with him.

Well, not the deepest. Not what Mother said.

"I suppose a man must enjoy readin' 'fore 'e be allowed to know where such a spot is," she said.

She braced herself for his answer. She didn't know what she'd do if he felt for books as his sisters did.

"I be in luck, then," he stated, taking a turn to eye the books before them. "I do enjoy a good novel. Howe'er, I must confess that I don't claim to enjoy 'em as much as me mother. Or ye, for that matter. Will that do?"

Yes, August. That will do just fine.

"I s'pose," she said much more calmly, then she faced the books again.

What was happening right now? Was she truly, dare she think it, *flirting* with August Moon? And was he flirting right back? Or was this simply the way he spoke with everyone? Admittedly, she found it difficult to care at the moment, his attention making her feel as special as a guinea in a pile of farthings.

"And yet ye still 'aven't shared the location o' the spot," August said, his smile drawing lines in his cheeks to mimic the curve of his lips. "But I won't press the issue further." He glanced at her sidelong. "Least not right now."

He winked at her. And Livvy died.

"Now," he said, mercifully turning to the books so she could breathe again, "which o' these many novels strikes your fancy, Miss May?"

Apparently not dead yet, Livvy narrowed her eyes, attempting to harness her vision to see the books instead of the man's flawless profile—straight nose, angled jawline, firm brow, masculine lips. She'd never been so attracted to a man. How fortunate he was not holding a book in his hands. *That* would have really done her in.

She still could not fathom that she was standing in August Moon's sitting room, choosing books to read from his mother's collection, all while he stood dutifully at her side. Surely she had dreamt up this whole scenario.

Yet, when August's questioning gaze fell on her, she snapped to attention.

Books. She was supposed to be choosing books.

Spotting a copy of *The Mysteries of Udolpho*, Livvy pulled it from the shelf. "I'd like this one, I think."

She was fairly certain she spoke the words aloud. She couldn't be sure, as his scent was making things hazy for her again.

He took the book and turned it over in his hands. That settled it. Handsome, kind, *and* holding a book.

Livvy died again.

When her heart resumed its pumping, she looked to the books once more, pulling down one from the middle of a Shakespearean collection of red-leathered spines.

"Ah, Shakespeare," August said, having recognized the collection. "Mother 'as far too many copies of 'is works, I be afeared."

"Oh, one can ne'er 'ave too many copies of a favorite."

August looked down at her with a half-smile. "It would appear that ye and me mother are one and the same."

She could only smile in return, still reeling at standing beside the man she'd loved for as long as she could remember. Not only that, but he also didn't seem the slightest put off by her odd behavior. She could certainly leave his home in peace now, just as he could leave her to rejoin his family. So why were neither of them moving? Was there any possible way he wasn't leaving her for the same reason she wasn't leaving him —because he was enjoying their conversation?

"Which play is this one, then?" August asked. He moved a step closer to her, curving his neck to the side to read the title.

"*Macbeth*," she replied, hoping he hadn't caught the tremor in her voice brought on by his proximity.

"Ah, yes. And 'ave ye read that one yet?"

"I've read all 'is work. Plays, sonnets, all of 'em."

August fell silent. Would this oddity of hers be the one to slam the casket closed on their friendship? She would be surprised if that ended up being the case. As far as her peculiarities went, this one was fairly innocuous.

"I do think ye might rival Mama in 'er devotion to Shakespeare," he said. "I don't believe she's read all 'is plays, let alone sonnets."

Livvy slid the book back into place. "I might beg to disagree, sir. Only the most devoted o' supporters would name 'er own children after an author's characters."

August looked down at her with a look of admiration. "Ye caught on to that, did ye?"

CHAPTER NINE

"I may have lost my heart, but not my self-control."
Emma, Jane Austen

"Yes, at once," Livvy explained, sliding her finger along the spine of the book.

August didn't respond for a moment, seeming to contemplate his response.

Perhaps Livvy was revealing too much. She really should do as Father said and behave more like a normal person. But then, she was having such a lovely time being herself.

"Be this somethin' ye wish to prove, too?" August asked. "As ye wished to prove ye weren't readin' in the bushes?"

She pulled in her lips to suppress what was sure to be the silliest smile that had ever stretched across a person's lips. Could this man be any more delightful?

"I *did* enjoy your playactin' 'fore," she said.

His eyes squinted before his smile even appeared. "Your wish be me command." He straightened again and put on that same dubious look from before. "Ye can't know *all* the plays. Surely ye be exaggeratin'."

She turned from the bookshelf and propped her hands on her hips in false annoyance. "I most certainly can. Ophelia be from *Hamlet*, and Portia be from *The Merchant of Venice*."

August looked to the side, speaking as if to himself. "If only I knew if that be accurate or not." He looked at her again with narrowed eyes. "Either o' those 'ave Puck?"

She smiled. "No, 'e be in *A Midsummer Night's Dream*."

He rubbed his jaw, and Livvy couldn't help but smile. The man was simply adorable, whether he knew Shakespeare or not.

He raised his chin. "Very well, ye've proven ye know me sisters' names. What about mine?"

"That be the easiest of 'em all. Either *Julius Caesar* or *Antony and Cleopatra*."

Finally, his pretended suspicion faded, and his smile returned. "Ye do impress me, Miss May."

Was he still playacting? He certainly seemed sincere. She stood on the tips of her toes to slide Macbeth back onto the shelves.

"Per'aps that be your intention, though," he continued. "To impress me."

Her cheeks blazed red. How the devil had he known that was precisely what she was attempting to do? She returned her attention to the books, but not before she saw the soft twinkling in his eye and the slight crease in his cheek that hinted of a smile.

He'd been teasing her. Again.

"Be ye in the habit o' teasin' unsuspectin' females, sir?" she asked, attempting to hide how delighted she was at being on the receiving end of his attentions.

His full smile finally revealed itself. "I think ye be the least unsuspectin' female on the Mount, Miss May."

She wasn't sure if that was a compliment or not, but she determined to take it as one.

Laughter sounded from the group behind them, and she turned to see Father's eyes still directed away from her. She knew she ought to be speaking about something other than books to August, but she couldn't bring herself to change topics.

"'Ave ye read any o' Shakespeare's works?" She pulled down a copy of *The Tempest*, which she'd only read once before.

He blew out a deflated breath. "I'm ashamed to say that I 'aven't. I'm afraid I don't 'ave much time for it." He stared up at the books. "Though Mother says if one truly wishes to read, one will do whate'er it takes to do so. Emma says so, too."

The magic around Livvy vanished like wisps of smoke on the air. Emma. Miss Pengelly. August had brought her into their conversation. Was that his subtle way of letting Livvy know about his attachment to the woman, or had it simply been a friendly mention?

Had Livvy been misreading the winks, the teasing, the flirtation all along, or was she misreading things now in assuming that he truly was attached to Miss Pengelly?

She'd promised not to believe anything the Moon sisters had said about August and his supposed relationship until she heard the truth from the man himself, so perhaps she ought to delve into that truth right now.

With a mouth as dry as sand untouched by the sea and a stomach filled with stones, she forced herself to begin the conversation. "Does Miss Pengelly read much?" she asked, forcing a light tone.

August paused, looking to the floor in thought. "I'm unsure, actually."

Livvy paused. Even after all the years they'd known one another and had been friends, he didn't know such a simple thing as Miss Pengelly's reading habits? That had to be a sign contrary to what his sisters had been saying, had it not?

"So 'ave ye a favorite Shakespeare play?" August asked, swerving around their previous conversation.

Instead of feeling flattered at his continued attention, confusion gripped Livvy's mind. She knew he'd been flirting with her. Just as she knew she'd seen admiration in his eyes when he looked at her. And as shocking as it was for her to hope that someone like August Moon could simply be interested in her—*her*, of all people—she knew August to be an honorable man. He would not be showing her this sort of attention unless he, himself, was unattached.

There was nothing more to it. His sisters had simply been misinformed. After all, this wouldn't be the first time they'd engaged in spreading false rumors about someone on the Mount, now would it?

Setting aside any remaining unease, Livvy faced August with a smile. "I've written a few lists to narrow it down, but—"

"Lists?" August interrupted.

She nodded, then hesitated. Was that not a normal thing to do either? "'Ow else would I decide if I didn't make a list o' the qualifications of each book?"

His lip twitched. "Ye do take this seriously."

Yes, she did. But maybe she ought not. Perhaps if she made light of her behavior, he wouldn't think her as strange. "Oh, I do. It be as serious as choosin' a spouse, I think."

Her ridiculous statement resulted in a chuckle from August, which was exactly what she'd been hoping for. "Very well, so ye've written your lists. And what did ye come to decide?"

Despite his obvious teasing, he did seem genuinely interested. Why else would he focus so much attention on her?

"*Hamlet* be me favorite. Followed closely by *Macbeth*."

August's brows arched in surprise. "Really? I was expectin' *Romeo and Juliet* or one o' the other romances to take the spot."

She guffawed, only realizing too late how very unladylike such a sound was. August didn't seem to notice, though.

Still, she cleared her throat and began again. "*Romeo and Juliet* be better described as a tragedy, I believe."

"One ye don't appreciate?" he guessed.

"Oh, it 'as many merits, as does any book. But I will say that the story was simply not for me. I'd ne'er go so far as to tell Shakespeare such a thing, though."

"I be sure 'e appreciates that."

"'E does. E'en deceased writers 'ave feelin's."

CHAPTER TEN

"We cannot judge either of the feelings or of the characters of men with perfect accuracy from their actions or their appearance in public; it is from their...half-finished sentences, that we may hope with the greatest probability of success to discover their real characters."

Castle Rackrent, Maria Edgeworth

August was pleased to have caused Miss May to laugh yet again. The sight of her dazzling smile was enough to make him desire the same for the rest of the evening and beyond.

He still didn't understand why his family had been so shocked that she would be joining them that evening.

"She 'asn't attended a social gatherin' in o'er a year, if not more," Mother had explained before the Mays had arrived. *"She doesn't enjoy socializin'."*

Seeing Miss May now, though, August had a hard time believing Mother's words. Yes, Miss May had been rather silent throughout dinner, but could she be blamed for not attempting to speak over her father and his sisters? At any rate, her ability to carry on a conversation, and a pleasant one at that, proved his mother may have been misinformed—possibly by his very sisters.

He glanced over his shoulders to where Ophelia and Portia spoke in hushed tones to one another, their heads close together as if plotting something secret—all while his parents spoke with Mr. Moon.

August still needed to speak with his parents about his sisters' behavior, but for right now, he was simply going to enjoy the opportunity he had to talk to Miss May on his own.

"I suppose we ought to be gettin' back to the others," Miss May said, obviously misunderstanding August's focus across the room.

But he wasn't quite finished with their conversation. She was so refreshingly different, this Miss May. He only ever remembered her as being a quiet sort of girl who kept to herself. But now, with her passion for reading and a wit that rivaled Emma's, August couldn't seem to pry himself away from her. At least not yet.

"Ah, but ye've only chosen one book to take with ye," he said, raising *The Mysteries of Udolpho* in his hand.

She lifted *The Tempest* in her own. "And this one."

He extended his hand for the book, and she allowed him to take it. "That be two," he said. "Mother said to take a few, so ye need at least one more." Was his attempt to keep her there for longer too obvious?

The shimmer in her blue eyes made him think she had caught onto his plan, but also that she didn't seem to mind it.

"Very well," she relented. "I'll continue lookin'."

She had such a lovely voice. It was a touch lower than most women but still thoroughly feminine.

August shifted to look at the bookshelf again, though he

kept his eyes on her from the side, noting the smooth angle of her jaw and the curve of her neck as she peered to the top of the bookshelves.

She pulled down another book, flipping through a few pages before sliding it back between the other books and finding another.

She seemed to be taking this task very seriously, just like her list-making.

Honestly, he'd never heard anything more adorable in his life. And there were worse things for a woman to obsess over than books. Buttons, for instance, like his sisters.

He eyed the books she'd chosen and quirked his head. "'Ow long will it take ye to read these?"

She kept her eyes on the bookshelf. "Depends on if I enjoy 'em or not. I've not read *The Tempest* in a while, either, so I'd say...a week?"

"A week?" he said, surprised.

"Be that too long?" Worry clouded her eyes.

How could she be so utterly adorable?

"Not at all," he replied. "It just means I get to see ye sooner when ye return 'em."

Miss May's wide eyes turned on him. She'd obviously taken his words exactly as he'd meant them. Was he being too forward? Was it terrible that he didn't care if he was?

"Unless ye don't wish to return 'em yourself," he said, leaving his comment open-ended.

To his delight, she shook her head with a smile. "No, I'd like to."

August's heart fluttered like loose petals of a blossoming apple tree in the spring. It had been a long time since he'd felt so giddy, so boyish. But there was something about this woman that was so unexpected, so refreshing, he couldn't help his reaction to her.

Why had no one warned him that he would fall for her charm, instead of warning him about her lack of societal norms?

"Be somethin' wrong?" she asked next, having obviously seen his stares in her direction.

"Forgive me for sayin' so," he said gingerly, "but ye be different than what I was told to expect of ye."

To his dismay, the light dimmed in her eyes. "People do love to talk," she said softly, gazing up at the books, "'specially when it be 'bout anyone but themselves."

August hesitated. So she knew what they said of her. What he couldn't understand was *why* it was said of her. Dare he ask?

He already knew that he would. If there was anything he'd learned from his years off the Mount, it was that life was far too short to *not* seek what he wanted. And he wanted to know Miss May, so know Miss May, he would.

But what about Emma?

His heart dropped.

Upon his return to the Mount, Emma and Nicholas had approached him in secrecy, revealing the fact that they'd fallen in love with each other over the last year. While thrilled for them, August knew the risk involved, for the Cuffs and the Pengellys had been at odds for as long as August could remember, and they certainly wouldn't look kindly on their children falling for one another—in true *Romeo and Juliet* fashion. Nicholas and Emma hoped their parents would one day understand, but no one was so naïve as to believe such a miracle could occur.

"If ye pretend to 'ave an attachment to Emma," Nicholas had explained, *"only for a month or so, then no one would e'er expect to see anythin' 'tween Emma and meself."*

August had been hesitant at first, not wishing to lead anyone astray or bring Emma's name into the gossip circles of the Mount, but after more conversation, he knew this was the best way to help his friends.

Only now, however, did he see the true effect of his agreement. He could not pay as much attention to Miss May as he wished to if he was going to keep up appearances with Emma.

But surely one evening speaking with Miss May would not injure his plan with Emma and Nicholas. He was three-quarters certain that it wouldn't. At any rate, he wouldn't risk injuring Miss May now by walking away without a natural departure.

He stared down at her again, ready to ask another question about her reading habits. To his surprise, she was no longer looking at the books, but over August's shoulder. He followed her gaze, finding Mr. May watching them with a focused look. He caught August's eye, then hurriedly looked away.

Had Mr. May been watching them the entire time? August knew how his behavior would appear to a protective father, and while he wished to know Miss May further, he couldn't very well risk upsetting his supervisor—or allowing the man to think that August had any intention where his daughter was concerned. Not while August's duty lay with Emma. He could only pray their ruse would not last long. A woman as delightful as Miss May would not remain single forever.

Consciously, he took a step away from her. Whatever Mr. May thought, August would be wise to tread carefully where the man was concerned. August had plans to live on the Mount for the rest of his days, and doing anything to upset his supervisor at the one job he wished to work would hardly be wise.

"I s'pose your father will be wantin' ye back with the others," he said softly.

She sniffed, though he couldn't tell if it was due to a watery nose or out of derision. "Yes. 'E doesn't like me speakin' o' books very often."

So, it had been out of derision, then. Before August could ask for more information—and possibly risk upsetting her further—he watched her reach up to take another book.

"I think I'll choose this one," Miss May said, pulling down a copy of *The Hermit's Cell.*

"A fine choice," he stated.

"Ye've read it?"

"No, but any story involvin' a hermit must be a classic."

She smiled at his teasing, though it faded faster than before.

He couldn't end the evening this way. Never mind his agreement with Emma and Nicholas. If his duty to them prevented him from being kind to another person, they wouldn't have wanted him to agree to it anyway.

"I must say, Miss May," he said, taking the book from her as he held all three together in his hands, "ye've inspired me. I think I'll make more time for readin' now."

"Will ye?"

"Yes. In fact..." He paused, peering up at the books. "Yes. If ye promise to ensure that I be 'ome when ye return these books, I'll promise to read one book o' your choosin' within the week."

She arched her brows. "A week? That be a lofty goal, sir."

"Do ye doubt me?"

"Very much."

He laughed at her forthrightness. "Go on, then," he said, motioning to the bookshelf. "Ye must choose one for me."

She gave him a look, as if to see if he was serious. When he motioned to the shelf again, she shrugged and turned to the books herself.

She looked through the titles before a smile spread slowly across her lips. "That one. Right there."

She pointed to the top shelf, and he ran his fingers along the spines.

"No, to the left," she corrected. He moved his finger to the left. "No. No. Yes, that one."

"This one?"

"That one."

August pulled down the thickest book he'd ever seen in his life and read the title.

Don Quixote.

"'Eavens above," he breathed. "I'm to read this in a week?"

She shrugged. "It shouldn't be too 'ard for ye. It be an easy read."

Was she serious? The expression on her face certainly made him believe so. Well, if he wanted to see this woman again, he certainly had his work cut out for him.

"I don't know what be more concernin'," he said, noting the freckles chasing after each other across her cheeks and the bridge of her nose. "That ye believe I be in need of an easy read, or that ye've declared this"—he heaved the book in the air—"an easy read."

She laughed, that contagious, charming laugh, but her smile faltered as she looked over his shoulder, no doubt at her father. "'Ave we a deal, then?"

He paused, then sighed heavily. "Yes, Miss May. We 'ave a deal."

"Excellent. And now that I've chosen me books, I think we'd better return to the others."

August nodded with reluctant agreement. Neither of them turned to leave, however, and their eyes caught each other's.

A moment passed between them, the same as when they'd been in the brambles, and a connection occurred without either of them saying a word. Was such a thing possible? He'd never felt that way with anyone before, so to feel that draw, that pull to Miss May after only a few hours in her presence, seemed odd in the best way possible.

"Before we return," Miss May said, her voice quieter than before, "I wish to thank ye."

He tipped his head to the side. "For holdin' your books?"

"No, for speakin' with me. And makin' me feel more like I..." She sighed, shaking her head. "Father tells me not to speak 'bout books so often when I socialize, as it makes me...but it be all I can speak..." She stopped again. "I don't speak very often to many people, and I don't 'ave many..." Yet again, her words trailed off, and she stared at the floor. "Thank ye."

August's heart twisted. Between Miss May's broken sentences, he was fairly confident he could piece together her fragmented words.

"Speakin' 'bout books makes me odd."

"They be all I can talk about."

"I don't 'ave many friends."

To hear such words almost slip past her pink lips, he could hardly bear it.

"Miss May," he said, dipping his head until she met his gaze, "it was me pleasure to speak with ye."

The smile he was rewarded with made his heart take flight.

She curtsied, then ducked past him to sit beside her father.

August followed with her books in one hand and his enormous novel in the other, all the while regretting the fact that they had to rejoin the others. Because while he could justify spending time with Miss May that evening, he wasn't certain he would be able to get away with it after that night.

Especially not now that Mr. May seemed to be, unfortunately, watching his every move.

CHAPTER ELEVEN

"Roses have thorns, and silver fountains mud;
Clouds and eclipses stain both moon and sun,
And loathsome canker lives in sweetest bud."
Sonnet 35, William Shakespeare

August's knees creaked as he stood from where he'd been kneeling near the lavender garden. He'd spent the better part of an hour carefully trimming the overgrown broom bushes near the plants so both could better breathe. Another few months would pass by before the stems of the lavender would reveal their stunning purple flowers, but the broom bush was in full bloom, its small, yellow petals releasing its intoxicating scent of vanilla.

As August straightened further, his back protested at being hunched over for too long. He pressed a hand along his lower spine with a long stretch from side to side. If he was creaking and aching this much at nearly eight and twenty, he'd hate to think how he'd feel gardening in his fifties.

Truthfully, he didn't *need* to garden for the rest of his life—

nor did he need to garden now. His father's inheritance would take care of them all if August wanted to laze about for the rest of his days. But then, he had never wished for an idle life.

And of course, if he was granted sights such as what the Mount offered him on the daily, he'd have no trouble being distracted from his aching limbs for the rest of his days, just as he had no trouble being so now.

He drew in a deep breath of the fresh, briny air that always permeated the Mount, then cast his eyes about him. Spring had arrived, and he couldn't have been happier to be back in time to see his home returning to its full glory.

From where he stood, surrounded by patches of long grasses, dainty bluebells, and white, towering rhododendrons, August could almost convince himself that he stood in the middle of Eden, were it not for the continuous rain that pelted against his flat cap and did its best to penetrate the shoulders of his thick coat.

Behind him, a perfect view of the sea stretched out in unending miles, grey wave after grey wave drawing closer to the Mount, as if pulled by some magical force, futile to resist.

How August knew the feeling.

It was almost May, which meant the bright pink azaleas would soon pop out to show their glorious petals and the pockets of sea pinks would continue to thrive across the edges of the Mount, where not even the fierce winds and battering waves could diminish their stalwart positions.

He stood within the castle's gardens, situated directly north of the fortress and surrounded with thick, stone walls. Beyond the vibrant camellias and the yellow lichen attached to the grey stone like paint on a canvas, the grand and imposing edifice of the castle towered above him at the highest point on the Mount.

August had been to Marazion often enough to know how

large the castle truly was, but from his viewpoint below—with only a small turret pocketed with six windows and two other towers in sight—the stronghold appeared a fourth of its size.

As one of only four undergardeners for the castle and the Mount as a whole, August was one of the privileged few to see such a view, and he would be forever grateful and humbled at that fact.

Aside from the rather gloomy weather, he found nothing at which to complain. Truthfully, not even the rain was giving him grief. How could any moisture dampen his mood when such storms breathed life into the Mount?

After another sweeping glance around him and another satisfied sigh—*Eden, indeed*—August gathered the spare branches he'd trimmed from the hedgerows that had fallen from his wheelbarrow, piled them back in, then pushed the barrow toward his next trimming task, the bilberries near the gates.

He hadn't felt such peace, such harmony, in years, and he knew it was due to once again being on the Mount and doing what he loved to do the most—feeling the earth between his fingers, allowing the scent of the wet soil to saturate his senses, admiring God's creations that he helped to cultivate and nourish.

Rain clicked against the leaves of the oak tree to the right of the pebbled pathway, the only other sound that marked the air aside from the waves below and the rhythmic creaking of the wheelbarrow's wood.

August was certain he'd never get used to such peace, such tranquility. He knew he was biased, but honestly, who could ever not love St. Michael's Mount?

"Moon?"

August looked up in surprise as Mr. May walked toward him, his boots crunching in the gravel as he approached.

August's thoughts instantly returned to Miss May—where they'd continually drifted all day. Indeed, her striking eyes and small smile had lingered in the back of his mind since the night before.

"Afternoon, sir," August said. He stopped on the pathway next to Mr. May, still raising the wheelbarrow in his hands.

"Ye be finished with the trimmin'?" Mr. May asked, his eyes settling on the broom bush.

August turned to look at his work, hopeful it met with Mr. May's satisfaction as he continued his perusal of the yellow blooms.

"Yes, sir. I'll be 'eaded to the bilberry bushes next to finish off the day."

Mr. May nodded in silence. August had been quite unsettled going to work that morning, wondering if Mr. May would be upset with August for monopolizing Miss May's attention the night before. Would he tell August to no longer speak with her because August was so clearly—though not factually—attached to Emma?

And yet, Mr. May had seemed fine all day, instructing August on his many tasks without a hint of derision. Now that he thought of it, though, the man seemed more distracted than usual.

"Did ye get the north section cleared?" Mr. May asked next.

"I did, sir." That had been his first task of the day. Apparently, Sir John wished for all the fuchsias to be replanted elsewhere to make way for his new cacti collection he'd acquired. The man was quite eclectic in both his private and public life—possessing botanical and geological specimens, restoring the church on the Mount only a few years before, being a lifelong patron of the artist Opie, and...well, fathering fifteen children out of wedlock with two different mistresses.

Despite all of that, August admired the man's ability to do

as he wished—as did many others on the Mount. For it was a dream few could realize themselves.

"Ye be an 'ard worker, Moon," Mr. May said, drawing August's mind to the present. "I be grateful to 'ave brought ye on."

Pride—the decent kind—swelled in August's chest. Perhaps Mr. May wasn't upset with him after all. "Thank ye, sir. I be more than 'appy to be 'ere."

And he meant it. He'd loved his apprenticeship in Bath, and working as head gardener for the Eastwoods in Coniston had been an incredible learning experience he'd never forget.

But going back to his roots, to where he'd grown alongside the trees, to where he'd stepped on the earth that he'd once ran across as a boy, that was something special.

Gardening had always been a part of his life.

But gardening on the Mount was in his soul.

He looked back to Mr. May, but the man had fallen silent, staring at the dirt beneath the broom bush.

August followed his gaze, wondering if he'd missed a branch. "Be there somethin' wrong with it, sir?"

Mr. May blinked, clearly distracted. "Hmm? Oh, no. I just be thinkin'."

August waited, but Mr. May didn't expound, which was uncharacteristic. Typically, he was running his tongue about what plants grew better in which parts of the Mount or about different flowers he'd discovered in his studies. August usually enjoyed such conversations, but today, he couldn't decipher what was wrong.

"Last evenin' be a fine night," Mr. May eventually said.

August stiffened. He lowered the wheelbarrow to stand on the wooden legs, fearing this conversation would need all of his focus and energy. "We were glad the both of ye could make it."

Well, he and his parents had been glad. His sisters, on the other hand...

"I can't believe 'ow Miss May 'as grown," August had said to his family after she and her father had left last evening.

"Grown duller in every way, ye mean?" Ophelia said with a laugh.

August had instantly frowned, shocked at his sister's ungenerous attitude. *"That wasn't kind, Ophelia,"* he'd returned.

What followed was Ophelia's attempt to assuage her guilt by shifting the attention to August, but he wouldn't think of her words right now.

Mama had chided his sister's unkindness before sending the girls off to bed, which provided August the perfect segue into his conversation with his parents. However, they didn't seem at all concerned about their daughters' behavior.

"They will grow out of it," Mama had said. *"I be certain of it."*

But August wasn't so sure. He simply couldn't understand why they felt the need to be so unkind to a woman who, he was fairly certain, did nothing to deserve any unkindness at all.

"Ye seemed quite focused on me daugh'er's conversation last night."

August's attention snapped to Mr. May. Had the man read his thoughts, or was that where his mind had strayed, too?

August swallowed, trying to buy more time before he responded. He needed to reply with care, unsure of why Mr. May had mentioned the topic in the first place. "We 'ad an enjoyable time chattin'. She be quite clever. Ye must be proud to call 'er your own."

There, that was very diplomatic of him.

Mr. May simply looked to the bright broom bush again. "Very proud," he mumbled, then he fell back into his thoughts.

August tapped his tongue against the roof of his mouth as

if counting the seconds that passed by in Mr. May's silence. Should August excuse himself to finish his tasks? Or did Mr. May wish for August to pry his thoughts from his mind?

Just as August decided to simply excuse himself, Mr. May spoke again.

"The only problem be..." he mumbled, "she, me Livvy..." He paused again, and August was reminded of the similar way in which Miss May had spoken the night before, as if they both had trouble formulating their thoughts when speaking of a topic with which they didn't seem entirely comfortable.

August waited in patience, not wishing to rush Mr. May as he finally continued.

"Livvy ain't very skilled, see," he said. "Least not in the ways o' proper society or talkin'."

August nearly balked. This was the third time he'd heard such a fact about Miss May. Now, more than ever, he simply couldn't understand it. How could all of these people be so terribly wrong about the woman? Had August missed something last night? No, no, he was certain his conversation with Miss May had been one of the best he'd experienced in years—and it had certainly not been with a woman who couldn't speak politely.

His confusion must have shown on his face as Mr. May shook his head. "No, I misspoke. Livvy knows 'ow to behave." His lips stretched into a grim line. "She simply chooses not to."

August paused. Very well, that made more sense. She had seemed to laugh and quip more than most women, and she definitely didn't bat her eyelashes as much as most. But then, how had she not behaved properly? By speaking of books when her father didn't approve? What was so very wrong about that?

"I be grateful for your kindness in speakin' with 'er," Mr. May continued. "Most people find 'er too odd to do so."

August was once again reminded of how his conversation

with Miss May had ended, with her admitting to not having very many friends—a fact he still could not wrap his mind around. He knew the Mount to be filled with kind, welcoming people. Was her experience so very different from his own?

"It be no trouble, sir," he reassured him.

He was toeing a fine line between expressing how greatly he'd enjoyed his time with Miss May and not wishing for Mr. May to assume that anything was going on between August and the man's daughter.

His words must have felt a little lackluster, however, as Mr. May grimaced. "Now, Moon, I don't bring this up lightly..."

Unease crept behind August, the same that accompanied seeing a sudden storm burgeoning on the horizon. He didn't know what Mr. May would say, but his instinct told him not to expect praise for his work any longer.

CHAPTER TWELVE

"We are not to judge the feelings of others by what we might feel in their place."
The vicar of Wakefield, Oliver Goldsmith

"I be at me wits end," Mr. May continued, his eyes still focused on the yellow flowers behind August. His long hair—quite similar to Miss May's in color and curls, fell out around his face from beneath his cap. "Ye see, other than meself, I've not seen me daugh'er interact with another soul as she did with ye last night."

August's ears were ringing. How could such a fact be true? And if it was...why him?

"I be certain ye saw me watchin' ye both."

"Yes, sir," August mumbled.

Mr. May nodded, as if unsurprised by August's affirmation. "I couldn't 'elp it, seein' 'ow often she smiled, 'ow she didn't try to escape the second ye were alone. I ain't ne'er seen 'er so 'appy. And I couldn't 'elp but notice that ye seemed to be enjoyin' yourself, too."

The knot in August's stomach secured itself ever tighter. This was what he'd been afraid of, the very thing his sisters had mentioned the night before.

"Ye seem awfully defensive o'er the girl," Ophelia had accused. *"Per'aps ye've taken a likin' to her. I do wonder what Miss Pengelly would think if she 'eard o' such news."*

Father had gently instructed the girls to leave their brother alone, but August knew this would not be the last he heard of such matters.

Truly, were it not for his agreement with Emma and Nicholas, August would've been flattered to learn of Miss May enjoying his company. Indeed, he would have been the first to admit his enjoyment of *her* company.

But he couldn't do that to his friends. He couldn't risk it. If news broke of August and Emma not being attached—though nothing official had ever been spoken and *would* never be spoken—the attention would fall on Emma more than ever, which meant that she would have to be even more careful with Nicholas than she was already.

So how was August to proceed now that Mr. May was involved? It was simple. He needed to stamp out the sparks before they grew into flames.

"I be that glad to 'ear she enjoyed the evenin'," he said gingerly, "and while I'd love to take credit, I do fear that 'er joy was simply due to speakin' o' books, and that be all."

But Mr. May shook his head. "'Twasn't just joy, Moon. I've seen 'er face countless times when she blabbers on 'bout 'em books she loves so greatly. But with ye, there be more to it. She be comfortable. And I ain't seen 'er that comfortable with another soul in years."

August stifled a sigh. While he wished desperately to be finished with this painfully uncomfortable conversation, he couldn't be so blunt as to injure Mr. May—or in turn, Miss May—by declaring his lack of interest in her.

Even though I 'ave a distinct interest in 'er.

Instead, August settled with something more indirect. "I do make it a point to ensure all those I speak with feel comfortable. I be glad Miss May did, as well."

Mr. May stared at him, his eyes narrowing slightly before he folded his arms across his chest. "Listen, Moon..."

August winced. Here it came. The blow.

"Me daugh'er be the single most unsociable creature on the Mount," Mr. May proclaimed. "And ye be one o' the *most* sociable. As such, I was hopin' that ye might...take 'er under your wing."

August paused. Take her...What? What in Heaven's name was the man on about? "Forgive me, Mr. May, but I be afeared I don't understand."

Mr. May took a step closer to August, glancing around them at the empty gardens before continuing. "I wish for ye to show me daugh'er what good can come from socializin'. Teach 'er 'ow nice it can be to speak o' somethin' other 'an books. Show 'er 'ow to become a respectable member o' society so she don't 'ave to deal with 'em rumors no more." He leaned ever closer, his voice dropping to a whisper. "'Elp 'er become a fine woman worthy o' findin' an 'usband."

August's lips parted in shock. The man could not be serious. August, teach Mr. May's daughter how to *catch a husband?*

He would have laughed had he not been so shocked. "Surely your daugh'er be more than capable o' findin' a spouse 'erself."

"Ye would think that," Mr. May mumbled. "Unfortunately, most men on the Mount know 'ow difficult she be. They've given up e'en tryin', just like everyone else 'as." He looked up at August. "Everyone but ye."

Heavens. He wasn't suggesting... "Ye mean, ye want Miss May and I to..."

Mr. May pulled back with a fierce scowl. "No, Mr. Moon," he said firmly. "I ain't suggestin' such a thing. In fact, I be suggestin' the opposite. I need ye to make 'er appealin' to men *off* the Mount."

"Off the Mount, sir?" August's mind was reeling. He could hardly make sense of what Mr. May was requesting of him, let alone why. Nor could he understand the strange and sudden slither of disappointment that snuck up behind him when he discovered that Mr. May did not intend August to wed his daughter after all.

He pushed the annoying feeling away. He hardly knew the woman. How could he be disappointed by such a fact? At any rate, this was better for everyone. Now his secret plan with Emma and Nicholas would be able to continue without a hitch.

"Yes, off the Mount." Mr. May's jaw twitched as he repeated August's words. "She must learn to see that livin' off the Mount'll bring 'er more 'appiness than stayin' 'ere e'er would."

August paused. So he was supposed to show her how living off the Mount would be better for her? He blew out a disbelieving breath. "I be sorry, sir, but I don't think I be the one to convince 'er to move off the Mount. I love livin' 'ere more 'an anythin'. To convince someone to leave a place I couldn't imagine leavin' meself again..."

But Mr. May shook his head. "Ye don't 'ave to convince 'er to leave. She'll *want* to leave. Eventually." He averted his gaze for a moment before facing August head-on once again. "All me daugh'er needs be someone she can trust, someone she be comfortable with"—he motioned to August—"to show 'er 'ow to be normal. When she sees that socializin' can be a joy, she'll be ready to marry. Since no one on the Mount would wish to marry 'er, she must find an 'usband on the mainland, where she'll realize she'll be 'appiest."

August didn't say a word. He *couldn't* say a word. How on earth could he make sense of all of this? Befriend Miss May, encourage her to socialize, then convince her to leave the Mount? In all honesty, a small part of him knew great joy to hear that Miss May had spoken more comfortably around him than anyone else her father had ever seen. And while August wished to know why that was exactly, he couldn't afford to pursue such knowledge.

From what everyone on the Mount was saying, Livvy didn't like talking to others—and from what her father was saying, she didn't sound like she wished to leave the Mount at all. So how could August even begin to approach such a task? And why, *why* did Mr. May think August was the best man for the job?

"Surely there be someone better to 'elp, sir," he said. "A woman, per'aps. Miss Pengelly or e'en me mother."

Again, Mr. May shook his head. "No. I've watched Livvy interact with everyone. I can feel it in me bones. 'Tain't no one to convince 'er o' these things 'cept someone she be comfortable with."

"But it be one night, sir," August said. "We spoke for only an evenin'. Surely she'd be more comfortable with others, given the chance. Or with ye, 'er own father."

Mr. May looked back to the bushes. "I've tried for years. 'Tain't I who can 'elp 'er. 'Tis ye."

August blew out a breath, still scrambling for some ounce of logic to throw at the man, though he knew he was fighting a losing battle. Mr. May seemed bound and determined to have his way, as illogical as it was.

But when his eyes met August's again, Mr. May seemed to have aged years in a matter of moments. His eyes were sunken, the half-circles beneath them deep and grey. “I be desperate, Moon,” he whispered. “I need me daugh’er to be ’appy, and this be the only way. I was at a loss for years ’til I saw the both of ye last evenin’. I know ye be attached to Miss Pengelly, but I swear, this won’t ’urt your relationship with ’er.”

August’s concern was alleviated for just a moment at the words. So Mr. May had fallen for August and Emma’s ruse. That had to count for something.

“Please, August,” Mr. May continued. “I need your ’elp. Me daugh’er...She do need a friend.”

His voice broke at his final word, and so did August’s fortitude.

Stifling another sigh, he rubbed the back of his neck with his wet glove, allowing the moisture to cool his tensed muscles. This was asinine. Ludicrous. Absolutely ridiculous. And yet, he nodded.

“Very well,” he murmured. “Very well. I’ll ’elp if I can.”

Help being the keyword. If it shifted to something where he was no longer helping Miss May, he would end the charade in a moment’s notice.

The relief in Mr. May’s eyes at August’s acceptance did very little to quell his steadily rising nerves. “Thank ye. I couldn’t ’ave done it without ye. Thank ye.” He reached forward, clasping a hand to August’s shoulder before stepping back. “Oh, and I know I don’t need to say, but this needs to be done in secret. Should me daugh’er discover...”

“I shan’t speak a word, sir.”

And he meant it. The last thing he wanted was for Miss May to discover what was happening behind her back.

Mr. May left to the other side of the garden then, and August continued pushing his wheelbarrow toward the gate and his next task, his mind as unkempt and wild as the overgrown bilberry bushes themselves.

He couldn't believe he'd just agreed to such a ruse. Lying about being attached to Emma was one thing, but going behind Miss May's back to convince her to socialize? To convince her to *leave* the Mount?

He did not know how he could do it.

One thing was for certain, while he wished to help Mr. May and his daughter, if Miss May didn't wish to leave the Mount, August would not continue with any of this.

He couldn't bear it.

CHAPTER THIRTEEN

"My friends were poor but honest."
All's Well That Ends Well, William Shakespeare

Livvy's breathing grew heavier as she made her way farther up the Mount, leaning forward with each new step she took to be able to make it the rest of the way.

She'd lived on the island her entire life, and still she found it difficult to make it all the way to the top without stopping for a quick breath due to the steepness of the alternating steps and steep pathways.

Fortunately, today she wasn't headed to the top of the Mount where the castle rested. Instead, she was making her way to the east side. Steps and slick hillsides due to heavy rainfall still met her way, but the journey wasn't as arduous.

Anyway, it was worth it to see the Otterhams. It always was.

As the elderly couple came into view in their usual location —out of doors, in the midst of a field of Jersey cows—Livvy's mood instantly lightened, and her footsteps quickened.

It didn't take long for Mrs. Otterham to see her, and Livvy's delight increased as the woman's face brightened.

"Oh, Livvy May!" Mrs. Otterham called out, waving her hand in the air. She approached the wooden gate that kept the Jersey cows in the large pasture encircled with a stone wall. "I was so 'opin' ye would stop by today. 'Ow we've missed ye."

As the Mount's cow-keepers, Mr. and Mrs. Otterham watched over the herd of Jersey cows that provided milk for the three hundred or so citizens that lived on the island. In Livvy's opinion, there were no better caretakers for something so important for the Mount.

Mrs. Otterham exited the gate just as Livvy arrived, the woman pulling her into a warm embrace, which Livvy heartily returned.

Every Wednesday, she visited with the couple and their cows, counting the Otterhams as her only friends—see, she *did* have them. Last week, however, on account of a head cold and excessive concern from Father, Livvy had had to miss out on her visit, and she'd felt their absence greatly.

"Ye be feelin' better, yes?" Mrs. Otterham said, pulling back and staring at Livvy with a scrutinizing gaze. "Ye didn't come out walkin' when ye be unwell?"

"No, ma'am. I be feelin' much better."

Mrs. Otterham reached up, placing her hands on both sides of Livvy's face and grinned. Her wrinkles splayed out from her eyes like bright rays of sunshine. "Ye do be lookin' beautiful, me darlin'. As usual." Then she placed a loving kiss to Livvy's forehead before shouting over her shoulder. "Mr. Otter'am! Ye be comin'?" She didn't wait for a response before turning back to Livvy. "Did ye finish your new book, then?" she asked next as her husband approached, the herd of cows following behind him in a slow migration.

Livvy nodded. "Yes and started another. And three more."

Mrs. Otterham laughed. "Ain't that typical of ye. Best reader I know."

Livvy beamed like a child being praised for finishing her schooling. Where Father couldn't appreciate her reading abilities, the Otterhams did in excess. In fact, they were the ones who fueled her passion for the written word.

"There ye be," Mr. Otterham said, finally reaching the gate. "'Ow be me favorite woman on the island?" He paused, turning to his wife, his greying hair flipping out in tufts beneath his cap. "'Sides me wife, 'course."

Livvy grinned. How she loved these good, happy people. "I'm well, sir. And ye both be farin' fine?"

"Oh, same as usual," Mrs. Otterham said. "Me 'usband's back be actin' up, but 'e be copin' well enough. And ye know me and me knees. Other 'an that, we be fine and fitty, as usual."

"I be that glad to 'ear it. I was sorry to 'ave missed seein' ye both last week." She motioned behind them. "And 'ow be the cows farin'?"

"Oh, they be just fine. Enjoyin' Mr. Otter'am as he fusses o'er 'em."

"I don't fuss o'er 'em cows," he protested.

"Ye do, too. Ye take better care o' them than ye did your own children. Look at the crown o' flowers ye just put on ol' Charlotte, there."

Livvy glanced behind the couple as the cows reached them, popping their large heads and woeful eyes over the wooden fence to see what their keepers were up to. The closest one to them, Charlotte, chewed a mouthful of grass in circles, rain gathering in drops beneath her chin before dripping to the ground below.

The large white spot blazoned across her brow was half-hidden by a crown made up of long grasses and small, white daisies. Livvy couldn't help but smile. The love and attention the Otterhams bestowed on these cows were more than admirable, it was enviable.

"I do think it looks lovely," Livvy said.

"As do I," Mr. Otterham said with a wink. "'Twon't last long on her fore'ead, but at least she be lookin' presentable for a moment."

"'Ave ye tried to put one on 'er calf, yet?"

"Lucy?" Mr. Otterham shook his head, leaning back to see behind the cows. "'Eavens, no. She'd eat the thing 'fore I could finish it."

Livvy smiled, stepping closer to the fence to see the little calf hiding behind her mother's leg. "Ah, she be darlin' without it," Livvy said, crouching down to see the little calf's face through the gate. Lucy—Livvy tried to remember all the names of the cows, if only for Mr. and Mrs. Otterham's sake—stared back at her, taking a few tentative steps closer to Livvy before her long, pink tongue curled out from beneath her wide, black nose and licked Livvy's outstretched palm.

"Afternoon," she cooed, grinning at the affection she'd received.

How Livvy loved the spring. The rain, the newly blooming flowers, the calves. All of it breathed life back into the Mount and into the people.

Straightening from her crouched position, she turned to see Mrs. Otterham wincing as a raindrop splashed in her eyelashes. "This rain," she murmured. "Thought we'd 'ave a moment's peace from it, but 'Eaven do 'ave other plans."

"The cows seem to be enjoyin' it, though," Livvy said. "Think o' 'ow clean they'll be with all this water. And the flowers'll thrive more, and the grass'll be greener."

Mrs. Otterham patted Livvy's cheek again. "Ye always do know 'ow to brighten me spirits, love."

Livvy could say the same about Mrs. Otterham. When Mother had died, Livvy had been asked question after question about what had occurred and how it had happened. Children and adults alike seemed bound and determined to receive answers. But the Otterhams, instead of asking questions, had brought a care package for Livvy filled with books, a new warm blanket, and a few fruits.

Livvy hadn't realized until she was older how poor the Otterhams were. Only then did she learn to truly appreciate the gift she'd been given by them. They'd also encouraged her to visit with the cows whenever Livvy wished to—a fact that helped to distract her from the pain of her mother's death. While there, they would speak of books and cows and the sea —never her parents, which she appreciated, too. Livvy wouldn't be the person she was today without their influence in her life.

Another drop of rain fell in Mrs. Otterham's eyes. She patted her stays, then turned to her husband. "I've misplaced me wretched handkerchief again, Brae."

Mr. Otterham came to his wife's aid, producing his grey handkerchief and delivering it to Mrs. Otterham, who used it to wipe the moisture from her eye.

Livvy watched the couple with admiration. She'd always loved how they loved each other. Livvy could count on one hand the number of times Father and Mother had been affectionate with Livvy—and she could not remember a single time when they were affectionate with each other.

Dismissing the sorrowful thought, she returned her attention to the cows. More and more of them poked their heads over the gate and above the stone wall, their ears sticking straight out, like a bird's airborne wings.

Livvy did her best to pet and name each one, only being corrected once by Mr. Otterham—"This one be Anna, *that* one be Beatrice." "Oh, does it really matter, Brae?"—as the three of them visited with one another.

Soon, the conversation shifted from the cows to the Otterhams' children and grandchildren, who lived on the mainland in Mousehole.

"I do wish they lived closer, but we must be grateful for what we 'ave, mustn't we?" Mrs. Otterham said.

"That be enough 'bout we, though," Mr. Otterham said. "Tell us more 'bout what ye've been up to."

Livvy's thoughts instantly shifted to the night before, dining with August's family, speaking with him about books, living out a dream she thought would never come to fruition.

"Oh, nothin', really," she replied. "Aside from readin' me new books."

The discussion settled on her reading, then, which Mrs. Otterham always feigned more interest in than Livvy was certain she had. Never mind that, though. If the couple were willing to listen to her retell all that she'd read after a week or two of reading, she would gladly do so. Especially if that meant not going into detail about a certain dinner party she attended.

They'd always been dull, dreadful, stressful affairs. But last night, well, she would simply say that August Moon had the transfixing power that may have changed her mind forever.

As she finished her summarization of what she'd read thus far in *Robinson Crusoe* and tried yet again to push August's handsome features from her memory, the rain poured harder around them, and Livvy had to take her leave, if only to allow the poor couple to get to a shelter themselves.

"Ye best 'ead 'ome 'fore ye catch another cold," Mrs. Otterham said.

"Do take care on your return, darlin'," Mr. Otterham added.

Livvy bade farewell to the couple, promising to return

soon, then made her way along the muddy pathway, carefully sidestepping the puddles and patches of slick grass.

She focused so intently on her footing, her eyes staring hard at the ground, that she remained unaware of everything else around her until a deep voice spoke right behind her.

"Miss May?"

Livvy started, stopping in her tracks and whirling around to discover August Moon standing before her, and her heart stuttered.

CHAPTER FOURTEEN

"A short silence does much improve conversation."
Gulliver's Travels, Jonathan Swift

"Mr. Moon," Livvy greeted, her heart still in her throat.

She hadn't stopped thinking of August since the night before. Had she caused him to appear due to her unending thoughts? Or had he sought her out because he hadn't spoken with her enough last night?

Honestly, Livvy. A little humility might do ye good.

"Evenin', Miss May," August said, tipping his cap to her. His eyes revealed their characteristic squint as he delivered a half-smile. "What ye be doin' out in such weather?"

"Oh, just..." She trailed off. She couldn't very well say that she'd been petting cows. "I just be visitin' with a few friends."

His eyes searched hers. Was he considering her words from last night?

She'd been so frazzled, so anxious to share with him what his kindness had meant to her, that she'd been daft enough to reveal more than she'd wanted to at the end of their conversation—specifically her near-slip of admitting that she hadn't any friends.

What she'd meant to say was that she hadn't any friends *her age*, but August could hardly surmise such a fact. Did he notice her contradiction? Or had he simply thought she'd been lying then—or worse, lying now?

Despite the rushing sound of the pouring rain, silence marked the air between them. Livvy shifted her legs anxiously. She needed to explain herself. She didn't wish for him to think her a tale-maker.

"The Otterhams," she said. "Those be the friends who I be visitin'."

He looked down at her in confusion for a moment. "The cow-keepers?"

A twinge of pride poked at her heart. This must be the odd behavior he would finally look down on. But whether she was in love with August or not, she would not be ashamed of her friends, nor would she forget who she was or for what she stood.

"Yes," she said with a straightened spine. "I visit with 'em at least once a week. They be the finest couple on the Mount."

His eyes softened. "I be ashamed to say I don't know 'em well, though I be certain your 'igh praise be warranted."

She sighed with relief. All was right in the world once again.

That is, until the silence returned between them. This was very strange, indeed. The evening before, August had shifted comfortably from one subject to another, not a single moment of awkwardness occurring. Apart from when she'd seen Father watching them, of course.

She glanced up the pathway from where August had come,

half-expecting Father and his all-seeing eyes to appear next, even though she knew he was at home. She'd left him in the sitting room with his pipe and a glass of brandy when she'd first left for the Otterhams at four o'clock.

Perhaps August was quieter than before due to exhaustion from his day of work. The time had to be nearing six o'clock. "Are ye only just now finishin' your work?" she asked.

August nodded. "I 'ad a few extra tasks to see to 'fore I left."

Unfortunately, the fact that Father left when there was still work to be done didn't surprise her. She recalled a time when he'd remained at work until well after dark, simply to keep himself surrounded by plants and flowers and trees. Now, he no longer seemed to enjoy his work—or anything, for that matter. Besides *talking* about plants, that is.

Still, she worried that he was giving too much responsibility to his undergardeners while not accepting any himself. "I trust me father 'tain't askin' too much of ye durin' your first few weeks at the castle," she said.

A strange look crossed over August's features, and his eyebrows raised a fraction, but he quickly shook his head. "No, 'course not. I enjoy bein' busy. At least when it comes to gardenin'."

"I be glad."

Again, silence hung between them. But, why?

She peered up at him, only then noting how very different he appeared than the night before, not only in his clothes, but in the way he held himself. Gone was his focused gaze and comfortable stance, replaced with flitting eyes and tense shoulders, his gloved hands fidgeting as his fingers tapped against his thighs.

He could merely be chilled due to the rain. But then, something within her told her he was anxious, though she couldn't begin to understand why. August was never anxious.

"Were ye on your way 'ome?" he asked, his smile tight, as if it felt foreign on his own lips.

She nodded. "And ye?"

"Yes." He hesitated. "Well, no. I was to meet Nicholas at the Sugar Loaf 'fore dinner."

His eyes shifted about them. Was he looking for someone? If he was, he would be disappointed, as the pathway was vacant, everyone having taken shelter in their homes and nearby shops.

Or was he ensuring that no one was there to happen upon him speaking with the Hermit of the Mount?

Her heart twisted. No, that couldn't be true. He'd spoken with her that first time in Marazion and then in his home. Both times, he'd been surrounded by his family and friends. Surely he wouldn't be embarrassed to speak with her now.

Unless, of course, her words last night had been incriminating after all, pushing August to the edge where he no longer wished to speak with her.

"Would ye like me to see ye 'ome?" August asked next. "Then ye can get out o' this rain."

Livvy hesitated. "If ye wish to."

He nodded, and together, they walked side-by-side. Instead of looking about them any longer, August's eyes now focused on the ground.

Livvy released a stifled sigh. She couldn't carry on with this any longer. She despised assuming things about people—especially when others did the very same to her. So she needed to practice what she preached and simply focus on what she *did* know. August was walking with her. He had *asked* to walk with her. That meant that he wanted to, so she would take that and run with it.

"'Ave ye started readin' *Don Quixote* yet?" she asked, determining to carry on the conversation.

She didn't really expect him to read the entire book in a week, let alone to ever finish it. It had not been an easy read for her in the slightest, and while she was glad she read it—like any book—she could not say it had made her list of favorites.

She'd just been unable to help herself from challenging August to read it.

To her relief and delight, a shred of the August from the night before appeared, his shoulders lowering a fraction and his eyes focusing on her. "As a matter o' fact, I 'ave. I managed three whole pages 'fore I fell asleep last night."

"Excellent. At this rate, ye'll be finished by next year."

He chuckled, his laughter rumbling harmoniously with the rain and the sea's waves. "I'm beginnin' to think ye set me up for failure, Miss May. I'd have to stay awake 'til well past eleven o'clock to make any progress."

Livvy clamped her mouth shut. There was no need to tell August that she'd stayed up until two in the morning for the last three days. "Are ye at least enjoyin' the story?"

He nodded, then paused. "I would be enjoyin' it far more if I 'ad the slightest idea what I'd read."

She laughed. She'd forgotten how good it felt to do so aloud.

"I be certain ye'll understand it soon enough," she encouraged.

"I do 'ope so."

He looked down at her with a kind smile, but as their eyes met, that same strange expression crossed over his features. Worry clouded his eyes, his smile disappeared, and his lips tightened. What had she said? What had she done to make him behave so unlike himself?

He peered down at the ground, rain dripping from the tip of his cap. "Terrible weather, ain't it?"

His words were stinted, as if pulled from his recesses of

politeness rather than the natural feeling they'd held yesterday. Was she truly making him that uncomfortable? Or was it something else?

"I suppose," she replied.

He tipped his head to the side. "Ye *suppose* it be terrible weather?"

Instead of meeting his gaze, which had seemed to upset him before, she cast her eyes around them. The grey skies and falling rain caused the world around them to deepen with greens in every shade, and without the glare of the bright sun, a calmness settled around the land like a cool blanket.

When she mentioned to Father how she loved the rain, he'd huffed about how odd she was. The Otterhams, however, thought such a declaration had been wonderful.

What would August do?

Knowing she was flirting with fire, she faced him once again. He would either think her more odd or more appealing. That was all there was to it.

"I know 'tisn't a popular opinion," she began, "but I quite enjoy the rain. At times I enjoy it more than the sunshine. At any rate, if ye live on the Mount, 'tis far better to learn to love the rain than to try to fight against it."

To her relief, his expression softened, and the ends of his mouth tipped upward. "That be sound logic, Miss May."

Livvy's heart warmed.

Father believed that she sabotaged any friendship she might have had on the Mount by revealing her oddities to others. But Livvy liked to think of it as giving people a proper warning. If she revealed her true nature—which she didn't think was all that odd in reality, even if Father did—and people still wished to be around her, then she knew she'd met a true friend.

So far, only Mr. and Mrs. Otterham had passed her test. And now, it would appear August had, as well.

"Tell me, Miss May," he continued, "do ye e'er tire o' the rain? Or...or livin' on the Mount in general?"

CHAPTER FIFTEEN

"...and miserable it is to be to others cause of misery..."
Paradise Lost, John Milton

Livvy peered up at August, half-expecting him to drop his gaze again. But this time, his brown eyes focused so intently on her, she couldn't help but think that her answer might mean a great deal to him, though she had no idea why.

For a fleeting moment, she wondered if perhaps she ought to deliver the answer she assumed he wanted, but then, why would she only now start being someone she wasn't?

"No," she replied simply. "I love the rain. It be me second favorite weather. And as for livin' on the Mount..." She peered around him, catching sight of the grey waves of the sea just beyond the thick oak trees and luscious, green grass, all cloaked in shimmering rain. "I could ne'er grow tired o' livin' 'ere. It be simply the most magical o' places. Havin' our lives dictated by the tide. Bein' separated from the rest o' the world. 'Tain't no place better, as far as I be concerned."

A flash of disbelief flickered in and out of his eyes as he

focused more intently on her. "So ye 'ave no desire at all to see what else be out there?"

Livvy's brows pulled together. Why was he pressing this issue? He sounded like...

She stiffened. He sounded like Father. Had they spoken to each other? Talked about her desire to remain and Father's desire to have her leave?

No, she was being ridiculous. Father avoided conversations about Livvy at all costs. He would never wish to speak about his odd daughter for fear of becoming even more embarrassed by her. So why was August asking her such questions?

"Tell me, sir," she began, deciding to shift the focus on him, "'ow did *ye* feel livin' off the Mount? Were ye satisfied livin' elsewhere?"

He looked at her for a moment, his brow twitching as if he battled an internal storm within him. After another moment, his features softened again, and a smile curved his lip. "No, Miss May. 'Twasn't fulfillin' in the slightest. The only thing I did for nearly five years was count down the days 'til I could return to the Mount."

Hearing his words, Livvy nearly leapt with joy, though she allowed only her heart to do so. "It do appear that we be in agreement, then."

His eyes shone brightly just as they'd done the night before. "Indeed."

Their gazes met. No longer did he try to look away. "Now, did I 'ear ye say that rain be your *second* favorite weather?"

"Yes," she replied warily.

"I thought as much. So not only do ye 'ave lists o' your favorite books, but ye also 'ave lists o' your favorite weather?"

She nodded, holding her breath. She and her blasted list-making. Although, he hardly seemed put off by the habit.

"That do make me wonder what your first favorite weather

be." He gave her a sidelong glance, as if to say, *"Go on. Ye know ye wish to tell me."*

Honestly, with that alluring smile, Livvy would tell him anything. Just before she'd melt away to join the puddles of rain beneath them.

Instead of responding, however, she merely shrugged with a smile.

"Will ye tell me if I guess it?" he asked.

She nodded. "'Course."

"Be it the sunshine?"

"No, that be me fourth favorite."

His eyebrows raised. "That does rank low." He rubbed his jaw. "Very well. Thunderstorms?"

She shook her head. "Closer. They be me third."

"Snow?"

"Fifth."

He narrowed his eyes as if deep in thought.

"'Ave ye no further guesses?" she asked.

"No, I merely be strugglin' to think o' what sort o' weather be left."

She smiled, enjoying herself far too greatly.

After another moment, he sighed. "Very well, I give in."

"Mist," she finally revealed. "I love it best when the Mount be shrouded in mist."

Understanding dawned in his eyes. "Ah, 'course. I should've known ye'd enjoy such weather. Ye be as enigmatic as mist can be."

She paused. There was yet another word she wasn't sure she could take as a compliment.

"I think I'd like to make me own lists now," August continued. "Per'aps then we can compare and see what we 'ave in common. Though I can already say the sunshine be me favorite weather."

"I can't blame ye for that. But are ye certain ye can manage writin' lists when the simple book o' *Don Quixote* be gettin' the better of ye?"

He would know she was teasing, would he not?

August paused, his lips parted in feigned surprise. Then he clicked his tongue in reprimand. "I'll 'ave ye know, madam, that I ain't..."

His words faded as he glanced beyond Livvy, and the color drained from his face. Instantly, the mood shifted back to what it had been before—tense, rigid, unbearable.

Livvy frowned. Following his gaze over her shoulder, she found Miss Pengelly to be at the end of it. The woman strode toward them, her eyes down as she walked swiftly through the rain.

"Emma," August said in greeting, just before she might have collided with them.

Miss Pengelly looked up from the pathway in surprise, slowing to a halt as her eyes took in August and Livvy standing beside each other.

"Oh, evenin'," she greeted, clearly surprised at having met with anyone else on the pathway in such rain. "I didn't see ye both."

Her smile was strained as it settled on August, who took a few subtle steps away from Livvy.

Her heart echoed hollowly in her ears. Of course. Now it all made sense. August's tense shoulders, his fidgeting person, and his shifting eyes. He'd been worried about being discovered not by just anyone around the Mount, but by Miss Pengelly. There was no other explanation for his behavior.

So his sisters had been accurate in their assumptions, then. August did have an attachment to Miss Pengelly. Why else would he appear as if caught doing something he shouldn't be doing?

A sickness rose in her stomach, though she did her best to quell it. August was honorable. She knew that. He would never encourage anything between the two of them if he was unavailable. So had she truly misread his flirtatious remarks? His desire to see her more? Or was he merely wishing for friendship, and *she'd* been the one to take it a step too far?

Either way, Livvy was ripe with humiliation. How foolish she was to have believed that August might like her. And how horrifyingly she'd behaved, flirting with another woman's intended.

"'Ow do ye do, Miss May?" Miss Pengelly asked, her own shoulders raised in the pouring rain. "I do 'ope ye ain't too wet from bein' out 'ere."

Livvy's spirits fell even further at the woman's goodness.

Miss Pengelly, even though she'd just spotted her intended alone with another woman, hardly seemed put out by the fact —smiling kindly and asking after Livvy's comfort.

Shame on ye, she scolded herself. Miss Pengelly deserved far more respect than Livvy had shown.

"Yes, I be tryin'," Livvy responded, her cheeks burning despite the cool rain. She glanced to August, but she didn't have to look at him long to decipher what his expression held —Livvy was imposing.

"I do be feelin' a bit chilled, though," she said, taking a step away from the others. It was time to leave. "Lovely to see ye again, Miss Pengelly. Mr. Moon." She curtsied, averting her eyes from August, then sailed off down the island as fast as any gunship, praying to not slip despite her fast footing.

She was such a fool. To think of her pride in believing that August might be interested in her when he had Miss Pengelly to have and to hold. She and August were obviously made for each other in looks and temperament—not to mention the fact that Miss Pengelly was as normal as a person could come.

As if to prove the facts to herself again, Livvy looked over her shoulder. To her dismay, she spotted Miss Pengelly slipping a small letter into August's hand.

A love letter, no doubt.

Livvy's heart twisted again.

CHAPTER SIXTEEN

"In trying to please all, he had pleased none."
Aesop's Fables, Aesop

August quickly tucked the letter he'd procured from Emma into the dry security of his inner coat pocket.

"Ye'll see it gets to 'im safely?" Emma asked in the hushed tone she always used when it came to speaking of Nicholas.

"'Course," August reassured her. Along with playing the diverting part of Emma's possible intended, he'd also agreed to act as liaison between the two, delivering letters and messages when Emma and Nicholas couldn't do so safely themselves. He was more than happy to help. Truly, he was. It was just that now...

His eyes returned to where Miss May had scurried away from them, the muddy pathway now empty, apart from the small footprints she'd left behind.

He'd felt great relief in discovering that Miss May didn't wish to leave the Mount. Now all he needed to do was tell Mr.

May, who would rescind his request for August's help, and all would go back to normal.

August could continue his help with Emma and Nicholas—which would only last another month or two, he was certain—then he could focus more on his desire to get to know Miss May better. Mr. May would soon realize the error of his ways and agree to have his daughter marry someone on the Mount. All would be well. All would be *perfect*.

A scoff escaped August's lips as logic caught up with his heart. Good heavens. Was he so obtuse? Mr. May had seemed determined for her to marry off the Mount. But surely if the man knew there was someone interested in his daughter *on* the Mount...

There he went again, speaking of interest in and marriage to a woman he'd known his whole life but had really only known for two days. What was he thinking? Or was that the very problem, that he wasn't thinking at all—that he was simply swept up in feeling joy and delight whenever he was around the diverting and charming Miss May?

He was exhausted, that was all there was to it. He'd had a full day of work, his stockings were wet in his boots, and he'd made matters worse by fretting all afternoon.

"August?"

He blinked. Heavens. Emma. "Forgive me. I've been deep in thought all day."

Her eyes focused on him before trailing down the pathway. "I be sorry for interruptin' ye."

August shook his head with a reassuring smile. "There be nothin' to interrupt."

At any rate, he was the one who ought to be apologizing. He'd been filled with such shame when he'd first seen his friend. He didn't want Emma to think he wasn't taking his task seriously. But then, was he? Because if anyone else saw him alone with Miss May, surely talk would occur about August and Miss May instead of August and *Emma*. Truly, what had he been thinking, agreeing to Mr. May's request?

There was nothing else to be done. He would speak with him tomorrow. The man seemed to deeply love his daughter, so once Mr. May knew how she loved the Mount, there would be no chance he would still wish to convince her to leave. All truly would be well.

Or so, at least, August hoped.

All he needed to do now was explain himself to Emma. "I was only speakin' with Miss May," he assured her as she maintained her silence. "But I won't do so again, least not alone. I can see 'ow it would look to others."

Emma's face contorted in a frown, and she looked away, but not before he caught sight of the tears in her eyes.

"Emma? Are ye well?"

She shook her head. "No. I...I'm so sorry to be draggin' ye through this. Askin' ye to put your life on 'old so Nicholas and I can...When we don't e'en know if..." She stopped, shaking her head.

August's heart reached out to her, and he *would* help her. But this rain was doing neither of them any good. He shouldn't have stopped Miss May from going home, either, forcing her to remain in such weather.

Although it *was* her second favorite.

He set aside his thoughts and focused on Emma, offering her his arm. "Come. Allow me to walk ye 'ome and out o' this rain. We can speak along the way."

Emma nodded, sliding her hand around his arm as she spoke of the latest crisis unfolding around her. "Father fought with Mr. Cuff again last night."

August winced. "What 'appened?"

Emma nodded. "They 'appened to meet at the Sugar Loaf.

Both of 'em refused to leave and were pulled into a scuffle. I...I do fear this'll set us back weeks. We can't tell 'em 'bout Nicholas and I until matters be calmer 'tween 'em. But that means that ye..."

She looked up at him with sorrowful eyes. Instantly, August chided his selfish behavior from before. Time was on his side concerning Miss May. He would be able to befriend her and get to know her further in a few weeks—when his friends *weren't* in need of his services.

"Do not worry yourself o'er me, friend," he said, resting his hand on hers. "I be 'appy to 'elp both of ye for as long as ye need."

She nodded, though worry still creased her brow. "Thank ye, dear friend. Nicholas and I be so grateful. And I know your efforts be helpin'. Mother asks after ye a great deal and ne'er mentions Nicholas. No one seems aware that we were on the mainland, either."

"That be a relief." Journeying together had been a risky endeavor, but the couple had needed *some* semblance of normalcy in their lives.

"I be prayin' fervently every night that this may end soon," Emma continued. "So we can move on. So ye can, too. Then you'll be free to pursue your own future." She paused. "With the people ye wish to 'ave a future with."

August wasn't sure he wished to rise to her baiting. Obviously, she'd seen something between Miss May and himself, whether on the mainland or only moments ago. He wished he could let Emma know about his newfound feelings for his supervisor's daughter, but things were still too uncertain.

"Can I do anythin' for ye, August?" Emma asked. "After all ye've done for Nicholas and me, be there any way I can pay it back?"

Nicholas was about to wave aside the offer that came every

time she thanked August for his help, but he paused. "Actually, there do be somethin'."

Emma's brow raised in surprise, but she nodded with fervor. "Tell me."

August looked around them as they neared the other houses—Emma's house at the opposite end of the Mount than his and Miss May's. The rain had lessened to a degree, and a handful of people began to mosey about the grounds.

Stopping, he faced his friend. "I wonder if ye might be willin' to befriend Miss May."

Emma tipped her head to the side, clearly surprised at his request.

"I know it might seem strange, but..."

Emma shook her head. "No, not strange at all. I'd be 'appy to. I only wonder..." She hesitated.

"Go on."

"Well, I do wonder if she be *wantin'* friends."

August pulled back. Everyone wanted friends. It was part of human nature. Wasn't it?

"I've attempted to befriend 'er before," Emma continued. "She likes keepin' to 'erself, as far as I be aware."

August nodded. While he appreciated his friend's insight, that was not his experience with the Miss May from last night or even that afternoon. She'd appeared more than pleased to speak with him both days.

And there was still that moment he couldn't shake from his mind. The crack in her voice and the vulnerable look to her eye when she had thanked him for being kind to her.

That, more than anything, told him to trust his instinct.

"I realize she might be difficult to get to know," he said carefully, "and I wouldn't wish for ye to pressure 'er or make 'er uncomfortable. But I know the two of ye would get along, if she do wish for a friend after all."

Emma nodded at once, her spirits clearly brightening. She was no doubt pleased to have something else to focus on other than the heavy burden on her soul. "I be more than 'appy to try again. For ye and for Miss May."

August smiled his gratitude. Nicholas was a fortunate man to have acquired the love of such a selfless woman. And August was a fortunate man to be friends with them both.

Would the three of them one day be fortunate to have Miss May enter their tightknit circle?

An idea popped into his head, and he grinned. "If ye do find it difficult for 'er to speak, simply ask her what she enjoys readin'. That'll be sure to solidify a place for ye in 'er life."

Emma looked at August curiously, but he merely continued toward her home. After ensuring she was safely within, August headed to the pub and Nicholas, a lighter step to his gait.

He had a task to see to, yes. But in that moment, he was more motivated to see it through than ever. For the very moment Nicholas and Emma were free to be together, August could finally do what he wished to do—and that was pursue Miss May.

Because if he was considering marrying a woman he'd known for but two days, he knew she had to be someone special, indeed.

CHAPTER SEVENTEEN

"Now there is nothing in this world I abominate worse, than to be interrupted in a story..."
The Life and Opinions of Tristram Shandy, Gentleman, Laurence Sterne

Livvy sat in the sitting room with her father the next late afternoon, quietly stitching away as she glanced again at *Robinson Crusoe.* The book sat in the center of the table beside her, though Livvy could have sworn it had been inching toward her since she'd laid it to rest there an hour before. Those sneaky books always tended to do the same whenever she reached the penultimate chapter.

Not even Father would fault her for laying down her stitching right this minute and picking up the book to finish it. But Livvy wouldn't do it. She refused to give in, performing a much more important task at the moment—being in the service of Mrs. Otterham.

Anyway, she was nearly finished. One more handkerchief to embroider with her friend's initials and favorite flowers, then she'd have five ready to go. Now poor Mrs. Otterham would at least have a few spare when the rain inevitably pelted her eyes again. Livvy could easily sacrifice putting off her book for a few hours to create but a small token of her appreciation for all the woman had done for her.

A sharp pain stung her forefinger, and she gasped, pulling the needle from where she'd stuck it into her skin yet again. Swiftly, she pulled her finger to her mouth, grateful none of the blood had fed into the handkerchiefs.

"It be nice to see ye doin' somethin' other 'an readin'," Father said across from her, managing to pull his pipe from his mouth to speak. "E'en if ye've 'urt yourself more times 'an I can count." His eyes shone at his teasing.

Livvy hmphed under her breath. Despite the fact that Father's criticism was thinly veiled with humor, she still couldn't return his smile. Stitching was for the birds. Or at least, it was for women who didn't mind such a tedious task.

She glanced again to the book before reining in her eyes once again.

I be doin' this for Mrs. Otter'am. I be doin' this for Mrs. Otter'am.

A knock sounded at the front door, but Livvy didn't look up, focusing intently on her stitching instead. At any rate, she knew who was visiting.

Their maid-of-all-work, Sarah, would answer the knocking, then she'd alert Father that one of his work associates or fellow supervisors had come calling—as they often did to discuss Sir John's many wishes to enhance his gardens. They would meet in the small study next to the sitting room where Livvy would hear them speak until dinner.

She'd offered to leave the sitting room many times so Father could meet in privacy in a larger room, but he always told her not to worry, that he was more than happy in the study. In truth, Livvy knew he met in there because he was embarrassed by her and didn't wish to feel even worse about excluding her from the conversation.

In truth, she far preferred not having to sit through business meetings. She truly did try to make Father proud, to not speak about books and to pretend like she was enjoying the conversation, but she found herself fretting too greatly about what others were thinking about her—no doubt because of Father's words.

"Ye be different from 'em, Liv, and 'different' makes others uncomfortable."

The problem was, Livvy didn't see herself as so very different. Peculiar, perhaps. But why not...unique?

At any rate, Mrs. Moon loved to read, Mr. Otterham preferred not to socialize, and there was bound to be someone else on the Mount who made lists of their favorite things. Why was Livvy the outcast when she was simply everyone else's single oddities all rolled into one, like a Chelsea bun with too many currants? Was there no one on this earth who *liked* an excess of currants in their buns?

A smile that reached warm brown eyes flashed through her mind, but she set it aside. That possible-currant-lover was already attached to another, and she would do well to remember it.

As these thoughts and more continued, Livvy carried on with her stitching in the sitting room, fully expecting the very same events to occur as always as Sarah entered the room.

To her utter shock, however, Sarah did not turn to Father. She focused her attention on Livvy, the maid's look of bewilderment no doubt matching Livvy's. "Miss Pengelly, Miss Moon, and Miss Moon be 'ere to see ye, Miss May."

Livvy's stomach heaved like a barrel caught in the harbor water. "Me?"

She glanced to Father for an explanation, but he looked as astounded as Livvy felt.

"Show 'em in, then," he said.

Sarah nodded, curtsied, then returned to the front door.

Heavens above. What could such a group of women want with Livvy? Were they there because the Moon sisters had heard from Miss Pengelly about August speaking with Livvy alone? Had the three of them joined forces to threaten Livvy to keep away from August? She wouldn't put it past the sisters to do such a thing, but then, Miss Pengelly was so kind.

As footsteps clicked down the small corridor, she scrambled to remove the handkerchiefs, thread, and needle from her lap, standing just as the women entered the room.

With five individuals in their small sitting room, the space seemed to close in on itself—especially as the visitors blocked the doorway, Livvy's only chance at escape.

But then, would she need an escape? To her surprise, Miss Pengelly seemed more than happy as she smiled pleasantly in greeting. How could the woman appear so at ease after yesterday? August and Livvy had done nothing wrong, but she couldn't understand it. If *she'd* caught her intended with another single woman, she would have been furious—especially if that other woman was in love with August, too.

Ophelia and Portia cast their eyes about the room without moving their heads, as if shifting an inch would cause the cobwebs in the corners to fall upon them.

Livvy would have to make a note to tell Sarah to ensure the cobwebs were removed before anyone else could make a surprise appearance.

"Evenin', ladies," Father said, having stood from his chair, as well. "Lovely to see ye all."

"Evenin'," Miss Pengelly returned. "I be sorry if we be intrudin'."

Livvy looked for Father to answer again, but he stubbornly clamped his lips shut and subtly motioned for her to respond. She knew speaking was customary for one's own guests, but honestly, Father knew how she didn't like to speak in large groups.

And five was a very large group, even if that included herself and Father.

"No, ye ain't intrudin'," she finally mustered forth.

Miss Pengelly smiled. "We were simply wishin' to see if ye'd like to come with us to Marazion tomorrow to do a bit o' shoppin' for ribbons and such."

Livvy froze, just as she always did when people invited her to participate in activities she had no desire to involve herself in. She recognized how kind it was, and honestly, if it was just Miss Pengelly, Livvy might have actually considered it—if only to show the woman she wasn't despicable enough to continue to fawn over August, now he was attached to another.

But with the Miss Moons looking as disinterested as possible, Livvy knew there was no chance she would accept the offer. She could only wonder what Miss Pengelly must have said to the girls to get them to agree to invite Livvy in the first place.

Then again, why was *Miss Pengelly* inviting Livvy? The woman was seven years Livvy's senior and had not invited her to anything in years, apart from the obligated invitation on Marazion. Was Miss Pengelly marking her territory with August? Or...

August appeared in Livvy's mind, and she stiffened. Had *he* asked Miss Pengelly to befriend her because Livvy had let it slip that she didn't have any friends?

Before she could stop it, pride welled within her heart. August was being nice, she knew that. And so was Miss Pengelly. But why did people always think she needed charity?

That she needed them to beg their own friends to be friends with her? Was it so very wrong of her to wish for people to be friends with her simply because they *wished* to be?

With these crushing thoughts, Livvy gave an apologetic smile to Miss Pengelly. She didn't even bother looking at Ophelia and Portia again, to whom she didn't want to give the time of day. "Thank ye for the offer," she began, "but—"

Father stepped forward with his hand outstretched, cutting off her words. "Ye'd love to go, wouldn't ye, Liv?"

CHAPTER EIGHTEEN

"You must learn not only to judge but to act for yourself."
Evelina, Frances Burney

Livvy frowned. She knew Father wanted her to get out into Society, but did he have to embarrass her in such a way, treating her like a child?

"I would, yes," she said, her smile fading. "But I've a few matters to attend to tomorrow that can't be put off. So I be afeared I can't."

Miss Pengelly nodded understandingly. Ophelia and Portia exchanged looks with each other, as if to say, "We knew she would decline."

Father frowned but finally fell silent.

"Perhaps next time, then," Miss Pengelly said.

Livvy appreciated the woman's kindness, especially her acceptance of Livvy's refusal. Most people were offended when she declined their offers, deeming Livvy cruel or thoughtless. The truth of the matter was that Livvy could never agree to socialize in an environment where she knew she wasn't wanted.

Which was why speaking with August had been so simple, so comfortable. Because she'd actually felt wanted.

But that was in the past now.

"'Fore we leave," Miss Pengelly said, "I do wonder if ye've heard o' the assembly in Marazion, a fortnight from tomorrow."

Livvy tensed. "I 'aven't." That was a lie. She'd seen the notices outside of the inn in Marazion. After she'd humiliated herself emerging from a thicket of bushes.

"We'd love it if ye could come," Miss Pengelly said. "We always 'ave a nice time. I think ye might, too. Don't ye, ladies?"

"Absolutely," Ophelia said with a stiff smile.

Portia just nodded weakly.

Clearly, the girls wanted to leave.

Father was about to interject again, but Livvy spoke before he could. "Thank ye. I'll consider it."

Considering.

Considered.

Done.

She would *not* be attending the assembly.

An awkward silence traveled round the group, then Miss Pengelly nodded. "We shall leave ye to your evenin', then. Good day, Miss May, Mr. May."

"Goodbye," Livvy mumbled.

The ladies left, their footsteps traveling back down the corridor. Before the front door closed, Livvy had already built up her defenses. She would need them with Father.

To her surprise, however, he merely sat down in his chair in silence. Where was his usual lecture? His critique of her not going out in public?

Instead of asking for either of those things, she sat in

silence, finishing up the final handkerchief. Before long, however, the silence grew unbearable. The lecture would come at some point. She may as well get it over with now.

"'Ave ye nothin' to say 'bout me refusal, then?" she asked.

Father shook his head.

"Surely ye must. I can see ye thinkin' a great deal o'er there."

He sucked on his pipe, staring into the fire. "I just be thinkin' 'bout when ye used to play with the other children on the Mount."

Livvy looked away. The memory was not a pleasant one, if only because of the feelings of longing and regret that accompanied it. She had once been the most sociable child on the Mount. But after Mother's death, the gossip began, and she couldn't bear it any longer.

"What 'appened, Liv?" he asked softly. "What 'appened to make ye not want to go out anymore?"

She'd been asked this question before by him, and she always said the same thing. "I dealt with Mother's death differently than ye, Father. Ye took comfort in friends at the Sugar Loaf. I took comfort in books."

But there was more to it than that. There was always more. Like what Mother revealed on her deathbed for only Livvy's ears to hear. Or like what the children began to taunt her about.

"That don't explain why ye behave such a way now, though," he said. "Your mother's been gone for ten years. Surely ye 'ave healed enough to go to the mainland with those girls now."

She bit back a scoff. Yes, much time had passed. And she had healed much from Mother's death. But then, some of those wounds would no doubt be reopened if she returned to Society. Questions would come back. Rumors would abound. And

Livvy would feel the brunt of them all. Especially if the secret she held closest to her heart was revealed—the truth about Livvy's past.

"Ain't it better for me to remain away from others, so ye aren't embarrassed by me more?" she asked.

She held her breath, awaiting his response.

Father kept his eyes trained on the flames in the small hearth. "Ye won't get any better if ye don't 'ave practice," he finally returned.

Livvy's breath seeped from her lips, shriveling her heart in the process. Each time she mentioned to Father how she embarrassed him, she hoped he would contradict her words—*"Ye don't embarrass me, daugh'er."*

Yet each time, she was disappointed again and again.

What was wrong with her? Why could she just not push past her pride, fears, habits—whatever they were—and simply behave in a way that would not continue to ruin Father's life, as she was clearly doing now?

"I just can't understand it," Father continued. "Why did ye agree to go to the dinner party at the Moons and not to Marazion with the same girls?"

Livvy shifted uncomfortably in her seat. She didn't like conversations like this. Conversations that made her think on her actions. Made her *question* her actions. "I...I 'ad more time to prepare for the dinner party, rather than just the sudden invitation to go to Marazion."

Not to mention the fact that August had invited her to come to his house. But she would never mention that to Father. He would be horrified to learn of her secret love for August, no doubt scold her for falling for an unavailable man. Then there was the very real fact that Father wanted her off the Mount. How could she if she fell for a *resident* of the Mount?

"At any rate, ye *wanted* me to go to the party with ye," she continued. “Those women didn’t want me to come with ’em. Not really.”

“They seemed genuine enough to me.”

But she shook her head. “No. I be certain August Moon told ’em to ask me.”

Father’s eyes hardened, his skin ashen. “What?” he asked sharply.

Livvy pulled back. Had she said something wrong? Was he upset that August had helped her? She frowned in confusion. “I only said that I believe Mr. August Moon asked ’em to befriend me.”

Father’s lips thinned even further. “Why would ’e do such a thing?”

Livvy hesitated, though she knew speaking the truth at this point was unavoidable. She sighed. “I may have let it be known at the dinner party that I don’t ’ave as many friends as per’aps the average person does.” Understatement of the year. “I just assumed ’e felt sorry for me and asked ’is sisters and Miss Pengelly to include me in their lives.”

Now that she thought of it, perhaps that was why August was being kind to her in the first place—simply because he felt badly for her.

The thought, though she prayed it was not true, sapped away the last of her energy. Her limbs pulled down to the earth, and her spirits sank even further.

Father, however, visibly relaxed at her words, whatever she said obviously helping him. “’Tain’t a bad thing for ‘em to wish to ’elp ye, ye know,” he said, his eyes softening.

“I know.” Her shoulders slumped forward, and her mind wavered from the pride she felt before. “I just...Be it so ludicrous to wish for people to be me friends simply because they wish to be, rather than being *forced* to be?”

Father looked at her with an odd look of discomfort. “No,

Livvy. There ain't nothin' wrong with that." He looked away, staring down at his pipe. "Ye be a fine woman with a passion for life, and that be a wonderful thing to 'ave. And I do believe everyone wants to be loved for who they be." He looked back up at her. "But all o' we need to make changes within ourselves to better fit in with the society we be born into."

The hollowness in Livvy's chest increased. Her father's words weren't exactly the inspiring pieces of advice for which she was hoping. Still, he gave her credit for having a passion for life, and that was...something. "So I must change who I am in order for people to accept me?" she asked.

"Changin' yourself ain't exactly a bad thing," he said softly. "Everyone needs to change to be better."

Very well, she could give him that. But to change all the things about herself that weren't necessarily bad—her preference of rain over sun. Her desire to read more than socialize. Befriending cow-keepers. Laughing at her own jokes. Not wanting to speak her secrets to perfect strangers. Why did she have to stop being herself simply so people would accept her? Why couldn't she be just a little bit different, a little bit...odd?

"Trust me, Liv," Father continued in a soft voice, "the faster ye conform to Society's standards, the happier ye'll be."

Livvy stared at her father, struggling to keep her lips sealed. How could she trust the man when he, himself, was not happy? He, who conformed to everything? He stayed in his station, never rose above. He spoke when he was told to do so. Didn't read when he wasn't expected to. Never took a step out of place. And what had that gotten him? A wife who hadn't loved him and a daughter who embarrassed him.

How was that inspiring to Livvy in any way?

"I think I be goin' to rest for a bit," she said, eying her book on the table. Rest or read, the two were synonymous for her.

But Father raised a hand to stop her. "Just a moment. I

know I've mentioned to ye 'fore 'bout me cousins who live off the Mount."

She eyed him warily. Countless times he'd mentioned his distant relations who lived in landlocked Nanstallon, and countless times, she'd denied the suggestion. Now was not the time to discuss such things again. Surely he could see that. "Father..."

"'Ear me out," he said. "If ye promise to accept whate'er invitation comes to ye next, shoppin', attendin' a ball, whate'er it may be—if ye agree to go, I'll drop ye leavin' the Mount. At least for a time."

Livvy paused. Now that was an intriguing proposition. But did she truly wish to agree to socializing, especially when it could very easily be with the Moon sisters?

To have Father stop trying to get her to leave her home, she knew it would be worth it.

"Very well," she said. "I agree."

Father smiled, then leaned back against his chair as it creaked in protest. "Ye won't regret it, Liv. Ye'll learn to enjoy it, I be certain of it. Now get some rest."

Livvy nodded, gathering her stitching supplies and discreetly slipping her book beneath the handkerchiefs before making her way to her room, plopping down on her bed, and finishing the final chapters of *Robinson Crusoe*, delving deep into the words instead of dwelling on her present and far more depressing life.

CHAPTER NINETEEN

"He has no more manners than a bear,"
Evelina, Frances Burney

August had attempted to speak with Mr. May the day before, intending to share what he'd discovered about his daughter, but August hadn't been able to pull the man away from his work for a single moment.

Today, however, he was determined to relieve himself of his duty to convince Miss May off the Mount. Arriving early to work, he set his eyes on the doorway to the garden, prepared to wait outside until Mr. May arrived.

To his surprise, however, Mr. May was already there, his eyes finding August's in an instant.

Excellent, they would be able to take care of this swiftly, then.

And yet, when August took note of Mr. May's lowered brow, his stomach churned. What now? Had August done something he disapproved of? Or was Mr. may now going to task him with some other asinine request—convincing his maid to become lady of the castle, perhaps?

"Mornin', Moon," Mr. May greeted as August reached the door to the garden.

The blue light of a clouded dawn cast its reach across the white and deep purple hellebores that stood as sentinels on either side of the black, wooden door. The entryway was tucked nearly a foot inside the flawless archway covered in ivy, the layered stones stretching over the door like an arm reaching round for a tight embrace.

"Mornin', sir," August returned. He paused a few steps away from Mr. May and the closed door. "Lovely mornin'."

Mr. May hmphed in response. "Ye be 'ere early."

"Yes, sir." Well, there was no point prolonging this anymore than it already had been. August was more than ready to put an end to this whole debacle here and now. "I was hopin' to speak with ye."

Mr. May's stern brow raised a fraction, revealing his surprise, but he wiped it away in an instant. "That be the very reason I arrived early."

The foreboding tone to his voice did nothing for August's nerves. "Do go on, sir."

He thought Mr. May would have denied the option of going first, but the man did no such thing. That shouldn't have come as any surprise to August.

"I'll get right to it," he said, his eyes focused intently on August. Such a contrast from when he couldn't meet his gaze the last time they'd met in the gardens. "Did ye tell anyone 'bout what I asked ye to do?"

August pulled back, affronted at the question. He knew Mr. May didn't really know August all that well, despite his growing up next door to the man. But really, had the man so little faith in him?

"No, sir. I said I would not, and I did not."

Mr. May scrutinized him a moment, then his shoulders lowered. "Thank ye for bein' honest with I."

August nodded, though his defenses remained high. He did not appreciate his integrity being questioned. "May I ask why ye were askin'?"

Mr. May removed his cap and slid his fingers through his hair. "Miss Pengelly and your sisters came to me 'ouse yesterday, askin' me daugh'er to join 'em in Marazion. Some'ow, Liv thought they asked 'er 'cause *ye* asked 'em to."

August flushed. That Miss May was a perceptive little pisky. Despite feeling caught out, he couldn't help but admire her intellect.

"I will say, sir, that I did just that." Mr. May frowned, so August rushed forward. "I asked all three of 'em to 'elp befriend Miss May, though I said no reason as to why."

His sisters had been less enthusiastic than Emma had been, but after Mother overheard his request, she insisted her daughters be more kind, so Ophelia and Portia had reluctantly agreed.

Mr. May replaced his cap on his head. "I asked for ye to do the job, Mr. Moon. Not to pawn it off on 'em."

The *job*? August winced. Mr. May considered pushing his daughter off the Mount a job?

"I'm well aware what ye asked me to do, sir. But I didn't think it would 'urt to 'ave other women befriend Miss May, either."

August could see the struggle within Mr. May's very eyes before he finally relented. "Very well. I s'pose that might benefit the situation, too. But ye must be more careful in future. I cannot 'ave 'er discoverin' what we be up to."

August cringed. The whole matter was just *rotten*. Which

was why he could not go on a moment longer. "Sir, 'bout what I 'ad to speak with ye about..."

Mr. May nodded, motioning for August to proceed.

He drew a deep breath. "I managed to speak with your daugh'er on me way 'ome from work two days past."

Mr. May's eyes brightened. Clearly, he was not expecting what August would say next. "And what progress can ye share?"

"Well, none, sir."

Mr. May's expression fell.

"That is to say, I discovered somethin' else."

"And what be that, then?" His tone grew impatient. August needed to move on, and quickly.

"From me conversation with 'er, I was quite convinced that she be o' the persuasion to *not* leave the Mount." He looked away, his mind dwelling on those moments with her in the pouring rain, neither of them seeming to care about the fact that they were becoming swiftly soaked through, both of them simply enjoying their conversation with one another yet again.

"In fact," August continued, "she didn't hesitate to explain why she loved the Mount and that she 'ad no desire to leave it at all."

Mr. May's expression hardened. "She's been sayin' that since she was a child. But as I said 'fore, she'll quickly learn that life off the Mount'll be better for 'er. And ye'll be the one to convince 'er o' such."

August hesitated, speaking as carefully as he could. "Be ye certain, sir? 'Tisn't it better to take 'er opinion into account?"

Mr. May's eyes grew cold. "Ye be thinkin' ye know what be better for me daugh'er than I, 'er own father?"

This was not how August had foreseen the conversation going. Swiftly, he shook his head, panic flapping in his chest.

"Not at all, sir. I was merely statin' how greatly she loves the Mount on the chance that ye might've not known."

"Well, thank ye," Mr. May said, though he hardly sounded grateful at all. "But just so ye be aware, I know me daugh'er's desire to remain on the Mount, as well as 'ow she says she loves it 'ere." He took a step closer to August. "But I do know 'er better than anyone. And I know she'll not be 'appy 'ere in't future. So I'll stick to me plan to show 'er 'ow much better she'll be on the mainland, socializin' and marryin' a mainlander."

His words were final. There would be no changing his mind.

August only had one option left. "Very well, sir. I respect your decision to do what ye see fit for your own daugh'er. But as for me involvement, I be afeared I can't honorably go on with this."

If he'd seen Mr. May frustrated before—*cold* before—August had been wrong. He'd expected the man's face to grow red, perhaps for him to become frazzled, even shout a bit.

But a calmness crossed over his features, a lack of feeling in his eyes that frightened August to his core, though he couldn't be sure why. After all, what could the man do?

Still, it would be best to deescalate the situation while he still could. "I do 'ope ye can forgive me, sir, for not bein' able to do this for ye. But I be certain a man as wise as ye can understand why it'd be difficult for me to do this. Again, I 'ardly know your daugh'er. And while I agree that ye must know 'er very well, I...I cannot in good conscience work without 'er knowledge to convince 'er to leave the Mount. Howe'er, I'll be more than 'appy to continue bein' 'er friend. As I said 'fore, I enjoyed 'er company a great deal."

He finished, hoping his words would have some effect, but Mr. May's expressionless face remained.

"Sir?" August prompted when another moment passed by in silence.

Mr. May didn't look away, nor did he speak for another few moments. When he did speak, August wished he wouldn't have urged the man to continue.

"I misplaced one o' me gloves on me way 'ome from work yesterday," Mr. May said.

August stared. What was he supposed to say to that? Before he could think of a response, Mr. May continued.

"I went back up to the third tier in the walled gardens after dinner but couldn't find it," he continued. "Then I remembered I ended me day at the lower tier. I thought I'd just leave it there, find it this mornin' 'stead. Then I convinced meself that I needed the exercise."

August felt more and more uneasy as Mr. May's story continued. What was he going on about? Was he even aware of what he was saying, or had he lost all sense when August said he was no longer going to help?

"While there," Mr. May said, "I came across somethin' shockin'. Somethin' most people on the Mount would be very keen to 'ear."

August's heart trilled uncomfortably against his chest, making it difficult to breathe.

He knew. Mr. May knew.

"I also assume," Mr. May continued, "that what I saw—*who* I saw—would wish for their actions to remain secret."

August bit the inside of his cheek, his head spinning. "I be sorry, sir," he said, raising his chin and feigning ignorance, "but I don't know what ye be talkin' 'bout."

"Don't ye?"

August shook his head. It was mostly true. Honestly, August could be wrong about Mr. May knowing. The man could just be finding some way to coerce August into helping him.

"Then per'aps a little enlightenment might 'elp ye," Mr. May said, taking a step closer and lowering his voice. "'Cause I do believe that I saw a woman who's supposed to be engaged to *ye* wrapped up in the arms of a man 'er family would most certainly not approve of."

CHAPTER TWENTY

"My soul abhors a falsehood."
The Castle of Otranto, Horace Walpole

A slew of curse words flew through August's mind. Blast. Blast and blast again. Blast Emma and Nicholas for not being more careful. Blast their secrets. Blast the Cuffs and Pengellys for being so childish as to allow their petty feud to last so many years.

And blast this man.

August tried to hide his concern, but the satisfaction curving Mr. May's lips was palpable.

"I o'erheard the two of 'em speakin' whilst together," he continued. "Now, I don't claim to know all 'em details. But I do know that ye be more involved than I be sure ye'd like to let on. And I be sure ye know that if their parents discover their dishonesty—what they really be doin' in the dead o' night —'twouldn't be good for any of ye."

There it was, the reason behind Mr. May's story.

Extortion.

But surely August was wrong. Surely the man he grew up next to, the man who was the father of one of the sweetest women August had ever met, could not resort to something so disgusting, so base, so inherently evil as removing someone's ability to choose for themselves what they could or could not do.

"I still be uncertain what this 'as to do with anythin', sir," he said, deciding to play ignorant. "And certainly, it be none o' your business what those two do."

"That is where ye be wrong, Moon." Mr. May folded his arms. "I've noticed Mr. Cuff arrivin' late to work the last few weeks. I've let it pass for now, but I believe these late nights for 'im do be affectin' his productivity. That bein' said, I might just 'ave to let the man go."

So not only was Mr. May in possession of such facts that could ruin the happiness of Emma and Nicholas altogether, but he also had the grounds to remove Nicholas from his position as undergardener?

Bile rose in his throat. Nicholas had worked for that position for years—longer than August had. The two of them had dreams of working together as boys and had loved every minute of those dreams coming to fruition.

"Ye can't do that, sir," August said, frustration rising within him, as well as unexpected emotion. "It'd ruin 'is life." Obviously, telling Mr. May such a thing was futile. The man was clearly beyond feeling anything.

"I can," he said, putting pay to August's words. "And I can do more 'an that beside. 'Specially when I see that your work be sufferin', too."

August's jaw slackened. "Me work? I be doin' fine work, sir, and ye can't deny it."

"No, I can't," Mr. May said, honesty shining in his eyes for the first time that morning.

August could hardly breathe. His place of work at the castle was now at risk? He couldn't bear it. He couldn't bear to leave the Mount again—leave his family again—after only now just returning. But then, if he didn't have work at the castle, he would *have* to leave, for where else was a gardener to find work on the Mount when the only place to work was under the supervision of the deplorable man standing before him?

"Truly," Mr. May continued, "it'd be a shame to lose two fine workers right after another. But as I said 'fore. I be desperate for me daugh'er to be 'appy. And I be willin' to do whate'er it takes."

"E'en ruinin' the lives o' three people who don't deserve it?" August spat out. He was trapped, humiliated, like a wounded pup backed into a corner, hunted down and facing a rabid wolf.

"I be sorry it did come to this," Mr. May said, but August refused to acknowledge the truth in his eyes. "And I swear, if ye do your best where me daugh'er be concerned, your secret—Mr. Cuff's and Miss Pengelly's secret—I'll take 'em all to me grave."

As if the man's word meant anything to August now. The defiance still trying to sprout within him sparked, telling him to fight back. Perhaps Mr. May was lying. He wouldn't remove two innocent individuals from their places of employment and then reveal a forbidden love. Or would he?

Perhaps August could report him to someone. Sir John, another supervisor?

As if they'd believe a young, newly hired undergardener over a man who'd worked as head gardener for over fifteen years.

August looked into Mr. May's eyes, saw the desperation still saturating his features from the day before, and finally admitted the truth. There was nothing else to be done. He should have known this would happen. What other sort of man would force his only daughter from her home—the home she loved more than anything—simply because he thought it would be best for her?

His daughter. Miss May. Her soft features and blue eyes filled August's mind, and his heart pinched. She was yet another innocent victim in all of this.

"What say ye, Moon?" Mr. May asked, his jaw twitching with impatience. Or was it guilt?

August truly had no choice in the matter. If it was merely *his* job at risk...but then, it wasn't. There was nothing he could do but relent. He couldn't risk Emma and Nicholas's happiness. He couldn't risk Nicholas losing his work. And August's family would suffer if he had to leave, too.

But then, how could he knowingly trick Miss May to be his friend, to leave the Mount?

"Moon?"

August clenched his jaw. He couldn't voice it, he couldn't verbally agree to such debauchery, so he merely nodded.

"And ye swear to not tell me daugh'er?" Mr. May asked.

Again, August delivered a single nod.

Mr. May nodded. His vibrant blue eyes so like his daughter's—but holding so much more darkness—closed for a moment. "Thank ye."

"Do not thank me, sir," August said. "I do not do this for gratitude. And I do not do this for ye."

A flicker of shame crossed over Mr. May's features, but it was gone in a flash. "Well, the decision 'as been made. The deal be done. Ye know what ye must do?"

Lie to Miss May. Trick her into being his friend. Encourage her to socialize. Convince her to marry off the Mount.

He nodded again.

Mr. May turned toward the door, paused, then faced August again. "One more thing. I think it be best for ye to continue me daugh'er's belief that ye be attached to Miss Pengelly. I be sure ye can understand why."

He needn't explain further. August caught his meaning at once. Miss May needed to know August was attached to keep the two at arm's length from one another because Mr. May still wished for his daughter to marry someone off the Mount.

Did that mean the man was concerned that Livvy was falling for August?

He didn't allow himself to dwell on the thought, delivering another silent nod instead.

Mr. May motioned to the doorway of the gardens. "Ye best be 'bout your work, then. Busy day ahead o' we all." Then he unlocked the door and led the way forward.

August didn't follow him. He couldn't. He was far too tempted to attack the man from behind, to shake some sense into his addlepated brain.

What did Miss May do to deserve such a father? What did *any* of them do to deserve such horrible treatment?

His final words to Mr. May echoed in his mind. No, he was not doing any of this for him. So why *was* he doing it?

He was doing it for the sake of his friends.

He was doing it for the sake of his family.

And he was doing it for the sake of his childhood dream to work on the Mount.

More than anything, however, something else spurred him on.

Miss May.

He may not be able to tell her about her father's depravity, but August could sure as heaven be a true friend to her. And he would not allow the woman to be tricked into something she didn't wish to do.

So he would produce his own plan. And if she just so happened to wish to leave the Mount simply to be free of her despicable father's presence, then so be it. But it would be her choice—and her choice alone.

August would make sure of it.

CHAPTER TWENTY-ONE

"It isn't what we say or think that defines us, but what we do."
Sense and Sensibility, Jane Austen

Sunny Saturdays were a novelty on the Mount—especially in April. *Especially*, especially when the tide cooperated.

As such, whenever all three occurred, it seemed that every one of the Mount's three hundred residents would come out to feel the warmth of the sun on their shoulders and relish in the weather that did not require frequent dress-changes and shoe removals due to being sloshing wet with rain.

Yes, sunny Saturdays were what many islanders dreamt of.

But to Livvy, sunny Saturdays were the stuff of nightmares. While she loved the feel of the sunshine on her face—such weather *was* number four on her list—she found it extremely difficult to enjoy it when there were just so many people around.

As such, whenever the fateful day occurred that the stars aligned and the sun shone at the end of the week, Livvy hunkered down in her room with a book and enjoyed the sunshine by sitting near the window and feeling the warmth that filtered in through her yellow-flowered curtains. From there, hidden behind said curtains, she was safe from prying eyes and probing questions. And she was safe to partake in another favorite pastime of hers—people-watching.

Here was yet another way in which Livvy was a complete contradiction. She couldn't speak in large groups, yet she loved *observing* large groups. She didn't like to receive much attention from others, yet she loved watching them and the things they did.

She knew this was what made other people think she was odd, but she'd assumed this strange, hermit habit a few years past, and she was perfectly fine to resume it again that morning. That is, until Father discovered her and demanded she go outside and enjoy the sunshine, even if she read while doing it.

"And don't ye dare think o' travelin' to Marazion to 'ide away where'er ye may," he'd said, having long suspected her secret spot.

As if she would dream of going to Marazion now. If sunny Saturdays were busy on St. Michael's Mount, they would be absolutely heaving on the mainland.

As such, Livvy begrudgingly put on her bonnet, tucked her book beneath her arm, then, sulking, left her house.

She attempted a few different locations. One near the Giant's Well halfway up the Mount, but that had been teeming with servants all fighting to complete the task of gathering water in the pleasant weather. Then she'd attempted the cliffsides, but wherever she tried to plunk down in the grass, a new group of young men and women would sit nearby and chatter and flirt and giggle until Livvy was nauseous.

Finally, of all the places she found to suit her needs, she humorously settled on one of the busiest places—the harbor. If she'd learned anything in her years of people-watching, however, it was that those near the harbor were the busiest of all, and busy people very rarely noticed Livvy.

Snagging an empty bench on the far southwest side of the harbor, just a stone's throw from her house, Livvy positioned herself in the middle of the seat so the chances of someone sitting next to her became less likely. Then she pulled out her book—she'd finally started *The Mysteries of Udolpho* today—and settled in for what she figured would be a mere thirty-minute reading stint, a time that would surely satisfy Father before she snuck back to her room.

Just as Livvy had witnessed from her window, the harbor teemed with individuals. Built in the shape of a *U* with two arms jutting forth and nearly joining together at the top, the harbor was typically home to hundreds of boats—sometimes so full, kids could be seen jumping from boat to boat until they moved from one end of the harbor to the next.

Right now, however, on that special sunny Saturday, the harbor was nearly free of every single boat, as everyone wished to take advantage of the fine weather and warm sea waves.

Despite the harbor being free of vessels, the water within was full and calm, boasting of colors that could rival the dazzling sapphires Sir John had no doubt purchased for his mistress.

Livvy couldn't help but marvel at the beauty of the water that changed from day to day, depending on the weather. She could see the harbor better with the view from her room upstairs, but she couldn't deny how fine it felt to be out of doors.

Typically, she would duck her head as people walked by, avoiding any chance of conversation. But that afternoon, oddly enough, she didn't mind smiling in greeting to others. She still lowered her head to allow her bonnet to cut off her view more often than not, but she found herself enjoying people-watching even more than reading.

Blasphemy.

Very well, not more than reading. But she was not so prideful to admit that the happenings around her were far more appealing to her *at the present moment.*

There was just something special about the joy and child-like behavior that sunshine brought out in people. Something contagious and lovely.

Snippets of conversations reached her ears as the crowds continued to migrate to and fro on the harbor.

"Lord Steere's heir married beneath 'im, ye know. That baron 'tain't at all content with 'is choice."

"I can't imagine a more beautiful day to take a wander."

"The dog escaped me mother's again. That be the fourth time this week."

Women walked by in their light-colored dresses as children skipped up and down the pathway along the harbor, their mothers following after them with tutting tongues, though they didn't seem as frazzled as usual.

A few dogs barked beside their owners nearby, rolling around in the grass as they no doubt enjoyed the weather, as well.

Along the harbor wall to her left, men faced the vast sea and cast their fishing rods over the edge of where they stood, their hooks and bait plopping into the water with splash after splash.

She observed them all standing in a row beyond her, each of them laughing with friends as jokes were shared and entertaining anecdotes were exchanged.

Livvy was about to look away, but when she heard a joyous commotion occurring farther down the row of men, no doubt caused by a recently caught fish, she leaned forward to search for the fortunate man who was now the envy of all the other fishermen.

As the victor emerged from the row, holding the fish in the air for the others to see, Livvy's heart tumbled.

August. She shouldn't have been surprised that he was the one who'd caught the fish.

She did her best to look away but was unable to, captured by the pure bliss that radiated from his features. Mr. Cuff stood beside him, clapping him on the shoulder in congratulations as others did the same. All the while, August shared his appreciation with more delightful grins. She could stare at those smile lines all day.

Then his eyes met hers. She gasped, swiftly looking away and pulling her book up to make it obvious that she was reading instead of staring at him, even though she had *very* obviously been doing the latter.

After a long moment, she dared a glance back at him, finding him returned to fishing along the line of other men. He'd seen her, as sure as the sun shining that day, she knew he'd seen her. A small mark of disappointment colored her mood that he hadn't dropped everything to come and speak with her, then she chastised her silliness.

If he had come over, she would no doubt have to acknowledge the fact that she'd been found staring at him—just like she was doing right then.

She looked away again, only to draw her eyes straight back to him. This was absolutely not what Father had in mind, sending Livvy out in public, but she wasn't about to complain about it. Especially when August removed his jacket, and she was able to admire his physique even more.

A grin begged to be released on her lips, but she bit it away. She should not be ogling the man. He was engaged—whether secretly or nearly, it was one and the same.

A little voice on the pathway before her pulled Livvy's attention forward to where a girl no more than four years old was singing and dancing nearby. Her mother—who appeared quite fine in her lavender-colored gown—was in a rather animated conversation with another woman. Livvy didn't recognize them, which meant they were no doubt mainlanders.

"Don't spin too near the edge, dear," the mother said, pausing her conversation to advise her daughter who spun in circles.

"I won't, Mama," the girl said, though she still danced in her own little world she'd created in her imagination.

"Perhaps ye ought to stop dancin', too," the mother said.

"Not when I have these new shoes, Mama. They're too wonderful to *not* dance in."

The mother didn't seem to notice that her daughter didn't pay her advisement any heed, carrying on in conversation with her friend.

But Livvy, however, watched the scene with amusement. The girl seemed quite happy with her new, black shoes, and nothing would deter her.

As she continued to twirl about, however, she tripped on an uneven stone, and she made for the ground, her little feet scrambling to catch her fall as one of her new shoes slipped off.

Livvy gasped, making to help but the mother fortunately saw first, catching her daughter just in time. However, in the commotion, as the mother righted her daughter, the girl's shoe bounced across the pathway before diving directly over the edge to plummet into the water below.

"No!" the little girl screamed.

"That is why I told you to stop dancing," the mother whispered, her cheeks growing red.

The girl's lips pulled down, and Livvy's heart twisted before the mother closed her eyes and drew a deep breath.

"No matter, dear," she said, clearly attempting to calm down. "It is only a shoe."

"But it was my *new* shoe," the girl said, her tiny voice breaking.

Livvy set her book down. She couldn't bear the heartache that little girl must be feeling right now—nor the stress of the mother who had clearly just spent good money on the shoes.

Livvy wasn't certain of how she'd be of service, but she couldn't stand by any longer without helping.

"Did ye lose a shoe, love?"

Livvy's heart once again jumped into her throat. She shifted her gaze to where August stepped down from the harbor wall onto the lower pathway, his eyes focused solely on the little girl.

Thank heavens Livvy hadn't stood yet. She was certain she'd faint from his sudden appearance.

"Yes, sir," the girl responded.

Livvy watched with bated breath, scooting forward to the edge of the bench. The scene was so familiar, so similar to what had happened when she was a little girl—when she'd first fallen for August Moon. She really shouldn't have been surprised that he'd find another little girl in need.

He walked to the edge of the pathway, peering down into the water where the shoe no doubt bobbed up and down in the lilting waves.

"It was a new shoe, too," the little girl said, clearly unintimidated by the adults now gathering around her.

"That's quite all right, darling," the mother said, looking around at the growing crowd, her cheeks an even brighter red than before. "We shan't cry over a lost shoe."

"Ah, but it'd be a shame to lose it permanently," August said.

Livvy watched from behind the gathering crowd as August placed his hands on his hips, then shrugged. "Ye know what? It be far too nice a day to stay out o' this water."

Then without hesitation, he rolled up his sleeves, removed his boots, stockings, and cravat, leaned over the edge of the harbor, then jumped down straight into the water.

CHAPTER TWENTY-TWO

"What reinforcement we may gain from hope, If not what resolution from despair."
Paradise Lost, John Milton

The crowd gasped, smiles abounding on all the spectators—Livvy included. She fought against her desire to see what had become of August in the water, but all too soon, she gave in. Picking up her book and holding it against her chest, she raced to join the others, standing off to the side until she could see over the edge herself.

August emerged from the water as she peered down at him, the crowd speaking with the little girl who stared on with excitement. Murmurs of the kindness and quality of August surrounded her, but Livvy was simply focused on watching him.

Floating in the water, he wiped the hair back from his brow, then swam toward the shoe that had floated toward the edge of the harbor and now bounced against the stone wall.

His white shirt billowed around him in the soft waves as he

wrapped his strong fingers around the shoe, then he shifted in the harbor and headed toward where the steps—half-covered in water—led back up to the walkway.

Livvy tried to tell herself to return to the bench. Or better yet, return home. But then, surely she needed to see the shoe reunited with its owner.

Still standing on the outskirts of the crowd, she watched him reach the steps and emerge from the water like Adonis, water dripping from his person, clothing clinging to every inch of him.

Look away, Livvy.

But she couldn't. Besides, why should she have to when no one else was? She was merely watching to ensure the little girl received her shoe. That was all.

So why was she only staring at the curves and ridges of August's back, so clearly defined and visible through his sopping wet shirt that was now entirely transparent?

As he finally reached the top of the stairs where the little girl and her mother stood waiting, Livvy's heart had never warmed so greatly—except, perhaps, when he'd helped her as a child, too.

He leaned down and extended the shoe to the beaming girl, the gathered crowd breaking out into a simple applause.

August hardly seemed to notice them, however, his eyes focused on the girl. "'Ere ye go, love."

The girl took it with a smile that stretched from ear to ear. "Thank you, sir!"

"'Course, ma'am. But ye'll probably want to dry it out 'fore ye wear it again." He winked at the girl, and the mother laughed, who expressed her gratitude for his service, as well.

A few people spoke to August—"Good on ye, lad," and "Well done, August"—before the crowd began to disperse.

That was Livvy's cue to leave, and swiftly.

With her book still close to her chest, she veered left and made for home instead of the bench. She was far too excited to sit down and read right now.

In truth, she didn't know if she could ever read anything again, what with the image of August's rescue—and of course, his transparent shirt—now emblazoned in her memory forever.

She waited for her turn to move past the disbanding crowd, but as the people scattered from left to right, the pathway forward cleared for her to move, but at the end of it stood August, and he was looking directly at her.

Her instinct was to look away. Or perhaps it was to *run* away. But when she spotted that twinkle in his eye and a raised hand in greeting, her legs tremored.

He'd acknowledged her. In public. That meant that she needed to do the same, right? She pulled up whatever bravery she held in her resources, then smiled in return.

To her utter shock, however, that must not have been enough for August, for in the next moment, he made his way toward her. *Her*, of all people.

Livvy had been convinced that after they'd been caught speaking by Miss Pengelly, August would never speak with her again. So what on earth was he doing right now?

Surely this would cause more rumors than anything, the fact that he was coming to speak with her when all of the Mount could see them.

Not to mention the state he was in.

As he drew nearer, she couldn't fight her eyes from dropping to his torso. All those years off the Mount had done him much good.

His white shirt clung to his person, outlining his physique—tapered torso, barreled chest, broad shoulders, far broader than she'd ever known before.

The man was...what, perfection? Excellence? Superior? Flawless?

How many words had she read in the last ten years for her now to be completely useless in finding one that fit?

Or perhaps that was the problem. One word could never suffice when explaining such a man.

"Miss May."

She pulled her eyes from his chest and smiled. "Mr. Moon."

They stood there in silence for a moment, neither of them speaking, both of them merely looking at each other.

Say something, Livvy, before he walks away.

"That must be uncomfortable for ye," she said, motioning to his sodden clothing. "Bein' all wet and..." Her words failed her as she peered at the contours of his chest.

"Wet and..." he prompted.

She blinked, looking back to his eyes that held a twinkle she knew her words had placed there.

She needed to hide her admiration of him. And swiftly. "Wet and...sodden."

He pulled back, clearly disappointed. "Sodden? That 'ardly sounds flatterin'. Are ye certain ye can't think of a nicer word than sodden?"

Well, *now* she could. She could even go so far as to find a word beginning with each letter in the alphabet.

Alluring. Beautiful. Charming. Delectable. Enticing. Fascinating. Gorgeous. Heart-wrenchingly mesmerizing.

She could go on and on. But that would hardly be appropriate.

Instead, she settled with a simple, "No."

To her delight, his smile grew.

Before her eyes could fall on his person again, she looked to the harbor. The rest of the crowd had disappeared, the mother and daughter halfway to the other side of the pathway by now.

"That be very gallant of ye. What ye did."

August merely shrugged. "'Tain't nothin'. Poor thing was so pleased with 'em shoes, dancin' about. I couldn't 'elp but come to 'er aid."

So he'd seen her dancing, too. No wonder he'd jumped into the harbor, compelled by the carefree nature of that little girl. Could this man be any more wonderful?

"She did seem to be enjoyin' 'erself," she said. "Dancin' and singin' like no one else existed."

"Would we could all be like that."

"Indeed," she murmured. Then she paused. "Though ye *do* be like that."

"What do ye mean? I be a terrible dancer and singer."

She frowned. "I don't know 'bout dancin', but I know ye be a fine singer."

August stared down at her, his eyes alight with intrigue. "How do ye know that?"

The blood rushed from her head. Wretched loose tongue. She'd let slip one of her secrets, hadn't she? "Oh, from hearin' ye at church?"

Why had she ended her words in a question? That hadn't sounded convincing at all.

A look of intrigue lit his eyes, but he asked her no further questions, much to her relief. She would hate to have to explain just what she'd needed to do to discover how wonderful of a singer he truly was.

Silence filled the air between them again, which inevitably led her eyes to drop to his torso once more. He certainly hadn't been an idle gardener to look like this.

Look at 'is face, Livvy.

That wasn't much better, however. At least not for her nearly nonexistent resolve to not ogle the man. Water dripped from his lips and the tip of his nose, trailing down his neck into the folds of his clothes. If she had a handkerchief she'd offer it to him.

But then she wouldn't be able to enjoy watching the traces of moisture slipping into the curves of his smile lines and clinging to his thick hair.

Shame about that.

'E be watching ye, Livvy.

The words brought her back to earth, and she looked up to see him watching her with a half-smile. There was no way for him to know her thoughts, unless her expression had revealed just how much she'd been admiring him.

Blast.

"Well, I be certain 'er mother appreciates the service," Livvy said, clearing her throat and forcing her thoughts to clear. "And the girl, too. She'll remember it, I be certain." Then she mumbled, "I know I did."

August leaned his head to the side, running his fingers through his hair which drew her attention to the ridges in his flexing arm.

She blew out a steady breath.

"What do ye mean?"

"Hmm?" she asked, still eying his arms.

"What do ye mean, ye know ye did?"

What *did* she mean? She closed her eyes to be able to focus. "Oh, nothin'."

Blast, how had she let that slip? The last thing she wished to do was reveal how close she held the memory of his helping her when he obviously didn't remember it at all.

His half-smile returned. "Well ye 'ad to 'ave meant somethin'."

He clearly wasn't going to let this go, so what should Livvy do? Perhaps if she stated it just right, he wouldn't think anything of her remembering such an occasion.

"Oh, it be nothin'," she said, looking away. "I just remember a time when ye 'elped me when I be younger. That be all."

"Did I?"

Just as she'd suspected. He didn't remember.

"Did I rescue your shoe from the sea, too?"

She smiled, looking away. "No."

"Did I pull ye from another tangle o' bushes?"

She shook her head.

"Did I 'old your books when your hands were full again?"

Heavens. How many times had the man come to her rescue? "No, just the once for that."

He ran his fingers through his hair again. "'Ow old were ye?"

How she wished she could say it was only a few years ago. That would make her seem far less strange. "Oh, just a little girl."

He looked away for a moment, water still clinging to his dark lashes as he stared into the harbor water as if attempting to remember. Before he could tell her another way in which she was indebted to him, she finally spoke.

"'Tain't nothin' special," she began. "I lost a few loose pages o' me book in the wind one day, and ye managed to catch 'em 'fore deliverin' 'em back to me, that be all."

At once, August's eyes brightened. "That was ye?"

She narrowed her eyes. There was no possible way he remembered. He was simply being nice. "I don't expect ye to recall it. It be so long ago..."

But August shook his head. "No, I distinctly remember ye chasin' after 'em papers down the causeway. I managed to step on one and caught the other midair 'fore they would've flown into the sea."

Livvy could hardly breathe. He *did* remember. "Yes," she managed to reply.

"I can't believe that was ye all this time. I'd forgotten until now. Ye were cryin' when I handed 'em to ye, if I recall correctly."

The blood rushed back to Livvy's head, warming her cheeks. "Was I?"

She looked away. She really needed to break her habit of telling falsehoods to make herself appear less ridiculous. The truth of the matter was that she remembered that day perfectly, and she *had* been crying. Quite a lot.

She'd been ten years old. Mother had died only a few months before. The book had been one of the novels the Otter-hams had given to her—*The History of Little Goody Two-Shoes.* She'd read it so often, and the copy had been so frail to begin with, that the pages had taken to falling apart one by one.

But it was special to her. It was *still* special to her. Priceless, even. Irreplaceable. And August had rescued it for her.

"Ye must've loved that book to 'ave been chasin' after its pages all those years ago," August said, his eyes warm as he peered down at her.

She bit the inside of her lip. Should she tell him the truth? The worst he could do was run away from her.

Or ask ye more questions.

She cringed. People's questions had been a major deciding factor in becoming the hermit she was today.

But then, August had never asked her imposing questions before. And if she spoke vaguely enough, there would be no need for him to ask anything at all.

Drawing a deep breath, she began. "It was that book that 'elped me to fall in love with readin'. From the Otter'ams, it was. It...it also 'elped me goin' after me mother's death."

There. She'd said it. She'd said it, and she was still alive.

Furthermore, August's eyes had softened even further with deep compassion and understanding.

"I be that glad I found 'em papers for ye, then," he said softly. "E'en more so now."

Unexpectedly, tears pricked at her eyes at his tender words. "I be always grateful for ye doin' the same, as well," she said, clearing the emotion from her throat.

She stared up at him again, water dripping from a strand of hair that had fallen over his brow. Would that she could brush it from his forehead, run her fingers through those luscious locks and—

A couple walked past them, pulling Livvy from her thoughts. The Dunstones greeted August, then settled their gazes on Livvy, but she looked away and closed her eyes for a moment, gaining her wits once again.

What was she doing? Falling into the same trap as before, becoming lost in his warm, brown eyes, and sinking back into her feelings of love and kinship with the man who was wholly unavailable?

She still couldn't begin to understand why he felt comfortable speaking with her now in front of all of those people. Perhaps that was because Miss Pengelly was nowhere in sight? Where was she? And why was she not with her intended on such a fine sunny Saturday?

At any rate, it was none of her business. And she had a book to get back to.

"Well, I-I must be gettin' back 'ome, I think," she said, taking a step back from him and averting her eyes from his still-clinging shirt.

"It was lovely to see ye again, Miss May," he said.

"And ye, sir," she said. "I...I do 'ope ye can get dry soon."

Then she spun on her heel and walked swiftly away, nearly running into two people as she scurried across the pathway.

When she reached her home, she slipped inside without a sound, fighting the urge to look back until she closed the door. From there, she could see August making his way back to the other fishermen. His shirt still clung to his body, revealing a lovely *V* down the center of his upper back.

Swiftly, however, she closed her eyes again and shut the door tightly behind her, telling herself she would go up to her room and read her book instead of looking out the window, where she would have yet another perfect view of the man she loved, and the very man she shouldn't.

Because she had too much respect for herself, for Miss Pengelly, and for August to continue this obsession any longer.

CHAPTER TWENTY-THREE

"Time will explain."
Persuasion, Jane Austen

August ran his hand down his face again, dispelling the remaining moisture that clung to his eyebrows as he gathered the clothing he'd shed and made his way back to Nicholas, though his thoughts lingered solely on the woman with whom he'd just spoken.

He didn't like to make anyone uncomfortable—in fact, he prided himself on helping people feel the very opposite around him. But seeing Miss May continually shift her gaze back to his transparent shirt had been more than pleasing, it had been flattering.

"Ye be a bit wet, August," Nicholas said as August reached him back on the top of the harbor wall.

August smiled at his friend's joke. "I suppose I ought to return 'ome for dry clothes. It be gettin' a bit uncomfortable in certain places."

"Or ye could be a man and let the sun warm ye up instead."

Again, August smiled. Nicholas was the gentle giant of the Mount. He was nearly half a foot taller than August and almost double the width around. While he appeared intimidating to folks who didn't know him, Nicholas was shy, soft-spoken, and kind.

It had certainly been a shock to discover that he and Emma had fallen in love. August had still been unable to unearth how Nicholas had been able to find the courage to speak with Emma when he had a difficult time speaking with anyone—aside from August, of course. With August, Nicholas was fully himself, free to tease, playfully mock, and complain all he wished.

Fortunately, August was able to do the same.

"Ye be one to talk, Nicholas," August returned, peeling the wet shirt from his person in an effort to dry faster. "I didn't see ye jumpin' out there to rescue a shoe."

"I'd ne'er be so reckless."

"Reckless or gallant?" Miss May's word echoed in his mind. Had she really thought him gallant?

In truth, it had been watching Miss May's concern over that little girl that had spurred August on to help. He'd noticed Miss May smiling to herself, and while he thought it had been due to what book she'd been reading, he quickly saw her attention focused on the little girl who had been dancing and singing to herself.

August had watched her with amusement, then saw the shoe fly into the water. He was making his way down to help, but when Miss May stood, August moved faster. But, why? To help the girl? Or to impress Miss May?

"I suppose ye were actin' gallantly," Nicholas conceded.

"It be all in a day's work for me," August joked.

He sat down, then, using the outside of one stocking to dry off his legs and around his neck, though the water from his hair and pants trickled down to wet them once again.

"I noticed ye were speakin' to Miss May just then."

All at once, August's mood shifted. He scrambled to return to the joy he'd felt before, but even then, he knew it had been fleeting and even false at times.

After all, how could he be truly happy when he was being extorted?

"She was just watchin' to ensure the girl received her shoe," he returned.

He didn't like lying to Nicholas. He despised it. But then, how could he tell his friend the truth when August had somehow embroiled his friend and his friend's intended in this entire mess?

He shook his head. No, he had not embroiled them. Mr. May had.

He glanced toward the Mays' house situated right next to his family's, trying hard to release the anger that was still pent-up within him from Mr. May's actions.

A movement caught his attention in the corner of his eye, and he shifted his gaze to the top window where yellow curtains fluttered. Beyond them stood Miss May, her eyes directed at him, but she darted swiftly out of the way and the curtains closed.

He smiled to himself. If Mr. May made him as livid as he'd ever been, Miss May was swiftly making him *happier* than he'd ever been. Which was a problem in and of itself. He found far too much joy being around the woman he was supposed to help convince off the Mount.

But then, he wasn't going to do that, was he?

After another attempt at getting dry, August set his stockings aside in frustration, though he knew they had nothing to do with his dropping mood. How he wished he'd never spoken with Mr. May. Things had been going so well. He could have continued to befriend Miss May naturally, all while helping Emma and Nicholas come together. Then when his friends married, August would have been more than fine to pursue Miss May. But now? Now he was falling for the charm and sweet nature of a woman he could never have.

A woman who knew he could sing.

He glanced once again to the window, but Miss May was no longer in sight.

August considered himself secure in his talents and abilities in every way but one—singing. That wasn't to say he wasn't good at it. In fact, he thought he was fairly talented. But for one reason or another, singing in front of others—family, friends, and strangers alike—always made him vastly uncomfortable.

So how did Miss May know he could sing? She'd said she'd heard him in church, but August made it a point to never sing louder than a whisper during Sunday services. The only place he did sing was when he was gardening, but only ever when he was certain he was alone. Had she somehow heard him? Snuck up on him without him being aware?

"August?" He focused his attention on Nicholas, his friend narrowing his eyes. "Are ye well?"

"Why wouldn't I be?"

"'Cause I've been talkin' to ye for the last five minutes and ye 'aven't 'eard a word I've said."

August blew out a quiet breath and approached the edge of the wall, ready to begin casting his line into the water, if only to distract himself from his thoughts.

"Forgive me, Nicholas," August mumbled. "I've been distracted o' late."

"Distracted with a certain girl, I take it?"

August cast a sidelong glance at Nicholas. "I take it ye and Emma 'ave been speakin' o' me."

Nicholas smiled sheepishly. "Per'aps we 'ave. But only 'cause we care 'bout ye. We've noticed ye've seemed..."

"Preoccupied?"

"Not yourself," Nicholas said instead.

August couldn't have agreed more. It was true. He'd not been himself for days now, ever since Mr. May's request and subsequent threats.

"We figured it be 'bout Miss May and," Nicholas paused, clearing his throat, "a newfound attachment to 'er."

August didn't speak for a moment, his eyes following a group of men leaving from the edge of the harbor.

With more privacy, he was inclined to share about his interactions with Mr. May, then he thought better of it. He'd not wish to embroil Nicholas and Emma more into this mess than they already had been.

"Do ye?" Nicholas pressed. "'Ave an attachment to the girl, I mean?"

How August longed to answer in the affirmative. "No, I don't," he answered truthfully. He couldn't have an attachment to her, thanks to her father. Now had Nicholas used a different word—an *attraction* to Miss May—August would have, indeed, said yes.

He couldn't deny the way his heart had taken flight when he'd first seen her blue eyes watching him. Nor the way he felt his soul lighten each time she spoke of another list she'd made.

"I don't believe ye," Nicholas said, drawing August back to the present. "There be no way a man can look at a woman the way ye just looked at 'er and *not* 'ave an attachment. At any rate, if ye do, Emma and I decided we can't keep ye 'elpin' us for much longer. 'Tain't fair."

"Ain't nothin' to do with fairness." Actually, it had everything to do with fairness. But he wouldn't have his friends suffer due to Mr. May's behavior, too. "But don't feel rushed 'cause o' what ye believe. I be 'appy to 'elp as long as ye need me."

"Then why can't ye tell me that ye 'ave an attachment to Miss May?"

August stared down at his fishing line, invisible past a certain point, though the water gave away its location by rippling away from the string. How was he to get out of this conversation without lying to his friend? "It be complicated," he finally settled with.

"Complicated 'ow?"

Why on earth was Nicholas pressing the topic so greatly? August had never known him to be so assertive.

But then, he knew why. Nicholas could sense something was wrong with August, so he would discover what was wrong because he wanted his friend to be happy. It was the same reasoning as to why August was allowing Mr. May to extort him, because he wanted his friends to be happy.

With a sigh, he glanced from side to side, ensuring the space around them had widened so others might not overhear their conversation. He knew Mr. May had forbidden him to speak with anyone about what August was to do, but frankly, August couldn't bear it any longer.

He may have been stripped of his freedom, but Mr. May would not strip him of his friends.

"I wish I could tell ye 'ow complicated matters really be," he said softly.

Nicholas sobered. He must have sensed August's tone. "Ye can tell me anythin', August."

Not this. "I know, but as I said, it be complicated. One day, I'll be able to share more, but not now."

He could see the intrigue in Nicholas's eyes—and the worry—but fortunately, his friend nodded, his signal that he was letting the matter go.

But August wasn't quite finished yet. "I will say one thing, though. Ye and Emma need to be more careful when ye be sneakin' 'round."

Nicholas frowned. "We be careful every time."

But August shook his head. "I 'ave it on good authority that ye've been spotted."

"By whom?" Nicholas asked, his voice dropping to a worried tone.

August grimaced. "I cannot say, me friend. Only that ye must be e'en warier than 'fore. If the wrong person gets hold o' this..."

"Ye be worryin' me, August," Nicholas said, his lips pulled down. "Who saw us?"

But August could say no more. "No one of importance, I assure ye," he lied. "And I be takin' care of it, so ye don't 'ave to fret. Just...promise me ye'll be take more care."

Nicholas shifted back to the water, clearly upset that he didn't know. August felt for him, but he could say no more. His friend wouldn't keep his job or the love of his life if he discovered the truth.

"Very well," Nicholas grumbled. "I don't like not knowin', but I'll agree to trust ye on the matter."

August nodded, grateful for his friend once again not pressing the issue.

The mood around them hung low, nearly blocking out the sun entirely, so August drew a deep breath, shrugged off the unhappiness around them, and focused on the water.

"Now, when are ye goin' to catch up with me and snag yourself a fish?" he asked.

To his relief, Nicholas cracked a smile. That was good. It

was exactly what August needed. Because if Emma and Nicholas weren't happy, and if Miss May wasn't happy, then what was this all for?

CHAPTER TWENTY-FOUR

"If I could but know his heart, everything would become easy."
Sense and Sensibility, Jane Austen

"Thank ye for bringin' these, Liv," Father said, his eyes peering down at the basket of cherry tarts Cook had made that morning.

Livvy nodded, grateful Father appreciated her act.

When she'd first awakened to the smell of the tarts that morning, her stomach had rumbled, and moisture had flooded her mouth in anticipation.

She'd headed straightway to the kitchen, ready to sneak a few of the tarts for her reading in Marazion that day, but Cook had stopped her, heaving over a basket already overflowing with the dessert.

"Your Father do need these delivered to 'im," Cook had stated. "Sarah be out sick today with an 'eadcold, so the task do fall on ye, I be afeared."

Livvy had made to protest. She couldn't go to the gardens,

for she would inevitably see the very man she had promised herself to avoid—August Moon.

But there was nothing else to be done. Father liked to provide tarts for the other gardeners once a month, and he'd be very cross, indeed, if they were late in delivery. So she'd relented, failing to untangle her jumble of nerves as she made her way to the castle gardens.

Even now, as she stood before father in the midst of the sweet-smelling flowers and thick shrubbery, her stomach was clenched, for despite her best efforts, her gaze continually glided past Father's shoulders to where August and Mr. Cuff stood speaking to one another, half-hidden behind a large, oak tree, yellow and white daffodils surrounding the trunk.

Truthfully, she shouldn't even be watching them—or rather, watching August. She'd seen him from the window only that morning with Miss Pengelly as she'd discreetly delivered another love letter into his hands. Though it pained Livvy's heart to see such actions, it had been yet another reminder. A reminder that she was nothing to August. A reminder that she needed to eradicate her feelings for him altogether to maintain a shred of self-respect.

"I be glad to see ye out," Father said, drawing her attention to him again. He took a bite of one of the tarts, a piece of the pastry falling from his lips to the ground. "Where ye be 'eaded after this?"

"I thought about seein' the Otterhams," she replied.

"Give 'em me best."

"'Course."

Her eyes once more slid over Father's shoulder to the men still standing by the tree. They clearly wished their conversation to be kept private, their eyes continually darting about, ensuring no others pried. The only reason Livvy was not discovered was due to the fact that she stood mostly behind Father's figure.

Still, if they wished for privacy, she should allow them that much.

And yet, before she could look away, her attention was stolen by them shaking hands—more specifically, to the small letter August had covertly delivered to Mr. Cuff during their handshake. Mr. Cuff ducked to hide fully behind the tree then, and August walked away in the opposite direction without a sliver of culpability on his face.

Livvy narrowed her eyes. What were they speaking of that required no other ears to hear them? And why had they felt the need to deliver a letter between them secretly?

At the thought of the letter, her mind flitted back to Miss Pengelly, and an inkling took seed in Livvy's heart. Could it be...was it possible that the letters exchanged were between Mr. Cuff and Miss Pengelly—and not August?

But how could that be? The Pengellys and the Cuffs had been at war with each other for years, long before Livvy could remember. Was it possible that the two of them had somehow formed an attachment?

She racked her brain, attempting to recall any moment she'd seen the two of them together, but Father's words prevented her.

"Well, I've 'ad me fill," he said, brushing the remaining tart crumbs from his chin. "I'll take 'em round to the others, but I need to make sure..." He trailed off, glancing over his shoulder directly at August. "Moon!"

Livvy froze as he called to the very man she was trying to avoid.

August turned, his face stoic as he saw Father, then his gaze shifted to Livvy's as he noted her for the first time that morning. Instead of the smile that naturally spread across his face each time he'd look at her, he visibly swallowed, and his eyes darted back to Father's as he made his way toward them.

"Sir," August greeted. Then he turned to Livvy. A small smile reached his lips, though still nothing like before. "Miss May, pleasure to see ye."

Livvy had no notion as to why he appeared so nervous. Unless, of course, he felt the same way around Father as Livvy did—as if she were constantly being watched for any sign of mistakes.

"I needed to speak with ye 'bout the edgin' round the graveyard," Father said to August. "'Ave ye seen Cuff?"

August wrung his hands together. "I-I believe 'e be in the lower tier."

Livvy tried to keep her expression unchanged, despite August's lie to her father. Obviously, August did not wish for Mr. Cuff's position behind the tree to be discovered. Was it because of the letter he'd delivered?

"Blast," Father murmured. "'E needs to be workin' on clearin' the pathway up the Mount." He rubbed his jaw, then glanced again to August. "Would ye mind stayin' with me daugh'er for a moment? Keep 'er company 'til I return? I should only be a moment."

August's jaw twitched, but he nodded all the same.

Livvy, however, was not so easily convinced. "Father, I need to be goin' anyway. I can just leave these 'ere—"

She made to leave the basket on the grass, but Father shook his head.

"Nonsense. Ye must keep 'em pastries safe 'til I return." He sent a lingering look at August, then turned on his heel and left the two of them alone.

Livvy stared after Father, dumbfounded. Keep the pastries safe? From what, the squirrels?

With a sigh, she turned back to August, though when she

saw the grimace written across his features, she wished she would have kept her gaze averted.

He tried to wipe his expression clean, but it was too late. Livvy had seen how he'd really felt about being forced to be with her.

Instead of trying to make sense of when he wanted to be with her and when he didn't, Livvy shifted to the side, as if allowing him passage. "Ye can leave. I know ye be busy workin'."

But August shook his head. "No, that be all right. I be 'appy to stay with ye."

The words sounded as stinted and rehearsed as an inexperienced playactor reciting Shakespeare. "It's fine, sir. Ye can go. I'll not tell me father that ye left."

Again, he refused. "I don't mind stayin' with ye."

She dropped her chin and looked up at him through doubtful eyes. "Mr. Moon, ye don't 'ave to stay 'ere just 'cause me father asked it of ye."

A flicker of disbelief flashed in his eyes—she hadn't imagined it, she was sure of it—before he drew a deep breath. "I know," he said softly, then he placed a smile on his lips that looked far more sincere than before. "Truthfully, I wish to stay 'ere and speak with ye."

"Ye do?"

His smile returned, and Livvy's heart softened. "I do. I enjoy our friendship."

Friendship. Livvy's heart took a step back, shifting into its rightful place. There was the truth of the matter. They were simply friends and nothing more. But then, why did his eyes linger on her? Why did he smile so warmly whenever he spoke with her? Was she simply imagining the admiration she'd seen before, dreaming up this entire scenario?

Doubt slipped beneath her defenses like a cloud of smoke,

preventing her from seeing clearly, and the same issue that continued to pop up into the back of her mind like a specter rose again.

She knew it would never go away unless she faced it and discovered the truth of the matter—that the ghost was simply a figment of her imagination...or that the specter, that her fears, were true.

"Miss May? Be somethin' wrong?"

Livvy stared up at August. He must have noticed the conflict within her playing out on her face. She never had been good at hiding her emotions.

"Yes," she replied. "Well, no."

CHAPTER TWENTY-FIVE

"Ask me no questions, and I'll tell you no fibs."
She Stoops to Conquer, Oliver Goldsmith

August's chest pressed against his lungs, his breathing nearly stopping. Something was wrong. Had Miss May discovered his and her father's subterfuge?

"Ye can tell me," he said, attempting nonchalance, though his legs felt as weak as a sapling's branch.

She looked away. "I just wanted to let ye know that ye don't need to be me friend 'cause o' what I said."

August paused. So she didn't know? But then, to what was she referring? "Forgive me. I ain't certain what ye be talkin' about."

She looked around them. The gardens were empty, aside from a few young men weeding the patch of bluebells at the far edge of the garden. Fortunately, her father had left for the lower garden after August's lie, otherwise he'd still be there, listening to them.

That was just what both of them needed, to have Mr. May

linger nearby to make them both even more uncomfortable than they already were.

Miss May leaned closer, and he did as well, ignoring the scent of lavender that blossomed from her person and tickled his nose. "When I spoke to ye in your 'ouse," she explained. "Told ye that I 'aven't any friends."

"Oh," he said, realization dawning.

"I ne'er should've said such a thing," she said, her voice barely above a whisper. "I be sure ye be feelin' the need to befriend me, and to 'ave Miss Pengelly do the same. But I don't want ye to feel any sort of obligation where I be concerned." She looked away. "I can't bear forced friendship."

August was still battling the conflicting feelings within him—relief that she didn't know what her father had forced August to do, and sorrow that she felt the need to worry about why he was befriending her in the first place.

Well, he would make one thing clear. He had befriended Miss May because he'd wished to befriend Miss May. Not out of duty or obligation. And certainly not because her blasted father told him to do so.

Still, he feared no matter how he tried to convince her otherwise, she would not believe him. So he'd try a different approach. "Be it truly so hard to believe that I'd wish to be your friend simply 'cause I enjoy your company?"

She hmphed under her breath. "Ask me father."

August's jaw tightened, and he fisted his hands to alleviate the instant stress that came upon him. Now, more than ever, he was determined to help this woman. But not in the way her father demanded, no. August would help her gain the confidence she needed to escape the man forever.

"What would 'e say if I did ask 'im?" he asked softly.

She delivered a dubious expression. "The same as everyone

else on the Mount. Ye be the charmer, and I be the recluse. The hermit. The...*odd one*."

His heart twisted to hear such words escape her lips, to feel the obvious pain she felt at being attached to those labels.

He'd never been fond of being called Charmer of the Mount either. It sounded far too pretentious. But then if Miss May thought that of him...

He shook his head. "Your father be wrong, Miss May." Her eyes whipped to his. Had his words been too heavy-handed? Did he even care at this point? "I be your friend simply 'cause I wish to be. Simple as that."

A smile settled on her lips, but it was short-lived as she shifted her gaze away. "And 'ow does Miss Pengelly feel about that?"

Emma? Why would she care if August was friends with—

Blast. Of course Miss May would be concerned about how Emma would feel with her supposed intended befriending another single woman. Because Miss May was the most honorable woman on the Mount.

He supposed it was just as well that she believed such a thing. After all, this was one of Mr. May's demands.

August stifled a sigh of regret that carried with it all his frustration for choosing to help his friends in the first place. It was all worth it, seeing the delight on Nicholas and Emma's faces when he delivered yet another secret note written by the both of them.

Still, how he longed to be honest with Miss May—tell her everything her father said, everything August had agreed to do, and everything about his friends' relationship.

But he couldn't. He couldn't risk Emma and Nicholas not being together, he couldn't risk Nicholas's job, he couldn't risk his own family no longer having him work on the Mount, and he couldn't risk injuring Miss May by telling her how truly despicable her father was.

If she would even believe August, of course.

Honestly, Mr. May's desires were not all terrible. His wish to see Miss May socialize and be happy was admirable. But he'd taken it too far with his threats and his attempts to force her into doing what he thought was best.

Why could he not trust his daughter to choose her own life?

Setting his frustrations aside, August responded carefully. "Miss Pengelly doesn't mind me bein' friends with anyone. And I 'ave it on good authority that she wouldn't mind bein' friends with ye either."

Miss May seemed to think this over for a moment. When she finally nodded, her eyes that matched the bluebells on the patch beyond them shone with light. "Very well. If ye be certain, I s'pose we can be friends."

He smiled at her feigned reluctance. The woman was adorable.

"Excellent," he said. His first step to helping her—truly helping her—was complete. But he would need to do more to show her how life could be for her outside of her house and her books.

And most importantly, outside of the guidance of her father.

"Now, since we be friends," he began, "I'll let ye know that I expect ye to do what friends do."

She watched him warily, though that sparkle still lit her eyes. "And what be that, then?"

He shrugged. "Talk to each other. 'Ave fun together. 'Elp and encourage each other to be better. Keep each other's word. That sort o' thing."

She scrunched up her nose. "I think I'd like to stick with bein' acquaintances, then."

He laughed. "No, no, Miss May. There be no backin' out now."

She pulled in her lips. "Very well. Then can I expect the same from ye?"

"'Course."

"So I can expect ye to keep your word 'bout readin' *Don Quixote*?"

Regret rushed over him, and he groaned. "Ah, I've completely forgotten 'bout that, 'aven't I? I be that sorry. 'Tisn't what a friend would do at all. I promise I'll pick it up again tonight."

To his surprise, a grin split across her pink lips. "There be no need. I gave ye that book on purpose."

"What do ye mean?"

"I thought it'd be amusin' to assign the largest, most difficult book for ye to read," she admitted. Not a hint of remorse shone in her eyes.

"Ye little pisky," he said, acting appalled, instead of how charmed he was by her playful nature. "Well, now I be more determined to finish it just to prove that I can."

"I wish ye much luck, then," she teased. "Ye'll be needin' it."

Footsteps sounded nearby, and August glanced up to see Mr. May headed toward them. Miss May followed his gaze, and the mood around them shifted instantly.

"Ye two be enjoyin' your conversation?" he asked, glancing between them both, his eyes lingering expectantly on August.

August took a step away, his stomach tight. "'Course, sir. I always enjoy me conversations with your daugh'er." He gave another smile to Miss May before taking a step back. "But I do 'ave work to see to."

"'Course, 'course," Mr. May said. "I be sorry for the delay. The gardens wouldn't run so well without ye."

August almost gagged at the forced compliment. He could perfectly see through Mr. May's actions, these false words no better than the threats from before.

Still, August nodded in response and walked away, stealing another glance at Miss May before leaving the gardens behind.

He would stay in the lower gardens today, if only to avoid any potential conversation with Mr. May when his daughter left.

He didn't need the added scrutiny.

CHAPTER TWENTY-SIX

"Unused to the situations in which I find myself, and embarrassed by the slightest difficulties, I seldom discover, till too late, how I ought to act."
Evelina, Frances Burney

It was midnight, and shockingly enough, Livvy had already undressed for bed.

For most ladies who remained at home all day, being undressed and in bed by midnight was not unheard of. But Livvy, well, she typically became so engrossed in her novels that she wouldn't even remember to undress until half past two in the morning.

That day, however, she'd had a full morning and afternoon visiting with others—first with her father, then August, then the Otterhams, and finally Mrs. Smith, a boatman's wife, whom she'd met with on the way down from the Mount.

Socializing always sapped her energy faster than dry sand swallowed water, even if the experiences were positive, like today's had been.

As such, when she returned home that afternoon, Livvy had locked herself away in her room and allowed herself the comfort that only removing her stays could offer.

As night fell, she'd wrapped herself up in her warm shawl and cuddled up in her bed with the window slightly parted to better allow the sound of the sea inside. There, she had remained for the last two hours—with no intention of ending any time soon. How could she when she only had a few chapters left of *The Mysteries of Udolpho*?

The gothic story, as she'd hoped, had turned out to be quite exhilarating. She could hardly wait to see what happened to Emily St. Aubert, not to mention the mysteries interwoven throughout the story. Who was behind all the strange voices Emily heard? And did she truly see a figure behind a veil?

Livvy wouldn't have to wonder for much longer. Nothing could distract her now from finishing—

A long creak sounded from the window, echoing from the path below, and Livvy's heart jumped straight out of her chest. Her mind envisioned ghosts opening people's doors and floating out across the harbor, but she swiftly rebuked her ludicrousness.

She was becoming far too absorbed in this novel. Fears of ghosts and specters and supernatural events. It was all rather ridiculous. The sound she'd heard had no doubt been a door opening. Not Livvy's, though. Theirs didn't make a sound. But the Moons?

Her heart jumped for a different reason. She tried to maintain her focus on the words, which for her should not be difficult. After all, she'd just discovered that St. Auburn was the Marchioness's brother. But as the creak sounded again, her eyes found their way to her open window once more.

Whoever had opened the door would be gone by now—or they would have entered the residence already. It was no doubt a servant. Or perhaps Mr. Moon had stayed out late like Father had that night and was only now just returning from the pub.

Whoever it had been, it was surely not August.

And yet, she *could* check...just to be sure.

With quick movements, she set her book aside, flung back her covers, and tiptoed to the window, carrying her candle alongside her.

Slowly, she peeled back the curtains and peered through the open window, her braid falling over her shoulder as she leaned forward.

She could only just make out the front area of the Moons' house, but to her utter shock, August stood outside the door, his hands on his hips as he stared out over the harbor.

Somehow, she'd known it was him, yet still, her heart rapped against her chest. She watched him for a moment, his eyes focusing ahead until he looked straight up to her window without warning.

The blood drained from her face, and she gasped, pulling the curtains back in place to ensure she remained hidden.

He'd seen her. She knew he had. Would he think that she had been staring at him for long? Just being her strange, hermit self? But then, she was certain she'd not made a sound, so what had made him look up to her room in the first place?

"Miss May?"

She started at his soft voice. Heavens above. He was calling out to her. What should she do? Pretend she hadn't heard? Go back to bed to read more of Emily and the horrifying Castle Udolpho?

Or should she respond? Have a late-night conversation with a man who was calling to speak with her?

A smile spread across her lips. Once again, she pushed the curtains back and peered down at the pathway.

August had moved slightly closer to her home and was

now facing it directly. “I thought that was ye,” he said, his eyes shining up at her, the light from the candle in her room pouring down across his sculpted features. “What are ye doin’ up so late?”

“I be—”

“No,” he interrupted. “Do not tell me. Be ye readin’?”

She was fairly certain her heart was going to burst. “’Ow did ye know?”

“Merely a guess.” He winked.

Her heart tripped. Was that what friends did with one another—wink when they teased? Or did he mean something more by the gesture? “And what ye be doin’ out so late?” she whispered, eying the harbor and pathway to ensure they were alone.

“I merely be takin’ a midnight stroll.”

She paused. He seemed to be telling the truth. Or was it but a half-truth and he was truly going to meet with Miss Pengelly?

The image of Mr. Cuff accepting the letter from August in the gardens flashed through her mind again. She’d been thinking about it often since that morning and had yet to be secure in her hunch that Mr. Cuff and Miss Pengelly were attached. It made perfect sense, what with how indifferent August seemed with the woman, but then, why did he never deny the fact that they *weren’t* a couple?

Perhaps she could receive another clue right now, ask him a question where she could deduce the truth from him further. She scrambled for a response, then peered down at him.

“Be ye walkin’ alone?” she asked.

He didn’t answer for a moment, then a sly smile stretched across his lips. “Not if ye decide to join me.”

Her stomach jolted forward, as if her body wished to join

him as much as her spirit did. Heavens, but this was not the response she'd been expecting.

And yet, it was the exact response she'd hoped for. Now she knew. There was no way August would invite another woman in the middle of the night to walk with him if he was engaged—or even attached—to another. She would not believe it. She *could* not believe it.

"Miss May?"

She looked back down at August, who stared up at her with a curious tilt to his head. "Did ye 'ear me?" he asked.

She swallowed. Yes, she'd heard him. She simply didn't know how to respond. She glanced over her shoulder, her door still closed tightly. Father was no doubt downstairs, still asleep on the settee as he recovered from his night of drinking. Cook had already left for the night, and Sarah was still home ill. There was no reason for Livvy to worry about being overheard, and yet...the man had just asked her to do something that could be conceived as highly improper.

At least she thought he did. She wasn't exactly sure now.

"What do ye mean, join ye?" she whispered softer than before.

He took a step closer, craning his neck to see her better. "I mean, Miss May, that I wish for ye to join me for a walk this evenin'."

This evening? Surely he meant this late night, or even better, early, early morning. What can he be thinking?

"Be ye mad, sir?" she whispered. "Be ye truly askin' me to go on a walk with ye, unaccompanied, in the middle o' the night?"

His grin was her undoing. "I s'pose I be a bit mad. Or per'aps I merely wish to get to know me new friend better by speakin' to 'er without the pryin' eyes of others."

That sounded logical enough. But it wasn't as if she could risk her entire reputation by sneaking out alone with a man.

But then, what reputation did she have to risk? The odd one on the Mount might benefit from such a scandal.

She closed her eyes and shook her head. She was thinking nonsense. No, she could not risk this. It was too much. But then, was this not what she'd dreamt of her entire life? Having the man she'd been in love with for years want to spend time with her? Of course there were better ways. In the daylight. With a chaperone. But where was the fun in that?

"Where would we go?" she asked after another moment of thought.

A devilish glint gleamed in his eye. "To the castle."

Her mouth dropped open. "Ye can't be serious." He meant to sneak all the way to the top of the Mount?

"Well, not exactly the castle, but near it. I can tell ye no more. Ye simply 'ave to trust me."

She blew out a breath from her nose, scoffing. "I hardly know ye, August Moon." Now *that* was a lie. She knew him, and she trusted him. "Who's to say me reputation wouldn't suffer?"

"We'll keep to the shadows."

Such a simple response. Such a logical response. Was it just her, or was he making complete sense?

"I can promise ye more fun than the book ye be readin'."

The book. She'd forgotten entirely about it. She needed to see how Emily fared in that castle. But a part of her—a part of her that was growing vaster by the second—wished to see how *Livvy* would fare in the castle. Or near it, rather.

She chewed her lower lip. She was out of her right mind. Clearly. And yet, how could she not accept August's request?

Her father's words slipped around her memory, and she

paused. He'd made her swear to accept whatever activity someone asked her to do next.

Well, walking was an activity. And she *had* promised to say yes. So say yes, she would.

"Very well, Mr. Moon," she whispered down to him. "I'll go with ye."

His eyes registered surprise, then he broke out into a smile. "I'll wait for ye down 'ere, then."

Livvy nodded, then swept the curtains closed. What had she gotten herself into?

CHAPTER TWENTY-SEVEN

"Some men are wise, and some are otherwise."
The Adventures of Roderick Random, Tobias George Smollett

What had August gotten himself into?

He removed his cap and ran his fingers through his hair as he waited in the shadow of the houses.

As he waited for *Miss May* to join him.

He really had taken leave of his senses. There was no other explanation as to why he would've asked the woman to join him on a walk in the middle of the night. Or even call up to her in the first place.

But seeing her watching him from the window, her braid falling over her shoulder, her eyes bright with curiosity, he'd been unable to help himself. He needed to spend time with her. His soul begged for it. And though he knew he'd regret it one day, right now, he was only looking forward to the opportunity he had to spend time with Miss May uninterrupted.

In truth, he never really thought she'd accept his offer to join him. But now that she had, he needed to keep his wits about him. Their reputations could be damaged irreparably for doing this—hers especially. Emma and Nicholas's relationship could also be affected. Not to mention the fact that Mr. May could very well have August's head for such a risk. He'd told August to earn Miss May's trust, but August highly doubted this was what he'd had in mind.

August blew out a slow breath. He'd not thought this through at all. If he could renege his offer, he would. But she'd clearly had a mental battle while trying to decide, and the excitement in her eyes that had appeared once she'd agreed... Well, he couldn't quell that now.

He would simply remain on high alert. He'd taken this walk a number of times in the few weeks he'd been home and had yet to see anyone else occupying the paths during his late-night excursions. Why would tonight be any different?

Movement from the corner of his eye caught him, and he turned to see the Mays' door soundlessly open. Miss May slipped out, then closed the door without a sound once again.

Had she practiced escaping from her home before? That had been the most silent departure he'd ever *not* heard in his life.

She walked toward him, her eyes darting about, a cloak wrapped around her with the hood pulled to just above her brows. He could make out very little of her features in the darkness until she faced him, then the light from the bright moon illuminated her stunning features. Loose curls hung about her high cheekbones and slender neck, and a long braid was only just visible within the opening of her cloak.

She hadn't taken the time to pull up her hair, then. Had she dressed at least? His eyes dropped to where her cloak was fastened beneath her collar bone, then he looked away. He should most definitely not be thinking such thoughts.

"Were ye able to leave unseen?" he asked, slightly on edge.

Mostly from instigating this ludicrous plan. Partially from the way his eyes continually shifted to her gloved fingers playing with the end of her braid.

"Yes," she replied. "When Father sleeps after drinkin', 'e wouldn't be able to 'ear the call of Cormoran if that giant was still rampagin' across the Mount."

She looked from side to side, clearly on sharp alert.

August didn't mind. With her attention focused elsewhere, he could more easily admire her features without notice.

"Shall we depart?" he asked.

She looked about them once again, then nodded, moving in the shadows where August had motioned for her to precede him.

"Ye needn't be frightened," he said, if only to calm his own nerves. "We'll not be seen."

"Oh, I ain't worried 'bout that."

"No?"

"Well, I suppose I be a little." She looked around them again, then back at August. "See, the thing is, I've been readin' one o' the books I borrowed from your mother—*The Mysteries of Udolpho*—and it can be quite...ghostly. I keep thinkin' that a figure'll appear round the corner and terrorize us."

Her eyes darted around them again, and she pulled her cloak more tightly around her. Blast, but this woman was adorable.

"I didn't take ye as one to believe in ghosts," he mused.

"I don't. But that book may 'ave 'elped change me mind."

"Well, worry not," he whispered. "I'll protect ye from any ghosts we might 'appen upon."

He'd meant it as a joke, but she nodded without a smile. Her shoulders finally lowered, then she peered up at him as they rounded the last of the houses on the harbor front. "Will ye tell me where we really be goin', then?"

"Ye'll see soon enough." He stopped, peered around the corner of the house, then faced Miss May again. "For now, I think it best we remain silent 'til we get farther up the Mount."

Miss May nodded in silence, and he led the way forward, sticking to the shadows and away from open windows as they made their way to the pathway that led up the Mount. The moon shone brightly, the skies uncharacteristically clear for an April night, and the stars sparkled almost as brilliantly as Miss May's eyes.

If he would have allowed himself to look at them, that is. He was far too focused on moving forward, anxious to remain unseen. Fortunately, each step they took led them farther from the village, and his nerves lessened little by little until they reached the darkness of the cobbled pathway that curved back and forth toward the castle and its gardens.

Oak, birch, and maples hung over the pathway with thick, nearly impenetrable branches, while both sides of the cobblestones were lined with massive, moss-covered boulders, a few resting benches, and various flowers, shrubs, and bushes. August had been tasked to care for a fourth of the gardens lining the pathway to the castle, and even after nearly three weeks, he was still discovering new varieties of plants he'd never before seen.

Those first two weeks, he'd been in his element. Completely and totally in heaven. But now? Now the gardens put a bad taste in his mouth, for he did not know how long his job there would last. Nor did he know if he *wished* for it to last. Working for Mr. May had sapped much joy from August's life.

So how must Miss May feel living with such a man? Did the same happen to her? Or was Mr. May the portrait-perfect father for her?

"Can we speak now?" Miss May whispered after a few more moments in silence.

"Yes, we ought to be safe to do so now," he whispered in response.

He glanced sidelong at her, the pathway opening up so they could walk side-by-side once again. She no longer looked from left to right. Had she forgotten the ghouls she'd been scared of before? Pity. He would have liked to give her more comfort. Maybe even hold her arm.

No, August, he chided. That would lead to nothing but heartache.

And yet, this endearing, charming woman had agreed to join him that evening, even though the decision—like his—had been utterly ludicrous. So he would take advantage of his time with her. He would forget Mr. May as best he could. He would forget about the dangers—to a degree. And he would enjoy his time with the woman. Because Heaven only knew if he'd ever have this opportunity again.

"Feelin' any regret with your decision to join me yet?" he asked, ready to distract himself from his thoughts.

"I regretted it the moment me foot left me 'ouse," she teased.

He smiled, though he couldn't help but wonder if there was a small degree of truth in her words. "We'll be there soon. Then we can return, and ye'll be back at 'ome with your books in no time."

"Where be 'there,' exactly?" she asked.

"Do ye not wish to wait?"

"I fear I ain't one for surprises."

"Unless they be in books?" he guessed.

She glanced at him sidelong.

"Ye don't like surprises in books either?"

She shook her head. "I read the last page o' the books I read sometimes."

A surprised chuckle escaped his lips. "Ye don't."

"I do. Not all o' them, mind. Just the ones that give me far too much angst."

He laughed again. "I ne'er would 'ave thought."

"Why?"

He shrugged. "Ye seem the type o' woman not to worry 'bout things. Whether in books or reality. Ye seem to live life without fear."

She stared up at him as they walked, but the darkness prevented him from seeing her expression. Had that comment offended her? Or was she flattered?

In the next moment, she must have tripped over a cobblestone that jutted forth from the pathway, for she stumbled a bit before catching herself.

"Are ye well?" he asked, reaching out his hand to steady her before pulling back.

He shouldn't be that near to her, even if it was to help her. Because he *wanted* to be near to her too much.

"Yes," she murmured. "I just can't see this blasted pathway."

"I should've brought a lantern," he said, mostly to himself. "But then we'd be easier to spot."

"Oh, I wasn't complainin' at ye for not bringin' a light. But ye could've at least trimmed them trees above us so the moonlight could shine through."

How he loved her teasing. "Forgive me, my lady. I shall see to it on the morrow."

"Very good, Mr. Moon."

Perhaps he really should have trimmed the trees. How he was dying to see her features again.

After a few moments in silence, they followed the curve of the pathway that temporarily steepened, and their breaths mingled.

He hesitated with what he was about to say next, but after

a moment, either his weakened mind or strengthening heart egged him on.

"Now that we be friends, ye can call me August, if ye'd like."

She didn't respond for a moment. He bit his lower lip, dying to know what she was thinking. This was very nearly destroying him.

"Very well," came her soft response. "Then ye may call me Lavinia. Or Livvy."

Relief swept over him. "Which would ye prefer?"

"Livvy."

"Ye don't like Lavinia?"

They rounded another corner, the incline raising and foliage thickening.

"I do," she said softly. "But it was always more me mother's name than mine."

At the mention of her mother, he paused. Until that point, he'd only heard word of her once before—when Miss May had spoken of August rescuing the pages of her book. But nothing beyond that. Mr. May had never once spoken of her, either.

Of course, August had heard the rumors about the woman, but what good were rumors when the truth was somewhere between them, hidden beneath the rubble like crocuses beneath the snow?

Clearly, the Mays didn't like speaking of the woman, though he could only guess as to why.

"Livvy it be, then," he responded, leaving the mention of her mother out of it.

They continued their progression, passing by the well and the Giant's Heart until Miss May, or rather, Livvy—he did enjoy the sound of that—spoke again.

"Will ye really not tell me where we be goin'? I be thinkin' ye be takin' me to break our way into the castle."

He stared straight ahead, keeping his voice level. "Be it considered breakin' in when one 'as a key?"

She stopped, and he followed suit, turning back to see her staring up at him—or rather, he assumed she was staring at him. He still couldn't see much of her face.

"Ye can't be serious," she stated.

"I can be. And I am."

"Ye mean to enter the castle?"

He smiled. "No, I mean for *us* to enter the gardens. But worry not. I've a key."

He was given said key to be able to enter the walled gardens when he was first hired on, just like the other trusted undergardeners. It wasn't a common practice, to any degree. But August knew Mr. May wished for others to have keys, as well, so the man could leave and arrive whenever he saw fit.

"But..." Livvy began, her voice still thick with worry. "But surely the castle guards will spot us."

"Ah, they don't linger much 'round the servant's entrance o' the gardens. I've ne'er seen 'em there."

She looked to the side. "But ye can't just enter the gardens whene'er ye feel the desire, can ye?"

He shrugged. "All I'm doin' is a bit o' work while there. I don't see why not."

Silence. Now, more than ever, he wished for a lantern.

"So that be the surprise? Ye brought me out 'ere to work?"

He chuckled. "No, I wanted to show ye somethin'."

"'Ow to weed a garden?"

Another laugh bubbled from within him. This woman was just a delight. "No, Livvy, not to weed a garden." How he relished her name on his lips. "Somethin' far more excitin'. But we must make haste, or we might miss it. Come."

He moved forward again, not waiting to see if she would follow him. Somehow, he knew she would.

Sure enough, a moment later, her footsteps skittered behind him until she reached his side. "'Ow be this in any way safe?"

"How be it not?"

"S'pose we get caught by Sir John within the gardens?"

"This late?"

"'E could be out with 'is mistress."

But August shook his head. "'E be in London. Everyone else will be sleepin'. No one else wishes to work at a time like this."

"Just ye?"

"Just me," he returned. "Now we must be quiet, or someone *will* 'ear us."

Livvy obeyed, remaining silent as they reached the garden gate, her eyes roving around them, though she wouldn't be able to see guards if they *were* there.

August unlocked the door with a soft click, though he was fairly certain Livvy believed the entire Mount had heard it. Unfortunately, the hinge was far louder.

As such, he only opened it a fraction before the two of them wiggled their way in one-by-one, after which, August promptly locked the gate once again.

"Now," he said, "I will show ye what I brought ye 'ere to see."

Down the pathways they traveled, taking one turn after another through the thick, maze-like gardens that were layered in three separate sections. They took the right that led to the higher pathway, all the while Livvy remaining silent.

Was she truly upset? Or was she simply tired? He supposed this was later than most women cared to stay up. Most men, too.

But he was convinced that as soon as she saw the spectacle he would reveal to her, all would be forgiven.

Finally, they reached the spot August had happened upon

his first night in the gardens. Nicholas had lost a correspondence from Emma within the gardens one afternoon and was beside himself with worry. August had agreed to seek out the note that evening weeks before, fortunately finding it before anyone happened upon it.

It was only then that he'd turned to see the view before him—the view few on the Mount were privileged to see.

He stopped, and Livvy faced him in turn. Near the red brick walls of the top garden, with pelargoniums and purple pericallis giving off their sweet scents and planted in waves so very like the sea, he peered down at her.

"*This* be why I've brought ye 'ere," he said softly.

With the light of the moon no longer hidden from the shadows of the trees, he could finally see her features, and heavens, was it worth the wait. How could she be even more beautiful than he'd remembered?

"What?" she asked, her curls fluttering in the breeze.

Using all of his energy, he tore his eyes away from her and motioned north to where the causeway stretched out to Marazion.

Livvy's eyes followed his, and the release of her breath from her lips told him all he needed to know.

He had been forgiven for bringing her out here.

CHAPTER TWENTY-EIGHT

"It is the very error of the moon. She comes more nearer earth than she was wont. And makes men mad."
Othello, William Shakespeare

"It be breathtakin'," Livvy breathed, removing the hood of her cloak.

August couldn't agree more. From their viewpoint, with the towering castle behind them—its windows void of any candlelight signaling to him of the sleepy state of the household—the causeway stretched out toward the mainland. A thin veil of water covered the hand-laid stones, but the nearly full moon above caused the pathway to light up like a silver ribbon in the night.

"I can't believe I've ne'er seen the causeway lit up like this 'fore," she continued.

August nodded. He'd felt the same when he'd first seen the spectacle. "Stunnin', ain't it?"

She didn't respond, so August looked over at her, and all at once, he was no longer captured by the pathway.

Livvy's gaze continued to move along the glowing causeway, her eyes filled with wonder, her formed lips parted in awe. Though they still stood within the shadows to avoid prying eyes from the castle above, the cool light from the moon created an ethereal halo around her, and he was once again taken by her.

It wasn't just her beauty that captured him, though. It was her spirit that radiated from her person each time she spoke, her goodness and vivacity for life making her glow brighter than August had ever seen in a person before.

He shouldn't be feeling such a way about the daughter of a man who was extorting him—about the daughter who he'd been tasked to deceive and essentially forbidden to fall in love with—but how could a gardener turn away from such a rare flower? How could the rest of the Mount, even Livvy's own father, not see what a wonderful treasure this woman was?

Or...or had Mr. May been correct in his observation, that Livvy had only ever shown her true nature to August?

Before he could dwell any longer on the subject and come to any sort of conclusion, Livvy turned to him with a grateful smile. "Thank ye for bringin' me 'ere," she whispered.

For reasons he couldn't begin to comprehend, a swell of emotion rose within him. She was grateful, that much he could tell. But there was something else in her tone, in her expression, that he couldn't put his finger on. It was almost as if she was experiencing life for the first time. The fact that August had been the one to give her the opportunity...it was touching.

"I be that glad," he responded. "I thought ye might enjoy it. I've ne'er been able to share it with anyone else 'til this evenin'."

Livvy craned her neck to meet his gaze. "Not e'en with Miss Pengelly?"

Her eyes delved into his, and August paused. Typically,

when Emma was mentioned, Livvy's eyes skittered about the ground and the skies. Did that mean...Did Livvy know? Had Mr. May told her?

He set the ridiculous notion aside. There was no chance of the man ever being honorable enough to speak any truth to his daughter.

Still, her unwavering gaze unnerved him. "No," he responded, staring back at the wispy pathway. "I've not 'ad the opportunity. Yet." He added the word to make his attachment to Emma sound more convincing.

Although, at this point, did he truly wish for Livvy to think that he was in a relationship with the woman? He knew Mr. May did. But then, what would Livvy think of August now, asking her on a scandalous outing while supposedly attached to another? Or had she only agreed because she'd suspected the falseness of their relationship from the beginning? He wouldn't put it past someone so clever as her.

Without a response, Livvy shifted her gaze from August to the pathway, then to the moon above. Her long, wavy curls fluttered across her brow and against her cheeks, though she didn't bother to brush them aside. Her braid was more visible now, and though he'd found her gorgeous before, there was something about the indecorum of her soft hair being worn down that beckoned him closer.

She appeared like a painting he'd seen once in the Eastwoods' house in Coniston, Birchwick Hall. He'd been invited to share his plans for their gardens with them, so on his way to the master of the house's study, he'd passed by painting after painting in the never-ending corridors. Most of them were the same—rigid men with frowns, women lounging on settees, children holding still and dogs quirking their heads—all rather...unrealistic.

But one had stood out to him from the others, a portrait of

a young woman with her back to the viewer, staring out at a storm-tossed sea. August had always imagined the woman lost in thought, admiring the sights around her that were as beautiful as she was.

That painting had held much intrigue for August over the years.

But now, that intrigue held nothing to the candle that he'd unwittingly lit to shine upon Livvy.

He'd made a mistake in bringing her here this evening. A horrible, terrible, lovely mistake.

"Mother always loved the moon."

Livvy's words had come so softly, he hadn't known if she'd meant to speak them aloud until she continued. "She said it be God's way o' sayin' that beauty and light can be found even durin' dark times."

He watched her, a soft expression across her features as she continued. "She'd stay awake until the early hours o' the morning on clear nights, just to watch the moon slide across the skies."

August wasn't quite sure when it had begun, but he only realized now how hypnotizing this woman's words were to him. She was intoxicating, now more than ever. She'd always appeared to have her guard up, skittering eyes, worrying over her father, remaining silent around others.

But now, she had dropped her entire façade, and August was seeing her—all of her—for the first time. She was irrevocably, entirely Livvy May, and he couldn't help but admire her all the more because of it.

"Sounds like ye take after 'er," he whispered. "Stayin' up late. Admirin' nature."

Livvy looked back down to the causeway, her eyes taking on a faraway look, as if she was, in actuality, standing in the sea. "Father says the same. That I take after me mother in many ways. I can't see it, though."

For some reason, she didn't seem upset by such a fact. But then, what did he know? He had never lost a parent. "Ye must miss her a great deal."

Her lips tightened. "Ten years does much to 'eal."

There was something in her tone that gave him pause, as if Livvy hadn't been referring to healing from her mother's death but healing from something else entirely. But, what?

"At any rate," she continued, "Mother wasn't around much, so it was just me father and I more often than not. As such, I'm beginnin' to lose much o' me memory of 'er."

August fought the urge to ask her where her mother was when she was not at home or with her family, but instinct told him to keep that question to himself. He'd heard the rumors of Mrs. May, but he'd never dignify them with the attention of forcing Livvy to speak of them aloud.

"Does that upset ye, not rememberin' 'er?" he asked instead.

She pulled in her upper lip, biting it for a moment before responding with a wary eye in his direction. "Not more than it ought to."

August tried to react accordingly, but he couldn't help his surprise from raising his brow. She didn't miss her mother? Or she didn't mind forgetting the pain associated with losing her?

He hesitated to ask her to clarify as she pressed her lips more tightly together, seemingly finished with the conversation. "Ye don't 'ave to speak more if ye don't wish to. I don't wish to pry."

She turned to face him. "That be what everyone says."

Her stare penetrated his defenses, as if she stared directly at his soul. He made to speak, wishing to reassure her that he meant what he said, but he clamped his mouth shut, allowing her to make the decision for herself.

Finally, a soft smile curved the corners of her lips. "But I be more apt to believe ye than others."

Warmth spread through his chest, despite the nipping night air. He didn't know why she believed him over anyone else, but he was grateful to have earned her trust.

As soon as the warmth pervaded his body, it was stripped clean from his person. He didn't deserve her trust. Not after what he'd agreed to do for her father.

He tried to remind himself that he really was helping her, that he would do what it took to guide her toward happiness, even if it wasn't what her father wanted. But despite his good intentions, he was still being deceitful, and his heart ached because of it.

"Be somethin' wrong?" Livvy asked. She must have seen his mood shift.

"Yes. I..." He drew a deep breath, longing to tell her the truth.

Nicholas.

Emma.

His family.

His job.

Mr. May's threats.

Livvy's feelings.

Livvy's heart.

All of them flashed through his mind.

He couldn't. He couldn't breathe a word about any of it. "No," he settled with instead. "Nothin' be wrong."

CHAPTER TWENTY-NINE

"...death, a necessary end, will come when it will come."
Julius Caesar, William Shakespeare

Livvy didn't believe him. August could feel it. He didn't blame her, either. He was apparently untrustworthy in every regard.

"I used to be quite social, ye know," she said, graciously allowing his falsehood to fade away. "I used to attend every gatherin' and loved talkin' and playin' games with the kids me age. But it all changed when Mother died."

Her voice fell, and her eyes drifted up to the moon again, as if her mind could only focus on her mother by peering at the light in the night sky. "Kids started treatin' me differently, obviously unsure of 'ow to speak to me any longer. I don't blame 'em, 'course, as they were just kids themselves. But it was difficult to continue on as I did 'fore. 'Specially when the rumors began." She eyed him sidelong. "I assume ye've 'eard 'em all."

How August longed to deny the fact that he had heard

them. Most of them centered around how Mrs. May had potentially died. There was talk of her falling ill to a mysterious sickness, whisperings of her running away from the Mount, even rumors of her taking her own life.

If August was being forced to lie about Mr. May's request, however, then he was determined to be honest in every other way he could be.

"I 'ave," he stated truthfully. "Though I be sorry to say it."

She nodded, unsurprised. "Father was beside 'imself after 'er death. 'E couldn't speak with anyone, so the burden fell on me own shoulders to tell the Mount what 'ad 'appened. E'en when I told the truth 'bout her death, though, no one believed me."

She stopped, and August hesitated once again. He knew he shouldn't press her. He knew he shouldn't ask her questions that might make her uncomfortable. And yet, a part of him—a very small part of him that he was allowing to have free rein for a moment—wished to sabotage their relationship from continuing forward, if only to sever ties so he no longer had to lie to her. If she lost her trust in August, he would always live with that regret. But at least Nicholas and Emma would be safe.

"And what be the truth?" he asked softly, regretting his nerve at once. He didn't deserve to know such a fact at all.

To his surprise and a small amount of dismay—and a large deal of relief—Livvy didn't appear offended at all. "I told others that Mother died of a fever that 'ad taken its toll on 'er body, and she simply couldn't recover." She kept her eyes on the moon. "But that be only a partial truth. Mother died 'cause she no longer wished to live."

August's mouth dried, his stomach roiling in sorrow for the woman standing before him.

"'Course, people were naturally curious," she continued,

"and naturally suspicious. They took to spreadin' their own ideas of 'ow she died. I don't blame 'em. She'd been so young. Seemingly so 'ealthy. 'Ow could she 'ave died of an illness? But I watched as the life faded from 'er eyes day by day 'til there was nothin' left but emptiness."

He winced at the hollowness of her tone. "Were ye there when she died?" he asked.

She nodded. "Yes, I was the only one. She spoke to me 'bout —" Her words ended abruptly, and she averted her gaze. "'Bout 'er life."

August was certain she'd been about to say something else, but he allowed her to remain silent on the matter. She was already pushing herself a great deal, that much was clear.

"Where was your father?" he asked instead, doing his best not to judge the man, though his opinion about Mr. May had already been secured in stone within the confines of his soul.

"'E was sleepin' off 'is drink," she replied simply.

Another stone slid deeply into the wall that was swiftly being built in anger against the man.

"I didn't expect 'im to join me for the funeral," she continued, "but I be glad that 'e did, if only so I wouldn't be alone. That be when I first 'eard the rumors, overhearin' folks talk about the *way* Mother left earth. When the children started pokin' me for answers—no doubt doin' their mothers' biddin'—I couldn't take it any longer. I retreated, locked meself inside me 'ome with no desire to e'er leave again."

She paused, though August wished for her to continue, if only to keep his mind occupied instead of dwelling on the miserable fact that he'd been entirely and utterly unaware of the grief this woman had felt right next door to him his entire life.

How could he have been so obtuse, so full of his own concerns and worries? He was ashamed of his stupidity.

"So there ye 'ave it," she said with a sigh. "The sorrowful tale o' the Hermit of the Mount. I took comfort in books, they gave me labels, and I've maintained 'em e'er since." She gave a mirthless laugh. "I s'pose I deserve 'em labels, though. I 'aven't made much effort to befriend anyone in the last ten years. If I did, they'd just be scared away 'cause o' them rumors and me strange behavior."

In all honesty, August couldn't even begin to picture Livvy scaring anyone off. She was far too kind. Far too thoughtful. But then, was that only with *him*, like Mr. May had said?

"I still be 'ere," he said softly.

Livvy glanced up at him. "Shockingly enough. But who knows 'ow long ye'll last. E'en Father 'as been scared away from me."

The last thing August wished to do was steer the conversation back to her father, but she seemed determined to do just that.

"'E be embarrassed o' me, ye know," she said.

August frowned. He did know. But he'd never admit that to Livvy.

"It be true," she said, looking up at him. Clearly, she'd mistaken his silence again as disbelief. "Tell me, 'as 'e e'er mentioned me at work?"

August shifted uncomfortably on the pathway, his cravat suddenly feeling very tight. "A time or two."

"And did 'e speak in secrecy, with no other pryin' ears?"

His breathing stinted. "I...I s'pose."

"Ye see?" she said, clearly unaware of the discomfort she was placing on August's heart. "Does that not strike ye as odd, that a man won't speak of 'is daugh'er unless doin' so in secrecy?"

Again, August couldn't say a word. Yes, it did strike him as odd. Everything about Mr. May struck him as odd and terrible and vindictive all rolled into one. Even still, while Livvy hardly seemed happy with her father, August didn't think she'd take kindly to August throwing him out to the dogs, either.

Was this the real reason Mr. May was asking August to help change his daughter—not because of his love for Livvy but because he was embarrassed by Livvy?

The bile in his stomach curdled.

"It be all right," she continued when he didn't respond. "I be used to 'is strange way o' showin' that 'e loves me. I only wish that I'd be allowed to be the person I wish to be without others—Father included—thinkin' I be strange. I be exhausted with tryin' to fit in, e'en though I ne'er will. I be a horse who wants to swim with dolphins 'round the Mount but am destined to remain confined to a one-stall stable, only let out to pull a desperately 'eavy wagon 'round for the rest o' me life."

Despite the heavy topic in which they'd been engaged, August's spirits raised a fraction, if only due to the imagery she created with her words. She really did have a way with them.

"Can I ask ye a question, August?"

His name in her soft voice sounded as sweet as the cherry tarts had tasted that morning. "'Course."

"What more do I 'ave to say to ye to 'ave ye run for the 'ouses at the bottom o' the Mount?"

He chuckled. "Be ye *tryin'* to scare me off?"

"No. I merely be curious to see what else ye can take."

"I think ye'd be surprised."

"I don't know. I do 'ave more secrets to reveal."

"Don't we all?" he mumbled without thinking.

Their eyes met, her gaze holding a weight to it he recognized all too well. But it was a weight he was tired of bearing that evening.

They'd spent far too much of their time speaking of sorrowful matters. Perhaps it was time for a change.

"Speakin' o' secrets," he said. He turned to face her, waiting to continue until her eyes met his. "'Ow did ye know I could sing?"

Her eyes rounded, and her chest rose as she drew a deep breath. "Oh, I..." Her words faded as she swallowed.

How he wished for more daylight in that moment, for he knew very well that another blush had graced her cheeks with its presence. For now, however, he would merely have to be satisfied with the way she peered up at him, the moonlight twinkling in her eyes .

"I told ye 'fore," she said. "I 'eard ye in church."

He took a step closer to her, shaking his head. "But I don't sing in church."

She looked away. "I be certain ye do."

He couldn't help but smile. "I be certain I do not. I ne'er sing in front o' people, so that leads me to only one conclusion. Livvy May, 'ave ye been spyin' on me?"

Even in the dim light, he could see her growing smile. She'd been caught out.

"I 'aven't the faintest idea what ye be talkin' 'bout, sir," she said.

His heart stuttered, her words confirming his suspicions. She *had* been watching him.

"I think ye do," he said, taking another step toward her.

He knew he should stay away, take a step back instead of a step closer. But the attraction he felt for her was powerful and potent and impossible to resist.

He flashed a smile. "I do wonder now if—"

A ruffling and a creak sounded nearby, cutting him off, and Livvy gasped.

"Be it a ghost?" she whispered. He felt her hand clutch the fabric of his sleeve.

If only it *were* a ghost.

His heart jumped into his throat. "No, it be a person," he whispered in response.

A very real and very tangible person.

Heavens above. They were going to be discovered.

CHAPTER THIRTY

"It's up to brave hearts, sir, to be patient when things are going badly, as well as being happy when they're going well..."
Don Quixote, Miguel de Cervantes

"August, I can't be seen!"

Livvy's distraught whisper shot warnings through August's already harried nerves. The noise might not have been a person. It could very well be an animal in the night. An owl or a fox, perhaps.

But when whispered voices reached his ears, he grasped Livvy's gloved hand in his own and tugged her at once into the shrubs nearby.

Knowing the gardens like the back of his hand, August sidestepped the mounds of azaleas tinted blue in the moonlight, hoping Livvy would follow his steps exactly as he paved the way toward a bundle of dogwoods pressed up against the edge of the stone wall bordering the garden.

There, he hunkered down, pulling Livvy beside him,

squished between stone and branch as the whispered voices grew louder. "We'll not be seen 'ere," he reassured her.

"Be ye certain?" He could barely hear her whisper above the blood rushing in his ears.

How could he have been so foolish to bring this woman out there? If anything happened to her, if he was the cause of more rumors spread about her or her family, he couldn't bear it.

"Yes," he breathed out shakily. "We'll be fine."

Or so he prayed. The small shrubs they hid behind were tall enough to cover the tops of their heads, though the leaves had not yet reached their full potential. Still, if they held stationary, the invader would not see them.

Invader. He and Livvy were the invaders.

Together, they waited side-by-side, their breathing still heavy, hands still intertwined.

Their hands. Somehow, in the fear of discovery, August had maintained his grip on her hand. She hadn't attempted to pull away either.

She must have simply felt more secure holding his hand, nothing more. But August...August was feeling something else. A powerful stirring in his heart that increased as he shifted in the dirt and his shoulder brushed against the woman beside him.

He'd been close to other women before, even kissed a few in the folly of his youth, but this was something different. This longing to be near Livvy, to know her further, was unlike anything he'd ever experienced.

"There be two of 'em," Livvy whispered.

August blinked. Two of what?

Whispers reached his ears in the silence, and he was brought back to the very real and very alarming present.

Two, Livvy had said. Two people. Two people who could very well discover them and ruin both of their lives forever. He needed to focus. Livvy was depending on him to rescue her from this situation that he alone had brought her into.

He peered through the dogwood branches that held buds of promised leaves, shifting back and forth before seeing that there were, indeed, two individuals walking on the pathway nearby. From the looks of them, one was male, the other female.

Who on earth could they be? Had Sir John returned and was now taking a midnight stroll with his mistress? Or had one of the other gardeners discovered how lovely a nightly walk through the gardens could be with a significant...

His heart dropped. It was Emma and Nicholas.

Conflicting feelings rose within him, his mind spinning as he tried to process them all. On the one hand, he couldn't be more relieved to know that his friends were in the gardens, for he trusted them more than anyone. They would never reveal to the Mount that August and Livvy had been discovered alone in a compromising situation.

On the other hand, a wave of dread rushed over him. Livvy couldn't discover that Emma and Nicholas were together. Not only had Mr. May instructed August to keep to himself the charade between him and Emma, but also, if Livvy discovered the truth, August would have to ask her to keep their secret, too. How could he ask that of her when he was already lying to her?

Then another thought occurred. Even though he trusted Emma and Nicholas, he didn't necessarily wish for them to know he was there with Livvy. They would ask him questions, particularly why he was hiding in a bush with a single woman. But August couldn't answer truthfully without jeopardizing them both.

The easiest solution would be for Livvy to not discover the couple at all.

He shifted in the dirt soundlessly, ready to point out the moon above, the dirt below—anything to pull her attention away from the others—but he froze when she leaned toward him, their shoulders pressed against each other.

"That be Miss Pengelly and Mr. Cuff."

August cringed. Blast this woman's astuteness. "I...I don't believe so." He narrowed his eyes, feigning ignorance. "It be another gardener, per'aps."

The words fell flat even for his own ears. Though, he couldn't be entirely certain, as his head still spun due to their shoulders touching.

Livvy looked over at him, but he couldn't meet her gaze. "Ye don't 'ave to pretend any longer. I know they be in a relationship."

He opened his mouth to protest again, then stopped. He'd promised himself to be honest with Livvy in every other way he was allowed to be. So honest, he would be.

With a heavy sigh and sunken shoulders, he nodded. "Yes, it be them."

Her hand loosened her grip on his at the knowledge of their safety. Did she wish for him to let go of her, then?

With great reluctance, he did just that, though he regretted the decision immediately. "Forgive me for lyin' to ye 'fore," he said.

"Ye don't 'ave to apologize. Ye were keepin' the secret for your friends."

Would she still feel that way if he told her that was the very reason he was doing her father's bidding? "'Ow long 'ave ye known?" he asked.

"I've suspected somethin' for a week now, but tonight settled it. I knew ye be too honorable to ask me to join ye tonight if ye be truly attached to Miss Pengelly."

For the second time that night, he was grateful for the

darkness, if only so his blush could remain unseen. She thought him honorable?

"Seein' ye and Mr. Cuff exchange letters in the gardens this mornin' was what convinced me, though," Livvy continued.

Of course. He'd told Nicholas it was a stupid idea.

"No one will see us in plain sight, August."

No one, indeed.

Livvy shifted, and their shoulders pulled apart.

August stifled a sigh. "And 'ere I be, thinkin' I be so clever keepin' their secret."

The moonlight pushed its way through the boxwood branches, revealing a slight smile on her lips. "Ye were," she assured him. "No one else would s'pect a thing. But ye be no match for me spyin'."

He almost laughed at her admission, but he remembered just in time to keep quiet.

So Livvy had watched him sing *and* help—or rather, not help—his friends keep their secret. What else had she seen him do? Nothing too embarrassing, he hoped.

He also hoped she was right in her assumption that no one else knew about Emma and Nicholas. Either way, he would certainly be even more careful than before.

He eyed his friends, the two of them having taken a lower path so only their upper bodies were visible from their vantage point. Their whispers continued just loud enough for August to know he and Livvy had not yet been discovered.

"I be terribly sorry for all o' this," he apologized again. "They've both sworn me to secrecy. Me own family don't know that I be tasked to..."

He trailed off as she nodded understandingly. "That ye be tasked to convince the Mount that Miss Pengelly and ye be attached so no one would s'pect 'er o' fallin' for Mr. Cuff."

Astute, indeed.

"Yes, exactly. If their families discovered the attachment, I fear the worst might 'appen."

She gave a single nod. "Understood. Ye don't 'ave to worry. I'll ne'er tell a secret that ain't mine to tell."

Apparently, she was apt to reveal that she was perfection personified. How was she so good with a father like Mr. May? "Thank ye. I be certain they'll be grateful to ye when this all be o'er."

She nodded, gratefully not asking any further questions. August couldn't be more relieved that at least one of his secrets was out in the open. And he hadn't even had to break his promise with Emma or Nicholas to have it done.

"So I s'pose we stay 'ere 'til they leave?" Livvy asked. "I don't really wish for 'em to know we've been hidin' 'ere alone together." She rushed to include, "E'en though we ain't doin' anythin'."

Relief rushed over him. Thank heavens for her sense. The last thing he wished for her to think was that he was embarrassed by being found with her, but with this being her decision, they could both get away with what they wanted—remaining unseen.

The truth of the matter was, though, that if Mr. May hadn't done what he'd done, and Nicholas and Emma hadn't asked August to help them...August would have already made his intentions for Livvy known, and he'd be shouting it from the top of the Mount.

But he couldn't. And he would never be able to.

They remained in silence for a moment until they could no longer hear his friends' whispers.

Livvy peered deep through the branches. "Did they leave?"

August frowned. "I don't believe so. But...what be that noise?"

"What noise?"

He leaned to the side, listening intently as Livvy did the same.

"It do sound like they be eatin'," she whispered.

August's lips parted, and he pulled a face. "Oh...That ain't eatin' they be doin'."

Livvy looked at him in confusion, then her eyes rounded. "'Eavens above. They be kissin'?"

Sure enough, as August strained to see in the darkness, he could just make out his friends' shadows merged into one as they stood kissing.

Loudly.

"'Eavens above, be right," August whispered.

Livvy held both hands to her face in horror. "Oh, this just can't get any worse, can it?"

August couldn't help but agree, and yet, as the stress of the evening slipped away, the heavy emotions from before draining from his spirit, a sliver of humor slipped into his heart, and a smile grew on his face.

"What ye be smilin' at?" Livvy whispered, staring at him condemningly. "This be terrible."

Humor bubbled up within August even more, a grin breaking out across his lips. "When are ye goin' to learn that nothin' good comes from hidin' in bushes?"

Despite her frown, a hint of a smile shone through her eyes. That is, until the kissing grew louder. She gave a disgusted moan under her breath again, lifting her hands to her ears next. "They sound like two dogs lappin' up water."

The accuracy of her description was his undoing. He stifled a laugh, but only just, a puff of air slipping through his nose.

"Two dogs *enjoyin'* lappin' up water, ye mean," he corrected.

She moved her hands to her mouth in what August thought was an effort to stop herself from groaning with disgust. But when her shoulders started shaking up and down, he knew she was laughing.

"What ye be doin' laughin' now?" he asked, leaning closer until their shoulders touched again. "'Tisn't humorous. 'Tis romantic."

Her shoulders shook even harder.

How he loved making her laugh.

"I can't bear much more o' this," she managed to say after another moment passed by. "We need to get out of 'ere 'fore I be sick."

August nodded. He had no idea how long his friends would remain there in each other's arms. But now was as good a time as any to make an escape.

He scoured the grounds around them, settling on the best route before relaying it to Livvy. "If we keep to the wall and slide behind the other bushes, we can leave without 'em seein' us. We'll 'ave to move slowly, though. And be careful to avoid the plants."

Livvy nodded her understanding. "I'll sprout wings and fly if it means I don't 'ave to listen to 'em any longer."

He grinned. "Now that'd be a spectacle I'd like to see."

"Get me out o' these gardens, and ye will."

They shared a smile, a moment passing between them in the darkness before Livvy looked away. "Lead the way, sir."

He did as he was told, and the two of them crouched low to blend in with shrubs, bushes, and flowers, as they moved forward, pausing every few steps to ensure they could—regretfully—still hear the kisses going on between his friends.

With their boots caked in mud, they finally and mercifully reached the gate. Sidling through the doorway, they continued on in silence until they were off castle grounds. Only then did they pause to catch their breath.

"Thank 'eavens," Livvy breathed as she wiped her boots on the grass.

August straightened his back that had been cricked as they tiptoed through the gardens. "Be ye more relieved to not be discovered or to not 'ave to 'ear 'em any longer?"

"Ye know, it be difficult to say."

He smiled, taking a turn to wipe his boots free of mud, too. "Well, let's see it, then."

She turned to look at him. "See what?"

"Ye promised me sprouted wings and flyin'?"

Her eyes twinkled. "Sorry to disappoint, but I can do no such thing."

He raised an appalled hand to his chest and dropped his mouth open. She responded with another delightful smile.

After their boots were cleaned off and their backs no longer ached, they began their descent of the Mount, walking mostly in silence, though a few conversations centered around *The Mysteries of Udolpho*, which, to his delight, had caused Livvy to cling to his arm again with each tree's shadow or whisper of wind that crossed their paths.

By the time they reached the houses, they were both yawning from the lateness and exhaustion of the night.

Instead of taking her directly to her home, August paused to the west of the houses, near the outside of the large sail repair loft that cast great, dark shadows around them.

"I be sorry for keepin' ye out so late," he whispered.

But Livvy shook her head. "I 'ad a wonderful time. That spot might e'en move into me top favorites."

"But not *the* top," he teased.

"No, 'twasn't that amazin'," she teased right back.

Their eyes met, their bodies standing close to the outer wall of worn stone.

August knew his time alone with Livvy was coming to an

end—just as much as he knew it *needed* to come to an end. He'd gone too far that night. He'd fallen for her too greatly. And now he feared she had fallen for him, too. If that happened, how would Mr. May react? And how was August to ever convince her to leave the Mount?

But then, he shouldn't worry about such things unless he knew the truth—unless he knew how she really felt about him.

"Before ye go..." he began.

She looked up at him. "Yes?"

"Ye told me this evenin' that ye were sociable 'fore your mother's death, that ye avoid most socializin' now..." He paused, trying to convince himself not to ask the question he already knew the answer to. But then, did he? "So...why do ye choose to socialize with me and no one else?"

Livvy was silent for a moment. He honestly wouldn't be surprised if she didn't respond at all.

"'Cause ye accept me for who I be," she replied softly.

Her response was worse than he'd even expected. His chest constricted as if strong hands had wrapped around his heart and were now squeezing the life from him like a dried fruit with no more sweetness to give.

How little she knew him, the man who was tasked to change *exactly* who she was.

"I must go now," she whispered.

He nodded in silence, unable to respond.

"Thank ye again, August. This...this 'as been one o' the best nights o' me life."

Without awaiting a response, she scurried around the corner and disappeared into the darkness toward the houses.

August wanted to remain hidden, to forget the evening had even occurred, but he peered around the corner and watched as her shadowed silhouette vanished into her home.

Once he knew she was safe, he fell back against the side of

the boathouse and stared up at the stars that shone beyond the edge of the roof.

He'd gained Livvy's trust. He knew he would be able to convince her to socialize with others now, perhaps even to attend the assembly off the Mount where she could find more men whose hearts she could charm her way into.

Mr. May would be thrilled. Perhaps Miss May would be happy, too. Because once she discovered August's ruse—and if he'd been convinced of anything that night, it was that she *would* discover it—there was no chance she'd want to be with him.

And that caused his heart to ache more than anything.

CHAPTER THIRTY-ONE

"Secret griefs are more cruel than public calamities."
Candide, Voltaire

Every spring near the anniversary of Mother's death, Livvy made it a point to visit the graveyard on the Mount, gathering a bundle of flowers and laying it to rest before her mother's moss-covered grave marker.

Typically, Livvy liked to complete the task in early March, but this year, she had been delayed by her illness, her new books, her time with August, and, perhaps more than anything, her hesitation to reassess the feelings that were brought to the forefront of her mind every time she visited Mother's grave.

Perhaps that was why she'd opened up with August last night. Or perhaps it was simply because she knew she could trust him with the information. Well, *some* of the information. She still was unwilling to share what Mother had told her on her deathbed—words Livvy would never even share with Father.

Even still, speaking with August had renewed her spirits, and she woke up bright and early to accomplish the task set before her. Her first stop was to visit the Otterhams, who once again asked after her reading.

Livvy told them that she'd stayed up late the night before to finish the final chapter of *The Mysteries of Udolpho*, which, of course, had proved to be as wonderful as she'd thought it would be.

Although, she did sidestep the fact that the book, while exciting, paled tragically in comparison with her night out with August. That was also another thing she did not share, that she very easily could have caused herself a personal scandal by sneaking out in the middle of the night with a man who was pretending to be quite attached to a woman who was secretly engaged to another man.

Her mind still spun at the thought. She'd felt such relief to know that August wasn't attached to Miss Pengelly, her guilt from before fading in the night's sky.

But then, with that worry gone, another surfaced, and it was one she was not yet ready to face.

After her visit with the Otterhams, Mrs. Otterham thanking her profusely for the handkerchiefs—*"They be the most beautiful I've e'er received. I don't e'en want to use 'em!" "Ye best use 'em, Talwyn, so ye stop usin' me own."*—Livvy walked through the rain to where the sea pinks grew along the cliffs' edges.

There, she picked a few of the small, spindly flowers, the first of many that would soon carpet the Mount in round bursts of trembling blossoms.

Gathering the long stems together, she pulled out a thin ribbon from her reticule and used it to tie the sea pinks as one before climbing back down the Mount to where the graveyard was situated, directly south of the causeway.

Rain trickled from the clouds above, as if reluctant to douse the Mount after the clear evening before. But Livvy didn't mind the moisture. She always chose rainy days to visit Mother's grave. Rainy days meant less people there.

Instead of focusing on what was to come, she kept her mind on her time with August, but far too soon, the graveyard came into view, and her thoughts on the night before ended.

She had done this for a decade now. She thought it would get easier with time, but each anniversary that came, Livvy still felt that same uneasy feeling stirring in her heart.

Even now, she stood outside the small gate to the graveyard, staring at the back of the marker she knew to be Mother's.

The good memories returned first, just as they always did.

Mother teaching her how to stitch, though she couldn't stitch a lick herself. The time they spent laughing in the middle of a sermon at the sight of two red squirrels bickering over acorns outside the church windows. When they used to race across the causeway and Mother would feign exhaustion so Livvy would win.

Mother was considered odd by those on the Mount, too. But she didn't care. She taught Livvy not to care, either, to embrace her true nature and to let people think what they may. And Livvy had, for a time.

But after Mother's death, after the words she'd spoken, Livvy stopped taking her advice.

The sorrowful memories came flooding in next.

How Mother would leave for weeks at a time, claiming to visit relatives on the mainland, though she'd never let Livvy or Father join her. How Mother always fought with Father when she returned.

How desperately she'd hated living on the Mount.

"I be trapped 'ere," Livvy would hear her say at night through the thin walls in their house. *"And ye and Livvy be the cause of it."*

Tears filled Livvy's eyes as she clutched the sea pinks tightly to her chest. Would Mother even like the sea pinks Livvy placed on her grave each year? Or did she truly despise flowers and plants like she'd told Father?

"What sort o' man wastes 'is life away by gardenin'? Flowers and bushes and trees. They be pointless. 'Elpless. Just like ye."

Then the worst memory of them all returned. When Mother beckoned Livvy into her room, her eyes gaunt and cheeks colorless.

"I 'ave to tell ye somethin', Lavinia, me darlin'," she'd whispered. *"Somethin' ye must swear to ne'er tell another soul. Somethin' not e'en your father must know."*

As clear as day, she was sent right back to that moment, but it came as no surprise to Livvy. Every year she went through this, the pain, the sorrow, the regret, reliving those frightful words Mother had spoken that had rattled all Livvy held dear.

"Ye might not be who ye think ye be, Lavinia."

Those feelings of fear and worry returned tenfold until Livvy finally managed a prayer heavenward. A prayer to forgive, to forget, to release her anger, and to focus on the truth—that her mother had ghosts in her past, just like everyone did.

But that was not Livvy's fault.

Within a few moments, with the rain rushing around her, sliding off her bonnet and clicking against the rhododendrons and hedges that surrounded the graveyard, that familiar sense of peace returned to Livvy's heart, and she breathed a sigh of relief.

Each year, it became easier and easier to find that peace, as did her ability to release the anger she'd held for years.

With a newfound sense of purpose, she walked through the gate and entered the graveyard, her eyes focused intently on the marker. She walked around the other stone crosses of villagers and beyond the large monuments erected for the family of the St. Aubyns until she reached the simple, curved headstone Father had purchased for Mother.

IN MEMORY OF
LAVINIA MAY
WIFE & MOTHER

Small patches of yellow lichen and green moss gathered on the edges of the marker. The grass was frayed around the edges and no flowers were in sight. The state of the stone didn't surprise Livvy, though. Why should it look as fine and clean as the other markers in the graveyard when she only visited once a year and Father...well, never?

Mother would roll over in this very grave if she knew she had been buried on the Mount.

"I shall go mad if I spend another moment on this forsaken island with ye."

The pain tried to rise again in Livvy's heart, but she gently set it aside as she would a child who needed loving correcting. Now was not the time to dwell on how deeply she missed her mother, how greatly she desired for a better relationship, how desperately she wished that her mother would have been there for her more.

Instead, she would focus on the times she *had* been there for Livvy, even if they were few and far between.

"I brought ye flowers again, Mother," she whispered, staring down at the grave. "I hope ye like 'em."

She bent down, placing them before the grave and setting a small stone on the stems, lest the wind blow them away. Straightening, she drew a deep breath. "I did somethin' foolish last night, but I think ye would've been proud. Ye always did want me to be more adventurous." She released her deep breath. "I fear I ain't so very much. But I be tryin' to accept meself, as ye taught me to do." Her chin quivered, but she firmly stopped the emotion. "I 'ope ye can learn to be proud o' me, Mother. Where'er ye may be. 'Cause I be proud o' meself and the strides I be takin' to make meself a better person."

She thought for a moment about what Mother would be like if given a second chance to live. Livvy liked to think that Mother would have changed. That she wouldn't have been so caustic the second time around. That she would have shown more joy, more patience. And that she would've loved Father and Livvy more.

But such a thing could not occur. Mother could not have a second chance at life on this earth. But Livvy...Livvy still had that opportunity. And she would not fall to Mother's ways, no matter how often Father said how similar Livvy was to her. She had the choice as to whom she would be.

And she would be Livvy May. Lover of the Mount. Odd one on the Mount. And she would be happy being just that.

A soft humming sounded above the noise of the rain, and Livvy started, looking around for the culprit. When she caught sight of movement on the outside of the graveyard—a gardener on his hands and knees by a patch of daffodils, the man only just visible through a small parting in the hedgerow—her heart jumped.

August.

What was he doing there? He only ever worked in the walled gardens.

Her breathing stopped, sick swelling in her stomach. Had

he heard her? Seen her? Witnessed her hesitance as she entered the graveyard and her emotions that came soon after?

But then, she'd spoken so softly, she was certain he couldn't have heard her at such a distance. Furthermore, he seemed so intent on his work that he truly seemed unaware of her presence at all.

And the greatest clue she possessed that he had no notion that she stood there? His humming. Just as he'd said, he only ever did so when he thought he was alone.

Relief rushed over her. She didn't have the energy to explain her behavior to him in the graveyard. At least not right now.

A moment passed, but she remained where she was, taking the opportunity to watch him work as he bent over the dirt, tossing weeds over his shoulder into the wheelbarrow behind him. Rain dripped from the tip of his flat cap, though he wore no jacket, his sleeves rolled up to his elbows.

His hard work must have caused him to feel warm, even in such cool temperatures.

Unlike Mother, Livvy had always admired Father's position. She always assumed that a man who cared for flowers was a sensitive man. A considerate one.

August certainly fit the idea.

She was still in awe—though not surprised—that her night with him had surpassed any joy she felt in reading the end of her novel when she'd returned to her bed. The novel would end up being her fifth, perhaps even fourth, favorite. And yet, her time with August had been far more exciting. Far more...satisfying.

And that had surprised her more than anything.

Another moment passed, and Livvy looked away, if only not to be the strange woman lurking at him without his knowledge.

Again.

She really should be getting home. She needed to change into dry clothing and start on *The Hermit's Cell* so she could return the books to Mrs. Moon.

More than anything, however, she needed to return home so she could put off asking August about his feelings.

Her gaze fell to the headstones around her before resting again on Mother's. Before last night, before ever speaking with August, Livvy's life had been simple, uneventful, and quite peaceful, despite her intrusive thoughts of loneliness.

Now, after speaking with him, spending time with him, she found herself looking forward to each day more than ever before. She felt renewed in every way. The time she spent with him filled her life with such wonder and joy that she couldn't help but wonder, if she would have had the courage to speak with him before, to be herself around others unapologetically... could she have had this life for the last ten years?

She knew she had been too young for August to really notice her before, but still, she could have been friends with him, perhaps even with his sisters, if she'd but found the courage she needed to look past the rumors and the judgmental looks.

Father said in order for Livvy to make friends, she needed to change, but she'd always despised the thought. Instead, what if all it took was for her to *be* a friend? After all, that had worked with August.

Her eyes found their way back to him, where he still gardened unaware of her presence. Each time they'd spoken, he'd been the one to approach her. Could she find the courage to be the one to approach him instead?

Drawing in a deep breath, she squared her shoulders. Mother couldn't have a second chance at life, but Livvy could. She could be brave. She could live with no more regrets. She could be herself, accept who she was, just like Mother taught. But she didn't have to be who Mother was.

She just needed to be who *she* was.

CHAPTER THIRTY-TWO

"I am excessively diverted."
Pride and Prejudice, Jane Austen

Livvy left the graveyard and rounded the corner to the outside where August still pulled at weeds, kneeling down in the sodden grass, his fingers covered in mud.

Her footsteps alerted him of her presence, and he raised his gaze to meet hers. Pleasant surprise lit his eyes. "Mornin', Livvy."

"Good mornin'," she returned. She still wasn't used to the warmth that filled her soul as he spoke her name.

He stood, facing her as he rubbed his hands together to be rid of the mud accumulating on his fingers. "What brings ye out this mornin'?"

His smile seemed more strained than it had last evening. No doubt that was due to the cold.

"Just visitin' me mother's grave," she replied. Before he could express any condolences he did not need to express, she motioned to his bare hands still rubbing together. "Do ye not wear gloves to garden?" Father always did.

He peered down at his hands. "I do. But I enjoy the feel o' the earth in me 'ands too much to wear 'em often."

Of course he did. Because August was just the sort of man to enjoy something so lovely.

He kept his eyes averted, still staring at his hands. Was he truly concerned with the state of them, or was he avoiding her gaze on purpose?

Or was his hesitance caused by something else entirely—that he felt anxious about keeping up his appearance as Miss Pengelly's intended?

Livvy glanced around them. There was no one in sight, thanks again to the rain. Still, she wouldn't linger long, if only for August and his friends' sakes. She merely wished to speak with him, to discover if he'd felt the same way about last night that she did.

She shifted her attention to the primroses lining the graveyard wall, their white petals holding the very color of the sunshine in the center of their blossoms. The dark brown dirt surrounding the flowers had only recently been cleared free of weeds and spare leaves, as was evident by its almost fluffy texture.

"Be this your task today?" she asked, motioning to the flowers.

"One of 'em, yes."

"I didn't know ye worked at the graveyard."

His gaze dropped. "I volunteered to today."

Silence fell between them again, strained and rigid. But, why?

"Be ye findin' joy back on the Mount and workin' 'ere?" she tried again.

"More than anythin'."

"E'en more 'an Bath and Coniston?"

"Far, far more. I've dreamt o' workin' 'ere me whole life, so it be everythin' I've e'er wanted."

Livvy nodded. She truly wished to know the answers to all these questions, but first and foremost, they were simply a way to divert her from her intended course.

If only she had the courage to just ask him.

"So ye don't regret leavin' there, takin' on a lower position?" she asked.

He shook his head. "I only e'er planned to stay there for a few years. 'Sides, ye can't beat livin' on the Mount. I be sure ye understand that."

"More than anyone." She drew a deep breath, pushing her courage forth to finally ask him her question. *"Did ye enjoy spendin' time with me last night?"*

But as his eyes finally found hers, she was shocked to discover sorrow within his gaze. What on earth had caused such a feeling?

He must not have wished for this emotion to be seen, however, for he cleared his throat and placed a strained smile on his lips. "At any rate, I be 'appy so long as I can work with flowers."

Was she imagining things, or did he seem to be avoiding a certain topic, as well?

She stared down at the primroses again. At this rate, she'd honestly rather speak of anything else than what she'd been about to ask him. She wasn't certain she could handle the rejection she feared.

"Do ye enjoy workin' with flowers or plants more?"

He seemed to think for a moment. "I enjoy 'em all, but I s'pose I be partial to flowers."

Silence returned.

Was this how others felt when speaking with her about

any other topic than books? How terrible if that was true. She felt as if she were attempting to pull up a thousand-year-old tree with roots secured around the very granite of the Mount.

And it didn't help that creating entertaining questions was about as foreign to her as breathing water.

"Do ye 'ave a favorite flower?" she asked, praying her questions didn't sound as terribly awkward as she feared.

"I quite like azaleas."

"Oh, I do, as well. They've a lovely scent."

"Be they your favorite? I take it ye 'ave a list."

Relief filled her to see that familiar spark in his eye. Grinning, she nodded. "I do. But me favorite ain't azaleas."

His gaze dropped, then traveled back to her face, the light within his eyes brighter than ever before. "I'd wager I could guess your favorite."

She raised a challenging brow to hide her delight in August finally seeming to wake up. Whatever stupor he'd appeared to have been in before had finally faded away. Perhaps he had merely been tired. They'd had a late night, after all.

"'Ow do ye plan on doin' that?" she asked.

"By askin' ye a few simple questions."

She nodded without hesitation. "Go on, then."

"Very well." He brought his fingers to his chin, seeming to forget the mud that had been on them before that had now transferred to the bottom of his jaw. Only he could make mud on one's face appealing. Could she reach forward and wipe it away? No, that would most definitely be too forward. "My first question be, what be your third favorite color?"

She narrowed her eyes. "Third?"

"I assume ye 'ave a list o' favorite colors, too."

"'Course," she replied. "But why me third?"

"If ye'd refrain from questionin' me process, please."

That teasing look in his dark eyes made her want to bottle

it up and throw it into the night's sky so she could stare at it all night long with the stars and the moon.

"Very well. Me third favorite color be blue."

He nodded, mulling over her answer.

"Next question. Would ye rather ne'er see the sea again or ne'er eat your favorite food again?"

"Not eat me favorite food."

He raised his brow. "That be a swift answer."

"I'd give up anythin' to keep me view o' the sea."

"I feel the very same. That was the most difficult part o' livin' off the Mount for so long. I used to stare at paintin's o' the sea to satisfy me desire to see 'em waves again."

She smiled at the image of August staring at paintings instead of working.

The rain was beginning to seep through her cloak now, cooling her shoulders, but she fought the urge to shiver. Now that August had fully come alive again, she'd do anything to remain with him.

"Next question," he said. "Do ye prefer travelin' by boat or by walkin' across the Causeway?"

This time, Livvy was required to think for a moment. "I believe I'd rather walk. I enjoy the fresh air more that way, and it takes more time, which means I get to enjoy the sights for longer." She paused, picturing the causeway in her mind's eye. "And there be somethin' magical 'bout walkin' across a pathway that only hours 'fore 'ad been covered by the sea."

"Yet another favorite we share in common," August responded. He straightened, his expression growing serious as he looked around them. Finally, he leaned toward her with a whisper. "Do ye regret goin' with me last night?"

Livvy nearly gasped. That had been the exact question she'd been longing to ask August for a good quarter of an hour now. How had he had the courage to simply ask it straight out?

She was also starting to grow suspicious of his questions. Had he given up on his quest to find her favorite flower and was now simply asking her questions that he wanted the answers to? Either way, she couldn't fault him for the bravery she wished she could mimic.

Even now, she was trying to find a way around answering his question with the truth. Then again, what good would that do? She'd been skirting around the issue their entire conversation now and had felt no peace because of it.

Perhaps she should simply answer with the truth.

Just do not be odd, Livvy.

The same old warning echoed through the recesses of her mind, drawing her spirits low and pushing her to retreat, to revert into the shell she'd lived in for years.

Then another thought occurred. Why should she listen to such thoughts when they continued to drag her down—to change her into a person she didn't want to be?

She would much rather listen to something else. *Anything* else.

Then live the way ye wish to live. Live without regret.

Instantly, her spirits were buoyed, and courage replaced all hesitancy.

Facing him directly, she shook her head. "No, August. I don't regret a single moment I spent with ye last night." Then she peered deep into his eyes. "Do ye?"

CHAPTER THIRTY-THREE

"These flowers are like the pleasures of this world."
Cymbeline, William Shakespeare

Livvy could hardly breathe as she awaited August's response.

Fortunately, she did not have to wait long, as his features softened, and his easy smile returned. "No," he replied. "No, I do not regret it in the least."

Relief overwhelmed her senses.

"But I thought I be the one askin' questions 'ere," August continued with narrowed eyes.

More relief. This, *this* was the real August. How happy she was to see him return.

"Be on with it, then," she teased right back.

"Thank ye." He paused, clearly for dramatic effect. "Now for me next question. Do ye think me a fine singer?"

He flashed a charming grin, raising one eyebrow in a theatrical manner that caused her to laugh.

She was sorely tempted to tease him again, claim that he

was a terrible singer, that she'd never heard worse, but she simply didn't have the heart.

With a deep sigh, she responded. "No, August. I don't think ye be a fine singer. I think ye be a superb singer."

"Do ye, now?" he asked, clearly flattered. "Very well. *Now* I know your favorite flower."

He didn't. Did he? "Well, what be it, then?"

"Sea pinks."

Shock overcame her, her mouth dropping open. "'Ow the devil did 'e guess that?"

He shrugged. "I told ye that ye'd be impressed."

"But, no...This doesn't make any sense. Those questions 'ad nothin' to do with flowers. 'Ow did ye know?"

"I know me flowers."

As if he could know them that well. "Did me answers truly give me away? Or did ye already know some'ow?"

He stared down at her with another shrug, then a smile broke out across his lips. "No." He motioned down to the reticule hanging from her hands. "I saw the sea pinks embroidered on your reticule and simply guessed."

Raising her hands and the reticule in turn, she peered at the mediocre embroidery of the sea pinks she'd stitched on the fabric only a few years before. Then as the shock faded away, laughter bubbled up from her chest.

"Ye little sneak," she said, still laughing. "So all those questions be for naught?"

He fairly beamed. "Be it a crime to wish to know more 'bout one's friend by askin' simple questions?"

She scoffed, though it shifted once again to another laugh.

"'Sides," he continued, "I just taught ye a valuable lesson—do not believe everythin' everyone says."

She shook her head, still reveling in his teasing. "Ye be nothin' but a connivin' cheat."

"A cheat? I ne'er. I simply used deductive reasonin'."

"That be just what a cheat would say," she returned.

"But surely ye can appreciate the lesson."

"Hardly." How she was enjoying this. "In fact..." She paused, looking around her before settling on a mound of dirt—wet, though not sopping enough to be considered mud. "I think I'll teach ye a lesson in return."

Without another thought, she reached down, retrieved a handful of the dirt, and launched it at August's chest. He let out a shout of protest, turning in time for the dirt to hit him squarely in his back instead.

Afterward, he faced her with surprised delight. "What do ye think ye be doin'?" he asked, then he reached down for a crumbly clod of dirt and tossed it at her next.

As it hit her shoulder, she gasped. "Ye can't throw dirt at a woman."

"I believe I just did."

She looked back down to the dirt, moving to pick up more before August stepped forward with his hands in the air. "Wait just a moment. I relent. I relent!"

She stopped, then faced him with a grin. "Already?"

"I know ye well enough to know I'd lose any fight I'd choose to pick with ye."

She laughed, though she wasn't sure she should be as flattered by his words as she was. "I see ye've learned your lesson, then."

"Indeed. Don't try to teach Miss Livvy May a lesson."

She grinned. "Or per'aps it ought to be, Miss Livvy May doesn't take kindly to liars."

His smile faltered. Had she taken her teasing too far?

Before she could explain that she truly didn't think August was a liar, he looked away.

"Perhaps I can make me behavior up to ye," he offered

softly.

Livvy grimaced. "I was only teasin', August."

"I know. But I'd still like to make amends."

"Very well," she said, shifting her footing uncomfortably. He didn't need to make amends for anything. He'd always behaved like a perfect gentleman to Livvy, so why had he taken her words so harshly? "'Ow will ye do so?"

He motioned to her reticule, where the sea pinks stood out against the blue silk. "By reassurin' ye that despite the obvious clue of your reticule, sea pinks would have been one of me first guesses to be your favorite flower."

She didn't doubt him for a moment. "Why be that, then?"

He stared at the reticule. "'Cause sea pinks be special, see. And only the most special o' women choose 'em to be their favorite flowers."

Her heart thrummed against her chest. She still couldn't understand the man and his swift changes in his emotions toward her, but in that moment, she found herself unable to dwell on anything apart from the softness with which he gazed upon her.

"Do ye know much about the flower?" he asked, his voice barely above the sound of the rain's consistent tapping around them.

She shook her head. Father had always been more of a technical gardener than anything, knowing everything about how to care for nearly every plant that grew in Cornwall.

Livvy had always done her best to listen to his instruction, but she found herself more of an admirer of the colors, shapes, and smells, than how to care for them.

August held his hand toward the reticule, signaling to hold it, so Livvy removed the ribbon from around her wrist and delivered the reticule into his outstretched fingers.

He examined the flower, which Livvy desperately wished

she had done a better job at attempting to represent. Father had told her not to rush the work. Livvy had returned with, *"It don't matter what it do look like, Father. No one'll be lookin' at it but me."*

Nothing like having one's pride take a direct hit.

"I've always thought a person's favorite flower says much 'bout who they be," August said.

"Do they?"

He nodded, his eyes remaining on the reticule. "Sea pinks be the hardiest o' flowers. They thrive in the salty air and live uncertain on the edges o' cliffsides, unaware o' the dangers lurkin' below. Despite all o' this, the flowers remain firm, standin' tall despite the winds and harsh weather, attractin' bees and butterflies with their sweet nectar, and sharin' their beauty with people for miles around."

He paused, and Livvy's breathing grew ragged as he finally looked up to meet her gaze. "'Ow similar ye be to these flowers," he said softly. "Just like these sea pinks, ye shine with a brightness that makes ye stand out. In a similar manner, ye do suffer with the salty winds of others' opinions and the harsh storms that come from people's judgments."

His voice was so soft, so understanding, that emotion welled in her throat.

"E'en more," he continued, taking a step toward her, "like these sea pinks, ye stand tall despite everythin' and remain unashamedly *ye*. And that be somethin' I can't 'elp but admire. 'Cause a woman who chooses sea pinks as 'er favorite flower be a woman who *deserves* to be admired." He stared down at her, his eyes delving deep into her own. "A woman who deserves to be cherished."

As he finished, Livvy's soul was alight with bright rays of sunshine. Never had she been spoken to in such a way, so tenderly, so sweetly.

Surely this was the proof she'd been searching for—that he did feel something for her. Something far more than friendship.

"Does that make up for me cheatin'?" he asked, peering down at her, his voice hardly above a whisper.

Livvy nodded, swallowing hard. "Yes. Although...did ye not try to teach me a lesson 'bout not believin' everythin' everyone says?"

He paused, admiration in his eyes as he chuckled. "Those words did come back to bite me far faster than I thought they would 'ave."

"I'd say so."

He sobered once again. "Per'aps I ought to 'ave said that ye ought not trust those who can't be trusted...but that ye can trust those who...who simply be doin' the best they can with what they've been given."

Livvy narrowed her eyes. He was trying to tell her something. Why else would he look at her with such a heavy gaze and focused eyes? But then, what could he not say that he wished to?

"Can I tell ye how else ye be like sea pinks?" he asked.

She nodded, no longer able to speak.

"Sometimes, people can be careless toward the delicate flowers, troddin' on 'em or causin' 'em to be dirty." He eyed her temple. "And just like sea pinks, ye might collect dirt on your petals caused by careless gardeners who decide to become embroiled in a mud fight 'e knows 'e'll ne'er win."

She paused. Was he saying...Did she have dirt on her face? She swiped at her temple in an effort to clean herself. Why had he not told her sooner? Never mind that she hadn't said a word about the dirt his jawline still sported. She didn't think he was admiring the muck on her face as she'd been admiring the muck on his.

August reached into his jacket pocket and produced a handkerchief, pausing as he stretched it toward her. "May I?" he asked with a half-smile, motioning to her temple.

Had she not cleared all the dirt from her face? If she took his handkerchief, she was certain she'd be able to wipe it all away. But then, who was she to deny the man an act of service?

A blush stretched across her cheeks as she nodded, and her skittering heart made it nearly impossible to draw a solid breath.

Nothing else in the world existed in that moment beyond August as he gently wiped the cloth down her temple. Livvy wasn't even certain *she* existed.

He focused on her temple, then moved to her eyes. The handkerchief stopped, and the distinct warmth from his fingertip brushed against her cheekbone.

Chills erupted up and down her skin, and her lips parted of their own volition, as if she needed more air to circulate through her whirring body.

Slowly, his thumb continued to gently caress her skin, creating an ethereal feeling around the both of them.

Livvy had no idea if she truly did have mud on her face or not. Nor at this moment did she care. August could lie to her all he wanted, so long as he continued to touch her in this way the rest of their days.

How long had she been waiting for a moment like this to occur—*dreaming* of a moment like this? But never in a thousand years did she imagine it would happen. Never in a million hopes did she believe it actually would occur.

Yet, as August leaned toward her, his own masculine lips separating as he drew closer, she knew this *was* happening.

And it would be glorious and wonderous. Everything she'd ever wanted it to be and more.

She couldn't wait.

CHAPTER THIRTY-FOUR

"What we place most hopes upon, generally proves most fatal."
The vicar of Wakefield, Oliver Goldsmith

"Brother?"

The young woman's voice snapped Livvy from the trance August had placed her in. She pulled away from his touch just as swiftly as he dropped his hand, and the two of them shifted toward the last women on the Mount Livvy had the fortitude to face.

Ophelia and Portia Moon.

The girls' condemning looks fell upon their brother first, then shifted to Livvy, who veritably squirmed like a worm under their gazes. If Lady Catherine de Bourgh in *Pride & Prejudice* delivered judgmental looks comparable to what these girls delivered, Livvy had no notion as to how Elizabeth Bennet had borne it.

She tried to set aside any unfounded guilt—after all, August was an unattached individual—but truth be told, she felt horrible. What would these girls think of her, allowing

August to touch her when they were under the impression that he was nearly engaged to Miss Pengelly?

And even worse was the fear of what rumors the girls could spread that would injure all parties involved, directly and indirectly.

How Livvy longed to have faith that Ophelia and Portia would keep what they'd seen to themselves. They were August's sisters, after all. But such faith was futile.

Her head spun as she thought of the repercussions of her thoughtless actions. She never should have lingered.

No regrets, indeed.

"Ophelia, Portia," August said. His voice hardly sounded affected, though Livvy was certain the redness on his cheeks was fresh. "What ye be doin' out in this weather?"

Ophelia pursed her lips before responding. "Mother told us ye'd be workin' 'ere today. Thought we'd come visit to 'elp ye pass the time, though I see ye be gettin' 'elp in that regard already." Her eyes flashed to Livvy's.

Livvy knew she needed to say something to the sisters, but anything she'd say would simply be used against her. Instead, she turned to August with an apologetic look. He would have to fend for himself now, as her presence would only make matters far worse.

But perhaps she could give him a slight boost before she left.

Giving a curtsy to the man, she smiled. "Thank ye for the lesson, Mr. Moon. I'll ne'er forget it."

His eyes turned to hers, and a slight smile shone in his eyes. "'Appy to 'elp any time, Miss May."

After another shared look, Livvy turned to the sisters with a curtsy. The girls exchanged annoyed glances with one another, as if they were both quite perturbed to not be let in on the exchange she and August had just shared.

Despite her best efforts, Livvy allowed the knowledge to boost her pride, and she walked away with a smile, grateful she needn't remain a moment longer with the women.

Poor August. He was sure to receive quite the scolding. But if anyone could talk sense into his sisters, it would be him. Livvy had to believe he could convince them to keep what they'd seen to themselves, if only for Mr. Cuff and Miss Pengelly's sakes.

As she moved around to the front of the graveyard, Livvy reached down for her reticule, only to discover she no longer had it in her possession.

Concern rushed over her as she wondered where she'd misplaced it, then dread slithered into her heart.

August still held onto it.

Pressing her wet glove to her brow, she contemplated what to do next. Return to August that moment, or go to his house later to retrieve it?

She cringed. Both had the high probability of subjecting her to awkwardness, but perhaps things would be less uncomfortable if his parents and household weren't involved, too.

With heavy steps, she turned around and returned to the graveyard, sheltered from view by the thick hedge. She couldn't see the Moons either, and had it not been for their voices, she might have thought they had already departed.

"Ye be behavin' disgracefully, August."

"*Abysmalic.*"

Livvy recognized the sisters' voices at once, especially Ophelia's creation of another word.

Hesitating, she stopped just out of sight, a frown burrowing in her brow. August should not have to be subjected to such words—especially when he'd done absolutely nothing wrong.

She itched to step forward, to defend his goodness. But

wouldn't that merely prove to the girls that Livvy was in love with their brother? Wouldn't they then be spurred on even more to share with the Mount all they had learned, effectively ending August's ruse with Miss Pengelly?

She stewed in silent indignation. Perhaps it was better for her to send Sarah for her reticule later on. Either way, if only to no longer be forced to hear another word of criticism about the man she loved, she was determined to leave.

That is, until she heard her name.

She froze, leaning closer to the hedge as she listened to their voices above the pouring rain.

"Ye'll be the laughin'stock o' the Mount if ye continue bein' seen 'round with that Miss May," Ophelia was saying.

Livvy's stomach churned. She knew the girls didn't like her. They hadn't ever since they were young, and Livvy would win every game the children on the Mount decided to play together. But their disdain for her had grown tenfold ever since she'd taken more to books than socializing. She was different from them. Impossible to understand, even, so they simply didn't bother to try.

Though she'd grown used to the knowledge after all these years, Livvy's heart still ached because of it.

"I don't know what ye be talkin' 'bout, Ophelia," August said, his tone weary. "We were just talkin'. That's all I e'er do with Miss May."

"Really?" Portia challenged. "Just talkin'? 'Cause I be fairly certain I just saw ye caressin' that girl's face."

August didn't respond. So he wasn't denying it, then? Livvy's heart soared at the thought.

"It be despicable," Ophelia said, seething. "What would Miss Pengelly think? Ye already be upsettin' Mother and Father with your confuddlin' behavior. Fallin' for your long-time friend, then droppin' 'er and pursuin' the oddest woman ye could e'er know. What can ye mean by this behavior?"

Livvy winced. There was that word again. *Odd.* August must not have heard it, otherwise he would have said something to defend her.

"Ye girls seem to be forgettin' after all these years away from me that ye both be me little sisters, not me mother."

"Well, sometimes little sisters need to speak up for the good of the family," Portia countered.

"She's right," Ophelia agreed. "'Specially when it be affecting all o' we as ye continue bein' seen near that odd woman."

There it was again. Her stomach clenched. Why did August not stop them from speaking that way about her?

"What do it matter if I be seen with her?" he asked. "We just be friends. Ye both be seen with men *ye* be friends with."

Livvy rubbed her hand against her pinching chest. He'd only said he was merely friends with Livvy to keep up his façade with Miss Pengelly. Did he not?

"If ye can't see why that be detrimental to your relationship with Miss Pengelly," Portia began, "or why ye be hurtin' us in doin' so—"

"Our reputation, August, think of our reputation," Ophelia jumped in.

"—then we *must* 'ave this discussion."

"Surely ye must see 'ow odd she be," Ophelia continued.

"So very odd," Portia agreed.

August's sigh was audible. "What do it matter if she be odd?"

His words pierced Livvy's heart. He...he thought her odd?

"'Cause it be ruinin' us, August..."

The girls continued, but their words faded from Livvy's mind as one word circled round and round in her thoughts.

Odd. Odd. Odd.

She shouldn't have been so surprised to discover August thought the same as everyone else did on the Mount—the same as Father did.

So why did it hurt so very much to have August agree?

Backing away from the hedges slowly to avoid being seen or heard, she left the graveyard and made for home, the rain having soaked through her cloak and dress, now sliding coolly against her skin.

After all this time believing that she'd been able to reach August before anyone else had time to sully his opinion of her, she'd been wrong. He thought of her the same as everyone else did—the same as Father did.

She'd kept her love of August to herself over all these years because she knew Father would claim she had set her sights too high, that she would be better off marrying a mainlander.

But in her foolish musings the night before, she'd mistakenly hoped that she could finally open up to Father about her feelings.

How wrong she had been.

Her hope tried to counteract her negative thoughts, but there was no use. No matter all the fine words August had said to her, all the encouragement and kindness he'd shared with her. His private, truthful thoughts had now been revealed.

And that was what hurt most of all. That she had been so stupid to believe that the Charmer of the Mount could have possibly fallen for someone like *her*.

CHAPTER THIRTY-FIVE

"Of the many things hidden from the knowledge of man, nothing is more unintelligible than the human heart."
The Odyssey, Homer

A few days later, Sunday arrived, and August found himself sitting in church with his family. He'd encouraged his parents to sit next to his sisters that day as he took the end of the pew. He didn't think it would be suitable for him to sit beside Ophelia and Portia through services when he still had yet to forgive them for their ridiculous scolding of him.

The organ's rich tone was played throughout the church as the rest of the congregation merged into the building attached to the castle at the top of the Mount. The church was different than most others August had seen, what with the thick stone used for pillars, walls, and roofing instead of a weaker wood. Even the stain-glassed windows could rival Bath Abbey's.

Or so his proud Cornish heart liked to believe.

The church was originally built more than seven hundred

years before, though refurbished a time or two—the latest renovations finishing up only a few years before, as per Sir John's wishes.

The wait was long to meet at the church on the Mount, but it was well worth it. How those islanders, August included, loved joining together in their church. His favorite part was the bronze figure of St. Michael defeating the devil, though the saint still offered the creature the hand of mercy.

August stared at the statue. If the devil could be shown the hand of mercy after all he'd done...would August receive such mercy, too?

His eyes once again darted to the doorway as another person entered. Every time Livvy didn't appear, however, his anticipation only increased. That is, until he did see her, accompanied, of course, by her father.

Somehow, August had managed to avoid the man for days, the busyness of the castle's gardens at spring leaving next to no time to speak of little else between the gardeners.

August wasn't about to complain. Any more time he could buy away from Mr. May would only serve him well, as August continued to worry himself over how exactly he could satisfy the man's demands...all without doing anything he demanded.

As Mr. May filed down the row of seats a few pews ahead of August and his family, August sat a little taller, hoping to catch Livvy's attention. To his good fortune, she glanced up, meeting his eyes squarely. He smiled in greeting, hoping his sisters would notice just so he could rile them up further.

But Livvy didn't return his smile. Instead, she looked away without so much of a nod and faced forward beside her father.

August's smile faded away. Now he hoped his sisters hadn't seen what had turned into the strangest of rejections.

What was that about? Had Mr. May told her about coercing

August into his plan? No, her father had been adamant that the whole affair be done in secrecy.

So what else had made her not smile at him? Was she upset that he'd covertly returned her reticule to her via her maid and their footman?

When his sisters had happened upon them outside the graveyard, he'd realized just in time that he still held her reticule, so he'd swiftly tucked it into his jacket. He would have returned it himself, but he'd been afraid to happen upon Mr. May instead of his daughter.

That hardly seemed the type of thing for Livvy to be upset about, though. So was she merely annoyed with how his sisters had ended their conversation—and his affection—prematurely?

He knew *he* had been. He was happy to have her leave, however, for he couldn't have handled Livvy listening to their harsh, judgmental words. He'd asked his sisters to keep what they'd seen to themselves, but, sadly, he didn't know if he could trust them anymore. They'd seemed to have developed an obsession with spreading gossip that could not be satisfied, even if it included ruining people's lives.

He'd spoken with his parents about this only yesterday, and while Mother and Father had also expressed their concerns, they didn't understand the urgency that August felt to change his sisters' ways. After all, he couldn't very well reveal to them the damage that could be done to so many on the Mount if they started wagging their tongues further.

"Unfortunately," Mother had said, *"your sisters 'ave far too much o' me own sisters in 'em."*

August grimaced even now at the thought. Mother's elderly, spinster sisters who lived on the mainland in St. Ives were generally kind, caring individuals. But they had a propensity to share untrue facts about others more than anyone August had ever known. According to Mother, Ophelia and Portia had spent a summer a few years ago with their aunts and had returned quite altered.

"Your sisters'll see the err in their ways eventually," Father had said. *"At any rate, they must make their own choices and face the consequences as they come."*

But August did not have such faith in them. Not when their unkindness extended to Livvy.

As the service began, his eyes drifted to the back of her bonnet. Something had to be upsetting her. Why else would she have snubbed him? Did her father's presence have to do with it? Mr. May always put August in a bad mood, so that idea might not be so very far-fetched.

August's worrisome musings continued, though he did his best to listen to the sermon until it ended, and the congregation began to file out of the church one by one, thanking the vicar for his words.

Despite his best effort, August couldn't slip into the aisles until long after Livvy had left the building. He moved at a snail's pace with the rest of the congregation, feeling like one cow in a herd of a thousand until he finally exited and cast his eyes around the courtyard, a few people lingering while others were already headed down the Mount.

He caught sight of Livvy quickly, who stood with Mr. May and the Pengellys. She spoke with Emma, smiling despite her ducked head, which warmed August's heart. He knew how difficult it was for Livvy to speak with others. The effort she'd put in with him at the graveyard had been admirable, to say the least.

He'd been so distracted digging up weeds from the wet dirt, deep in thought about all the terrible things that might occur if he continued to pursue Miss May in secret, that when she appeared, he'd been unable to remain present and happy until well into their conversation.

Then, of course, he'd overstepped his bounds and caressed the woman—*caressed* her, for heaven's sake.

Even now, standing outside of the church doors with his family, the memory of her soft skin sent his pulse racing.

He watched her for a moment as she continued to speak with Emma, entirely captivated by her dark curls rustling in the cool breeze.

He'd had dreams of late where he'd spoken with Mr. May, told him of all that had been going on between himself and Livvy.

"I know ye've told me to find a way for your daugh'er to marry someone off the Mount, sir. But I be sorry to say that we've fallen in love with each other. We are to marry and remain on the Mount fore'er more."

The dreams always ended up with Livvy turning her back on August because of his lies and Mr. May throwing him over the cliffside.

Unfortunately, these dreams held a fraction of truth. Mr. May would never accept anything less than his daughter moving off the Mount, and Livvy would never forgive August for his deception. So what could he do?

Speak with her.

The words came with a force he couldn't deny. He knew that was the only thing *to* be done. But his thoughts always came back to how his honesty would affect Emma and Nicholas's secret.

Feeling worse than ever before, August decided to take care of one thing first—discover why Livvy hadn't returned his smile. Because his top concern was to ensure Livvy was happy.

Excusing himself from his family—his sisters watching him with eyes as narrowed as his elderly aunts'—he made for the Mays and Pengellys.

Livvy caught sight of him first. If he wasn't mistaken, and he was fairly certain he wasn't, he could have sworn that he saw panic in her expression.

She pulled her gaze away, whispered something to her father, curtsied to Emma, then turned on her heel to flee down the stairs in the direction of the pathway down the Mount.

August stuttered to a halt. There was no mistaking her actions. She was avoiding him. Which meant she was *upset* with him.

But, why? What on earth had he done?

His mind raced over his actions, combing through every possible thing that could be construed—or misconstrued—as cruel before he sighed with frustration. But then, what was the purpose in wondering when he could simply ask the woman instead?

With determined steps, August left the courtyard behind and slipped past family after family on his way down the Mount, careful not to trip on the cobblestones or slip down the slick pathway until he finally caught sight of Livvy weaving in and out of the crowds migrating down the path.

Heavens, but the woman was fast.

Fortunately, for his sake, she became stuck behind a larger group of individuals—elderly women and men—who took up the length of the pathway. With no chance to squeeze through, Livvy slowed her step and walked behind them instead.

Now was August's chance. Stepping quickly, he maneuvered around more individuals until finally, he caught up with her.

"Good mornin'," he said.

Livvy started, turning to face him with raised brows. "August."

She glanced around them, no doubt to ensure no one else was within their vicinity to have overheard her use of his given name.

Fortunately, no one else seemed to be in as much of a rush as Livvy did to make it home that Sunday.

"Mornin'," she finally returned, focusing her gaze ahead of them.

No doubt she was now contemplating squeezing past the elderly couples in front of them.

"I ain't sure if ye noticed 'fore, but I was tryin' to speak with ye back there," he said.

That was more diplomatic than what he wished to ask, *Why be ye avoidin' me?*

Livvy didn't respond. That was enough of an answer in the affirmative for him.

"So ye did notice," he said.

"Yes, but I...I needed to return 'ome."

Unease clung to August's chest like ivy to a stone wall. "Did ye receive your reticule from your maid?"

She nodded, mumbling a quiet, "Thank ye," before falling silent again.

Very well, that wasn't upsetting her, then. Perhaps he ought to take a more direct approach.

He dropped his voice. "Be somethin' wrong?"

"No, I be perfectly fine."

As if he could believe that. "Forgive me, but I can't 'elp but think that somethin' *do* be wrong. If I've done anythin' to upset ye..."

But she shook her head.

Again, he didn't believe her. "Be it me actions outside the graveyard?" he whispered. "I shouldn't 'ave touched ye—"

"I be fine," she snapped, her whispered voice harsher than he'd ever heard before.

August pulled back. Why was she reacting in such a way? He was only trying to help, to make amends for what he'd done —whatever that had been.

Drawing a few deep breaths, he forced his rising defenses to lower, quelling them with the patience he prided himself on. She was upset. That was why she'd snapped. He could help her be happy if he but tried a little harder.

"I only be tryin' to 'elp," he whispered softly. "If ye can tell me what I did..."

She didn't respond.

"Livvy?"

More silence.

He looked behind them, a group of boys and girls approaching as they made their way down the Mount with their loud laughter and chattering voices.

If he and Livvy were to fix this, they had better do it before the young group was upon them.

"We be friends, be we not?" he asked, trying a different approach. "If ye can tell me, I can listen as a friend."

She scoffed, averting her gaze.

His defenses rose again at the derision with which she treated him. "What?" he asked.

"Nothin'."

"It 'ad to be somethin'," he countered. Once again, he quelled his frustration that festered inside him like fungus on a tree, though he could not be fully rid of it this time.

She glanced up at him. "It be just an interestin' choice o' words, that be all."

He paused. Well, she'd spoken. That was progress. But then, what words had she been referring to, that they were friends?

He peered down at her. "We *do* be friends. Ain't we?"

Her lips thinned. "I thought so."

She was speaking enigmatically, he was sure of it. But as the group of boys and girls edged ever closer, August simply didn't have the time to solve such cryptic messages.

"Look, Livvy," he said, "I be askin' ye to tell me what be wrong. I don't 'ave time to play these games."

"I ain't playin' a game, Mr. Moon."

He raised his brow. "*Mr. Moon*?"

She raised her chin, the firm set to it telling him all he needed to know. She was in no mood to speak.

He'd been a fool to even attempt to pull something from her lips that she wasn't willing to give.

"Very well," he said, allowing his impatience to finally take the reins. "I can see I be wastin' me time at the moment. When ye be ready to be a friend yourself, ye know where to find me."

"Don't expect to see me any time soon."

Her words had been spoken in anger, and he knew more than anyone, words born from such an emotion were not to be trusted.

Yet still, they pierced through his heart.

The girls and boys reached them, but they had no effect on an already ended conversation. A break occurred within the elderly couples in front of them, and Livvy slipped between them and away from August in seconds.

August stopped, standing to the side of the footpath and shaking his head as the group of young individuals filed past him with laughter and conversation he couldn't help but envy.

Well, this was just excellent. What a wonderful Sunday this was shaping up to be.

He had no idea what he'd done to upset Livvy. She no longer considered him to be her friend. Mr. May would surely see his failed attempts at befriending his daughter. Nicholas and Emma would be outed. August would leave the Mount after failing all of his friends.

And worse than anything? He now had no hope that the stars would align to help him one day find a way to be with the woman he loved.

Excellent Sunday, indeed.

CHAPTER THIRTY-SIX

"There's no trust, no faith, no honesty in men..."
Romeo and Juliet, William Shakespeare

August walked back up the Mount to where his family and a few others lingered near the church. He had a mind to return home and stay in his room all day, if only to avoid questions from his family—he was certain they'd seen him run after Livvy that morning—but he needed to speak with Emma first.

He only hoped that when others saw him speaking with his supposed intended, any rumors his sisters might have already brought about would settle.

When he reached the top of the Mount, his family was already speaking with the Pengellys, his parents sharing a laugh with Emma's.

Ophelia's words from before returned to his mind. *"Ye already be upsettin' Mother and Father with your confuddlin' behavior."*

Regret spread throughout his guilt-laced soul. He hated

misleading his family—especially his mother. How much longer would Emma and Nicholas need him to lie to everyone he knew and loved?

"Moon," a voice called to him from behind.

August cringed. He'd thought Mr. May had already left the courtyard.

Turning around, ensuring he maintained a safe distance from his family to avoid them overhearing and asking him more questions he couldn't answer, August turned to face the man who was the cause of all of his problems.

"Mr. May," he greeted.

"I trust ye be 'avin' a fine sabbath," Mr. May said.

August clenched his teeth, attempting to calm himself at the feigned pleasant conversation taking place between the two of them.

How Mr. May managed to sit through church, praising God after all he'd done, was beyond August. He longed to shout out, *"This man be a deceiver!"*

But then, who was he to talk? He was just as much of a liar as Mr. May.

"Fine enough, sir," he lied yet again.

Mr. May glanced around them, then faced August with a whisper. "I do wonder if I might speak with ye for a moment."

August's jaw was beginning to hurt with how he ground his teeth together. "Perhaps we might wait until tomorrow." Speaking with the man would be just the thing to solidify this as the worst Sunday of his days.

But Mr. May shook his head. "'Twon't be long. I only wish to speak o' your progress with..."

He didn't need to finish. But then, he didn't even need to ask. Surely Mr. May could see the progress Livvy had made.

"What do ye 'spect me to say 'bout it, sir?" August whispered, keeping a pleasant expression on his face to mimic Mr. May's, though anger boiled within him.

He needed to maintain his cordiality with the man. After all, who knew what else Mr. May was capable of doing?

But August was tired. Tired and confused and, quite frankly, done.

"I be doin' what ye demanded," he continued. "I be tryin' to befriend your daugh'er. But I..." He paused, shaking his head. Before a few minutes ago, August could have told him how happy Livvy appeared, how they'd made great strides in their friendship. But now? "I can't force 'er to be me friend, sir."

To his surprise, Mr. May smiled. "It don't look like ye 'ave to force 'er at all. I only came o'er to say I be impressed with the strides ye be makin'." He leaned forward, the excitement in his eyes unsettling August. "Did ye see 'er speakin' with Miss Pengelly like it be nothin'? That ain't 'appened at church since she be a child. She be far 'appier now than she e'er 'as been. Ye ought to be proud o' the 'elp ye be givin' 'er."

If it truly was help, August would have been pleased. But he could not be proud of his deception. Yes, he truly wanted Livvy to be happy. But then, her father said the same. The truth of the matter was, neither of them could justify their actions by claiming altruism. They were being selfish. It was as simple as that.

"Listen," Mr. May continued, leaning closer than before. "I just wanted to say I be sorry that I 'ad to take...drastic measures in gettin' ye to 'elp me. Ye must see I 'ad no choice."

August could have laughed. Drastic measures? That was putting it lightly. Still, the man's apology hinted at his actually regretting his behavior. But not enough to change his ways.

August stared hard at him. "We always 'ave a choice, sir. Everyone always 'as a choice."

Just as expected, Mr. May's face shifted back to the frown

August knew all too well. "Spoken like a young man who 'as yet to learn the cruelty o' the world."

August made to respond, ready to tell Mr. May he was doing a fine job of alerting August to cruelty, but Mr. May straightened and spoke again. "There be one thing left I'll ask of ye 'fore we can set this whole business to rest."

August tapped his boot impatiently against the stone floor of the courtyard. "And what be that?"

"I've already spoken with your mother. She's agreed to chaperone me daugh'er at the assembly in Marazion at the end o' this week. It be your job to convince Liv to attend."

August's nails dug into the palms of his hands as he clenched them tightly together. His pride was taking a beating, for certain. But it was more than that. His heart, his morals, even his very soul, was being pushed to breaking point.

Never mind the argument he'd just shared with Livvy moments before. That woman had been through so much, suffered so greatly. How could August push her to do more when she'd already done so much?

"I'll take your silence as a *yes*, then," Mr. May said.

Instead of attempting to convince him to change his mind —August would have more success in asking a weed not to grow—he nodded in silence.

Mr. May gave a single bob of his head in return, then walked away down the Mount.

August stared after him, chewing the corner of his mouth.

Livvy was a happier person now. That was what her father had said. August was inclined to believe it, as he had seen her joy for himself. But then, was it socializing that was making her happier—or was it being around August?

Despite his attempt at humility, he was more inclined to believe the latter. In truth, he hadn't done much to encourage her to socialize with anyone but himself.

So what would happen if he did as Mr. May demanded and pressed her to speak with others at the assembly? Would she fall for someone else? Or was he worrying about matters of no importance because she didn't even wish to be his friend now?

Blowing out another breath of exhaustion, August turned back to his family and the Pengellys, praying they would not ask after his conversation with Mr. May. He wasn't sure he would be able to keep his true feelings about the man to himself.

Because one thing was for certain. Of all the words Mr. May had said, August disagreed with one the most—that he had yet to learn the cruelty of the world.

For he had.

And he'd learned it by falling in love with a woman who could never be his.

CHAPTER THIRTY-SEVEN

"I ought not to doubt the steadiness of your affection, yet such is the inconsistency of real love, that it is always awake to suspicion, however unreasonable..."
The Mysteries of Udolpho, Ann Radcliffe

Livvy had made great strides in going out of doors ever since that first dinner party at the Moons' house. Obviously, that had everything to do with her desire to happen upon August wherever she went. More often than not, that had worked out entirely in her favor.

Now, however, she was doing whatever she could to avoid him. Church had been a painful necessity—one she'd regretted attending instantly, just as she regretted her harshness with August.

Despite her questioning aloud if they were still friends, she still believed that they were, so why could she not have been honest with him, instead of forcing him to wonder why she was so unhappy?

Perhaps she'd wished for him to suffer just like she had

suffered, to feel an ounce of the pain she had felt herself. But how was that in any way the right thing to do? How would that in any way solve matters?

In all reality, August had done nothing wrong. His sisters had been overly harsh, yes, and though he hadn't defended Livvy, she couldn't believe that he'd ever meant to intentionally injure her.

Which was why he deserved an apology.

As such, as Tuesday rolled around and Livvy's pride had been swallowed up by her humility, she made ready to leave for the castle gardens in the late afternoon, intent on relieving herself of her regret once and for all. So long as August would accept her apology, that is.

Father caught her on her way out with another uncharacteristic smile. He'd been in a remarkably pleasant mood that week—whether that was due to the warmer weather or something else, she couldn't be certain.

Perhaps today's happy mood had been produced by his returning from work hours early once more.

"Goin' out again?" he asked.

She nodded. "I thought I might as well while the weather cooperates."

He beamed accordingly—especially when he eyed her hands and found no book or basket within them. "I be that glad to see ye doin' better, Liv. Keep this up and ye'll be just like the rest o' we."

Just like the rest of them. *Normal*, was what he was referring to.

Not odd.

His words echoed in her mind as she left her house and carried on up the cobblestones, slipping by a few gardeners with a simple wave as she continued her penitent walk.

Passing by the Giant's Well—the water supply that

provided for both the castle and the island—she soon reached the Giant's Heart.

To the untrained eye, the heart was quite difficult to spot—small, dark, and hidden amidst the scattered cobblestones. But Livvy made it a point to find the heart-shaped stone each time she walked by it, so she always discovered it in a matter of seconds.

This time, however, instead of walking past the heart, she stopped on the pathway and peered down at the brown, perfectly shaped stone. Though trodden upon daily by guests, visitors, workers, and the Mount's residents alike, the heart maintained its shape.

But then, for how long could it do so before it became so weathered, it no longer looked like a heart, after all?

Pushing aside the unsettling thought, Livvy stepped off the pathway to where a small alcove had been created for visitors to take rest as they continued their search of the heart. A massive granite boulder, taller than Livvy, jutted forth near the pathway, smaller rocks resting to the side of it.

Leaning against one of the lesser granite pieces, Livvy was better hidden by the pathway—and those traveling down from the castle—which allowed her a moment to gather her courage. If she was truly going to apologize to August, she'd better rehearse what she wished to say to him.

And yet, before she'd even thought of a single sentence, footsteps sounded from farther up the pathway, and her stomach clenched.

Somehow, she knew—she just knew—it was August.

Sure enough, in the next moment, he appeared around the rock, his eyes focused intently on the pathway, his brow furrowed.

He continued forward, having clearly not seen her, and for a fleeting moment, Livvy flirted with the idea of allowing him passage without speaking to him. After all, she'd be able to save her pride, then.

But what good would that do either of them?

Shaking her head at her cowardice, she stepped forward. "August?"

He started, looking up in surprise over his shoulder and stopping as he met Livvy's gaze. "Livvy, I didn't see ye there."

They stood in awkward silence, the pathway empty other than the two of them.

Say somethin', Livvy.

But the words refused to come as thoughts flowed instead. August must despise her after her words to him. And now, more than ever, as she stood staring at him in stunned silence, he must think her even *more* odd.

"Are ye well?" he asked, hesitance written across his features.

That finally shocked Livvy from her stupor. He was hesitant. Not frustrated. Not judgmental. Hesitant.

Surely that meant he wasn't upset with her, that she could speak her mind with him just as she'd done since the beginning.

"Yes," she finally responded.

He glanced over his shoulder to the empty pathway shrouded by thick trees and grey clouds above. "I believe your father already left for 'ome."

But Livvy shook her head at his assumption. "Yes, but, I...I came 'ere to see ye."

His brow raised a fraction. "Oh." He placed a small smile on his lips. "What did ye wish to see me 'bout?"

Why was he so kind? Even now, after she'd basically accused him of not being a true friend and stormed away when he'd tried to help her, he was still behaving as wonderfully as ever.

She let out a breath. Well, now was her chance to make amends, to show him that she intended to be as good a friend as he was. "I wished to speak with ye, to explain...'bout me actions on Sunday last."

Again, surprise lit his features. He glanced left and right across the empty pathway, then drew a few steps closer to her, though they remained a few feet away from one another. "Ye don't need to explain. Not unless ye wish to."

"I know. But I do wish to." He fell silent as she continued. "Ye see...I be ashamed to admit it, but when I came to fetch me reticule from ye at the graveyard, I o'erheard your conversation with your sisters. I should've left, or per'aps said somethin' on Sunday 'bout it, but me feelin's were hurt and I...well, I blamed ye for it. So I just wished to 'pologize."

There. She'd explained herself. Could this awful feeling finally leave her now?

Unfortunately, August didn't seem ready to end the conversation at all. Wincing those beautiful brown eyes of his, he drew closer to her. "Please, don't 'pologize for o'erhearin' what ye did. I ought to be beggin' forgiveness for what me sisters said more 'an anythin'."

She looked away. How she longed to clamp her mouth shut, to pretend that everything was now resolved, but she knew if she didn't speak up now, she'd feel just as terribly as she had all week.

"Thank ye," she said, "but I be used to their words. I...I was more upset 'bout what *ye* said."

He didn't speak for a moment, looking away with a distinct look of confusion. "What...what *I* said?"

She stifled a groan. Need she speak it aloud? "Ye just said I be odd. Well, your sisters did, and ye didn't defend me." She looked away, her cheeks aflame with heat. "I know it be ridiculous, but I s'pose it 'urt as I'd hoped ye thought different 'bout me. But it be fine if ye don't. I just—"

"Livvy."

His soft voice made her pause. "Yes?"

A half-smile stretched across his lips. "I did defend ye."

Her mind raced over the conversation, as it had over and over again for the last week. "No," she said softly. "Your sisters said I was odd, and ye...ye agreed."

He looked to the side. "Well, 'course I did."

Her brow puckered. He was openly admitting to it?

"I be sorry," he said, "but I simply can't see 'ow what I said be offensive. I agreed that ye were odd 'cause, well, ye *do* be odd."

Livvy frowned, her defenses rising like the tide to prevent her heartache from occurring once again. Perhaps she'd been wrong about this man all along. "And ye don't know 'ow I could be offended by such words?"

He peered down at her, his smile maddeningly distracting. "I s'pose, but I didn't mean it offensively as we *all* be a sort of odd."

Livvy struggled to maintain her anger. She was right in being offended. She knew she was. But then, was it his fault or her fault for taking insult when none was meant to be taken?

He took a step closer to her. "Be that why ye've been avoidin' me? 'Cause ye 'appened to o'erhear a tenth of our conversation?"

She looked away. How she wished she could bury herself beneath the cobblestones they stood upon, if only to hide her embarrassment. "Per'aps," she mumbled.

His smile grew, his eyes squinting delightfully. "Well, if ye wish to o'erhear a conversation, might I suggest givin' into your wiles and listenin' to the whole thing? At least then it might save ye from all o' this grief."

"I was *tryin'* to be a good person," she defended weakly, his teasing slightly easing the heat from her cheeks.

"And ye ought to be commended for it. But will ye now allow me to explain meself and share why I didn't deny me sisters when they called ye odd?"

Hearing the word again lowered Livvy's mood once more, but she nodded all the same. She'd love to hear his reasoning, if only so she could have the chance to prove him wrong.

"First off, there be nothin' wrong with bein' odd," he began.

She sniffed with derision. "Me father would beg to disagree."

August's smile disappeared. "There ain't," he insisted. "Bein' odd only means that ye be different from what be expected. Now who *wouldn't* want to be that?"

Livvy paused. She'd never thought of it in that way. She'd only ever considered herself bizarre. Strange. An outcast. Like the Mount thought of her—like *Father* thought of her.

"Furthermore," August continued, "*everyone* on the Mount be a little odd in their own right."

She eyed him dubiously. "As if I could believe that."

"No, it be true. Name anyone I know, and I'll share what be odd 'bout 'em."

She pressed her lips together, deciding to play his little game. "Very well. Your mother."

She'd caught him out now. He'd never disparage his mother.

But August smiled. "That be an easy one. Me mother can't 'ave different foods touchin' on 'er plate, otherwise she won't eat a single bite."

Livvy stared, trying to decide if he was in earnest. "Truly?"

"Oh, yes. Nothin' can touch at all, or she 'as to 'ave an entirely new plate to begin again."

Livvy tried to picture Mrs. Moon sending away a plate simply because her broccoli touched her fish, but the image nearly sent her into a fit of giggles.

"See? She be quite odd," August said.

Very well, Mrs. Moon's little quirk was different. But no one avoided the woman simply because of this little oddity like they did Livvy for hers.

"Who else do ye wish to know 'bout?" August asked next.

Livvy thought for a moment. "Your father?"

Another smile. "'E 'as to begin each mornin' with a cup o' tea that be scaldin' hot. 'E'll send it back if it be only slightly hot. And 'e won't start a sailin' journey on the right. 'E always 'as to start off to the left."

The load on Livvy's shoulders began to lift. "Your sisters?"

"Well, I be sure ye've noticed Ophelia makin' up 'er own words. And Portia, well, she can't abide the color blue."

"Blue?" That was Livvy's first favorite color to wear—third favorite color overall. Close behind the lovely shade of grey the clouds turned just before releasing their pent-up rain.

"Yes, blue," August said. "Now that be *very* odd. Who doesn't love blue? I've a waistcoat I wear o' the shade, and she do 'ardly look at me when I don it."

Livvy continued rattling off people, if only to try to stump August, but one after another, he succeeded in sharing the odd —or rather, different—things about people on the Mount.

Miss Pengelly? She wrote with her left hand and despised sweet foods.

Mr. Cuff? He couldn't bear his hands to be sticky and always wore stockings to bed.

The other undergardeners? They *couldn't* wear stockings to bed.

One by one, he continued as Livvy exhausted the names of those on the Mount. How August knew this about each person was beyond her. Every oddity he spoke of, he did so without judgment. But then, that was nothing new. He'd not once judged Livvy—not even when he'd called her odd.

"Anyone else?" he asked.

"What about ye? What do *ye* do that be odd?"

"Oh, I be the oddest one there be. Some'ow, ye already know 'bout me habit o' singin' only when others ain't watchin'." He paused, leaning closer to her. "I will get to the bottom o' that one day, I promise ye that."

Her heart skipped a beat at the look in his eye.

"But," he continued, "what ye don't know be that if I do sing in front o' people, I go terribly off tune."

"Truly?"

"Truly. Now, do ye wish to know the oddest thing 'bout me?"

She waited at the edge of her imagined seat.

He looked around, then whispered, "I love flowers."

CHAPTER THIRTY-EIGHT

"It is better to reveal a weakness than allow oneself be suspected of a vice."
Jacques the Fatalist, Denis Diderot

Livvy couldn't help the laugh that burst through her lips. "That ain't odd. That makes ye refined."

But August shook his head. "Ye might think that. But other men find it odd when I tell 'em I'd rather tend to me flowers than spend the mornin' shootin' or sailin' or e'en fishin'."

For some reason, learning that only made Livvy love him more.

"If that don't count for ye, though," he continued, "I've one that does." He paused. "I don't like puppies."

She pulled back. "Ye what?"

"Ye 'eard me. I don't like 'em. Not one bit."

She laughed in surprise. "'Ow can that be so? They be darlin'."

"No, they be *disgustin'*. They eat their own...deposits, if ye will, after leavin' 'em everywhere. They smell. They bite." He shook his head. "Don't like puppies."

Again, she laughed. "All right, ye win. That be the oddest thing I've e'er 'eard."

He smiled in response. "Ye see? 'Tisn't so very terrible to be considered odd when everyone else 'as their own oddities, too."

She peered up at him, grateful for his helping her, but a niggling doubt still tried to press its way through to the forefront of her mind.

"All those things ye mentioned," she began. "They don't seem too terrible, nor would they make me avoid any o' those people. They almost make 'em sound...endearin'."

"Ye think me dislikin' puppies makes me endearin'?"

She smiled at his teasing. "Ye know what I mean."

"I do. But the reason ye find 'em endearin' be 'cause ye be an endearin' person yourself."

Livvy longed to reach out and embrace the man for his kindness, but doubt wedged its way between her heart and logic. "I do feel that sometimes..." Her eyes dropped to the stone heart on the pathway, her own heart feeling as stiff as the rock. "Sometimes I feel like I be Cormoran."

August tipped his head in confusion. "The...the giant who terrorized the mainland by stealin' animals and eatin' children?"

She pointed her finger. "Ah, ye see? That be Jack the Giant Killer's side of it. What if they be just rumors, though? What if everythin' that was said 'bout Cormoran ain't true, and they dumped that poor giant down the hole into the ground simply 'cause o' what they believed to be true rather than what was in *reality* true?"

Livvy knew the story was just a legend, a tale those on the Mount enjoyed telling round bonfires and during parties to explain the heart on the pathway and the well of the Mount. But frankly, she was tired of having more in common with the giant of the Mount than with the people of the Mount.

"What if the giant be simply different?" she continued. "What if 'e be misunderstood? What if 'e wanted to fit in but couldn't 'cause 'e couldn't change who 'e be inside—a giant who liked makin' lists of 'is favorite things, readin' 'stead o' talkin', and misty weather 'stead o' sunshine?"

They stood there in silence for a moment, robins chirping their lovely tunes overhead, the sea gently rushing below them.

Still, August didn't speak.

"'Ave I finally caused the demise of our friendship," she asked, eying him sidelong, "tellin' ye I feel a kinship with a giant known for terrorizin' others?"

The corner of his lips curled up, those same small smile lines stretching across his cheeks. "Ye'll not lose me friendship o'er somethin' so trivial." His smile faded, and his eyes delved into hers. "I be merely thinkin'."

"'Bout what?" she asked warily.

"'Bout 'ow tragic it'd be if ye really did fit in with the Mount, 'stead o' standin' out as beautifully as ye do now."

Livvy wouldn't allow his kindness nor his generous words to melt her into a puddle at his feet again. She needed to keep her wits about her. She needed to know the truth.

"If standin' out be so beautiful, why do others avoid me 'cause of it?"

"Do they avoid ye?" he asked softly. "Or do ye avoid *'em*?"

Long had Livvy had such thoughts—and long had she always readily and easily set them aside. After all, why would she wish to dwell on the idea that her avoidance of others, and not her odd behavior, was what kept people away from her?

And yet, August's soft-spoken words could not be ignored.

With a deep breath, she nodded. "I know there be some on the Mount who don't like me for bein' different." The Moon sisters, being two of them. "But I believe most of 'em don't care a jot 'bout me bein' peculiar, but they stay away 'cause o' me own avoidance of 'em."

Saying the words aloud was like removing a rain-sodden cloak from her shoulders. Warm. Relieving. *Freeing*. She'd held onto those lies for so long, she hadn't realized until that point that they *were* lies.

"Ye be right," she said, her spirits thriving without the weight of the world to drag them down. "I do avoid 'em. And I do it out o' fear o' what they'll think o' me. That they'll believe me to be as peculiar as others do."

"As your father believes ye to be?"

She lowered her gaze. Just like that, the weight returned, and humiliation overcame her. To have her own father think she was strange, to have her own father embarrassed by her, she could hardly bear it. And yet, she could not deny it.

She delivered a simple nod in silence.

August drew a deep breath, staring off to the side so she couldn't see his full expression. Was he upset with Father? Or was he upset with her?

"I wish ye knew," he began, "that any person who does find fault in ye, or uses who ye be as a reason to not accept ye, simply lacks confidence in 'imself and must tear others down to feel right."

The words were uncomfortable to hear. Even still, she knew them to be the truth. Father did lack confidence—no doubt due to his wife's treatment of him. That was why he only drank, gardened, or remained indoors, staring at the fire and smoking his pipe instead of meeting new people—instead of finding a new wife who *did* love him.

Was that why, when he did go out, he only ever spoke of gardening—just like Livvy could only ever speak of books?

The thought struck her with such force, she nearly fell over. She wasn't like Mother, as Father suggested. Livvy was like *him*. Was that why he wished for her to change who she was? Because she reminded him too much of himself? Was that why he wanted her to leave the Mount—so he didn't have to be reminded that he wasn't secure in himself?

So he didn't have to have the constant reminder of why his wife had left him?

"Did I upset ye?" August asked softly.

She shook her head. "No. Ye be right, 'course."

He peered down at her, his gaze soft. "I know it be easier to say such things, but...try not to listen to the loud few who will do anythin' to break ye. Listen instead to those who 'ave your best interest at 'eart. To those who admire your love o' readin' and list-makin' and misty weather. To those who wish to see ye thrive as vibrantly as the sea pinks on the Cornish cliffs."

Tears flooded her eyes at his kindness, at his words.

Love. Admiration. Sea pinks.

Her head spun, unable to make sense of anything other than the spell August was casting over her. The truth within his words settled round her heart like a balm, soothing the neglected cracks that had been allowed to grow dry for far too long.

August was right. Father *was* insecure. And the ache she felt at his disapproval could not be so easily resolved. She had carried those scars with her for years, and would, no doubt, for many years to come, just as she would the scars Mother had left behind.

But then, was she not learning to overcome Mother's mistakes? Could Livvy learn to overcome Father's, as well?

Could she truly strive like sea pinks and live as she so desired without fear of what others thought of her—Father included?

"I...I wish I could show Father—Father and the rest o' the Mount—that e'en though I don't so much take with socializin', I...I wouldn't mind bein' invited every now and again to a party or a dance." She looked up at him, finding courage with each new word she spoke. "I wish I could tell 'em that e'en though I don't mind bein' left to me own, that doesn't mean I don't get lonely from time to time, or that I might need a friend or two." She hesitated. "But I fear I've lost me chance to say any o' that."

A twinge of sorrow lit August's eye, that same sorrow that he held a number of times before. That sorrow she couldn't quite decipher from where it had originated—or *why*.

"Ye 'aven't lost your chance, Livvy," he said, his solemn tone matching his expression. "Not with me." He looked away as he continued. "There be an assembly on the mainland at the end o' the week. In Marazion, at the inn. It could very well be your opportunity to...to live life the way ye've always wanted to. After all, ye always 'ave a choice." He looked back at her, eyes shimmering. "Everyone always 'as a choice."

Livvy hesitated, distracted by the moisture in his eyes, but he averted his gaze, swiftly blinking away what emotion he'd revealed.

She couldn't help but wonder why he'd felt whatever it was he'd felt, but her mind was soon taken instead by the assembly.

Her heart had picked up at the very mention of the dance. Of course she'd heard about it already from Father and Miss Pengelly, but having August bring it up, did that mean he wished for her to attend? Did that mean he wished to dance with her?

"I'd heard of it," she began. "But I wasn't sure if I'd 'ave the courage to attend. Will ye...will ye be there?"

August chewed his bottom lip, nodding. "I will be. And I'd love to 'elp ye find the confidence ye need to shine."

The words were rigid, as if rehearsed. But then, why would such words be rehearsed?

His words echoed once more in her mind.

"Ye 'ave a choice. Everyone always 'as a choice."

Without another thought, Livvy nodded. This *was* her choice. "I'll go, then. I'll go to the assembly."

August smiled, though he still averted his gaze. "Excellent. I be that glad to 'ear it." He swallowed, taking a step away from her. "As for now, I...I fear I must return 'ome. Me mother be waitin' for me."

"'Course," Livvy said, shrugging aside the disappointment she felt at his coming departure. "I be sorry for keepin' ye so long."

August shook his head. "It was me pleasure, Livvy." He tipped his head to her. "Until the assembly." Then he turned away and strode down the Mount's pathway.

Livvy stared after him, wondering why he didn't wish to walk with her. To keep up his appearance with Miss Pengelly, perhaps?

Still, as she watched his brown jacket stretched across his broad shoulders disappear around the pathway shrouded in thick leaves and lined with stone walls, she couldn't keep her emotions in line.

Excitement, concern, worry, fear.

Too many feelings ran through her. She felt like the sea during a storm, unable to keep her many waves in check.

August would help her at the assembly—she knew that much about him. So there really would be nothing to fear. And as for the help she needed *before* the assembly?

Well, she knew just who to ask for help with that, as well.

CHAPTER THIRTY-NINE

"Friendship is certainly the finest balm for the pangs of disappointed love."
Northanger Abbey, Jane Austen

The assembly arrived a few short days later, and Livvy was...Well, frankly, she was beside herself with panic.

Why she'd ever agreed to do this was beyond her. Never mind that August had asked her to. Never mind that she wanted to grow and improve. Never mind that a small fraction of her—the insane fraction of her—wished to make new friends.

She never should have agreed to go.

"Miss May, ye must breathe."

Livvy blinked, staring at the mirror she sat in front of. Her own reflection stared right back, as did Miss Pengelly's.

The woman gave Livvy an encouraging nod as she placed another bluebell—Livvy's second favorite flower—in her hair.

She did as she was told, drawing in a breath, her head finally ceasing its spinning.

"There ye go," soothed Miss Pengelly. "We can't do anythin' in this life 'less we breathe."

How true that was. But Livvy still struggled to do the simple task, what with how tight her chest was. "Thank ye, Miss Pengelly," Livvy said, peering up at the woman in the mirror. "I couldn't 'ave done any o' this without ye."

Miss Pengelly smiled. "I be more than 'appy to 'elp. And... call me Emma, if ye please."

Livvy nodded, still reeling at all that had happened over the last few days. After August had left the Giant's Heart three days past, Livvy had made straight for Miss Pengelly's house.

Miss Pengelly—or rather, Emma—had been startled at Livvy's visit, though she'd quickly invited her to sit before the two of them engaged in conversation. Despite the initial awkwardness, Livvy had eventually found her courage and asked Emma to help her prepare for the assembly.

"I fear I don't remember many o' the dances," Livvy had said. *"And our maid ain't one for doin' fine things with me hair. And me dress might be out o' fashion..."*

Emma had leaned forward in her seat with a grin. *"I be more than 'appy to 'elp, Miss May, in any way I can."* Tears had flooded her eyes, then, and she'd whispered, *"It be the least I can do after what August 'as told me...That ye've kept me secret 'bout Nicholas."*

After that, the walls between them had crumbled, and Livvy, oddly enough, had grown to feel more comfortable with Emma than with any other person on the Mount—excepting August and the Otterhams, of course.

Over the next few days, she and Emma had rehearsed the steps to the dances, practiced Livvy's hair, and spent time trimming her gown with different lace to give a more refreshed appearance.

Livvy had been anxiously anticipating the event, but now

that the day had arrived, she wasn't entirely sure she wanted to attend.

No, that wasn't true. She was absolutely *certain* she didn't want to attend.

"Ye'll be just fine," Emma continued to say in her soft, calming tone. "Mrs. Moon'll be me chaperone, too, as me mother won't be attendin' this evenin', so I can be by your side the entire time if ye wish it."

Livvy nodded, drawing in a deep breath. She'd imagined attending balls over the years, but every imagining had ended up with her alone in some corner, being spoken about how odd she was with no dance partner to speak of. It wasn't so very far-fetched, as the very same had occurred during the assembly she'd attended when she'd turned sixteen.

But that wouldn't happen tonight. She had a true friend in Emma, she was sure of it. And she wouldn't be without a partner for the entirety of the evening, as August had already promised to dance with her.

August.

At the thought of him, her nerves jostled inside of her. She hadn't seen him since that afternoon near the Giant's Heart, though not for lack of trying. If she didn't know any better, she'd have thought he was avoiding her, but then, that would hardly make sense after he'd asked her to attend the assembly himself. It was far more likely that he was being made busy at the gardens by Father.

At any rate, having not seen August was the only thing pulling her to attend the assembly that night. She needed to see him like flowers needed the rain.

"There," Emma said, drawing Livvy back to the present. Emma took a step back and eyed Livvy in the mirror. "What do ye think?"

Livvy turned her head left and right, an oddly light sensation filling her heart as she stared at her reflection. Her dark curls were piled high atop the crown of her head, ringlets framing her features and draping down the back of her neck. The small bunch of bluebells and sea pinks Emma had placed near the side of her gathered hair appeared as Livvy shifted back and forth, the flowers accentuating the darkness of her curls, as well as bringing out the color in her cheeks and lips.

Livvy had always considered herself to be average-looking. Not unattractive, by any means. But not beautiful like Emma or even how Mrs. Otterham must have appeared in her youth.

But now, staring back at her reflection, her blue gown lighting her eyes like the sun on the sea, she breathed out a sigh.

"Do ye like it?" Emma asked, no doubt concerned with Livvy's continued silence.

But Livvy could only shake her head in awe. "I love it. Thank ye, Emma." She stood, turning around with an appreciative smile. "Thank ye for everythin'."

"Aw, it be me pleasure."

They shared a smile, then Emma hesitated before reaching forward and embracing Livvy. Livvy wasn't sure what to do at first, unversed in such affection, but in a matter of seconds, she returned the embrace.

A moment passed by, a warmth settling around her shoulders like a blanket, then they pulled apart. Livvy was once again surprised as she noted tears in Emma's eyes.

"Are ye well?" she asked.

Emma nodded, swiftly wiping the tears away. "Yes, me apologies. I just..." She shook her head, looking away.

The last thing Livvy wished to do was impose. And yet, surely she could let her know she would listen to anything Emma had to say.

"Ye can tell me, if ye wish to," Livvy encouraged.

Emma turned back to her with a soft smile. "I know. It be just...Matters in me life 'ave been so difficult lately, and I've lost a great deal o' hope o'er so many things."

Livvy's heart twisted. How she wished she could help ease her new friend's pain.

Her new friend. It was still strange thinking such words, let alone hearing them spoken aloud, but the comfort she was brought knowing that she *did* have another friend expanded throughout her heart, increasing her desire to help.

"Be ye losin' hope with Nicholas?" she whispered carefully.

Father was downstairs in the sitting room, no doubt with his pipe full as he stared into the fire, but Livvy would hate to have him overhear Emma's secret.

Emma nodded. "In part. We love each other a great deal and want to be together. But we've both spoken to our parents, hintin' at matters, but..." She broke off, shaking her head. "There ain't much hope for us. Me parents will surely send me away if I tell 'em I be in love with a Cuff. So that leaves me only one choice..."

Livvy's brow rose. "Ye plan to run away with 'im?"

Emma glanced at the door, then nodded in silence.

Livvy released a breath. To be required to run away from one's parents simply to marry the person she loved. What a tragedy that would be.

"I be so sorry, Emma. Would I could 'elp ye."

Emma smiled. "Ye've 'elped more than ye know. I've been lonely for so long, not bein' able to be with Nicholas, all me other friends leavin' the Mount or marryin'...I be grateful we be friends now."

Livvy blinked. Emma was lonely? Livvy had never considered such a notion. Emma always appeared happy and friendly with everyone, the exact opposite of Livvy.

And yet even *Emma* was lonely.

Peering over at her new friend, Livvy saw her in another new light—a light that revealed their shared insecurities and sorrows. A light that revealed to Livvy that she and the woman had even more in common than she thought.

"We be friends, be we not?" Emma asked, her eyes wide and hesitant.

Livvy swiftly nodded her head. "'Course we be."

Relief flooded Emma's features. "I be that glad. I've wanted to be for so long. I just..." She paused with a sheepish expression. "I'll be honest, I always assumed ye didn't like me. Whether 'cause o' me age or me personality."

Livvy's heart hurt. So many wrong assumptions were made about her, so many misconceptions about who she was inside. People needed to judge her less.

And yet, they were not the only ones at fault. Now she had found her confidence—now August had boosted her courage—Livvy had to do her part in ensuring the truth was made known.

Shaking her head, she faced Emma directly, drawing a deep breath and praying for even more courage as she spoke the truth. "I couldn't care a lick about your age, Emma. Truth be told, I always wanted to be your friend, too, but I was so anxious around ye 'cause..." She looked away, finding the words difficult to say. "Ye be so perfect, and ye be friends with August when I wanted to be..." She shook her head, ending the words she wasn't sure she wished to say.

Emma placed a comforting hand on her wrist. "I understand. There was a time when I'd seethe at the mere mention of another woman speakin' with Nicholas."

They shared a smile, and an understanding passed between them. Livvy typically would have felt a great deal of embarrassment for having her attachment to August be known, but then, Emma didn't seem to think anything of it.

Did that mean August had told Emma that he'd had an attachment to Livvy, as well?

Her heart flipped at the thought.

Voices sounded from beneath Livvy's open window, a soft murmuring above the sea's waves.

"That must be the others," Emma said, glancing toward the window before looking back to Livvy with an excited glint in her eye. "Be ye ready?"

The peace Livvy had experienced for a single moment vanished like mist on the air, replaced with thick clouds of worry. "No," she groaned.

Emma grinned, pulling on her gloves and handing Livvy her own. "Come. In me own experience, the dread be worse than what ye dread in the first place."

Holding onto that hope, Livvy followed Emma as the two of them stepped down the stairs and through the small corridor to the front door. Passing by the sitting room, Livvy spotted her father, who, indeed, sat by the fire with his pipe.

"I'll wait for ye outside," Emma said softly, curtsying to Father before leaving the house.

Livvy faced Father with a smile, peering down at her dress as he stood to bid her farewell. "Will this do?" she asked.

He didn't respond for a moment, his eyes softening in a manner she'd not seen in years—perhaps even since the last time she'd gone to a ball. It was the look of a father who was finally proud of his daughter.

"Ye look lovely, Liv," he said. "Miss Pengelly did a fine job. I be that proud of ye for changin' and facin' your fears by goin' this evenin'."

"Thank ye, Father," she said. She wished she felt something more from his words, but all she experienced was a sense of sadness. After all, he was only proud because he thought she'd changed who she fundamentally was inside.

The voices outside their house grew louder as more young people and chaperones from the Mount gathered near the Moons' home—the meeting place where they'd decided to gather before they'd walk together across the causeway to the assembly.

She needed to join them before they left without her.

"Ye 'ave all the dances memorized?" Father asked.

"I believe so."

"And ye'll stay with Mrs. Moon?"

She nodded. Father had been the first to suggest Mrs. Moon as chaperone.

"I ain't one for dancin', see," he'd said.

"And ye won't speak too much 'bout your books?" he asked next.

"No, Father."

"'Cause ye know 'ow uncomfortable it do make people."

Livvy bit her tongue. She longed to tell Father how August didn't mind her speaking about books. In fact, he encouraged it. But that would open up an entire conversation Livvy wasn't sure she wished to have.

Because Father still wanted her to leave the Mount—he was no doubt planning on it. Surely he would change his tune once he discovered August's feelings for Livvy.

Her heart flipped at the notion of actually marrying the man she'd loved for so many years, but she quelled the feeling as best she could.

She was getting ahead of herself. She was nearly certain August had intentions for her, but she'd never dare bring them up to Father until she was *absolutely* certain.

After all, August had yet to even make an offer. Would tonight change that?

Laughter sounded outside, and she glanced at the door again. She didn't wish to extend this conversation any longer than necessary. She wanted to see August. "Worry not, Father. I understand. And I'll be well-behaved so ye won't be embarrassed by me."

How she longed to hear him deny her words. Instead, he simply nodded, then turned back to the fire, resting his hand on the mantle. "I look forward to hearin' 'bout your time off the Mount. I be certain ye'll enjoy yourself—and the mainland. Just like your mother."

Livvy tried to ignore his words, but they niggled at her already frayed nerves. True to his promise two weeks ago, Father hadn't pressed her to leave the Mount again. Perhaps she should have made him promise to no longer compare her to Mother, too.

Weight pressed down against her chest, leaving her feeling heavier than the boats in the harbor without water to float upon.

Instead of speaking her mind, however, she turned to the side, ready to be finished with the conversation. Where had her courage gone? Had she only confidence with everyone *but* Father?

Live without regret.

"I ain't like 'er very much, ye know," she said softly.

His sniff told her everything she needed to know. He did not believe her. "Ye just don't remember 'er like I do."

Livvy stared longingly at the door, knowing the others were no doubt waiting for her now. But she needed to speak. She needed to voice the truth.

"I do remember 'er, Father. And I like to think I 'ave more in common with ye than I e'er did with 'er."

He didn't respond. Did he not wish to be compared to Livvy? Did he not wish to see the truth?

"After tonight, ye'll see," he said.

"See what?"

He looked out the window, as if staring off into the past. "Ye'll see how similar ye be to 'er once ye go off the Mount. That be what made 'er realize how un'appy she be 'ere—havin' the life she 'ad 'fore marryin' me. Livin' with a greater society, more friends." He nodded, as if to reaffirm his words. "When ye meet others off the Mount, ye'll see what a better life ye can 'ave than 'ere. Ye'll see."

Livvy winced. She wouldn't. She wouldn't ever feel that way. But how could she explain that to Father? Unless, of course, she finally went this evening and returned with the fact that she still wished to live on the Mount.

Would that then end this ridiculous comparison to Mother —this fear that she would be like her?

The voices outside beckoned her once again.

"I must go, Father," she said. "Thank ye for your advice. I'll remember it."

He nodded in silence without another glance back, so with a heavy sigh, Livvy made for the front door.

Pausing with her hand on the knob, she drew a deep breath, attempting to push aside the heavy feeling Father had once more lobbed upon her.

Tonight was supposed to be perfect, and it still could be. All she needed to do was focus on the joy she'd felt before. The joy she looked forward to feeling as she danced with August. And the hope she had that all her woes would be taken away and replaced with peace that evening.

Because with August, she knew they could be.

CHAPTER FORTY

"There is nothing I would not do for those who are really my friends."
Northanger Abbey, Jane Austen

August was the first to look at the door when Livvy opened it. Though that came as no surprise. He had been unable to remove his eyes from the door since the moment he'd stepped outside and the group had started to gather near his home.

It was a tradition they'd participated in for years—those attending the assemblies and balls on the mainland would come together in front of the Moons before making the journey together across the causeway, whether by boat or by foot. Each year made for fun, enjoyment, and delight.

But this year was different. Instead of the excitement he typically felt and had missed while he was working in Bath and Coniston, he experienced only dread at the prospect of attending the assembly. For in the days since he'd seen Livvy at the Giant's Heart—the days he'd spent avoiding her at all costs

—he'd come to the realization that none of this—agreeing to Mr. May's terms, keeping secrets for his friends, being dishonest with Livvy—was worth it if she was hurt in the end. So he had made up his mind to tell her the truth.

All of it.

And yet, as she walked outside of her home, the look of vulnerability across her stunning features accentuated even more by her lovely hair and perfectly fitted gown, he wasn't sure if he'd be able to manage a single word around her in her state.

Such a perfect, flawless, beautifully blue state. Had she worn that color of gown to spite Portia? He'd worn his waistcoat of the color for that very reason.

Honestly, how was he to endure this evening, watching her dance with countless men while never being able to dance with her himself? For that was precisely what Mr. May had asked him to do.

"Ye must ensure she dances with only men from off the Mount," Mr. May had told him only that morning in the gardens. August had tried to avoid him but to no avail. *"That includes ye, too."*

Had Mr. May started to suspect something between August and Livvy? August couldn't be sure. At this point, however, he didn't know why Mr. May would care. It wasn't as if the man would allow his daughter to remain with August anyway. He would force her away whether she was miserable or not.

Just as Mr. May would force August to watch this beautiful, unique woman dance with every eligible man on the mainland. Or worse...August would be forced to watch her fall in *love* with someone on the mainland.

As his thoughts continued to race, Livvy's eyes met with his, wide and unassuming, but clearly seeking his approval.

Oh, how he approved. And oh, how he loved her.

Which would only prove to make this evening even more impossible to bear than before.

Livvy could not deny the look of admiration on August's face, nor the appreciation in his eyes, and for a moment, all her worries melted away.

That is, until August moved to stand beside Mr. Cuff instead of approaching her. He did so to keep up appearances with Emma, surely. After all, nearly the entire Mount was gathered together to walk to the assembly. This would be the perfect opportunity to ensure Mr. Cuff and Emma were not attached in the slightest.

And yet, could August not smile in Livvy's direction? Or simply speak to her as one's neighbor might? Or was he simply waiting for the assembly to do both?

Instead of dwelling on questions she had no way of answering, Livvy sought Emma out instead.

She moved through the gathered crowd lit in the golden light of the setting sun, all dressed in their finest attire, her heart pounding against her chest.

Ophelia caught her eye after a moment, but she turned away without acknowledgement, linking arms with a man as she twittered out a laugh. Portia was next, eying Livvy up and down before speaking with a friend, who also stared at her in surprise.

So many eyes, so much attention focused on her—curious gazes, a few smiles, but mostly raised brows at her unexpected presence.

How was Livvy to survive such attention?

"There ye be, Miss May."

Emma spoke behind her, and Livvy's concerns quelled, if only to a degree.

"All will be well," Emma whispered with a smile, looping her arm around Livvy's. "Ye stay by me side the entire night, if ye must."

So Livvy did just that.

Together, along with the rest of the group, they walked across the causeway to Marazion, and Emma, true to her word, allowed Livvy to linger at her side—and seemed more than happy to have her do so.

Livvy did her best to ignore the unsettling feeling that continued to grow with August's continued lack of attention in her direction—and the Moon sisters' judging looks—drawing Emma's strength to help her own. But when they reached the assembly and August vanished from her sight, she wasn't sure what to do.

Especially when a man from Penzance was introduced to her by the Master of Ceremonies and asked her to dance.

Livvy knew a keen disappointment that her first set wasn't with August, but she accepted the man's arm nonetheless with a fleeting look of panic to Emma.

To her relief, however, Emma had already procured a partner and had somehow maneuvered herself to stand directly beside Livvy in the set.

Despite her fears, Livvy remembered most of the steps to the dance, and though she wished she had been partnered with August, she managed to maintain her focus on the kind man who *was* her partner, even speaking a few words—*not* about books—before the song ended and the two parted ways.

"'Ow be the dance?" Emma asked, breathing hard from the vigorous steps.

Livvy thought for a moment, then she turned to Emma

with a grin she was certain wouldn't subside for quite some time. "Simply wonderful."

Emma beamed, reaching forward to embrace Livvy once again. This time, Livvy didn't hesitate to return it.

This night had the potential to be one of Livvy's finest. The dance had been invigorating, *exhilarating*. How she could only imagine what it would be like dancing with August.

Unfortunately, August had yet to reappear. With each new dance, another mainlander was introduced to her by Mrs. Moon, Mr. Moon, or the Master of Ceremonies. And with each new dance, Livvy followed her latest partner to the dance floor, always scouring the crowds for August—always coming up short.

She could understand his disappearance no more than she could understand why so many men were asking her to dance. She knew Emma's work had helped, but then, it seemed so strange to be the object of such attention—No, not just attention, *positive* attention.

Still, even with the attention, the joyful dances, the pleasant conversations, and the time she spent with Emma, she could not stop her spirits from drooping lower and lower like the wilting petals of a daffodil as the evening wore on and August remained hidden.

Where was he? And why had he not yet asked her to dance? Hadn't he promised her he'd do so?

A few hours into the assembly, Livvy had fallen so desperate that she'd even asked Emma if she'd seen him.

"I've no idea where 'e's been all evenin'," Emma had confessed. "E'en Mrs. Moon 'as been askin' 'round." Then she'd whispered, "I shall ask Nicholas when I find the opportunity."

But the opportunity never came.

More time passed by. The Otterhams, whom Livvy had not

known would be attending that evening, found her at one point, which proved to give her a most desired boost.

After complimenting her appearance and her bravery for attending, they asked about her latest books just before another man was introduced to her.

"I do be sorry," Livvy muttered to her friends as she was led away once again to the floor.

But Mrs. Otterham looked more than pleased. "We'll speak soon, love. Ye enjoy yourself this evenin'. Ye deserve it."

Then Livvy was whisked away yet again by another handsome, amiable, intelligent man who was *not* August Moon.

When the dance ended, and the man—Mr. Arnold, was it? —had asked for Livvy to save him another dance, she and Emma had excused themselves to retrieve glasses of lemonade with the intent to walk out into the small garden attached to the back of the inn.

However, with a heavy rain having started in the last hour, the girls instead settled on standing near a back window, away from prying eyes so they might rest from the current set of dances.

Livvy drank her lemonade as she observed those around her, reveling in the laughter and smiles abounding. She spotted Ophelia and Portia across the floor, laughing together in a group of younger men and women, clearly in their element that evening.

"'Ow ye be farin', Livvy?" Emma asked, taking a sip of her lemonade.

Livvy looked away from the sisters. "Quite tired. But more than glad I came," she answered truthfully. Matters were quite perfect, aside from August's disappearance, of course.

"Aw, I be glad to 'ear it." Emma took another sip, then her eyes shifted to stare at the rain that slid down the wood-paned windows.

Livvy watched her for a moment, wondering why Emma seemed sad herself before realization hit.

How selfish Livvy had been, thinking of herself all evening when she had not even considered the difficulty Emma would be facing that night, as well.

With a humble heart, she turned to her friend. "And 'ow be ye?"

Emma gave a weakened smile. "Fine. I only wish..." She dropped her voice to a whisper. "I wish I could dance with 'im."

Livvy knew at once of whom Emma spoke. How she felt for her, seeing Nicholas dancing with other women all while being unable to dance with him herself.

It would seem both she and Emma were doomed to be distanced from the men they loved that night.

Unless...

Livvy chewed on her bottom lip, an idea formulating in her mind. "Was the Oslo Waltz just announced?" she asked.

Emma pulled in her lips, thinking. "I believe so."

Livvy continued to mull over her thoughts.

"What ye be thinkin'?" Emma asked.

Livvy looked around the crowds, craning her neck before spotting Mr. Cuff near the dessert table, his eyes cast down, hands behind his back.

"Find yourself a partner," Livvy said.

She left before Emma had the chance to respond.

Swerving in and out of giggling ladies and flirting men, Livvy headed for Mr. Cuff. She knew, even in her limited experience, that what she was about to do was highly untoward—and far too direct—but she hardly cared if Emma could have a moment to shine.

"Mr. Cuff," Livvy greeted as she neared the table.

Mr. Cuff looked up, surprise registering across his handsome features before he smiled, his eyes averted shyly. "Miss May, good evenin'."

Livvy looked to the growing group of couples on the dance floor. They needed to make haste, or they'd miss it. But Mr. Cuff was even more reserved than *she* was when it came to Society. Would her plan even work?

"Be ye dancin' this evenin'?" she asked, motioning to the others.

He looked to those on the floor, his eyes catching on something—or *someone*—before his smile faded. He shifted his gaze back to the food. "Not this dance," he answered quietly.

Livvy had an inkling he'd just caught sight of Emma and her partner, but that only urged her to go on all the greater.

"Not e'en if I ask ye to dance?" she pressed.

His brows drew high. Livvy was clearly behaving in a manner she ought not. "Ye wish to dance with me?"

She smiled. "'Course, sir. But e'en more..." She leaned toward him, brazenly lacing her hand through his arm as she whispered. "I wish ye to dance with *'er*."

He frowned in confusion, then followed the motion of Livvy's head tilt toward Emma. Sorrow creased his brow. "I can't. There be too many others lookin'."

But Livvy shook her head. "It be the Oslo Waltz, Mr. Cuff. No one will bat an eye."

He paused, then a smile grew on his face as he peered down at Livvy. "Ye be a clever pisky, Miss May."

Livvy, clever? Not quite. Especially when she could only give credit to Emma. Days before, she'd explained to Livvy that this particular waltz consisted of a large circle—and sometimes inner circle—where every woman had the chance to dance with nearly every man.

So Emma would be able to dance with her love after all, and no one would suspect a thing.

Without another word, Mr. Cuff barreled through the crowds with Livvy and stood in the growing circle of couples.

Livvy stood beside him, grinning. Mr. Cuff didn't notice, though. He was too busy staring at Emma, who had caught onto their plan, as well, and was now watching Mr. Cuff with veritable love hearts in her eyes.

And for the first time that night, with August or not, Livvy was elated.

CHAPTER FORTY-ONE

"...for hope is always born at the same time as love..."
Don Quixote, Miguel de Cervantes

As the Oslo Waltz ended and a different dance was announced, August stood on the outskirts of the assembly, watching as Mr. Blisland approached Livvy with the Master of Ceremonies. Mr. Blisland bowed, then extended his hand to Livvy, a clear sign that he'd just asked her to dance. Livvy, just as she had all evening, accepted the man's offered hand and followed him with a smile to the dance floor.

For what seemed the hundredth time that evening, August ensured she arrived on the dance floor happily, then he turned away, unable—and unwilling—to watch yet another man dance with the woman he loved.

He shifted his footing to stand farther away from the assembly room, positioning himself down a darkened corridor of the inn, where he would not be spotted and subsequently judged for not dancing that evening. He knew it was his duty, as there were more women than men in attendance that night, but he didn't have the heart.

He leaned his head back against the outer wall, staring into the darkness as the cheerful music from within the dance hall mocked his dampened mood.

He'd already delivered more than a dozen men from off the Mount to dance with Livvy, apart from the last when she'd danced with Nicholas.

Certainly, that would appease Mr. May's insatiable appetite. Certainly, that meant that August could now leave for home so he could finally end this crushing night.

"There ye be, August."

August pulled his head away from the wall, though his shoulders still leaned against it as Nicholas approached. "Evenin', Nicholas."

"What ye be doin' in 'ere?"

August shrugged. "I do feel a bit rundown tonight. I might leave for 'ome."

"Without dancin' with your sweet'eart?"

He rubbed at his chest, the stabbing pain in his heart unceasing. "I 'ave no sweet'eart."

Nicholas fell silent. August knew what he was thinking, but he couldn't have the conversation again.

"Will ye tell me mother I've left for 'ome? And Emma? I know they both be lookin' for me." Had Livvy been, as well? "'Night, Nicholas."

He pushed away from the wall and his thoughts, walking down the hallway, his sole footsteps echoing how he felt that evening—utterly and entirely alone.

"And what about Miss May?" Nicholas said from behind. "What should I tell 'er?"

August slowed to a stop, though he spoke over his shoulder

instead of facing his friend. "Why should ye 'ave to tell 'er anythin'?"

He regretted his words the moment they left his mouth. He was being selfish. Cruel. He'd told Livvy to come to the dance. He'd told her he'd love to help her find confidence.

But all he'd done was deliver man after man to her. And had that not been for Mr. May instead of his daughter?

"She's been wantin' to dance with ye all evenin'," Nicholas said. "Emma told me."

More pressure weighed down against August's chest, more pain in his heart. "That be why I 'ave to leave," he said softly. "I can't dance with 'er."

"Why not?"

The words were on the tip of his tongue, but he couldn't release them. He couldn't risk destroying everything Emma and Nicholas had tried so hard to achieve together.

"'Cause I can't be with 'er," he said.

Footsteps behind him signaled Nicholas approaching him down the dark corridor. "Emma and I 'ave spoken. We appreciate all your 'elp, but we be endin' the ruse now, as it be destroyin' your life. If that be the reason ye can't be with Miss May, then..."

But August shook his head. Any other evening, under any other circumstances, August would have been relieved to hear he no longer had to pretend to be Emma's intended.

But he'd rather be beholden to Nicholas and Emma than Mr. May.

"Thank ye, Nicholas. I do 'ope it be what ye both wish. But...I still can't dance with Miss May. So I'll be leavin'. 'Night."

Then he walked away, heavier than ever, for now that his duties with his friends had passed, the only person standing in his way from being with Livvy was her impenetrable father.

And that brought him more despair than anything.

"What ain't ye tellin' me?" Nicholas called out, his footsteps joining August's.

"Nothin'."

"That be a lie. Friends don't lie to each other."

August's shoulders slumped forward, though he continued to walk, nearing the back doors of the inn as if they held the key to his happiness—though he knew nothing did, *no one* did, but Livvy.

"I ain't lyin'. I already told ye, I can't speak o' what be goin' on."

Nicholas's footsteps quickened, reaching August just before the door. He stepped in front of him to bar his departure. "I know what ye said. But I don't believe ye."

August stared at the door in silence.

"Do ye love 'er?"

August winced. He couldn't speak of Mr. May to Nicholas. But there was nothing preventing him from speaking of Livvy. Tears pricked his eyes as he chewed the inside of his cheek, then he nodded in silence.

"Then why don't ye dance with 'er?"

Again, August shook his head. "I can't, Nicholas. I can't speak o' why."

"There ain't nothin' ye can't tell me, August."

August clenched his jaw. How could he explain to his friend how wrong he was? Unless...unless *August* was the one who was wrong. He bit his tongue, shaking his head as fear overcame him.

"I can't. It...It'll hurt..." Still, the words refused to come.

"Hurt ye?"

August shook his head.

"Hurt Miss May?"

Another silent nod. "And more beside."

Nicholas stared at him, his frown growing. "Who?"

August couldn't bear it any longer, shaking his head as he took a step away. But Nicholas reached forward, clasping a strong hand on August's shoulder.

"August," Nicholas said, keeping his grip tight. "Tell me."

Internally, the battle raged, thought versus negative thought, hope versus fear, can versus cannot, until finally, August peered up at his friend.

Nicholas searched his eyes, then understanding dawned. "Me?"

August's jaw flinched as he clenched it over and over again. "Yes," he finally breathed. "And...And Emma."

Nicholas shook his head, his hand falling to his side. "But I don't understand. What could hurt us 'sides someone knowin'..." He paused, more understanding lighting his eyes in the shadows. "Someone knows?"

August nodded, the pressure still on his chest, on his mind.

"Who?"

Behind them, the musicians finished their song, and applause signaled the end of the dance. Now that he wasn't leaving the assembly, August needed to ensure another man was introduced to Miss May. After all, that was where his duty had come to lie.

But the mere thought of doing such a thing pressed the breath from his lungs, and he hunched forward. He couldn't do it. He couldn't do it any longer.

He couldn't help Livvy find another man to marry. Not when he wanted to marry her himself.

He couldn't keep up the lies between them any longer.

He couldn't keep the secret from Nicholas a moment more.

August needed to say it. He needed to speak the truth. To release himself from this burden he could no longer bear alone. "Mr. May," he finally whispered. "Mr. May discovered ye."

As soon as the words were spoken, more fear was felt, but a

rush of relief overcame him, as if free from the chains binding him for so long. To tell someone, anyone, what had been restricting him—*who* had been restricting him—was more than freeing. More than liberating.

It was heavenly.

He blinked furiously to rid himself of the tears pooling in his eyes as relief continued to flood him.

"'Elp me to understand," Nicholas said softly. "I want to 'elp."

August drew a deep breath, nodding as he finally found the courage to explain, all the while carrying with him the hope that his friend *would* be able to help him.

Glancing behind them, ensuring they still stood alone, August began his tale of woe, explaining what he'd been pressed into doing and the threats that hung over him. By the end, though still weighed down, the relief he felt was incomparable.

"Well," Nicholas said, running his fingers through his hair as he stared at the ground. "No wonder ye didn't tell me."

August nodded glumly, staring off at the light pouring in from the doorway to the dance hall. "I still be riskin' yours and Emma's 'appiness by tellin' ye. But now..." He shook his head. "Now matters be e'en more complicated, what with me fallin' in love with Miss May. I think Mr. May s'pects it, too, as 'e forbade me from dancin' with 'er this evenin'."

"But surely Mr. May would allow 'is daugh'er to marry ye and stay on the Mount if she loves ye, too."

"I've mistakenly thought the same thing. But 'tain't possible. If 'e resorted to extortion, 'e'll stop at nothin' to get what 'e wants." He paused, shaking his head as his stomach tightened. "But I must tell Miss May. I can't keep this from her any longer." He winced, looking up at Nicholas. "Forgive me. I don't want this to destroy anythin' 'tween ye and Emma, but I can't go on any longer. Miss May deserves to know what I've been doin'."

Nicholas hesitated. "We weren't supposed to share this with anyone. But Emma and I...We plan to leave the Mount."

August frowned. "What? Ye can't leave. It be your 'ome, where ye both wish to be."

"It 'ad been, yes. But we can't be apart any longer. We'll be tellin' our families in the comin' weeks, and if they don't accept our love for each other, we'll be leavin'. Together."

August couldn't believe it. And yet, what other choice did his friends have?

"So tell Miss May," Nicholas said. "There ain't nothin' to stop ye now."

August nodded. His friend was right. Now that Nicholas was secure in his own path, there was nothing to stop August from being truthful with Miss May.

And yet, as laughter and cheers sounded within the assembly hall, signaling the end of another jovial dance, August paused. He didn't wish to prolong the inevitable in telling Livvy the truth, but she'd appeared so happy, so carefree that evening. Did he truly wish to destroy her mood with talk of his deception?

An image flashed in his mind of her whirling around in her blue gown, and the pathway lit before him, clear and bright.

Never mind Mr. May's instruction not to dance with her. The man could threaten all he wanted now. He no longer held any power over August. He was finished being Mr. May's pawn. He was ready to reveal to the world how he truly felt about the woman.

And there was only one way to discover if she felt the same way about him.

"Excuse me, Nicholas," he said, turning to the doorway of

the dance hall, music and light pouring forth like a beacon. "I've somewhere I need to be."

He caught his friend's grin as he turned, but only one thing —one person—was now on his mind.

Miss Livvy May.

CHAPTER FORTY-TWO

"To be fond of dancing was a certain step towards falling in love."
Pride and Prejudice, Jane Austen

Livvy stood next to Mrs. Moon and Emma as they spoke of the rain pelting against the windows of the dance hall ever harder.

"That storm blew in quickly," Mrs. Moon said, her brow wrinkling. "Shame. It 'ad been such a beautiful evenin'."

Livvy nodded, pretending to agree as she held her tongue instead of saying what she wished to—*"The rain can be beautiful, too."*

The conversation continued, though Livvy's eyes wandered about the room at the sconces brightening the hall, candlelight glistening against sweating brows and shimmering ribbons. Everyone seemed to be having a wonderful time. Even Emma's spirits had improved since her dance with Mr. Cuff.

If only Livvy could feel that same delight. There was no reason not to, what with the number of men who'd been introduced to her that night.

Oddly enough, all of them had been mainlanders, aside from Mr. Cuff. Her father would certainly be pleased to hear such a thing—that not all of Cornwall thought her to be too odd to be acquainted with—but Livvy couldn't help but be suspicious of the fact that so many men wished to dance with her. Mrs. Moon no doubt had something to do with the introductions. She was grateful for the woman, but all Livvy wanted to say was, *"Can ye not get your son to do the same, per'aps?"*

Thunder clapped outside above the noise of the musicians and chatter of the crowds, and a few gasps sounded as eyes raised to the windows and doors, the noise rattling glass and fixtures.

Livvy looked as another flash of lightning lit the night sky, the warped windowpanes streaked with trails of never-ending rain as bright as the sun for a brief moment.

Heavens, the storm *had* gotten worse. It would certainly make for an adventurous boat ride back to the Mount.

Her eyes fell upon the dancers again lining up in their sets, this song being the first of the evening that she would have a moment to rest. Each couple had seemingly forgotten about the storm already, their laughter picking back up as the musicians took a moment to retune their instruments.

As the sets straightened out, Livvy's eyes reached the end of one, and her heart stopped beating.

There, at the end of the dance hall, with his eyes focused solely on her, stood August. He remained still, watching her, his chest rising and falling slowly as he drew measured breaths, then he moved forward in her direction.

The blood rushed from her head, and she turned away, fearing she had imagined the look of determination crossing his handsome features, but when she returned her gaze to him, his eyes still upon her as he weaved in and out of the crowd, she knew he was coming for her.

But to what end? To speak? To dance? To tell her...

She looked away again, praying for composure. And yet, by the time he reached her, her insides were entirely undone.

"Son, there ye be," Mrs. Moon said, spotting August as he stopped beside them. "We've been lookin' for ye all evenin'."

He tipped his head to his mother. "Forgive me. I've 'ad a few matters to see to. But I be finished with 'em for good." His eyes found Livvy's again. "And I be 'ere now."

She struggled to breathe as that smile she knew so well, that smile she loved so greatly, stretched across his lips. "Miss May, would ye care to dance?"

He stretched out his gloved hand toward her, and Livvy nearly burst into tears then and there.

Do not be odd, Livvy May.

No, that was not what she wished to think.

Live with no regret, Livvy May.

Swiftly, she delivered a silent nod, keenly aware of the smile on Emma's lips as Livvy reached her hand forward and August held it securely in his own.

Over a dozen times the very same had occurred that evening with other men. But with August, everything was different. Her spirit soared. Her soul warmed. And her heart rejoiced.

Together, the two of them walked to the end of the set, facing each other with unabashed smiles.

How she'd dreamt of this moment. How she'd feared it would never come. And yet, here she was, standing across from the man she loved, ready to dance before the world with the same man she was almost certain loved her in return.

But then, were they not supposed to hide such feelings for Emma's sake?

She winced.

"What be wrong?" August asked. Of course he'd notice the subtle change that had overcome her.

She looked down the set to ensure no one watched them. "Emma?" she mouthed out before speaking in a low tone she prayed only he would hear. "Are ye not s'posed to be dancin' with 'er to..." Again, she looked around them. "Keep up appearances?"

To her surprise, his smile only grew. "We needn't worry 'bout that any longer. I've been relieved o' me duties."

A weight she wasn't aware she'd been bearing lifted from her chest. "Ye be certain?"

He nodded, and the music began.

August bowed. Livvy curtsied. And when he reached his hands toward her to meet in the center of the set, the rest of the world faded away. They danced together as if one—one heart, one mind, one spirit—no other cares or worries or fears.

They were together, and that was enough.

Then another crack of lightning shone through the windows, followed instantly by a sharp clap of thunder, and the dancing slowed to a stop.

CHAPTER FORTY-THREE

"...such are the companions we wish when we join a party avowedly formed for pleasure."
The Coquette, Hannah Webster Foster

Livvy stopped along with the other dancers as the violins slid off-tune before stopping altogether, another thunderclap cracking through the room. Her footing froze, as did her hand in August's.

"My apologies, my friends," a loud voice boomed out over the rest. Livvy searched the crowd before finding the Master of Ceremonies as he spoke. "The storm worsens, as you can see. We were hoping that it would lessen, but for the safety of all those in attendance, I fear we must end the assembly early, as the boats to the Mount will be suspended shortly and the roads will only worsen for the carriages. Please, use a mannered approach when leaving, and..."

His words faded away as Livvy looked to August, her hand still in his. He very well could have been holding her heart with how secure she felt in his touch.

As those around them parted from their partners to find their chaperones and families, August and Livvy remained still and silent, understanding passing between them without a word, for they both felt the very same.

How cruel the evening had been to them. Giving them a moment in the promised land before tearing them apart once again. And now to end the night entirely?

A cruel evening, indeed.

"August, Miss May?"

Mrs. Moon's voice from afar cut through the commotion around them, and only then did Livvy break her hand free from August's. Cold instantly enveloped her, despite the heat of the dance hall.

"Come," August said softly, offering his arm to Livvy instead.

Together, they made their way around the throngs of individuals swarming the doors leading to the storm outside, each one more anxious than the next to arrive home in safety.

Finally, they reached the rest of the Moons and Emma, who walked together toward the doors calmly.

"The *unfairity* of it all," Ophelia whined to her mother with yet another invented word. Portia's lips pulled down into a deep frown, as well. "Why can we not stay?"

"No one be stayin', love," Mrs. Moon cooed.

"Ye two could stay behind and dance with only each other, if ye wish to," August said with a teasing glint to his eye.

Portia looked over her shoulder with a ready scowl, only then noting Livvy, who still held onto August's arm. Together, the sisters eyed Livvy's hand on their brother with narrowed eyes.

Mr. and Mrs. Moon must have noticed, as well, for they glanced furtively between August, Livvy, and Emma—who had apparently made it a point to show she was pleased with

August's attention to Livvy, smiling broadly in their direction. His family no doubt wondered what the devil was going on.

Livvy attempted to pull away from August, if only to hide from the attention she was receiving, but he rested a hand over hers, keeping her there.

She peered up at him as his family looked away, but he merely kept his gaze focused straight ahead, though she didn't miss the small smile on his lips.

Perhaps having the evening cut short wasn't so bad after all, so long as August kept his hand over hers.

And so he did as they and the others waited in the whipping wind and rain for the boats to take them back home.

"It be freezin'," Ophelia groaned as the first half of the boats left with their passengers in tow. "Can't Portia and I go on ahead with our friends? They'll be there faster."

"No, we be stayin' together as a family," Mr. Moon said.

Ophelia and Portia both pouted once more, then cast their eyes, again, at Livvy—as if they blamed her for the storm.

Livvy had seen them only a handful of times at the assembly. She hadn't realized until now that she didn't mind that fact.

A few moments later, another bolt of lightning lit the night's sky, illuminating the group huddled together in mounds of tightly knit jackets and cloaks, appearing as miniature dark hills in the mist.

Livvy flinched at the thunder booming above them, but August pulled his arm closer to his side, securing his hold of her.

"'Tain't safe to be out 'ere much longer," Mr. Moon said, eying the skies.

Another flash lit the world around them, revealing the boat creeping ever closer to the mainland as it tossed to and fro on the water. Livvy's stomach tightened at the thought of traveling across such torrential waves.

"We can't board that, Father," August said under his breath, though Livvy was close enough to hear.

Mr. Moon nodded in silence.

Sure enough, as the boat was docked, those remaining on the mainland were swiftly informed that they would need to seek shelter until the storm weakened, as the sea was no longer safe to travel across.

Only then did Livvy's worry mount. What were they to do?

"No way back?" Ophelia cried out. "I be wet and cold. And me slippers be ruined from all this rain. Of all the nasty tricks 'Eaven be pullin' on we *innocentin'* folk—"

"Hush, Ophelia," Mrs. Moon said with a shake of her head. She glanced up at her husband. "I suggest we go back to the inn. Find a few rooms to sleep in tonight so we may all rest well. When the storm lessens, we can 'ave word sent to the Pengellys and Mr. May that their daugh'ers be well."

Emma and Livvy gave Mrs. Moon a grateful nod, though Livvy longed to tell the woman not to bother for her sake. The Pengellys would no doubt be beside themselves with worry. Father, however, wouldn't be fussing over Livvy at all. He'd no doubt be completely unaware of her absence until morning, if not later.

"A fine idea," Mr. Moon agreed, then the Moons, Emma, and Livvy made their way through the lashing rain, arms up to shield their eyes until they reached the inn.

Once inside, much to Livvy's dismay, she had to release her hold on August as he and Mr. Moon went to the front of the inn, asking for rooms with the rest of those from the Mount who'd been unable to leave for home.

Portia and Ophelia folded their arms and frowned fiercely as they waited, not bothering to speak with anyone at this point in the evening. Livvy didn't mind. At least they weren't attempting to make her feel ridiculous for reading in the bushes again.

In a matter of minutes, the men returned with one room key, and Mrs. Moon hesitated. "One room, me dear?"

Mr. Moon's smile—so like his son's—did not fade. "Yes, I be afeared so. There was only one room left in the entire inn, so ye ladies can take it. August and I will stay down 'ere."

"'Eavens, that filled up swiftly," Mrs. Moon breathed.

"Many on the mainland chose to stay 'stead o' bravin' the roads," Mr. Moon explained.

Portia scoffed. "As if they should be served first."

"Well, they *were* 'ere first," August said.

Livvy knew by the twinkle in his eye that he was teasing his sister. Whether Portia was aware of the fact or not was beyond her, as his sister merely folded her arms and looked away.

August glanced to Livvy, who smiled at his teasing instead.

"'Ow are we to sleep on the beds 'ere?" Ophelia asked next. "They be so *discomfortable*, Mother."

"Cease your frettin'," Mrs. Moon said. "We'll make do."

Livvy admired the woman's positive nature. How far her daughters had fallen from their parental trees.

"Miss May!"

Livvy turned at the sound of her name spoken by a voice she knew all too well. "Mrs. Otter'am," she greeted with a broad smile, shifting her eyes between the elderly couple. "Mr. Otter'am. I be that glad to see ye again."

The couple appeared just as wet as the rest of them who'd been standing out in the rain, though Livvy hadn't seen them before, no doubt due to the darkness.

Despite her sodden appearance, Mrs. Otterham still smiled. "Did ye enjoy all your dancin' this evenin'? We ne'er saw ye rest, what with 'ow many men wished to dance with ye."

Livvy's cheeks warmed, and she averted her gaze from August. Was he aware of how many men she'd danced with? Did he care?

Clearing her throat, she stood to the side. "I did 'ave a fine evenin', thank ye." Keenly aware of the eyes upon her back and the silence between the Moons and Emma, Livvy turned back to the others. "Forgive me, allow me to introduce to ye all me friends, Mr. and Mrs. Otter'am."

After the introductions, the families spoke for a moment together. Mr. and Mrs. Moon, August, and Emma were as gracious as ever, while the Moon daughters yawned on with clear boredom.

Mr. and Mrs. Otterham didn't seem to notice, fortunately, as they carried on their conversations until a loud clap of thunder rattled the walls of the inn once again.

"This do be a fierce storm this evenin'," Mrs. Otterham said, her smile faltering. "I do 'ope 'em cows'll be fine."

"They'll be fitty, me love," Mr. Otterham said. "We'll see 'em bright and early in't mornin'."

Livvy faced them more directly. "Will ye be stayin' the night, as well, then?"

Mr. Otterham nodded. "We were just about to ask for a room for the both o' we."

Livvy's heart dropped. They hadn't received a room yet? "Oh..." She glanced warily at the Moons. "I be afeared they've all been taken. We...we received the last one."

Mr. and Mrs. Otterham exchanged concerned looks, then Mr. Otterham shrugged. "Well, I s'pose we'll be swappin' stories in front o' the fire tonight, me love."

Mrs. Otterham smiled, though worry still clouded her eyes

as she lowered her voice. "But your back, Brae...Sittin' in 'em chairs all night, what'll it do to ye?"

"Ah, bother. Don't ye worry 'bout it."

Yet Mrs. Otterham clearly was—as was Livvy. But what could she do? She couldn't very well offer a room that wasn't hers to the Otterhams. But then...there was someone else who could.

CHAPTER FORTY-FOUR

"Absorbed in the single idea of being beloved, her imagination soared into the regions of romantic bliss..."
A Sicilian Romance, Ann Radcliffe

With a concerned look, Livvy peered up at August, but he was already looking at his mother, who seemed to catch on at once. With a twinkle in her eye, she looked to Livvy, nodded, then motioned to the couple.

Livvy breathed a sigh of relief at the woman's awareness—and her kindness—as well as her son's.

Livvy faced her friends with a smile. "Mr. Otter'am, Mrs. Otter'am...ye must take our room."

Instantly the couple protested, but Mrs. Moon stepped in. "No, please, do. It be the least we can do for a fine couple such as yourselves. 'Sides, Mr. Moon and me son'll be down 'ere anyway. We'll be more than 'appy to stay with 'em. Won't we, ladies?"

Emma nodded at once, as did Livvy, though she tried to

show less enthusiasm than she felt at the prospect of staying in August's company all night.

Ophelia and Portia, however, smiled weakly and turned away, no doubt to hide their displeasure.

Again, Mr. Otterham tried to protest, but Mrs. Otterham looked up at her husband. "Oh, Brae, I do think we must accept. It be such a lovely offer. And ye know with your back and me side, we'll be better off e'en with the inn's beds."

Finally, the man relented, though he pulled out payment and insisted the Moons take it.

"Thank ye all," Mrs. Otterham said. "Ye be too kind."

After another moment of gratitude expressed, the Otterhams left for their room, and the Moons and their small party remained behind.

"Well, now what are we to do?" Ophelia asked with another huff.

At least she had the decency to remain silent until the couple had gone.

"We do exactly what your father and brother were goin' to do," Mrs. Moon said. "Sacrifice for another."

Portia and Ophelia exchanged glances, clearly sharing each other's thoughts. Then they looked to Livvy condemningly.

Livvy would not take credit for creating the storm, but she knew it *was* her fault that the sisters would now have to remain upright on uncomfortable wooden chairs all night in a public room.

Pausing, she pulled on her empathy as she would a pair of gloves, imagining what the sisters would be feeling right now —giving up their beds for practical strangers and giving up their night of fun and dancing with handsome men simply due to an unplanned storm.

Livvy would certainly be more put out if she didn't have August to salve her disappointment.

Drawing a deep breath, for she knew she could be rejected yet again, she faced the sisters. "I do understand 'ow ye feel," she said with as much effort as possible. "And I be sorry we gave up the room. But I can't thank ye enough for doin' so. Mr. Otter'am would ne'er admit to it, but I know 'is back be painin' 'im somethin' fierce. Stayin' up all night on a chair would 'ardly do 'im well. Ye be fine girls to give up your room for 'im."

The sisters didn't speak for a moment, looking at each other awkwardly before nodding. "'Course we be 'appy to 'elp someone so deservin'," Portia mumbled.

"Indeed," Ophelia agreed.

"That be me girls," Mr. Moon said with a grin. "Now let us find a place by the fire."

The girls sighed, linking their arms on either side of their father before walking forward. Emma fell into step beside Mrs. Moon, leaving August and Livvy at the rear.

Shame.

As they followed the procession, August leaned down to speak with Livvy softly. "It would appear that ye've found the way to me sisters' 'earts."

She peered up at him, admiring the creases next to his eyes as he smiled. "And what be that, then?"

"Excessive flattery."

They shared a smile, then joined the others as they shifted a few seats closer to the fire.

Livvy thought August had been teasing before about finally capturing his sisters' favors, but as the evening progressed, she found a marked difference in how the girls treated her. She wasn't sure if it was the flattery she'd given them or the fact that their parents were watching them closely, but either way, she was happy with the change.

As such, Livvy felt her defenses lower little by little as she joined in the family's conversation. She could see how well

Emma fit in with them, and were it not for Livvy's knowledge of Emma's love for Nicholas, she, herself, might've felt a keener jealousy at how greatly the Moons had accepted the woman as their own.

And yet, as the night progressed, Livvy began to feel that she, too, belonged with the Moons. Or was that simply how everyone felt around the congenial family? Either way, Livvy embraced it as they remained awake until well-past midnight, speaking, laughing, and conversing like old friends.

Livvy found herself piping up in the conversation, as well, even when it wasn't centered around books. Father's pride would swell when he heard of this.

Would he be just as pleased when she told him she found someone to love—even if it was someone from the Mount? For all Father's faults, she believed that he truly did love her, so why would he not be happy for her?

With her hope flourishing brighter than the fire in the hearth, Livvy continued to enjoy the rest of the evening until one by one, the others fell asleep around her, heads drifting to rest against shoulders and upon the walls.

Livvy sat behind a small table next to Emma, who had fallen asleep with her head against the wall of the inn. Livvy, however, remained awake, propping her head on her hand as she rested her elbow on the table and leaned onto it, staring at the fire.

August and his father had left the women a few moments before, clearing the tables free of their empty cups and depositing them near the bar. There, the two men had remained, sitting away from the others in continued conversation.

Livvy missed August's presence instantly, and though she longed to join him and his father and speak the rest of the night away, she remained where she was. It was enough to hear his deep laughter drifting toward her every so often as she stared at the warm flames lapping the walls of the hearth.

She didn't know how long she sat there, listening to August's comforting tone, feeling a peace she'd not known since she was a child, until footsteps thumped softly against the floor nearby. She raised her head from her hand and looked up to see August standing nearby.

"Did I wake ye?" he whispered.

She shook her head, glancing back to the bar, where Mr. Moon spoke with a few other men. Had August left to join Livvy specifically?

"No," she replied. "I was simply restin'."

He stood, staring into the fire then on the opposite side of the table from her. "Are ye comfortable enough?"

She nodded. "Not as much as your sisters, but I'll manage."

She motioned to the other Moons, Ophelia sprawled out across a bench along the wall, a guttural snore escaping her nose with her head in Portia's lap. Portia, though seated upright, leaned most of her weight against her mother, her head on Mrs. Moon's shoulder and her mouth propped open as she maintained a deep sleep, as well.

August smiled. "Charmin', they are."

Livvy grinned in response. August looked down at the chair beside Livvy, then pulled his gaze away when she saw him staring.

If he wasn't the most adorable man.

"Would ye care to sit 'ere?" she asked, motioning to the seat beside her. The chair *was* a solid foot apart from hers, not to mention the fact that it was the only one left aside from Mr. Moon's seat next to Mrs. Moon. "I could use the company."

"Will ye not try to sleep?" he asked, clearly hesitating.

She shrugged. "I ain't very tired."

After another moment, he relented, taking a seat beside her, half-hidden behind the table. As he settled on the chair, it creaked, and the intoxicating scent of his cologne slipped beneath her nose.

How she wished to swim in that scent for the rest of her days.

"'Ow ye be farin' with all o' this?" August asked in another whisper, his eyes still on the fire as he rested his arms across the table.

He'd removed his jacket and rolled his sleeves midway up his forearm, her eyes instantly drawn to the ridges of his muscles.

"Livvy?"

She pulled her eyes up, finding him watching her.

He'd asked her a question. "I be fine, now that I be warm."

"I be sorry 'bout it all. We should've 'ad the foresight to leave 'fore the storm worsened."

"'Tain't your fault. I didn't wish to leave early, anyway."

He peered down at his hands as he laced them on the table. "Ye enjoyed yourself this evenin', then?"

"Very much." Especially the latter end.

"Was the assembly everythin' ye 'oped it'd be?"

"Moreso," she whispered.

He nodded. "I be glad to 'ear it. And...and ye enjoyed the dancin'?"

Livvy could hear the hesitance in his tone. But then, why was it there at all? "Yes, I did. Very much."

Another nod. He pulled in his lips before he spoke again. "Ye did seem to be enjoyin' yourself with each dance."

Livvy paused. He'd been watching her? Now it was her turn to hesitate. But then, why should she when he'd made the slip? "Ye saw me, then?" she asked.

His lips parted, and he dropped his gaze. "Just a time or two."

As if she could believe that. "Ye must've been hidin' then. I couldn't find ye all night."

Again, he looked away. "Yes, as I said, I 'ad a few things to see to. But I do be sorry 'bout it."

What needed seeing to in the middle of a dance was beyond her. But then, he clearly wished to keep his secrets. Who was she to ask him to share them when he was not ready? Even she had secrets she still held close to her chest.

Images of her mother flashed through her mind, but she set them aside. Now was not the time to dwell on the past. Now was the time to enjoy the present. To enjoy these quiet, intimate moments with August.

"I did 'ear ye were introduced to many men off the Mount," August said next.

Had he heard that, or had he *seen* it? "Yes, quite a few."

His jaw twitched. "And did ye find anyone ye wished to get to know further?"

His tone was tight, even in a whisper, as if he was hesitant to ask. So then, why was he asking? Simply to make conversation?

Or because he wanted to know if she liked anyone beyond him?

She stared up at him, attempting to decipher his feelings from merely staring at his profile as he watched the flames sliding along the large logs in the hearth. His shoulders were high, as if tensed to await her response.

If her dream had come true and August did have feelings for her, he was asking this out of jealousy. But could that ever be true? Could this man she loved truly not wish for her to be with anyone other than himself?

She knew she ought to relieve his suffering, but part of her had to know the truth of the matter. And part of her couldn't help but relish in the idea that the man she loved could not bear the thought of her being with anyone but himself.

"Yes," she replied in a whisper. "I did find someone."

CHAPTER FORTY-FIVE

"I have so much in me, and the feeling for her absorbs it all; I have so much, and without her it all comes to nothing."
The Sorrows of Young Werther, Johann Wolfgang von Goethe

August's heart ached. Was it true? Had Livvy met someone that evening whom she wished to see again? Whom she wished to know better? Whom she...whom she could perhaps love one day?

He clenched his teeth, fisting his hands tighter together until the whites appeared in his knuckles. What a fool he'd been. To listen to Mr. May, to introduce those men to Livvy, to not sweep in and catch her before *she* could be swept up by another man.

As regret gave way to anger for his stupidity, rage burned through his limbs. Why had he not done more? Why had he not made his intentions with her known from the start? And who was this man who'd managed to turn her eye?

"Would I know 'im?" he asked, attempting a light tone, though he feared his anger deepened his voice too greatly.

Livvy didn't respond for a moment. Then she whispered, "Yes."

His chest tightened further. So he knew the dastardly man, did he? Perhaps August could approach him. Tell him to keep away from the woman he loved. Perhaps...

He stopped, feeling Livvy's eyes on him. Slowly, he turned to face her, and realization hit. She'd been speaking of him. Relief rushed through him, followed swiftly by a small degree of indignation when he saw the playful light in her eyes.

"Ye little pisky," he said softly.

A stunning grin split across her lips. "It be what ye deserve after makin' me wait to dance with ye all night."

His smile faltered. "I be sorry 'bout that. Truly. But I 'ad to..." He hesitated. He knew he needed to tell her the truth. He had to tell her everything. But he'd already decided that that night was not the time, nor the place. His family was too close, as was Emma.

So he would keep it to himself for one evening more. And tomorrow, he would tell her the truth, beg her forgiveness, and pray that she might still feel for him how she felt for him that night.

Right now, however, he could speak the other truth burning within him, growing brighter and brighter with each moment he spent with her.

Drawing in another deep breath and pulling up the courage he'd felt before, August shifted on his seat to peer closer at Livvy.

"Truth be told," he said, capturing her eyes with his, "I wanted to ask ye to dance from the beginnin'. And though I can't tell ye now why I didn't, I can say that the dance I shared with ye, though cut short, was the finest I've e'er shared with anyone."

A blush brushed across her cheeks, and she looked away,

though a soft dimple appeared as she smiled. "I don't 'ave as much experience as ye with dancin', but I can say I felt the same way with ye."

His heart skipped a beat, and he stared down at her bare hands held together in her lap, the gloves she'd worn resting on the table beside them. How he longed to reach out to her, to touch her, to hold her as he had during their dance.

"May I ask ye a question, Livvy?" he asked instead, staring at the fire dancing in her eyes.

She nodded in silence.

"'Ow did ye know I could sing?"

Her lips parted in surprise, then she shook her head. "Ye don't give up, do ye?"

He couldn't help but smile. "'Tis a blessin' and a curse. Or so me mother says."

She hummed, her smile fading away. "Ye'll think I be e'en odder than ye already do."

"'Tisn't a bad thing to be odd, remember?"

She nodded, appearing deep in thought as she stared into the flames. "I used to watch ye when I was younger," she whispered, even softer than before. "When ye'd tend to the flowers behind your 'ome. I used to sneak into me father's room and watch ye from above."

August had suspected as much. He only ever sang when he was alone. But to hear her admit to watching him lightened the burden he still carried round his shoulders.

"I ne'er did it for long, mind," she continued. "Just long enough to 'ear a few lines. It was after me mother died, and listenin' to ye, for one reason or another..." She shrugged. "I don't know. I felt comforted."

August stared at her, tears pooling in her eyes like water clinging to sapphires. He'd longed to be some sort of comfort for this woman, to bring her peace in whatever way he could.

So now, to hear that he'd done so without even realizing it, he could no longer keep himself from her.

Slowly, he reached forward, resting his hand over hers in her lap.

She stared down at his fingers, and he wondered if she felt the same energy, the same heat, surging through her skin as he felt upon his. She didn't move for a moment, closing her eyes and drawing in a deep breath before she opened her hand further, allowing his fingers to curl around hers.

Finally, she looked up at him, a slight smile on her lips which he readily returned.

"Thank ye," she whispered.

"For what?"

Had he done something more? His swirling thoughts and burning heart filled with love for this woman were muddling all of his senses.

She shook her head. "For everythin'. For dancin' with I this evenin'. For helpin' me find the courage to come." She paused, looking down at his hand still over hers, and she tightened her hold of his fingers. "Father's been so disappointed with me lately, and I..." She trailed off again, shaking her head. "I just be glad to know ye be helpin' me. Acceptin' me for who I be and not tryin' to change me like 'e 'as."

Her words faltered in the last sentence, and August's spirit shrank. He had never wanted Livvy to change. He'd wanted her to be herself from the beginning. To thrive as Miss Livvy May of St. Michael's Mount. And thriving, she seemed to be doing.

But then, what would Mr. May say to her thriving on the Mount instead of off? And what would he say once he discovered that August and his daughter...that he and Livvy...

A dark fog clouded his vision, and he could no longer see the light he'd felt before.

"August?"

He blinked, trying to see Livvy and the brightness she always shared with him.

"Are ye well?" she asked.

How he longed to tell her the truth. How he longed to be honest with her, declare his undying love for her and beg her for her forgiveness.

But now was not the time.

"Yes," he said softly, mustering another smile. "Merely concerned for ye to get some sleep."

She eyed him for a moment, clearly not believing him until she nodded, settling back further in her chair with a wince, clearly uncomfortable.

His heart reached out to her. "Come," he said, touching his shoulder closest to her with his free hand. "Ye may rest 'ere, if ye like."

She looked at him in surprise, her gaze dropping to his shoulder before a shy smile reached her lips.

Slowly, she leaned toward him, shifting in her seat again as her head softly rested against his shoulder. The moment he felt her press against him, he knew he'd made a mistake.

His love for her, his need to be near her forever, grew exponentially. So what would happen to him if he could not be?

His worrisome musings continued as Livvy's head rested harder against him, and her breathing grew deep and steady.

He knew relief for only a moment as she slept soundly upon him, for in the silence of the evening, with his family—and his desired family—resting around him, his weight only grew heavier, for he knew this perfect moment would never be again.

CHAPTER FORTY-SIX

"My courage always rises at every attempt to intimidate me."
Pride & Prejudice, Jane Austen

Livvy had been correct in her assumption that Father wouldn't be aware of her absence until the following afternoon. Fortunately, after her night with the Moons and August, she hardly cared.

She and the others marooned on the mainland were able to take a boat across the water the following morning before the sun had awakened to touch the sea. They parted ways after they reached solid land, and August's eyes lingered on hers until she entered her quiet home.

Father, of course, was nowhere in sight. She didn't discover him until he came down from the gardens for luncheon, asking how the evening had gone and whom she'd met.

He listened with more care than Livvy had ever experienced, Father urging her to speak of each gentleman with whom she'd danced. By the end, however, all Livvy wished to do was tell Father of August and the attachment that had grown between them.

Still, she did not know how he would react, hearing that she'd fallen for someone on the Mount instead of off.

Gathering all of her courage, she began. "I...I also danced with August Moon."

His eyes clouded over, seeming to harden a degree. "Did ye now?"

The change that had come over him was not a good sign. Not a good sign at all. Still, she would push forward. "Yes. I was disappointed, though, as the storm cut it short."

His eyes shifted to the doorway. Was he finished listening now? "Shame," he said. "Least ye was able to dance with others, eh? Any other men from off the Mount?"

Livvy chewed her lower lip. Clearly, he didn't care a lick about any man *on* the Mount. "No, Father."

He nodded, seeming to think for a moment. "Well, I'd consider last evenin' a success, then, wouldn't ye?"

Yes. Livvy would consider it a success. But not for the same reasons Father did.

Before she could tell him the truth, he headed down the corridor. "I'd love to discuss this more with ye, but I've got to be gettin' back." He paused at the door. "Ah, I nearly forgot. Sir John be gone from the castle again. 'E's allowed the doors to be opened for a tour this afternoon for family o' those who work for 'im. I said ye'd attend."

Livvy paused. Family of those who worked for the castle? She'd definitely be up for that.

She bade farewell to Father, then set aside her frustrations for not being able to speak with him about August. Perhaps this was for the better. Perhaps this had happened for a *reason*.

After all, she'd hate to share her love for August, only to

have August discover the truth about her past and no longer wish to be a part of her future.

The heavy feelings that accompanied the thought refused to budge. She knew August, just as she knew he would never leave her for something her mother had told her ten years prior.

But Livvy also respected August far too much to allow their relationship to grow further until he was in possession of all the facts.

So her final secret would become August's, as well. How she prayed he would come to accept it as she had.

Livvy had toured the castle before, but that did nothing to stop her from admiring the beauty within the private doors once again.

The beautiful entryway. The Chevy Chase room with the frieze depicting the hunting scenes around the entire upper wall. The grand blue drawing room painted the color reminiscent of a creamy blue sea at sunrise.

Each window revealed another view of the sea, of Penzance, or of Marazion, each more spectacular than the last. And though the rain caused a cold mist to surround the Mount, preventing much of a view at all, Livvy marveled at the sights.

When she wasn't marveling at August, that is.

He and his family had decided to join the tour. Father had not. Those facts alone had turned this day into an even better one than she'd hoped for.

Except for, of course, the fact that she still had to accomplish the task she'd set before herself.

She did her best to explore the grounds with a focused gaze, moving with the group and speaking with others in another attempt to find her courage. But with her mind so preoccupied, she was finding it more difficult than ever to enjoy much of anything.

Emma had been unable to make it, and the Moon sisters were mostly preoccupied with their other friends, but Livvy didn't mind, taking the opportunity to observe August—who spoke with all those around him—and Mrs. Moon, who was as kind as she always had been.

As they explored the library with its red velvet chairs and leatherbound books in shades of brown, black, and maroon, Mrs. Moon asked how Livvy was faring with the novels she'd borrowed.

"I be nearly finished with *The Hermit's Cell*," Livvy said. "I be sorry it be takin' me so long."

But Mrs. Moon shook her head. "Ye just take your time. After all, ye be a much faster reader than I."

Livvy typically was, but those last few weeks with August had prevented her from reading very much at all, which she found herself not minding so very greatly.

Sacrilege.

As they moved through the corridors to the next room, Livvy found herself looking at August again, attempting to focus elsewhere, but as he looked in her direction and smiled, her heart twisted.

She couldn't do this any longer. She needed to know. She needed *him* to know.

The tour moved them to the balcony outside, a large, open area without any cover from the rain pouring from the skies above. From the balcony, Marazion to the north and the sea to the east could be seen, as well as the stunning walled garden below.

Most people simply skittered to the upper balcony—which

led around the castle walls and to the next indoor section of the tour—so they avoided getting wet at all.

Livvy, however, lingered when she caught sight of August hovering near the edge of the balcony, peering down at the gardens—no doubt admiring the work he and others created in tending to the flowers, shrubs, and trees.

She looked around, only a few stragglers remaining aside from her and August. She could wait to tell him, use the excuse of others being nearby to stop her words. But then, would she ever find the courage to speak such things aloud again?

Drawing a deep breath, she squared her shoulders and stepped through the rain. She would get this over with, and she would get it over with now.

"Enjoyin' the view?" she asked, walking up to stand beside him.

August looked down at her in surprise, though his smile was quick to spread across his lips. Those lines she'd grown to love so much caused his smile to appear ever brighter.

"I am," he said.

She smiled, glancing over her shoulder as another member of the tour group shifted farther away.

"I s'pose we ought to follow 'em," August said.

Livvy nodded, then paused. "May I speak with ye for a moment first?"

He stared down at her curiously. "Right 'ere?"

"I know 'tain't the perfect place, and I know it be rainin', but..." She glanced around them, ensuring once again that they were far enough from the few who remained before she continued. "I can't keep this in much longer."

The curiosity grew in his eyes.

She knew she should probably be more nervous than she was at that moment, and yet, she knew August. Better than she knew anyone else on the Mount. And she knew there was nothing he wouldn't accept about her, nothing that he wouldn't understand or allow her to explain before deciding his opinion about her.

"Be everythin' well?" August asked, his smile having faded.

She nodded. "Yes. Well, 'twill be. I only..." She looked away and drew a deep breath. "I've been needin' to share somethin' with ye for quite some time now. So I'd like to share it with ye now."

He nodded, his swallowing visible.

She needed to do this swiftly, if only to calm his own nerves.

"Ye recall when I mentioned bein' the only one to see me mother 'fore she died?"

He nodded in silence.

She stared out at the sea as she continued. "I've been wantin' to tell ye more 'bout what she said for quite a while now, 'specially after last night, and, well...I thought it be time for ye to know that I might not be who I be said to be."

CHAPTER FORTY-SEVEN

"I was oppressed with the sensations I then felt; I sunk under the weight of them."
The Sorrows of Young Werther, Johann Wolfgang von Goethe

August listened intently, his heartrate rising as Livvy continued.

When she'd first said she had something to say to him, he could've sworn he was going to be called out in that moment and told that she knew all about his lies and deceit.

But now, he wasn't entirely sure.

"Ye see," Livvy whispered, "Mother told me that...that me father might not be me father after all."

August stared, the breath from his lungs expelling as surprise shook his senses.

Livvy watched him closely, clearly trying to gauge his reaction. As such, August drew a measured breath and merely raised his brow. "That must 'ave been quite a shock to ye," he replied, not knowing what else to say.

Livvy, not Mr. May's daughter after all? Of all the terrible things to be told just as one's mother lay dying. How had Livvy coped?

"It *was* a shock," Livvy agreed, "'specially at the age o' ten. She told me that she'd..." She paused, her cheeks turning a bright shade of red. "That she'd been with a number o' men on the mainland 'fore I was born—all without Father's knowledge—and she couldn't be certain who me real father was."

August scrambled for words, actions, prayers, anything to respond to what she'd just revealed. But what could be said to account for how he felt about her suffering through such a horrifying betrayal—all while she was just a child?

Before he could think of a response, she continued. "That be the real reason I stayed away from others. I was already hearin' cruel words 'bout 'er takin' 'er own life. I couldn't 'ave handled it if they'd heard word o' Mother's admission."

August blew out a slow breath. It was no wonder she'd hidden away. A grown adult would have done the very same. But then, surely Mr. May had been there to help his daughter.

"'Ow did your father bear the news?" he asked carefully.

She eyed him sidelong. "I ne'er told 'im."

August was more surprised by this fact than Mrs. May's unfaithfulness. "Ne'er?"

"No. I couldn't. I s'pect 'e be aware o' Mother's later betrayal, but to upend 'is world as mine was due to 'er words? I didn't 'ave the 'eart."

August could hardly believe his ears. "'Ow did ye manage?" he asked, his heart breaking at the thought of a child keeping such knowledge to herself simply to keep her father happy.

She was a better person than he could ever be.

"I didn't manage much at all in the beginnin'," she responded truthfully, staring out at the sea half-covered in mist. "For years, I despised me mother for tellin' me. I retreated more and more into me books, convinced I was alone in the world without a family. As I grew older, I 'ad the thought to seek the men Mother 'ad been with, hopin' to find a sense of identity, but..." She cringed. "She'd told me she didn't remember the names o' most men she'd been with."

August's stomach roiled. How had this beautiful woman blossomed as brightly as she did, being born into such tainted soil?

"A few years ago," she continued, "round the time when ye first left the Mount, I think, I reached a breakin' point, plummetin' deeper into the darkness. I knew right then I 'ad a choice to make. I could either sink lower and ne'er feel joy or light again. Or I could rise up and choose to believe. So that be what I did. And do ye know what 'appened?" She looked up at him with a smile.

Wholly engrossed in her story, August shook his head, hanging onto her every word as the raindrops tapped against the stone surface they stood upon. "What?"

"I started to see what 'ad been before me eyes all along, the similarities me father and I shared—not only in looks and features, but in mannerisms and tendencies, too. And more than that...I saw what 'e did for me. 'E raised me, provided for me, loves me. And that speaks louder than blood e'er could."

August stared down at her, rain dripping from the tip of her bonnet, her dignity and grace in the face of such turmoil not only inspiring, but astonishing.

Then something else happened he had not expected—he considered Mr. May in a new light. He considered Mr. May with *compassion*.

It was no wonder the man pushed so hard for Livvy to leave the Mount. He'd experienced pain of the acutest sort, having his wife not only *not* love him, but leave him for other men countless times.

There was no excuse for Mr. May's behavior, nor his deception of his daughter, but...there was a reason.

"So there ye 'ave it," Livvy said. "The tale o' me distasteful mother and the pall she's cast upon me life." She turned to face him more directly. "I don't relish tellin' ye such things. Nor do I believe I be the illegitimate daugh'er of a wanderin' woman. But then...I'll ne'er know for certain, will I?" She shrugged. "At any rate, I thought ye ought to know the truth since, well, we've been honest with each other from the start, 'ave we not? I want that to continue 'cause I appreciate the trust 'tween us more than ye could e'er know."

August could bear her words no longer. He turned away, the pain he felt leaving him unable to stand as he leaned against the railing.

She trusted him. She trusted him when she absolutely should not.

"Ye...ye be disappointed," Livvy breathed out, misinterpreting his silence and his shift away from her. "That be fine. I can understand why."

August turned to face her with a frown. "I ain't disappointed."

But she backed away from him. "No, it be fine, I assure ye." Tears filled her eyes as she tried to smile. "I understand it can be a shock. 'Twas for me, too. Take the time ye need."

He shook his head, but she didn't allow him to say more, turning on her heel and walking swiftly across the balcony that had emptied during her revelation.

August winced, her footsteps clicking and resounding against the echoing fortress, water splashing up against her skirts from the puddles she strode across. "Livvy, wait," he called out.

But she didn't.

August couldn't bear the thought of her thinking he was

upset with her in any way. Swiftly, he jogged toward her, reaching out to grasp her arm softly with his hand. "Please, wait."

She stopped, though she pulled away, flicking a few tears from her cheeks. "Ye don't 'ave to explain, August. I understand."

"No," he said at once, grimacing at the pain he was already causing her. "Ye *don't* understand."

More tears spilled down her cheeks. "Please, don't cry," he said in near desperation. He reached forward, wiping them from her cheeks, though his wet hands did very little to dry her tears.

Was this a metaphor, a promise of what was to come—that he would be able to do nothing to ease her pain, only make matters worse?

And yet, he still had to try. As he continued wiping his thumbs gently across her cheeks, her eyes met his, wide and vulnerable. Trusting, even still, and he winced again at the pain in his chest.

They stood there for a moment, his fingers slowing their caress until his hand cupped her face. How he loved this woman. How he longed to help her, heal her, love her forevermore.

He needed to pull away, to release his hold of her, but he couldn't. The attraction he felt was too great.

"What ye said," he whispered, looking deep into her eyes, "what ye told me...There ain't nothin' ye could say, nothin' ye could reveal, that would e'er lower me opinion of ye." He brought his other hand up, cradling her face gently between his fingertips. "Ye be the most wondrous o' women."

More tears glistened in her eyes, though this time, he knew they were not borne from pain but from love—the same love he felt for her.

The same love he needed to share with her.

Slowly, he leaned forward, her eyes dropping to his lips before closing altogether.

"Livvy," he breathed, her warm breath on his lips as she parted hers. "Me darlin' Livvy."

Then their lips touched. Rain slid down his cheek as he leaned to the side, exposing his features to the elements, but he didn't pull back. He couldn't. Not when he finally had Livvy to himself.

He held her gently between his hands, her fingers gripping his sides as she held onto him tightly, as if she was as unwilling to release him as he was to release her.

Her skin was soft, her lips even softer, and he released a sigh deep within his chest as he felt her love for him in their shared kiss. Her love, her affection, her trust...

All at once, reality came crushing down on August. What was he doing?

Slowly, he pulled back, leaning his brow against hers, unable to meet her gaze out of shame. "I can't do this."

She pulled back, but he kept his eyes down, refusing to look at the confusion, the hurt that would no doubt be shared on her features.

"I can't..." He began again, removing his cap to allow the rain to pour down upon him all the greater. "Livvy, there be somethin' I need to tell *ye* now."

She nodded, worry clouding her blue eyes. He stared into them, seeing the love within them for one last moment.

For he knew, when he shared with her the truth, she would never look at him with love again.

She would despise him. And he would deserve it.

CHAPTER FORTY-EIGHT

"The truth may be stretched thin, but it never breaks, and it always surfaces above lies, as oil floats on water."
Don Quixote, Miguel de Cervantes

Livvy's heart pounded, though from the exhilaration of August's kiss or the look of worry in his eyes now, she couldn't be sure. How could elation so swiftly transform to fear? How could peace so swiftly transform to chaos?

"August?" she prompted as he maintained his silence.

He stared down at her, his brow contorted with pain, no hint of the usual smile on his lips.

"I be so sorry, Livvy. I be so sorry."

She could hardly breathe. "August, what be wrong? Ye be scarin' me."

He drew a few deep breaths, ensuring they remained alone on the balcony before continuing. "I've been wantin' to tell ye for some time now, but I...I've been afeared. I just..." He shook his head, wetting his lips, the rain sliding down the ridge of his nose. "I wanted to be honest with ye, so I 'ave to let ye know. Your father, many weeks ago...'E asked me to befriend ye."

Livvy frowned. "I don't understand."

"That night at me family's 'ome, the dinner party?"

She nodded. How well she remembered that evening, how it had turned fate upside down and brought her and August together.

Hadn't it?

He continued. "Your father saw 'ow well ye and I got on, so 'e asked me to befriend ye."

Livvy's breathing grew ragged, though she forced herself to remain calm. So...so their friendship was not true? August had not desired to know her after all?

"Not only that," August continued, tears flooding his eyes, "but 'e asked me to also..." He grimaced. "To 'elp ye find joy in socializin' and to make ye more presentable so ye might find a spouse off the Mount."

Her head spun, the cold wind being the only thing to keep her from expiring on the stone beneath her feet. How could this be so? Father wouldn't do that. *August* wouldn't do that. Would he?

"So ye were just pretendin' to be me friend?" she asked, the breath squeezing from her lungs at the weight pressed upon her chest, as if the Mount now rested against her, burying her deep within its caverns like Cormoran.

August stepped forward, but she drew back, and he winced. She didn't want to hurt him, but she could hardly make sense of anything in that moment.

"No," August said at once with a pleading look. "No, I wasn't pretendin'. I swear to ye, Livvy. I wanted to be your friend from the start. The moment I saw ye emergin' from those bushes, I wanted to know ye further. Then your father..." he looked away, grimacing. "'Twasn't 'is fault. I chose to go along with 'im. To 'elp 'im get what 'e wanted. But I swore to only do so if it 'elped ye. Only e'er if it 'elped ye. But things got out o' hand."

She looked away, shaking her head, the last few weeks spinning about her mind like the wheels of a runaway cart. Every moment she'd spent with him—the odd behavior, the strange looks, the times she'd seen the sorrow in his eyes that she'd been unable to make sense of—it was all due to this secret. This...this lie.

Every walk they'd taken, every conversation they'd shared, flashed through her mind. "So be ye a questioner for Father?" she asked, her stomach in knots. "Did 'e ask ye to find out me secrets and report back to 'im?"

August instantly shook his head, his brow furrowed. "No, it be nothin' like that." He stared into her eyes, as if determined to have her believe him. "I promise ye, Livvy. Everythin' we did, everythin' ye said, I've not told another soul one word of it. The only thing I e'er told 'im was that ye wished to remain on the Mount."

Her concerns were quelled, but only for a moment, for how was she to believe him when he'd kept this secret from her for so long?

Then another thought occurred. "The assembly. The men dancin' with me..." She didn't have to finish, for August was already nodding.

"That be your father's final...request for me," he explained. "'E wished for ye to dance only with mainlanders, hopin' it'd be the final push to get ye to leave."

She huffed out a disbelieving breath. How foolish she'd been to think that any of them might have been interested in her. How foolish she'd been to think that *any* of this had been true.

"Why?" she asked, peering up at him, her hands trembling

as she continued to consider all that his revelation entailed. "Why did ye do it? To embarrass me further?"

"No, I—"

"Then to prove I really do be the odd one o' the Mount 'cause me father 'ad to *request* ye to be me friend?"

He drew another step toward her before holding back, his brow drawn high with emotion. "No," he stated emphatically. "No, I *wanted* to be your friend, Livvy. And your father..." He winced. "I can't blame 'im for wantin' 'is daugh'er to be 'appy, but 'e...'E gave me no choice but to do as 'e said."

The words brought her back to when she'd spoken with him near the Giant's Heart, and sorrow nearly consumed her at how much had changed—how much truth had been shared—since that fateful moment where she'd decided to trust August wholly and attend an assembly she thought *he'd* wanted her to attend.

Instead, it had all been a ruse.

"Just as ye said 'fore, August," she whispered, staring up at him, her whole body shaking with tremors. "There always be a choice. Ye *always* 'ave a choice."

His shoulders fell forward, and she thought she saw a tear slide down his cheek, though she couldn't be certain with the rain pouring down upon him.

"Ye be right," he said, his features falling in sorrow. "I did 'ave a choice. And I made a poor one. But I ne'er meant to 'urt ye. I love—"

"No," she interrupted, backing away. "Don't ye say it." She couldn't bear to listen to what she'd dreamt of hearing for years, only to now wonder if he spoke the truth or not. "I can't believe anythin' ye say anymore, August. I can't trust ye."

His eyes, rimmed in red, pleaded silently as he looked down at her. "I know," he whispered. "And I can't tell ye 'ow I regret me actions."

But regret wasn't enough. Not when their relationship started off with a lie—*Father's* lie.

She turned away from him, no longer able to bear seeing his sorrow, for it too deeply matched her own. "I think it be better if we don't speak again."

"But, Livvy—"

"Goodbye, Mr. Moon."

She left him on the balcony, fleeing through the rain and abandoning the tour altogether as she headed down the Mount seeking shelter, home, her books.

For only in them would she find the solace she needed to escape her pathetic existence—the existence she'd stupidly, foolishly, and mistakenly believed might have been better than a life she'd read about in her novels.

How wrong she had been. How dreadfully, disappointingly wrong.

CHAPTER FORTY-NINE

"Books were sweet unreproaching companions to the miserable, and that if they could not bring us to enjoy life, they would at least teach us to endure it."
The Vicar of Wakefield, Oliver Goldsmith

August went through the motions of his day with a feeling of numbness. Telling Livvy had done exactly what he'd feared—broken her heart and crushed her spirit. And now that he *had* told her, and he *had* injured her, he had nothing else to live for.

His family tried speaking to him through dinner that night, but August had excused himself, leaving for bed early without explanation, though he knew they all watched him and wondered what was wrong.

He couldn't tell them, though. They wouldn't understand. None of them would. Because he was the one at fault. He was the one who had caused his own heartache, *Livvy's* heartache. And how stupid he was to have done so.

He sat on his bed, unable to move anything but his eyes as

he turned to find the book Livvy had asked him to read as a joke. *Don Quixote.* He hadn't even read more than a few chapters, though he'd promised her to read the entire tale.

Yet another way he'd damaged her trust in him.

How long ago those moments now seemed, standing with her near Mother's books, speaking of trivial matters like names and novels and reading in bushes. If only he could go back to such a time, when matters were simple, carefree. If given a second chance, he would refuse Mr. May and his pressuring, stand up for Livvy's right to remain on the Mount, and beg her to marry him, day one.

But it was too late. Far too late. He'd failed Livvy, failed himself, and failed his future.

He'd hoped the knowledge of her father's coercion would have softened the role that August had played in their deception, but after what she'd said—that everyone always had a choice—he'd known that the extortion would merely sound like an excuse. A valid one, but an excuse, nonetheless. Made by a man too weak to take responsibility for his own deplorable actions.

So he'd taken responsibility. And he'd paid the price for doing so.

He shook his head, turning away from the book to stop the never-ending grief within him, though he knew not even sleep would help him overcome this sorrow.

All that would help him would be Livvy's forgiveness. Livvy's love. But he had forfeited the right to both. And he would never see them again.

The following Monday, after remaining home from church, holed up in his room all day, August went to work, desensitized to all around him.

Livvy would have told Mr. May about matters now, and the man would be deservedly furious. As such, August fully expected to arrive at the garden gate, only to have Mr. May remove him from his position as undergardener.

Had the man already begun spreading the news about Emma and Nicholas? Or was he saving that to threaten August one more time?

Either way, he'd come to terms with losing his job.

Though he'd not yet come to terms with losing his Livvy.

To his surprise that morning, when he arrived at the gardens, Mr. May was nowhere to be seen. As such, August went about his tasks as best he could, but not even the feel of the earth between his fingers or the sound of humming bees visiting the purple foxgloves nearby could give him the strength he needed to move on because all he could see were the sea pinks trembling on the edge of the cliffside.

Just as Livvy had trembled when he'd told her what he'd done.

"Moon!"

August started, shifting his gaze from the sea pinks to Mr. May as the man approached, his gaze dropping to the pathway he walked across so August couldn't see his expression.

This was it. This was when August would lose the job he'd been working toward since he was a child. This was the beginning of his final days on the Mount, for he would now have to go elsewhere to seek work.

But none of it mattered any longer. None of it mattered but Livvy.

August shifted his stance in the grass, then stood to face Mr. May. "What can I do for ye, sir?"

To his utter shock, Mr. May raised his head and smiled. Was this some sort of cruel trick? Was the man happy to finally remove August from his job? Had that been his ploy all along?

"Ye can accept me gratitude," Mr. May said, stopping before August. "That be what ye can do."

August reeled. Was the man having a laugh? Or had Livvy not told him, after all?

"I've ne'er seen me daugh'er so determined to socialize," Mr. May continued. "Not only was the assembly a success, but she agreed to go to the castle tour without bein' forced, *then* she chose to spend the entire day yesterday out o' doors, too. I s'pect she be out with the Pengelly family." He shook his head, a proud smile on his lips. "I can't thank ye enough, August. Ye've worked a miracle."

That answered that question. But then, why had Livvy kept silent on the matter? Was she as upset with her father as she was with August and couldn't stomach speaking with either of them?

Mr. May reached into his jacket pocket, then, and extended a folded paper toward August. "Payment. For your troubles."

August balked. His *troubles*? He shifted his eyes from the paper that no doubt held banknotes to Mr. May, who seemed pleased as anything to be delivering money to a man he'd forced into tricking his daughter to leave the Mount.

"Don't think I didn't 'ear 'bout your dancin' with me Livvy at the assembly, though," Mr. May said with a playful narrowing of his eyes. "But I'll forgive ye for that mis'ap since ye followed through in every other regard." His hand still extended the banknotes forward, and he wiggled them when August still didn't take them. "What be the matter, Moon? Ain't your arms workin' no more?"

August remained still. "'Ave ye spoken to Miss May recently?"

Mr. May eyed him. "As I said 'fore, she's been quite busy socializin'. I've not spoken with 'er much since she returned from the ball. Why do ye ask?"

Spoken with her much—or spoken with her *at all*?

Before, August would have been dealing with an internal battle within him right this moment, but now, a numbness prevented him from feeling much at all.

After all, what could injure him more than how he'd already injured Livvy?

As such, he faced Mr. May with a stalwart—albeit slightly weary—determination. "I can't accept that, sir," he said, motioning to the banknotes. "I *won't* accept that."

Slowly, Mr. May's hand fell back to his side, and a rigid look stiffened his features. "May I ask why not?"

August squared his shoulders and faced the man directly. "For a number o' reasons. For the shame I feel in doin' what ye asked o' me. For the disgust I feel when I think o' what I did. And most of all, for the simple fact that I refuse to be paid for doin' somethin' I bitterly regret doin'."

Mr. May stared at him with a deadened look. "Are we goin' to take issue with each other again, Mr. Moon?"

"I take no issue with ye, sir. Not now that your daugh'er knows the truth."

Mr. May lowered his eyebrows, his lips parting. "Ye didn't."

"I did," August answered confidently. "She deserved to know what we've done to 'er."

Mr. May's jaw twitched continuously, his hand balled into a fist as he deftly slid the paper and money back into his coat. "And ye thought ye'd be the one to do it?"

"Yes. 'Cause I knew ye wouldn't."

Mr. May shook his head. "'Ow dare ye," he growled, his tone low and menacing, his teeth clenched.

But August maintained his ground. "I be sorry it ended up

this way, sir, but I ne'er should've agreed to your terms to begin with."

"Ye be right about that." Mr. May took a step closer to him. "'Specially since ye ain't be man enough to keep your word. Ye *swore* she'd ne'er know."

August refused to fight back, forcing himself to maintain his self-control. "I understand your anger, sir. But I did what I saw fit. I did what your daugh'er deserved. She—"

"There ye go again, thinkin' that ye know what be best for me daugh'er." He reached forward, grasping August's lapel in his fist.

Though August could have pulled back with ease, he aloud the man to do as he wished. Part of him longed for a blow to his face, his stomach—anything. At least then he could feel something other than his heartache.

"Allow me to tell ye somethin', August Moon," Mr. May seethed, his voice low so as not to be overheard by anyone in the lower gardens. "Ye be finished. Finished with your work 'ere. Finished on the Mount. Finished with your friends. Ye won't e'er work for the castle again. Ye won't e'er work at another garden on the Mount again. Nor will Mr. Cuff."

August gritted his teeth, maintaining his ground as Mr. May continued. "Did ye think I'd not share their secret? Did ye not think I be serious? Ye'll ne'er see 'em together. Ye'll ne'er see—"

"Father?"

Instantly, the air between them changed, and a flicker of fear flashed through Mr. May's eyes as he recognized his daughter's voice.

He released his hold of August at once, then turned back to face Livvy.

August straightened his coat, then stepped to the side to face Livvy, as well.

Her eyes—bloodshot no doubt from the tears she must have shed for days—flickered between them, landing longer on August. Two days had gone by without them seeing one another, but even then, it seemed an eternity had passed, what with how greatly he missed her. But perhaps that was simply due to the fact that he knew their time of seeing each other often, of laughing in each other's company and holding one another's hands, was now gone.

"What ye be doin' 'ere, Liv?" Mr. May asked, his tone laughably light.

With a weary look, she shifted her gaze from August, focusing on her father instead. "May I speak with ye?"

"'Course, love." He walked away, turning to look at August over his shoulder. With a look of warning, he tossed his head to the gate, signaling that he'd meant what he'd said before—August was no longer an undergardener.

Then he reached his daughter's side and urged her to follow him.

Livvy didn't look back at August, nor did Mr. May have to tell him to leave twice.

August was finished. He knew that. Finished with his work in the gardens, finished with his life on the Mount, finished with his hope of being with the woman he loved.

Finished. And he had only himself to thank for it.

Livvy followed Father to another section of the gardens far away from August, neither of them stopping as they walked in silence.

A strange calmness had fallen over her in the last few moments. It wasn't quite peace, for that would mean she was content with her life, and she was anything but that. Yet, she felt more in control than she had in years. More in control as she finally accepted what her life would now become.

She hadn't been close enough to hear a word of the exchange between August and Father, but she'd seen the anger on both of their faces, and she knew August must have revealed to Father that he'd let Livvy in on their...what had it even been, an agreement? A plan?

Whatever it had been, she'd made the decision that morning—after hiding away from Father the day before—that she was finished mourning over the loss of some dream that could never have been a reality.

She believed August did have feelings for her—to a degree. But they'd been born from something she could never be happy with, something she could never trust. They were born from Father's trickery.

Once they were far enough away from anyone who might overhear them, Father stopped and turned to face her, his anxiousness apparent on his flitting eyes and forced, lightened tone.

"So what brings ye 'ere, daugh'er?" he asked.

"Ye know why I be 'ere, Father." She was finished with the façade, finished with the games and lies.

He frowned, appearing as if he wished to deny her words again, then he lowered his shoulders and tightened his lips. "It be that August Moon. 'E ruined it all. 'E..."

He trailed off as she shook her head, raising a hand to stop him. "Please, allow me to speak. I didn't come 'ere to cast judgment or spew more 'atred. I simply came to 'pologize to ye."

Father narrowed his eyes. "What for?"

That same sorrow she'd felt before threatened to overpower her, but she pushed on, unwilling to deviate from the course.

"For bein' a disappointment to ye. For behavin' in such a

way that embarrassed ye so greatly that ye felt the need to go behind me back to change the way I be, just so ye could receive some peace."

Speaking the words aloud pained her even more than she thought they would. And yet, it also brought a semblance of peace to her, having the issue no longer tucked away, to have it be spoken aloud for the both of them to face together.

"In order to show that I truly be sorry," she continued, raising her chin, "I've agreed to accept your offer o' livin' off the Mount with your cousins. If they'll still 'ave me."

Father stared, as shocked as Livvy had been the day before when the thought had first entered her mind. But now, as she spoke them aloud, she knew this was what she needed to do. This was the only way she could move on, the only way to move forward.

"Be ye certain?" he asked.

She nodded. "Quite. It be the only way to make ye 'appy."

He tipped his head to the side. "'Tisn't about *me* bein' 'appy, Liv. 'Tis about *ye* bein' 'appy. Ye know ye be like your mother, and livin' 'ere would ne'er suit ye for the rest o' your life. I just...I can't 'ave ye resent me as she resented me for keepin' 'er 'ere."

Livvy closed her eyes, trying to allow his words to settle around her. Hearing him speak of Mother in such a way was a rarity, and her heart reached out to him and the fear he obviously still felt at the hands of his late wife.

Perhaps he was right. Perhaps she was more like Mother than she thought. Perhaps she never would be happy on the Mount.

She was closer to believing that now than she ever had been before, what with August no longer in her life. She couldn't bear seeing him day in and day out, always having the embarrassment of how their relationship started—and then how it ended—at the forefront of her mind. So leaving the Mount was the answer.

"I'll ne'er resent ye, Father," she said. "But I'll leave the Mount, if ye so desire it."

His frown lessened. "Do ye desire it?"

She looked away. "Yes." It was mostly the truth. She wanted to stay but not under the current circumstances.

"Then may I ask...what changed?"

Tears pricked her eyes, but she swiftly blinked them away. Now she would never reveal to Father how she'd fallen in love with August. How he and Father both had broken her heart and her spirit so she could no longer fight back. For what good would come from admitting to such things?

"The assembly in Marazion," she lied. "It did reveal to me 'ow 'appy I could be on the mainland."

A smile played on his lips, a cruel opposite to her grieving heart. "I was hopin' it'd 'ave that effect."

She closed her eyes and turned away, wincing at another pierce to her heart. She didn't wish to be there any longer. She wished to be home while she still could, reading at the seat by the window with the view of the harbor.

She still needed to finish Mrs. Moon's books, but right now, nothing called to her more than the familiarity of *Hamlet*. After all, reading a book she'd pored over before was like watching the tide come in—she knew just what to expect, but the comfort that expectation brought to her heart was unmatched, unparalleled, even unforgettable. And she needed that comfort in her life right now more than anything.

"Liv, ye be starin' off again," Father said, clearly perturbed.

She blinked. "Forgive me, Father. I'll leave ye to your work now. If...if ye'll write the letter to your cousin and request me presence there as soon as possible?"

"'Course, love. 'Course."

She nodded her gratitude then stepped away.

"Liv?"

She turned back around to face him. "Yes?"

"I be so proud of ye."

Livvy felt the final breath of energy escape her spirit. "Thank ye, Father."

Then she turned away and headed back through the gardens, praying she would not see August. For if she did, she knew she'd be reminded yet again of how he'd always expressed his appreciation for her being her true self—and just how greatly that opposed Father's own pride in her.

For Father's pride only appeared when she was swallowed up by his own ambitions and fears.

At least with her departure one of them would finally be happy.

Though she knew in her heart, that one would never be her.

CHAPTER FIFTY

"It is far better...to be disappointed in love, than never to love."
A Vindication of the Rights of Woman, Mary Wollstonecraft

August stared out the front window in the sitting room, watching the raindrops race each other as they slid down the glass.

He'd done this a number of times in the two days since he'd been removed from his position, hoping somehow the rain would ease his suffering, if only to distract him from his ever-present thoughts of Livvy.

As if those thoughts had some power of their own, a flash of blue cloth dodged past the window he stood behind, and he started. Livvy's profile was just visible beyond the hood of her cloak as she ran through the rain. He leaned forward, watching as she entered her home next door to his, and just like that, she once more slipped out of his sight.

For those few blissful seconds, he'd forgotten the pain he'd caused her, and he'd imagined that they were still where they'd been before, two hopeless individuals in love.

But all of it was a dream. Just like his desire to take back his foolish actions.

"August?" Mother spoke softly from behind, having seated herself near the fire with Portia and Ophelia.

"Yes, Mother?"

"Won't ye 'ave some tea?"

He hesitated. "No, thank ye."

Silence followed his words, as they'd done each time in the last few days. His family was not used to such sullen behavior coming from him, but August couldn't help it—nor could he speak of it. Even when he'd told them he'd lost his job at the gardens, he'd been unable to tell them the truth, so ashamed he was of his behavior.

"Mr. May no longer saw me fit to work there," he'd stated simply. Which, more or less, was the truth.

"'Ow can that be so? Surely somethin' can be done," Mother had said often in the last two days.

August never answered her. He still had not. For the only response that came to his mind was that he would have to leave the Mount. Never mind his dreams. Never mind his passions. None of it mattered now, which was why he stood there, staring at the rain on the windowpane, hoping to catch another glimpse of Livvy, for it was the only thing that made him feel *something.*

"'Ave ye spoken with 'er since the assembly on the mainland?" Mother asked, as if able to read his very thoughts.

"Who?" he returned, deciding to play ignorant.

"The woman ye've been pinin' after for days. That be who."

He kept his back to his mother and sisters, unwilling to see their expressions for fear of what those expressions might do to him—encourage him to speak what was on his mind. Make him share his feelings with them. Force him to face his own stupidity.

He'd much rather live in this constant state of numbness. Or so he liked to tell himself.

"I ain't pinin' after anyone," he responded.

"That be a lie," Ophelia muttered under her breath.

"Miss May," Portia stated louder, as if anxious to get him talking. "'Ave ye spoken with Miss May since the assembly?"

Were they only interested in the gossip it would serve them? Or were they genuinely concerned?

"Yes, I've spoken with 'er once or twice," he stated.

"But not in recent days?" Mother clarified.

"No."

"And why be that?"

He shrugged, unable to find a response.

"Well, if ye wish to e'er speak with 'er again, ye'd best make it quick," Ophelia said.

"Ye'll miss out otherwise," Portia added.

"Girls," Mother whispered sharply.

August paused, an unsettling feeling coming over him. Slowly, he turned to face his family. "What do ye mean?"

Mother looked at her girls with a reproving look, then faced August with a wary eye. "It may be just rumors."

"What?" he asked, looking between the three of them as his patience thinned. "What be ye not sayin'?"

Mother looked to Ophelia, who peered up at August with hesitance—the first hesitance she'd ever exhibited while sharing gossip.

"I 'eard that Miss May be leavin' the Mount," his sister said with a wince.

His heart dropped, the blood rushing in his ears as he took a step back. "Whom did ye 'ear such a thing from? Surely ye be mistaken."

But Portia shook her head next. "She ain't. We 'eard it from Mrs. Otter'am, who 'eard it from Miss May 'erself."

No. Surely they'd all heard wrong. Surely Miss May wouldn't leave the Mount, her home, her favorite place to be. Otherwise, how had Mr. May convinced her to do such a thing so swiftly? Or had it been August's cruelty that finally pushed her over the edge?

The truth of the matter nearly crushed him under the weight of his guilt.

"Where?" he asked.

"Where is she to go, ye mean?" Mother asked.

He nodded.

She looked at her daughters, then responded. "Mr. May 'as a cousin who lives on the mainland. Somewhere near Bodmin. She's to depart in a fortnight."

An ache occurred in his chest, one that could not be subdued, one that prevented any breath drawn. She couldn't leave. He wouldn't allow it.

Swiftly, he stepped from the room.

"What are ye to do, August?" Mother asked, rising at once, her teacup clattering against the plate as she set it down.

"Nothin'." He reached for his jacket and cap that hung near the front door. "I'll be back 'fore dinner."

Then he stepped into the cold rain and closed the door before he could hear another word.

Livvy, not live on St. Michael's Mount? It could not be so.

Without thinking through his decision, he charged toward the Mays' house, knocking on the door with a pounding heart.

Mr. May would be at the gardens still, which was fortunate. August wasn't certain he'd be able to control his rage if he saw the man now.

After another knock from August, the maid opened the door with a pleasant smile. "What can I do for ye, sir?"

"I must speak with Miss May. I—"

His words failed as Livvy herself stepped in the background, appearing with wide eyes in his direction. "August?"

The maid looked between them.

"Ye may leave us, Sarah," Livvy said, then she faced August with a wary look, waiting for her maid to depart before speaking again. "What ye be doin' 'ere?" she asked softly.

August faced her, still standing in the rain. "Be it true?"

She opened her mouth, then closed it again before sighing. "Ye 'eard."

"That ye be leavin' the Mount?" he asked, his chest swirling with emotion—anger, sorrow, regret. "Yes, I 'eard."

She looked away. "It be time."

"Why?" he breathed. "After all this time, why?"

She tipped her head to the side, her eyes growing weary. "Ye know why."

"'Cause o' me," he stated, swallowing hard as he acknowledged the truth.

She didn't respond.

"Please, don't leave," he pleaded. Though no one was out in such weather, he lowered his voice to a whisper, refusing to allow another person into their private conversation. "Ye ought not suffer 'cause o' me own stupidity. *I* will. I must leave the Mount anyway."

But she shook her head. "No, ye must stay. Ye 'ave a life 'ere, your work at the gardens, your family. I...I 'ave nothin'."

August paused. Did she not know he'd been removed from his position as undergardener? His jaw tightened. Of course Mr. May wouldn't have told her. He'd no doubt blamed August for the entire situation.

Before he could explain himself—share why he had to start a new life elsewhere, Livvy continued. "'Tain't just 'cause of ye that I be leavin', though. It be the rumors that'll start and..." She looked away, her chin trembling as August's heart broke further. “Me father. ’E don’t want me ’ere. ’E’ll be ’appier with me gone.”

Fire sparked within him at the thought of Mr. May and his despicable behavior. Curse the man. And curse August for not standing up to him and helping Livvy fight for what she actually desired.

Helpless beyond anything, August dropped his hands to his sides, rain sliding down his fingertips. He lowered his brow and removed the anger from his soul. “I be so sorry, Livvy. ’Bout all o’ this. I ne’er meant to ’urt ye. Truly. I ne’er once wished for ye to change, for ye to leave the Mount. I only e’er wished to ’elp ye find your ’appiness. But I went about it in the wrong way. Your Father and I both did. And I can’t tell ye ’ow bitterly”—his voice broke—“I regret doin’ what your father demanded.”

Again, that same desire pushed forth to tell her the truth of Mr. May’s extortion, but he swallowed it back, refusing to blame another for his own actions.

He remained on her doorstep, breathing heavily as he stood before her, rain rushing around them, as it always seemed to do whenever he was with her, as if she caused the drops to fall due to her love of it.

She didn’t respond for a long moment, her eyes unfaltering as they peered at his very soul, as if she could sense by a simple gaze if he was in earnest or not.

So he remained still, allowing her to read him, to feel his sorrow, his pain, and his regret, all the while praying she would understand.

Finally, her features softened, though a sadness filled her eyes. “Thank ye,” she whispered. “I...I believe ye. And for what it be worth, I be glad that ye told me the truth o’ what ye and Father did, as I know ’e ne’er would.” She took a step back inside, and a panic gripped his heart. “I wish for ye to know that I'll ne'er regret the time we spent together. Ye made me live for the first time in me life, and I'll always be grateful to ye for that."

Her words were the conclusion to their story, a final goodbye. But they couldn't be. This couldn't be the end. "Please," he begged. "Please, don't go. Don't leave the one place ye love."

"I must," she whispered in return, her lips pulling down as she fought her emotion. "'Tain't no other way."

He wouldn't believe such a statement. He couldn't. "I'll find a way. I promise ye, I'll find a way for ye to remain 'ere."

"No, August. Ye must accept me decision." She glanced over her shoulder. Had she heard her maid approaching? "I must go."

He stared at her as she inched the door toward him. "I'll find a way, Livvy," he stated again. "I promise ye."

But she didn't respond before closing the door.

CHAPTER FIFTY-ONE

"Seldom, very seldom, does complete truth belong to any human disclosure; seldom can it happen that something is not a little disguised or a little mistaken."
Emma, Jane Austen

Emma came to visit Livvy the following day. Despite Father believing that Livvy had visited with the woman often over the last few days, Livvy had only ever left the house to be with the Otterhams, deciding to spend as much time with them as she could before she left the Mount.

As such, when Emma *did* come, Livvy did her best to be herself, but she could feel her defenses rise the moment she saw her friend—who just so happened to be August's friend first.

Had Emma come merely on his behalf? Or was she truly there to see Livvy because she wished to?

She led the way to the sitting room, situating herself on the seat Father typically resumed by the fire. As Emma sat down across from her, Livvy's eyes snagged on the book near the table across the room. *The Hermit's Cell.* The last one she'd not read of Mrs. Moon's books. How Livvy wished she could have finished it earlier so she could have delivered it back already. Never mind that now. Father would be the one to ensure the books were given back to their proper owner. Livvy wouldn't step foot in the Moons' home again.

Instead of guessing why Emma had chosen to visit that day instead of any other, Livvy went straight to the issue herself. "I s'pose ye've 'eard 'bout me and August. The rumors that've started."

Emma winced. "I 'ave."

Livvy averted her gaze. She wasn't surprised that the rumors had begun, or that they were spiraling out of control already. That was the nature of Society. Servants overheard, details were spread, truths were warped over time, and gossips were satiated with twisted pleasure.

The same thing had happened this time. Livvy had heard Cook speaking with Sarah this morning. Apparently, the latest chatter was that Father had paid a handful of men on the Mount and off to take interest in her, since no one in their right mind would wish to do so of their own accord.

It wasn't too far from the truth, but still, the words stung. So much so that Livvy could hardly leave her home any longer out of fear for the humiliation she'd face.

"I wish ye to know," Emma said softly, "I don't pay heed to these rumors." She leaned forward in a whisper. "August spoke with Nicholas and me last night, told us o' what occurred. I be so sorry, Livvy. I ne'er thought..." She shook her head, tears glistening in her eyes. "I ne'er thought anythin' like this could e'er 'appen."

Livvy looked away, questions swirling round her mind. "So ye didn't know 'fore...'bout the agreement 'tween 'em?" That had been her worst fear, that Emma had been in on it since the beginning, too.

But her friend shook her head at once. "No. The only thing August e'er told me was that ye be in need of a friend."

Livvy's cheeks burned. How humiliating this was, to have Father and August beg others to befriend the hermit of the Mount. Still, having Emma tell the truth meant a great deal to her. "Thank ye for bein' honest with me. 'Specially when no one else 'as been."

Emma leaned back. "Well, under the circumstances, I be glad I *can* be."

Livvy nodded, then paused. "Under the circumstances. What do ye mean?"

"Well, I ain't bein' threatened."

An unsettling feeling slipped beneath Livvy's heart, and she shifted in her seat, though it did nothing to dispel her discomfort. "Who be bein' threatened?"

Emma stared. "Well, August was. But then, ye know that... Do ye not?"

Livvy frowned, shaking her head as an ache pierced her heart.

Emma, clearly hesitant, winced again. "I-I be sorry. I thought ye knew. August said..."

Livvy's heart was in her throat, her head spinning. "Tell me, Emma. Please, make haste."

Emma's eyebrows drew together, sorrow crossing her features. "August told Nicholas and me last night, after hours o' coercin' it out of 'im, that...that your father discovered the truth 'bout me and Nicholas. 'E threatened to expose us if August didn't agree to go along with 'is plan to force ye to leave the Mount."

The breath rushed from Livvy's lungs, her heart breaking in two. For days, the man she'd known August to be had mixed with this distorted image of a person she couldn't make sense of—a person who had hurt her for seemingly no reason.

His apology to her the day before, the humility he'd expressed, had helped to remind her of who he really was—a good man who'd made a poor choice.

But now, seeing what Father had done...

She squeezed her eyes closed, the pulsing in her forehead refusing to relent. "Why didn't 'e tell me?" she whispered, rubbing her fingers to her brow as the realization of the gravity of the situation settled around her.

"Knowin' August," Emma said, "'e probably thought it be more honorable to take the blame 'imself."

Livvy let out a breath. That was exactly why he'd kept the knowledge to himself. Because he *was* honorable.

And Father? Why had he not told her?

Unfortunately, she already knew the reason—and it was certainly not for honor. He'd made this decision, just like every decision, out of fear, out of the desperate desire to not make the same mistake with his daughter that he'd made with his wife.

Her mind flashed back to the conversation with August on the castle balcony.

"'E gave me no choice," August had said.

"There always be a choice. Ye always 'ave a choice."

He'd tried to be honest with her, he'd tried to tell her the whole truth, but she'd put an end to it with her pride.

She groaned, burying her face in her hands. Yes, August *did* have a choice. But was it a fair one when each choice resulted in terrible consequences no matter what choice he made—consequences her own father had placed upon him?

How could Father ever do such a thing?

"Livvy?" Emma rested a soft hand to her shoulder. "Are ye well?"

She shook her head, still hiding her face. "No. I...I can't e'en bear the knowledge. To know me own father'd do somethin' so despicable...." Then another thought occurred. She lowered her hands and faced Emma with wide eyes. "Did Father tell the Mount?"

Emma removed her hand from Livvy's shoulder, shaking her head. "No. As far as we be aware, not a word 'as been said 'bout our relationship."

Relief filled her for only a moment, replaced swiftly with shame over her father's behavior. "I be so sorry, Emma. 'Bout all o' this."

Emma reached forward, taking Livvy's hand in hers. "Ye musn't fret, Livvy. 'Tisn't your fault. None o' this be your fault. Surely we can all find a way to move forward together, though. To 'elp each other."

How Livvy wished that were true. But what had happened could not be undone. The rumors had already begun, and Father still did not wish for her to remain on the Mount. Even if Livvy could withstand the gossip, even if she believed that August did have true feelings for her, she couldn't stay.

"No," she responded, her voice falling flat. "'Tain't no way to move past this. I can't stay on the Mount."

Livvy had cried so frequently over the last few days that no more tears came, despite Emma's own eyes flooding with emotion. "Ye really do be leavin', then?"

Livvy nodded. "There be too much sorrow I can't face. Too many lost dreams. I can't put August or 'is family through such rumors connected to me name. And...and Father don't want me 'ere. That much be clear by the lengths 'e took to be rid o' me. It'll be better for everyone if I leave."

Emma dabbed at her tears with her handkerchief. "Where will ye go?"

"Me father expects word back from 'is cousins any day

now," she responded with a half-smile. The somber mood between them grew, though Livvy did her best to pick up both of their spirits as she would the corners of a blanket, shaking them free of dust and sorrow. "They live in Nanstallon, so not too far from the Mount."

Not too far. Nearly fifty miles was too far from the home she loved. But this home she loved was now tainted. Colored grey by even greyer hearts.

But ye love the color grey, Livvy.

"I understand why ye wish to leave," Emma said softly. "Why ye *must* leave. But...but I do 'ope ye ain't be leavin' 'cause o' August."

Livvy shook her head at once. In truth, that had been the deciding factor at first. She couldn't bear to live so close to him with the ever-present memory and knowledge of how their relationship had been tricked into growing.

But now, she was not running away from August. She was running away from her fear of pain.

"No, I ain't leavin' 'cause of 'im. I understand why 'e did what 'e did. And I don't blame 'im for it. But there be too much humiliation to o'ercome. If I leave, 'e'll be able to move on. The rumors'll subside as 'e continues workin' at the castle gardens, livin' with 'is family, and bein' 'is usual charmin' self."

"Oh, but—" Emma stopped, clamping her mouth shut.

"What be the matter?" Livvy asked, concern growing within her again. Was there something else she didn't know? Something else of which she needed to be made aware?

Emma chewed the inside of her lip before glancing to the door, as if to ensure they were truly alone. "Do ye not know what else your father did to August?"

Her throat constricted, rendering her unable to speak as she shook her head.

Emma hesitated. "August didn't want ye to know. But...

your father removed 'im from 'is position as undergardener. 'E don't work in the gardens no more."

Another blow struck Livvy straight in her heart, and she leaned back in her chair. "But, why? August did all Father asked of 'im, did 'e not?"

"'E did everythin' but keep the knowledge from ye," Emma said. "When August told your father that 'e'd told ye 'bout their agreement, your father demanded that 'e not come back to the gardens. Apparently, your father was goin' to remove Nicholas, as well, but thus far, 'e still 'as 'is position."

Crushed once more, Livvy's stomach heaved. August had lost his job because he'd decided to tell Livvy the truth. How had she ever doubted the man? How had she ever doubted him to be as good and gentlemanly as she always thought him to be?

Frustration boiled within her. She was doing what Father wanted by leaving the Mount. Now it was time for Father to do something for her.

Setting her tasks in order, she knew what needed to be done.

She needed to have a word with Father.

She needed to have a word with August.

And more than anything, she needed to have a word with herself. For if she was going to maintain her stance on leaving the Mount, she needed to remember why she was leaving in the first place.

For being near August, she was bound to forget.

CHAPTER FIFTY-TWO

"Angry people are not always wise."
Pride and Prejudice, Jane Austen

August did his best to quell any rumors he heard about Livvy, but they spread like spilt water over a smooth table. The more he tried to stop one dripping, the faster more would spill on the other side until all of the Mount seemed to have heard one version of the lie or another.

His sisters, fortunately, did not seem to be participating in said rumors, though that had backfired, as August's name soon became embroiled in the mess, as well.

"Be it true, August?" Mother asked him after church the following Sunday. "What they be sayin', be it true?"

But August didn't have the heart to respond. Livvy and her father hadn't attended services that day, and August knew there was only one reason for that. Livvy had heard the rumors, too.

Here was yet another one of his many wrongdoings, yet another way in which he was causing her pain.

Without responding to his family, all four of them casting curious and worried gazes in his direction, August excused himself to spend the rest of the day in his room again, unable to face what now lie ahead in his future—a future without Livvy May.

Before he could climb the stairs, however, a knock sounded at the door, and August paused. His heart lifted. Could it be... had Livvy come to visit him at last?

And yet, when their footman John answered the door, revealing Mr. May's stoic face in the doorway, August stiffened.

His first reaction was to flee, as he'd been doing since the beginning of Mr. May's rotten behavior. But a quick memory check reminded August that he no longer had anything to fear.

The man had already taken everything from him.

As such, he faced him with a matching look of severity.

"Is Mr. August Moon in?" Mr. May asked John.

But August was already moving to the door, if only to prevent John from allowing the man in. "I'll take it from 'ere, John, thank ye."

John nodded, glancing between them before leaving the corridor.

Between John and the Mays' maid, the servants would be having a grand time with how much fodder they were earning from their drama-filled employers.

"What can I do for ye, Mr. May?" August asked stiffly. As if he would do anything more for the man who'd effectively ruined his life.

Mr. Moon raised his chin, standing outside of the house with a tight jaw. "It would appear that me daugh'er 'as learned o' your termination at the castle gardens and wishes to reverse me decision."

That was not what August had been expecting to hear. Emma must have told Livvy about his no longer working at the castle, despite his desire to keep it to himself for as long as possible. He simply didn't want Livvy to pity him. Not when he deserved her derision.

Still, he couldn't fault Emma for telling her. She no doubt must have only been trying to help.

His heart lifted for a single moment at the thought of Livvy championing him, but then, he hardly deserved such kindness.

"Now," Mr. May continued, "I be certain ye know I cannot easily do such a thing, as ye've forfeited me trust permanently."

August looked away with a scoff, shaking his head at the man's audacity. He had a mind to push him out in the street and show him how he really felt about his trust. Instead, he clenched his fists tightly together and listened as Mr. May continued.

"Howe'er, as ye might be aware, I'll be escortin' me daugh'er off the Mount soon." He paused, as if to rub August's face in the matter. "As such, she's alerted me to the fact that I'll need more 'elp at the gardens, and as I don't 'ave time to train anyone else up, I be willin' to bring ye back on for a trial period. If ye do well, I'll open your position again. If not, well, I be certain ye can find somewhere else to work *off* the Mount."

August's eyes hardened.

Mr. May hardly seemed to notice, though, as he backed away, clearly finished with the conversation. "Now, if ye'll excuse me." He tipped his head slightly, then made to leave, but August, with a burning fire within his heart, could no longer allow himself to stand idly by.

"Just a moment, sir."

Mr. May stopped, slowly turning around. "Yes, Mr. Moon?"

Footsteps shuffled behind him, and he became keenly aware of his family's eyes and ears upon him, but August no longer cared.

What did it matter if anyone heard? What did it matter what they thought of him or who knew what? All he cared about was standing up for Livvy when she could not.

"Thank ye for the offer," August said, "but I'll not be acceptin' it."

Mr. May smirked, causing August's rage to burn all the brighter. "I told Liv ye'd say that. That your pride'd get in the way."

"'Tisn't me pride," August said. "'Tis me love for your daugh'er."

Mr. May frowned in confusion, then his face contorted with anger as he realized what August was saying. He opened his mouth to speak, then glanced over August's shoulder, no doubt seeing the rest of the Moons standing behind him.

August's courage grew.

"Ye be out o' your mind, Moon," Mr. May said. He tried to walk away, clearly not wishing to speak with August with an audience gathered.

But August would not be stopped. "No, I ain't. I be in a better frame o' mind than ye, forcin' your daugh'er off the Mount when it be the last thing she wishes to do."

Mr. May looked around them, waiting for a passerby to walk away before he stepped closer to the house once again, pointing a finger at August. "I told ye, it be none o' your business what I do with me daugh'er."

August barked out a laugh. "It be me business when ye forced me to lie to 'er, forced me to trick 'er to leave the Mount." He took a step forward, and a flash of fear flickered in Mr. May's eye. "And it be me business the minute I fell in love with 'er."

Mr. May's nostrils flared, and he narrowed his eyes, his words spitting, though he kept his voice low. "I should've known ye'd betray me in such a way. Fallin' in love with 'er. Ye 'ad one job. Convince 'er to want to leave the Mount."

"No," August said. "The job I agreed to was to make Miss May 'appy. And she'll ne'er be 'appy off the Mount. Nor will she be 'appy with a father who be embarrassed by 'er."

His jaw twitched. "Ye know nothin', Moon."

"I know more than ye think," August said. He needed to tread carefully, not wishing to betray anymore of Livvy's trust by revealing what she'd said about her father. "I know it do pain 'er each time ye reveal 'ow ye don't love 'er for who she be. But *I do*, sir. I love 'er *'cause* of who she be."

Mr. May scoffed. "If ye think I'll allow ye to be with 'er, ye be mad." He pointed his finger at August, dropping his voice so no one else could hear him. "Ye stay away from 'er. Ye stay away, or I'll make ye suffer more than I e'er 'ave 'fore."

August gave a mirthless smile. "Ye needn't worry 'bout that, sir. She don't want to be with me. The damage we've done to 'er be irreversible."

For the briefest of moments, Mr. May's eyes revealed his regret, the pain he must have felt somewhere in his cold heart breaking through his angry defenses, but he looked away.

August continued, his voice low. "Ye could not make me suffer any more than that."

Instead of the satisfaction August had expected from Mr. May, the man merely glanced back at August's family, then drew another step away.

"Good day, Mr. Moon," he said shortly, then he headed in the opposite direction of his house.

August watched him until he disappeared into the Sugar Loaf, then he turned to face his family. Sure enough, his sisters and parents stared at him in silence, wide-eyed and open-mouthed.

He'd put this off for too long. It was time for him to come out of the stupor he'd lowered himself into and ask for help from his family.

He could no longer do this alone.

CHAPTER FIFTY-THREE

"Let us never underestimate the power of a well-written letter."
Persuasion, Jane Austen

After speaking with Father, veritably forcing him to hire August back at the castle gardens or she would refuse to leave the Mount once again, Livvy had written a note for Emma to deliver to August, requesting that they meet for a brief moment of conversation.

However, the next day, when she went to deliver the note, Emma handed one to Livvy from August instead.

With a racing heart, she returned home, not opening the correspondence until she reached the safety of her room.

She tried to quell her aching heart as she saw the masculine script across the paper, longing to see the man behind the missive as she read and reread his message.

Livvy,
I have started and restarted this letter countless times, wondering what could be said to ye to express how I've felt

without ye these few days past. But each time, words fail me.

There is nothing I can say to express how I miss ye. How I long for your smile to brighten me days again. How I yearn for your conversation about books and weather and favorites lists.

But I know such a thing is not possible when so much has been unanswered between the two of us. I have spoken with me family about matters, and they have encouraged me to tell ye the truth.

So, dearest Livvy, I shall do so, if ye care to learn of it.

The matter with your father started out slowly. He requested me services to help ye find friends, which I accepted—albeit reluctantly—because I genuinely believed he loved ye and wished for ye to be happy. I also accepted because I was already planning on getting to know ye further. When I told him of your desire to remain on the Mount, and of me decision to do no more for him, that is when the threats began. That is when me shame multiplied.

Livvy continued reading, her mind reeling as August explained moment after moment what had occurred, how he felt disgusted with himself for weeks, how her father had coerced him into following his pressuring time and time again, though August had done his best to tell him no.

Tears flooded her eyes, unable to be contained as she cried at the memory of the sorrow written across August's features at times when they were together. Now all of it made sense. His behavior, his conversations. All of it made perfect sense.

And yet, did that not make matters more difficult? Knowing August truly did have feelings for her, despite Father's malicious workings?

She peered back down at the letter, continuing August's words.

There ye have it. The truth of all matters I've been through in the last few weeks. I know ye cannot trust me, but I ask that ye know I've only ever done what I thought it best to do.

I know ye do not wish to see me. I know I've forfeited all right to call ye mine or to have your love in me life. But if ye can honor me request to see ye again, to allow me the chance to speak with ye one last time, I would forever be in your debt.

Forgive me, but I told your father how I felt about ye. I hope this did not make matters worse for ye, as it did for meself. Due to me words, he has forbidden me from speaking to ye again. But, me darling Livvy, I cannot bear the thought of not doing so.

Will ye allow me one final chance to speak with ye? To share with ye all I've wanted to share with ye since the moment I met ye? I will be waiting for ye on the west side of the Mount, beyond the sail repair loft and over the wall at midnight tonight. I pray ye will come. But if ye do not, I will take your absence to mean that ye no longer wish to see me, and I will respect your wishes.

Until then, I remain hopefully, faithfully yours,
August

Livvy stared at the ending.

Hopefully, faithfully yours

How she wished to call August hers. How she wished to be with him forevermore, wrapped up in his embrace, filled with his love for the rest of her days.

But it could never be.

Father had approached her the night before, asking if she'd fallen for August. Now she knew why.

"I be leavin' the Mount, Father," she'd responded. *"No matter what feelin's I did or did not 'ave for 'im."*

This had seemed to satisfy him, and he'd shifted instead to read the letter that had just arrived from his cousins.

She didn't mind him ending the conversation swiftly. Since discovering his cruelty to August, Nicholas, and Emma, Livvy had found it difficult to speak with Father at all.

Yet another reason she was grateful to be leaving the Mount, even if it was sooner than she thought. Not only would she be able to leave the memory of Mother behind, but she would also be able to leave the ever-present knowledge of disappointing Father, as well.

Ye ne'er disappointed August.

The thought slipped through her mind before she had the chance to stop it. She didn't know if she'd disappointed August or not. Would he have even told her if she had?

Closing her eyes, she prayed for clarity of mind. She needed to speak with him, to apologize for her father's behavior—as she knew Father would not have done so in the slightest. She also needed to ensure that August would be secure in his job at the castle once she left.

Father had said August had denied his request to still work in the gardens. *"Turned 'is nose up at it, 'e did."*

But honestly, Livvy didn't know what she could believe and what she couldn't—at least where Father was concerned. It was far safer to ask August herself. She'd never forgive herself if he didn't keep the job he fought so long to earn. Especially because he lost said job due to simply being honest with Livvy.

Blowing out a slow breath, she eyed the correspondence again.

Yes, she would meet with August tonight. She needed to see him one last time, to let him know he would always hold a special place in her heart. Even if they couldn't be together.

And more than anything, she needed to say goodbye. For on the morrow, she would be leaving the Mount forever, bidding farewell to her home, her favorite places, and her favorite people.

To add the love of her life to it as well would break her heart all over again. So she would say goodbye tonight and pray that she could survive the heartache.

August rubbed his hands together, staring out at the misty sea. In the darkness of the night, he could see very little beyond what the nearby light of the castle cast across the shores.

But he could hear the waves, and that was enough. They signaled the familiarity of the sea. Though he could no longer see the vast ocean, he knew it was still there, could hear the lapping water, smell the briny scent, feel the mist spraying up in the soft wind.

He closed his eyes, focusing on the way his senses were enlivened at night due to the sea, rather than the anxious knot his stomach tied itself into over and over again, like a rag wrung free of water, though still trying to fetch some from its dry fibers.

Would she come?

The thought continued to penetrate his hopeful defenses, creating threads of doubt through the tapestries of his heart.

He'd been waiting there for half an hour, praying, hoping she would make an appearance, though he knew she did not need to. Though he knew he did not deserve it.

The movement of air alerted him first to the change around him. He turned, afraid to believe it was her, yet unable to stop the hope that lit his soul like the sun.

At first, he could see nothing but darkness, shrouds of mist cloaking him and the cliffside where they'd chosen to meet.

Then out of that darkness, a movement occurred, and he could just make out a cloaked form emerging from the mist, drawing ever closer to him.

"August?" came her whispered question.

His heart took courage, his spirits taking flight. She *had* come.

CHAPTER FIFTY-FOUR

"The eagerness with which we endeavor to escape from misery, taught him to encourage a remote and romantic hope that {she} yet lived for him."

A Sicilian Romance, Ann Radcliffe

"I be 'ere," August whispered at once.

He reached out his fingers, finding Livvy's in the darkness as warmth surged up his arm. He clasped onto her hand with his, drawing her near.

As they drew closer, she pulled her hand from his and removed the hood of her cloak. The light reflected in the mist finally revealed her features—concerned and beautiful.

"I didn't think ye'd come," he whispered.

She looked up at him, vulnerability etched across her features, just as it had done countless times before. But this time, he was the one who had caused that pained look.

"Forgive me for bein' late," she whispered. "Father didn't fall asleep until later this evenin'." She looked away, as if hiding something, but August set the thought aside. He wasn't there to ruminate. He was there to speak the truth—to have *both* of them speak the truth.

His eyes caressed her features, drinking them in as a man lost in the desert. Livvy was his water. His sunshine. His life.

Would his words have any effect? Would they change her mind and convince her to remain?

There was only one way to see.

"Thank ye for comin'," he said. "I...I've a lot goin' through me mind now. I just be glad to see ye. I—"

"August," she interrupted, and he stopped at once. "I feel I must be frank with ye, right from the start."

He swallowed, nodding for her to continue, though an inkling within him told him to stop her, prevent her from saying what he knew she was about to say.

"I came 'ere tonight as I wished to speak with ye, too."

Again, he nodded for her to continue.

She drew a deep breath. "I first must apologize to ye for me father's behavior. I 'ad no notion that 'e...that 'e be extortin' ye, forcin' ye to do 'is biddin'. 'Ad I known, I ne'er would've been so upset with ye. Any man would've done the same as ye did under the same circumstances, so I want ye to know, I don't fault ye for that."

August couldn't help but stare. Who was this angelic woman? And how did he deserve to even stand in her presence? Was she in earnest? Had she truly forgiven him for what he'd done?

"Furthermore," she continued, "I wanted to ensure that me father did ask for ye to work at the gardens again. As I fear I cannot trust 'is word any longer, but I...I believe I can still trust yours—in this regard."

In this regard. He hadn't missed the addition to her statement. That meant she couldn't trust him in any other way.

"So..." she pressed. "Did 'e offer ye the position again?"

August hesitated, knowing her disappointment would be great if he told her the truth. But if he did not, would she not see straight through him? "'E did," he replied earnestly. "But I told 'im I could not accept any position where I'd be workin' with 'im again."

He could see the disappointment across her features, and tears flooded her eyes. "I be afeared o' that. But please, please work there again."

"I can't, Livvy. Surely ye can see why."

She lowered her gaze. "It be all me fault. If I could just be different, then Father'd not be so disappointed in me. Then 'e ne'er would've 'ad to press ye to do what 'e wanted. Ye could still 'ave your job. Your family would be 'appy. Your friends would be secure. None of it be fair. 'Tain't fair, August. It be me own fault, and ye be sufferin' 'cause of it."

August's heart overflowed with love and sorrow simultaneously. Each time he'd seen her, she'd fought back tears, always blinking them away, always being strong. But she was breaking now, and he couldn't bear it a moment longer.

Swiftly, he reached for her, wrapping his arms around her as she crumpled into him. "I be so sorry, August. It be all me fault."

He shook his head as her slight frame trembled against his body. "No, Livvy," he whispered, placing a kiss to the top of her head, wet from the moisture in the air. "No, 'tain't your fault. Don't think for one moment it be your fault. This 'as 'appened 'cause o' the choices o' others, not 'cause of ye."

"If I wouldn't 'ave been such a disappointment to 'im..."

Again, he shook his head. "No," he said softly but firmly, unwilling to let her take any of the blame. "Ye ain't a disappointment. Your father be tormented. 'E's let 'is own fears and struggles color 'ow 'e feels 'bout ye and sees ye. 'Tain't your doin', any more than the tides be your doin'."

Her shoulders shuddered as she continued to cry, and he held her all the tighter, blinking away his own tears as he leaned into her.

He longed to take back his own decisions that contributed to her sorrow in that moment, but he could not. So he would do what he could to make up for it.

In silence, they stood, August's arms wrapped around her as comfortingly as he could manage until her cries softened, though still, she remained resting against his chest, her arms slipping beneath his open jacket and encircling his waist.

He closed his eyes, drawing on the warmth, the comfort he felt with her so near to his heart.

"Thank ye," she whispered into the darkness.

August held her tighter.

"'Ow I wish ye'd reconsider workin' at the gardens," she continued. "It be your dream, after all."

He breathed in the scent of her hair, allowing it to fill every crevice of his heart. "It *was* me dream. Now, I 'ave another."

She didn't respond, though he knew she'd caught his meaning. Another moment passed by, but Livvy did not make to move. Did that mean...Was she feeling the same comfort in his embrace as he felt in hers?

Taking courage from the thought, August drew a deep breath. "I know ye cannot believe anythin' I say. I know ye can't trust me. But I..."

He paused. She pulled away but just far enough to peer up at him, her arms still wrapped around him. "I *do* trust ye, August. More than I e'er trusted anyone."

He stared down at her, the sincerity written in her eyes striking him so he could not speak. He took in the sight of her features staring up at him, as stunning as they had been that first day he'd seen her in the bushes. Eyes, vibrant and telling. Hair, dark as the night's sky. And lips...

He stared at them, parted and inviting. How he longed to taste their sweetness again. How he longed to feel her love for him in that way once more.

Was it possible? Could he truly have the woman he loved be his forever?

His conversation with his family the night before flashed through his mind.

"The only question that remains be this," Mother had said, *"do ye love 'er? Do ye love Miss May?"*

August had nodded firmly. *"I do."*

Mother and Father had exchanged glances, then, and Father grinned. *"Then ye must fight for 'er, son. Fight for 'er as if your very soul depends upon it."*

Well, August's soul, his happiness, his life *did* depend upon Livvy being with him. So he would fight.

"Marry me, Livvy," he stated, unable to keep himself from saying the words a moment longer. "Stay on the Mount and marry me."

She took in a quick breath of air, her chest rising against his as she peered up at him. Her eyes fell to his lips for a brief moment, and desire stirred within him.

"I'll spend the rest o' me days makin' up for me errors," he said. "I'll spend each day strivin' to make ye 'appy once again."

Her lip twitched, and she drew in a trembling breath before she shook her head.

"I can't."

CHAPTER FIFTY-FIVE

"In this world of semblance, we are contented with personating happiness; to feel it, is an art beyond us."
The Man of Feeling, Henry MacKenzie

August had expected her to say the words, knowing the depth of her conviction. Yet still, they stung bitterly. "Ye can. Together, we can do anythin'."

She shook her head, her eyes dropping to his lips again as she slowly blinked. "No. The rumors..."

"Hang the rumors," he stated, tipping his head to the side to better see her lips as she raised her chin toward him.

How he wished she would disregard the gossips. How he wished she would let go of all else and cling to August this way forever.

"I would," she whispered, her fingers clutching to the folds of his shirt near the small of his back. "But ye know it be more 'an that. Me father. 'E don't want me 'ere anymore."

Curse her father, destroying everything the two of them had ever wanted. "But *I* want ye 'ere, Livvy. Ain't that enough?"

Her eyes softened, her brows drawn high. "I wish it was."

"It *can* be." Desperation clawed its way from his heart, clamoring toward the woman in anguish. "If we love each other—if ye love me—we can see through anythin', your father's desires included."

A flicker of hope flashed in her eyes, buoying him up as he continued. "For if there be one thing I've discovered o'er the weeks o' knowin' ye, it be the power ye 'ave within yourself to be *ye*, despite all odds."

"I fear I don't 'ave much courage anymore, August. Or much strength. I..." She broke off, shaking her head. "I don't e'en know who I be anymore."

"Then allow me to remind ye," he said softly. He reached his hand up, resting on her jawline, his thumb caressing her smooth skin. "Ye be Miss Livvy May," he whispered, his thumb edging closer to the corner of her lips. "The woman who stands tall in the face of adversity, just like 'er favorite flowers. Ye be the woman who creates lists of 'ow joyous life makes ye. The woman who ain't afeared o' bein' 'erself, e'en when everyone else be." His thumb trailed over her chin, her own eyes dropping to his lips. "Ye be the woman I've fallen in love with more deeply and desperately than I e'er thought possible. For o'er the last few weeks I've discovered that to know Miss May is to *love* Miss May."

A tear slipped from the corner of her eye, trailing down the opposite side of her cheekbone. She didn't raise her hand to wipe it away. Nor did *he*, his eyes merely staring at the trail of moisture it created down her cheek, like the drops of rain he'd watched sliding down the window, making their mark on the glass.

"Tell me not that these tears are caused by me," he whispered.

She sniffed. "They are caused by ye. But only from 'ow greatly I love ye."

Passion burned in his heart, sliding through his very soul at her words.

"This be me final secret, August Moon. The secret I've kept with me longer than any other. The secret that I've loved ye for ten years, e'er since ye rescued those pages o' the book for me."

How blind August had been. How focused he'd been on himself and his own life. Yes, she had been far too young to pursue years ago, but then, had he known, surely he could have avoided all of this pain.

But then, without the pain of losing her, would he have ever known the joy of having her love?

Slowly, his eyes once more fell to her lips. This time, their kiss would be different. This time, it would not end in sorrow. He would not pull away to tell her all of his wrongdoings, and he would kiss her as she deserved, with all of the love he held for her.

This time, he would kiss her right.

Livvy's heart stuck in her throat as August leaned closer to her, his brows low over his eyes, his lips parted as he drew in a ragged breath.

She knew she should pull away. She shouldn't allow another kiss to occur between them, especially when...when she would still be leaving in the morning.

But as August's eyes, dark and penetrating, focused and determined, fell again to her lips, she could no longer think properly.

If she was to leave in the morning, if she was never to see this man again, she would forever regret not giving into her desires in that moment, giving into her love and passion for the man.

So she would allow it. She would allow herself a single moment in time where she wasn't being dictated to by her father. Where she wasn't being controlled, humiliated, spoken about.

Where she was, instead, loved and cherished.

No one else could make her feel so but August.

All other thoughts fled her mind as his hand slid across her jaw to rest near the back of her neck, his fingers pressing against her to urge her closer to him, softly, gently.

Livvy did as he requested, tipping her head back slightly, her hands sliding forward to rest at his waist.

Slowly, he leaned toward her, his warm breath on her lips a perfect contrast to the cold mist around them. Was it coincidental that she would kiss the man she loved in her very favorite weather?

In her heart, she knew it was not. In her heart, she knew Heaven wished for her to have this one moment of joy and made it all the more perfect for her.

August's thumb propped beneath her chin, caressing her softly until her lips parted from his slight pressure.

The moment they did part, August closed the distance between them, and his lips pressed into hers. Years of waiting culminated into this moment, even more than their first kiss. For even then, she had felt August holding back, an invisible force keeping him from fully enjoying the kiss.

But this one. This one was different. For August was hers, if only for a moment. And it was a moment she would relish forever.

She slid her hands up his chest slowly, and his responding sigh deep in his throat stirred the desire within her to greater depths. Slowly, she moved her arms over his shoulders, standing on the tips of her toes to link her fingers at the back of his neck, pulling her body against his.

August responded in turn, moving his arms to wrap about her securely, his hands sliding from the small of her back to her hips, never straying past the point of propriety, which allowed her to more fully enjoy his affection.

For just as she said, she trusted August. With all of her heart, she trusted him. She knew if she stayed, she could combat any rumors that had already occurred and would no doubt occur. If she stayed, he would help her, fight her insecurities alongside her, encourage her to grow, love, and experience life better than she ever had before.

But if she stayed, she would always have the constant reminder, the constant discouragement, the constant darkness from her father. The thoughts would always be there.

I ain't good enough for 'im.

'E don't want me to be 'ere.

'E doesn't need me, just as Mother didn't need me.

How could she stay with August when each day with him that should be filled with light, would also be filled with darkness?

August broke apart from her for a moment, trailing kisses along her cheeks and brow before finding her lips once more, deepening their kiss with the love she knew he possessed for her.

But it was a love that could never be.

Tears sprang to her eyes, sliding down her cheeks, but she didn't brush them aside, afraid any movement would end their affection.

A few moments later, however, August pulled back, looking across her features with a worried expression. Had he felt her tears? Or had he sensed them?

She allowed her arms to loosen around his neck, resting

them lightly atop his shoulders as he moved his hands to her sides.

"More tears?" he whispered.

She nodded. It was time. Time to depart. Time to say goodbye to the love of her life forever.

"I must go," she whispered.

His brow furrowed. "Yes, I've kept ye up too late."

Had he truly not understood her meaning? Or was he simply denying the fact that she would still be leaving?

"Allow me to see ye back?" he asked.

But she shook her head. "I can't risk Father seein' ye." As if that could ever be her true answer. The fact of the matter was, if she spent a moment more with this man, she would change her mind forever.

As such, she backed away. "Thank ye, August."

"For what?" he asked, his face barely visible in the darkness as she increased the distance between them.

Cold overcame her senses, and she shivered. "For lovin' me as I be."

He didn't respond for a moment, but when he did, his voice was filled with emotion. "We'll figure this out, Livvy. Together. We'll be 'appy. Ye wait and see."

How Livvy wished to believe him.

"I'll send ye a message soon," he said. "And...and per'aps I can see ye tomorrow."

Livvy didn't respond. She turned on her heel and left August to himself on the cliffside, releasing silent cries as she did so.

For there would be no tomorrow. At least, not for them.

CHAPTER FIFTY-SIX

"I know not my own heart if it be not absolutely free."
Clarissa, or, the History of a Young Lady, Samuel Richardson

Livvy closed the door to her home in silence, forcing herself not to look back at the outer blue walls that had always brought her such great joy.

She wasn't certain if she'd ever see them again. At least not in the years to come. For she would not come back to St. Michael's Mount unless there was no chance she would see August.

She couldn't bear it.

"Ye be certain ye packed everythin' ye need?" Father asked, raising the small portmanteau he carried for Livvy, his own bag in his opposite hand.

Both of them were headed across the causeway to Marazion early that morning, where they'd catch the coach to Nanstallon. Father had brought just enough in his bag to carry him through the journey, as he'd depart the moment she was safely delivered.

"Yes, Father," she said. "I 'ave everythin' I need."

She didn't have much to begin with, and there was very little she needed.

"Say your goodbyes, then," he said. "I'll wait for ye by the causeway."

He walked across the pathway along the harbor, leaving Livvy with the only person who'd come to bid her farewell—the only person she'd told when she would be leaving.

She turned to her friend with a soft smile. "Emma. Thank ye for comin' to see me off."

"I wouldn't 'ave missed it." She hesitated. "I know someone else who wouldn't 'ave wished to miss it either."

She didn't have to say the name of whom she'd been referring to. Livvy's eyes traveled the length of the Moons' home, settling on the window she knew belonged to August.

Immediately, however, she looked away, keeping her voice low in the darkness of the morning. The sun had not yet risen—nor had half the Mount, August included.

That was precisely how Livvy had wished it.

"I know," she said, tears pricking her eyes, the emotion being her unwanted yet constant companion for days now.

She reached into her reticule, ensuring Father still had his back turned to them before extending a small, folded paper to Emma. "This be for 'im. Will ye see that 'e gets it?"

Emma nodded, hiding the note at once in her hands. "I will. But...be ye certain ye don't wish to speak with 'im yourself?"

Livvy nodded. "I did last night, but 'twill be too 'ard to do it again. 'E won't understand, but I do 'ope me letter sheds more light than I could in person."

After her time with August, she'd spent the better part of the night writing the message, though she knew, even though she'd poured her heart and soul into it, August still wouldn't understand.

How could he? He'd always been loved by both his parents. He'd always been cared for. They'd always been proud of him.

But she had never felt any of those things from either of her parents. So perhaps this action, this leaving the Mount, would finally earn her Father's respect.

Or per'aps not.

The voice inside her head spoke out again, pouring down upon her like an overwatered flower, rotting out her hope.

"Ye know," Emma said softly, "'e's done 'is best to prove 'imself to ye."

Livvy nodded. "I know."

"'E's e'en gone so far as to tell people the truth o' what 'e's done to stop the untruths goin' 'round. 'E's enlisted 'is family and me and Nicholas to 'elp, too."

Livvy paused. A niggling feeling nudged its way into her heart, whispering more doubts into her mind. She didn't know he'd done any of that.

"But I'll not attempt to convince ye to stay when ye've already set your mind to leavin'," Emma said, breaking through Livvy's thoughts. She reached forward, taking Livvy's hand in hers. "I'll miss ye, me friend. Write when ye arrive, so I know ye be well-settled."

Livvy nodded, squeezing Emma's hand tightly in hers, though her mind still fidgeted, as if she had a pebble in her shoe of which she could not be rid.

"Ye must write to tell me when ye and Nicholas depart from the Mount," Livvy returned, and Emma nodded.

Another moment passed by, the girls staring at each other with looks of sorrow. Livvy did her best to swallow her emotion, though a stone still welled up in her throat. "I can't thank ye enough for your friendship, Emma. I only wish we could've 'ad more time."

"As do I."

They shared a solemn smile, then Livvy reached forward, embracing Emma tightly before pulling away and giving her a nod of farewell.

Without looking back, Livvy walked past the Moons' home, praying with all of her might that she would escape before August discovered her absence.

Be that really what ye wish for?

She tried to set the thought aside. After all, she'd already made her decision. She was leaving. That very minute. And she was doing so for Father. So why, now, was she second-guessing everything?

Telling herself it was merely worries for the future, she reached the causeway, where Father stood waiting for her.

He gave a short nod, then led the way forward without a word.

Livvy fell in step beside him, staring out across the slightly curved pathway, lit in blues and greys as the sun approached the horizon from below.

It was the first of May today. She'd always loved this month—her favorite, in fact. When she was young, she'd called it *her* month, due to her last name and because her birthday was in the middle of it.

As she grew older, however, she learned to appreciate the month because she'd passed by another anniversary of her mother's death and life didn't seem so bleak.

Now, life seemed nothing but.

"I know what ye be thinkin,' Liv," Father said after a few more steps in silence. "But ye be doin' the right thing."

Was she? Still, she nodded, if only to convince herself that Father had her best interest at heart.

She knew he wanted her to be happy. She *knew* that. But sometimes...

She shook the thought from her mind, continuing across the uneven cobblestones of the causeway.

How often she'd taken this route with a skip in her step, knowing she was merely going to Marazion to enjoy the view of her home.

But now, she was leaving it, with no hope of returning.

"Ye'll be 'appier off the Mount," Father continued, unsettling her further. "It be better for ye to escape 'em rumors, too. There be no stoppin' 'em, after all."

A thought occurred then that Livvy tried to suppress. But it continued to grow, to fester within her until it cankered her soul.

"Father," she breathed. "'Ave ye e'er tried to stop 'em?"

He looked down at her with a creased brow. "What do ye mean?"

"The rumors," she responded, staring straight ahead. "'Ave ye e'er tried to stop 'em?"

He looked at her, his eyes scrutinizing, as if attempting to decipher what her question meant. He looked away the next moment, then shook his head. "Ye know better than I, daugh'er, what comes o' tryin' to deny rumors. It only makes 'em grow all the more powerful. Like weeds, they be."

Livvy knew such a fact. When she was younger, she'd attempted to deny the rumors, but it only made her sound all the more defensive. And yet, what would have happened had *Father* attempted to stop them? What would have happened had he spoken up, had he shared the truth, and defended his daughter?

That same unsettling feeling came once again—or had it never really left? It scratched at her nerves, leaving marks and scars along her choice to follow her father.

"Did ye 'ear the most recent rumors 'round the Mount?" she asked, a numbness creeping over her body, her tears drying up as if her eyes had discovered their long-searched-for drought. "That August and I fell—"

"I don't pay 'eed to 'em. Nor should ye."

That was admission enough for her. He did not wish to hear her speak of her and August, just as she'd suspected before.

"But what if the rumors aren't rumors?" she asked, her heart thrumming in her ears.

"Ye be out o' your right frame o' mind, daugh'er," he answered gruffly. "What ye think ye felt for that Moon boy was just a lie, created by 'is own lies."

Perhaps, had Livvy not spoken with August the night before, had she not heard the truth of the matter from August about Father's trickery, she might have believed Father. But now? Now she could not trust a word that escaped from his mouth.

"There were also rumors that ye tried to pay others on the Mount to befriend me," she continued, "and that ye extorted August to do your biddin'."

She had not mentioned it before now. She had not seen the point of doing so, what with her leaving the Mount and Father forever. But now she needed to hear him speak the truth.

"What about them rumors, Father?" she pressed. "The rumors that were spread so vapidly, me own servants couldn't 'elp but speak 'em."

Father scoffed, his face half-hidden in the shadows of the morning. He didn't look at her, focusing on Marazion that creeped ever closer. "This be why ye'll be better off elsewhere. *Everyone* will be better off without ye to be the subject o' their gossip time and time again."

A cool wind blew across the causeway, and Livvy shivered

as it slid past her neck. Or had she shivered due to Father's words?

Everyone will be better off without ye.

What he meant was, *he'd* be better off. With his daughter gone, he'd no longer have to suffer hearing rumors about her. He'd no longer suffer humiliation at her hand.

Again, the thought came.

Why had he never defended her to others?

The excuse of the rumors only growing was a pitiful one, at that. For what were rumors and falsehoods when the truth was shared? Even if the Mount hadn't believed him, even if the rumors had grown, at least she would have felt the comfort in a father who'd defended her.

As August did.

Her footing stopped, her lips parting as the realization struck her with such force, she could no longer move.

August had defended her. She'd known this before, but seeing it so clearly propped up against Father's cowardly silence, she could hardly bear it.

"Did ye forget somethin'?" Father asked, stopping as he shifted to face her.

Livvy couldn't respond, her tongue bound as she blinked mutely.

"Livvy," Father pressed. She looked up at him as his frown deepened. "We mustn't miss the coach."

The coach. Marazion. The Mount. All at once, the fog seemed to lift from her hazy mind, and clarity rushed forward. "I be sorry, Father, but I can't leave the Mount."

Father's eyes shifted from confusion, to realization, to anger, all in a matter of seconds. "Ye can," he stated. "And ye will."

But Livvy shook her head. "No. No, I can't leave."

He sighed, taking a few steps forward, clearly encouraging

her progression across the causeway. "Ye just be havin' second thoughts. Once ye reach Nanstallon, ye'll be 'appy. Ye'll see."

"No," she said, and he stopped to face her again. "No, Father. I be 'appier on the Mount, just like I've always said."

His nostrils flared. "And just as I've always said, ye don't know yourself like I do. I saw it with your mother, the un'appiness she felt 'ere. I'll not see ye experience the same."

Livvy squeezed her eyes shut at the mention of her mother again, the unwarranted comparison. "I ain't me mother."

"No. But ye be your *mother's daugh'er*."

Had Livvy not been closing her eyes in that moment, she might have missed the slight derision in his tone, the hesitation in his words. But she hadn't missed it. Not this time.

Slowly, she opened her eyes, looking at Father as the light around them shifted from blue to a soft purple.

Sure enough, the look in his eyes revealed exactly what she feared. "Father," she said softly. "Ye 'eard 'er, didn't ye?"

He looked away. "I don't know what ye be talkin' 'bout," he said. "Come. Ye made a promise to me cousins and meself. Ye must leave the Mount."

But Livvy could no longer hear him, her ears ringing. "Mother," she said in a flat tone. "Ye listened to 'er the day she died. Ye 'eard what she said to me."

He didn't meet her gaze, but that was proof enough. As realization hit her once again, Livvy shook her head, attempting to contemplate all the revelation entailed. "All this time," she breathed. "All this time, ye knew what she said to me, and ye ne'er said a word? Not a jot o' comfort, not a whisper of encouragement?"

His jaw twitched, and he looked away. "Well, what did ye want me to say? I couldn't deny 'er words. Nor could I confirm..." He hesitated. "Who ye really be."

Her heart twisted, wringing out the tears she'd thought

had dried from her eyes for good. All these years, Father had known the burden Livvy had carried, wondering if she was her father's daughter, and he hadn't said a word.

But then, that also meant that all these years, he had been unsure if she was his daughter or some other man's he'd been tasked to raise on his own.

Her heart ached. For herself and for her father. "No wonder ye've always been embarrassed o' me," she whispered. "No wonder ye be wantin' rid o' me. 'Cause ye still don't believe I be yours."

CHAPTER FIFTY-SEVEN

"But [she] had in herself that which softens all difficulty, and beguiles all fatigue—an active mind, a strong sense of duty, and the habit of meeting and of overcoming adverse circumstances."
Self-Control, Mary Brunton

Father didn't say a word.

Everything made sense now. That was the real reason he wanted her gone. For if she left, so left all possibilities of their past being discovered, and he would avoid once and for all the fear of others finding out that he might have raised a daughter who was not even his.

Instead of the anger she was tempted to feel for his behavior, for his embarrassment of her and not believing she was his, she prayed to Heaven for peace, where Father had none. And she prayed for comfort, where Father had none.

Until all at once, compassion filled her heart.

Instead of the heartless soul she expected to see in her father, she witnessed only sorrow in his eyes and the weary lines in his brow. And instead of the cruel behavior she knew she could focus on, her heart reached out to him, for he had not healed from what Mother had done to him.

How could that be so, that Livvy had made strides where Father had not—*could* not?

Slowly, she walked toward him. Resting a hand on his arm, she eyed his dark curls that so resembled her own, his blue eyes that mirrored hers, and waited until he looked at her.

"I can't imagine the 'eartache ye experienced at the 'ands o' Mother, the woman ye loved."

He looked away, but again, she waited until he looked back. This time his blue eyes were burdened with red markings as he fought his tears.

"I, too, suffered untold grief," she continued. "But I learned that, despite our own physical similarities and outward appearances, I chose to call ye Father 'cause ye be the only father I've e'er known. The only father on earth I care to know. For it be ye who comforted me when I 'ad night terrors. It be ye who 'eld me 'and at Mother's funeral. And it be ye who furnished me love o' readin'. Ye did all o' that despite what could possibly be discovered—that ye be raisin' someone else's daugh'er."

His jaw twitched over and over again as he clenched his teeth together, working through his emotions.

"I don't blame ye," she whispered. "Nor do I resent ye. Any man would've 'ad a difficult time. But..." She drew a deep breath, determining to be firm and resolved. "But we can't go on livin' like this any longer."

He peered down at her, his eyes hardening, though she continued resolutely. "I be stayin' on the Mount. I be facin' the rumors, standin' up to 'em. And I...I'll be marryin' August Moon."

Just as she'd expected, fire flashed in his eyes. "I forbid it," he said at once. "That man betrayed me, and yourself. Surely ye can see it."

She remained calm, knowing no good would come from them both being livid. "No, Father. 'E didn't betray either one o' we. 'E be the only honest one."

He frowned, shaking his head. His eyes flicked over her shoulder toward the Mount, then straight back to her. "If ye marry 'im, ye'll end up just like your mother. Miserable and six feet under."

She winced at his harsh words, knowing they were born of grief. "No, I shan't. I'll be 'appy with August. I'll be 'appy on the Mount. Just as I always 'ave been."

Again, his eyes flicked over her shoulder, but he turned away. "The rumors'll destroy ye. Your oddities'll be the talk o' the Mount fore'er."

His words threatened to break her peace, but she held strong to her knowledge of August's love. "For so long," she began softly, "I've 'eld to the knowledge that I be the strangest person on the Mount—e'en the strangest in Cornwall...'cause ye've fed me that truth for me whole life. But now I see, with August's 'elp, that I can be odd, I can be different, and still be accepted."

Father's nostrils flared, the tips of them turning white. "If ye marry 'im, ye'll 'ave to leave the Mount anyway. 'E'll 'ave no work for 'im at the castle."

To her utter shock, such news did nothing to weaken Livvy's determination. But how could that be? After all, she had fought for so long to remain on the Mount because that was where she was happiest.

But then, perhaps it wasn't the Mount that made her happy. Perhaps it had always been the hope, the prospect of being with August—even through all those years he'd been gone—that had kept her on the Mount.

Because she loved him more than she even loved the island.

The truth of those words settled any remaining doubt in her mind. "Then off the Mount, I will live," she said. "I'll be 'appy, so long as I can be with the man I love."

"Love," Father scoffed.

A soft noise on the wind reached her ear, but she ignored it, forcing her eyes to remain on Father. "Yes, love, Father. What ye felt for Mother. What she ought to 'ave felt for us. What I know ye still feel for me."

Again, his eyes flashed over her shoulder, and he turned away. "Mark me words. Ye'll live to regret stayin'. And ye'll regret e'er fallin' for that man."

He tossed his head behind her, and she paused. August? Was he—

She was about to turn around when Father stepped away from her, catching her attention.

"Where ye be goin'?" she called after him.

"I be goin' to see me cousins," he said over his shoulder. "Beggin' forgiveness for me daugh'er's fickleness o' character and findin' commiseration with 'em due to me daugh'er ruinin' 'er life."

Without awaiting a response, he walked toward Marazion.

Conflicting feelings arose within Livvy. Sadness at Father leaving her in such a way. Shock that he was seemingly allowing her to stay on the Mount and marry the man she loved. Gratitude for Father's love for her, no matter the strange ways he showed it, and sorrow for the damage Mother had done to both of them.

But most of all, she felt hope. Hope for a future where Father would be happy for his daughter and proud to call her his own. Hope for a future with August. And hope that true happiness would be theirs no matter what the future held for them.

"Livvy! Wait!"

Her heart jumped.

August. It *was* him.

She turned around, her heart catching in her throat at the sight of August barreling down the causeway toward her, his shirt open at the top as his cravat flew out behind him, lost across the exposed sand and rocks of the sea at low tide.

"Livvy!" he shouted again. "Ye can't go!"

The desperation in his voice filled her parched soul, and tears streamed steadily down her cheeks.

She made her way toward him, fighting the smile on her lips until she could no longer bear it. She started into a swift walk, shifting faster and faster, catching herself more than once on the cobblestones but still moving back toward home. The sight of August, with the Mount behind him was all she needed to keep pressing on.

The sun was finally rising above the sea, casting bright rays of glorious sunbeams across the pink and yellow clouds above, highlighting the Mount in all its beautiful, hazy, magical glory. August still ran toward her, a look of determination across his features until finally, *finally*, they reached each other.

Without hesitation, she closed the final distance between them, jumping up and wrapping her arms around his neck at once.

"Please, don't leave," August said, speaking the words into her neck as he held her against his body, cradling her in his arms. "If ye can't stay for me, stay for yourself. Don't leave the Mount. Ye need to be 'ere. The *Mount* needs ye to be 'ere."

"I won't," she whispered back. "I'll not leave ye e'er again."

August froze, pulling back and staring down into her eyes. "Ye mean..."

She nodded, smiling through her tears. "Yes, August. I be stayin'."

He glanced beyond her to where Father still made his way to Marazion. "With your father's blessin'?"

She sobered, noting Father's angered stride as he moved farther and farther away. "No. But one day, I pray it will be."

She turned to face him again, staring up into August's eyes.

"Ye be certain this be what ye want?" he asked, vulnerability in his expression.

"I've ne'er been more certain of anythin' in me entire life," she said. "Other than me love for ye."

And that was the truth. For even if August could find no work on the Mount, even if they needed to move elsewhere, she knew she could bear it, for with August, she could make it through anything.

"I love ye, August Moon," she said, raising her hand to his face.

He shook his head, seeming to gulp in her features as he looked at her. "I love *ye*," he responded. "Me favorite bush-readin', list-makin', hermit."

She laughed, grasping August by the lapels and pulling him down for a kiss.

Apparently, he needed no further persuasion. He wrapped his arms around her tightly, taking over the kiss with a passion that curled her toes and warmed her very soul.

As their kiss ended, and August pulled away, Livvy sighed. "Must we stop?" she murmured.

August chuckled. "I fear we must. Or all o' Cornwall will see us."

She sighed again, eying the Mount growing brighter and brighter, no doubt awakening its residents and pulling them from their beds and homes. "Very well. Though I can't imagine what other rumors would be worse than what's already been said 'bout the two of us."

"I can imagine a few," he said with a wink.

She swatted him playfully on the arm, if only to distract herself from her overheated cheeks. How he managed to make her blush every time was beyond her.

And yet, how she hoped it would continue for years and years to come.

He reached down, taking her hand in his and pulling her toward their home.

She did not know, nor could anyone know, what the future held for them. But what Livvy did know was that as she walked hand-in-hand with August, the sun glistening brightly on the rocks beside them and the Mount glowing before them, whatever future *was* before them, she could not wait for it.

For any future with August Moon was not only worth fighting for—it was worth *living* for.

EPILOGUE

"...how suddenly one comes to be happy, just, perhaps, when one is beginning to think one never is to be happy again!"
The Italian, Ann Radcliffe

"Be ye ready?" Livvy asked, straightening August's cravat as they stood in the corridor near the front door of their house.

"I believe so," August said, eying his pocket watch once again before tucking it securely in his waistcoat pocket. He glanced anxiously around, patting his jacket pockets for who knew what.

Livvy couldn't help but smile. Over five years together now, and he still expressed his nerves in the same manner.

"Breathe," she said, making the motion with her hands for him to breathe in and out. "All will be well."

He nodded, though his breathing still appeared stinted.

She pressed her lips together, wishing to help ease his agitation, though it was entirely warranted—new jobs always were.

Days after Livvy's decision to remain with August all those years ago, Father had written to the castle, requesting his removal from his head position over the gardens. Within a month, the job had been fulfilled by Mr. Caddy, a gardener who had come highly recommended from an estate near London.

Fortunately, through a surprising turn of events, August had managed to secure his job as undergardener once again and had worked for Mr. Caddy devotedly over the last five years.

Just last week, however, Mr. Caddy announced his intention to return to London, recommending August to replace him as head gardener.

Livvy had been thrilled, and August, elated. After all these years, his lifelong dream was now being realized.

And yet, his nerves this morning appeared to be eating him up.

But there was one certain thing she knew would always make him feel better.

Reaching forward, she placed both of her hands on his face and pulled him down, kissing him soundly on the lips. Sure enough, within a moment, his arms encircled her waist, and he kissed her in return.

Just as he deepened their kiss, however, footsteps skittered past the corridor, and giggles erupted, followed by swift gagging noises.

"Don't look, Miranda! They do be kissin' again!"

"No, me like it!"

Livvy pulled away from August and peered down at their two children, Piran, their four-year-old son, and Miranda, their daughter who'd just turned three.

August smiled down at them, his arms still wrapped

around Livvy. "If ye don't like seein' us kiss, son, ye best look away."

He moved toward Livvy again, and the kids ran back down the corridor with squeals and groans.

But Livvy sidestepped August just in time. He opened his mouth with a look of longing. "Just one more?"

"No, I know that look," she said, taking another step away from him. "We don't 'ave time for any o' that business. Ye must leave for work. I was merely distractin' ye for but a moment."

"Your distraction worked far too well," he said, snatching her hand and drawing her closer. He kissed her deeply once again before breaking off due to her smiles.

"Kissin' doesn't work when ye just be smilin' all the time, love," August said.

"Then ye ought not make me smile so much."

They shared a grin, but soon enough, his eyes clouded over once again. "All right, I really do need to be goin' now," he said.

Livvy nodded. "Yes, ye musn't be late for your first day. What'll all 'em men think?"

"I just be concerned with what Nicholas will *do*."

"Scold ye again, no doubt," Livvy said with a smile.

Nicholas had been given a promotion as well in the last few weeks, working directly below August. While the two were still wonderful friends, August always took a more lighthearted approach to gardening, while Nicholas secured a more serious role.

Either way, the two worked wonderfully together, and Livvy and Emma had often talked about how grateful they were to have their husbands be as close as she and Emma had grown to be over the years.

Nicholas and Emma had married a few months after Livvy and August had, though not with their parents' approval.

While there had been some hope to resolve matters, the Cuffs had stopped speaking with their son altogether, and the Pengellys only welcomed their daughter in their home without her husband.

Still, despite matters being difficult, Nicholas and Emma had been truthful with their parents, and instead of running away in the dead of the night, they'd married on the Mount and remained on the Mount, always maintaining the hope that one day, their parents would accept their relationship as one of love, and relationships would begin to heal.

Either way, Livvy had been thrilled to have their friends remain on the Mount after all their hardship, especially now that the new Cuff children—also a boy and a girl—got along splendidly with Piran and Miranda.

"All right," August said, drawing a deep breath. "I'll be off now—"

"Oh, do ye 'ave but one more moment to spare?" Livvy interrupted.

August hesitated, but nodded, nonetheless.

She smiled her gratitude, if only to hide what she was really doing in keeping him there longer. "I received word from me Father."

August's features fell. "And?"

Livvy couldn't hide her grin for long. "'E'll be marryin' Miss Harris after all. Next month."

August's brow rose, and a smile stretched across his lips. "Ah, well that do be good news. It be about time."

Livvy couldn't help but agree. "We be invited, 'course, so I'll need to send our response today."

A strained look crossed August's features—a look that was no stranger to them both, as it appeared whenever she mentioned her father.

But August replaced it with a smile faster than ever.

"'Course we'll be in attendance. We wouldn't miss it. After all, 'e didn't miss our weddin', did 'e?"

Livvy's heart was overwhelmed with warmth once more for this wonderful man before her.

Over the years, August's relationship with Father had continued to be strained, but each time they saw one another —especially after Father's direct apology last year—matters had become better and better.

Apparently, leaving the Mount and remaining in Nanstallon with his cousins permanently had been the best decision he'd ever made. While his decision had shocked Livvy—more often than not leading her to many tears that first year—her relationship with him had improved vastly.

A few weeks after his departure, he'd sent a missive to Livvy, explaining his reasoning for his behavior, expressing his regret for not loving her as he should have, and then stating that he was doing what he could now to change for her and be the father she'd always deserved—promising to be there for her wedding.

More than that, he'd offered his home—Livvy's home—to her and August as a wedding gift, then delivered a letter of recommendation for August, so he would have no trouble obtaining a job from Mr. Caddy all those years ago.

This change of heart had not surprised Livvy. She'd always known he'd loved her. What neither of them knew was that Father needed to get off the Mount—while Livvy needed to stay.

And now, Father was thriving, just as she hoped he would be— working, socializing, *marrying*. She could hardly believe he was the same man whenever she saw him again.

But then, he wasn't the same man. And she couldn't be more grateful for the change that had come over him.

"If that be all..." August said, once more bringing her to the present.

He motioned to the door, signaling his need to depart.

"Oh, yes. 'Course, 'course. Ye must go."

He opened the door, then she held up her hand. "Oh, wait! I've remembered another thing. Dinner tonight. With your parents. Your sisters will be comin', too."

August stifled a sigh, though he still drew on a smile. "Yes, I remember."

"And ye'll be on time?" She struggled keeping her own smile at bay, knowing she was testing his patience like the best of them.

"Yes, love."

He turned once more to the door.

"Oh, and Miranda do be needin' new shoes soon," she added.

He turned back to her, glancing down to his watch once more, then opened the door just a crack. "We can do that soon, then. Anythin' else?"

She tapped her finger to her chin. "Just one moment, I know there be somethin' else...What was it...I know it be *somethin'*..."

"Livvy, I do be sorry, love, but I really must be goin'." He opened the door wider.

"No, no. Wait. It'll come to me," she said. But she could no longer keep in her smile.

Glancing at her husband with her best innocent look, she waited until he narrowed his eyes, then a grin split across his face, though he did his best to scowl. "Ye be doin' that on purpose, ain't ye?"

"I'd ne'er."

He closed the door with a nearly soundless click, then faced her with a look that sent anticipation sailing through her limbs. "Just for that, I'll take that other kiss from ye now." Then he strode toward her with a determination that fluttered her heart.

Swiftly, he placed one hand behind her back and leaned into her with a warm kiss until she fell backwards into his arm, then he lowered her halfway into a dip in the same absurdly charming manner that he'd kissed her in front of the entire Mount on their wedding day.

After a moment, he straightened, both of them breathless as he grinned. "*Now* I must go."

She allowed him to leave that time, though she stepped outside the door and stood by the blue-colored outer walls, waving to a few passersby before she watched her husband walk down the pathway away from her.

When he reached where the pathway curved away from the terraced houses, he turned around, delivered a little wave and an excited smile, then disappeared around the corner.

Livvy sighed with happiness, greeted another couple who walked by, then went back inside the home that she and August had made their own.

Leaning against the door, she went through the list of tasks she needed to see to that day.

Continue her redecoration of the sitting room.

Finish up the weekly meal schedule with Cook.

Speak with the schoolteacher of the Mount to ensure Piran was doing fine with his lessons.

And read. Definitely read.

She pushed herself away from the door and headed to the kitchen first, but not before her eye caught onto the table in the sitting room—and the stack of new books she'd just borrowed from Mrs. Moon placed on top.

The temptation was too great. She would see to the rest of her list later.

Right now, she needed to see how Miss Anne Elliot was faring with Captain Wentworth being in Bath.

She had a feeling she was just about to get to the good part —in her books and in her life.

How grateful she was for both.

August had never had a more exhausting—or more satisfying —day of work. He hadn't realized how greatly he'd missed being head gardener, but being so for the castle's gardens was a new beast to tackle entirely. Though even still, it was a beast he was more than ready and more than happy *to* tackle.

Upon his return home—yes, he had been right on time— Livvy greeted him with a warm kiss, and his children wrapped their little arms around his legs as he carried them about the house, their laughter filling his soul and his heart, just as they always did.

He filled Livvy in on the details of his day as they'd made ready for their upcoming meal at his parents' home, then the four of them had traveled next door, arriving at the same time as Ophelia and Portia.

The girls moved forward, embracing August, Livvy, and the children as their husbands followed close behind.

His sisters had both moved to Penzance with their husbands years before, though they made it a point to visit the Mount and their family a few times a month. August and Livvy always enjoyed seeing them when they did, for even though they still enjoyed a good gossip, their off-putting behavior had shifted toward kindness to Livvy, and that kindness had eventually morphed into sisterly love—which August would be eternally grateful for.

Portia held her one-year-old propped up on her hip, and Ophelia held her back as she waddled toward them.

"Ye be lookin' ready to pop, Ophelia," he said, eying her swelling stomach.

Ophelia groaned. "I look it and feel it, but me physician says I must wait another three weeks, if not more. *Ridiculousity* of the man."

Her husband, the red-headed Mr. Hopkins, smiled endearingly at his wife. "Ye can do it, love. Ye can do anythin'."

They shared a kiss, and August looked away. While he was glad both of his sisters had settled so well and with such kind husbands, he certainly didn't need to witness such a thing.

Together, the three small families entered the Moons' home, where more embraces and smiles were shared with Mother and Father. Talks of August's job abounded, then shifted to the latest books Portia and Ophelia had taken to reading—"It took ye both long enough to see the pull of 'em, daugh'ers"—before the meal was served.

After even more pleasant conversations around the table, the families decided to take advantage of the fine May weather and set off to see the sun set over Penzance.

With Mr. and Mrs. Moon rounding up the children and gripping onto their hands with firmness, the party walked to the west side of the Mount, beyond the sail repair loft—where Livvy and August had first declared their love for one another.

August passed by this location every day he went to work, and every day, he counted the blessings that had occurred upon his meeting the love of his life.

He always ran out of time before he could finish.

Even now, as he stood beside Livvy, their hands intertwined as they stared at the setting sun, a warm, orange light casting its glow around them, he couldn't believe all that had occurred over the years to make him so gloriously happy.

He hoped Livvy was, too. After all, just as he'd promised all those years ago, he'd done his best every day to make her happy. To help her know how much he loved her and how grateful he was for her.

"What ye be starin' at, August?" she asked, eying him sidelong.

He smiled at her teasing. "Just this stunnin' woman beside me."

"'Tain't polite to stare."

He looked away. "Right. I won't, then."

She slipped her hand beneath his jaw and directed his eyes toward her again. "I didn't say I didn't like it."

He smiled, reaching down to kiss her cheek. "Be ye 'appy?"

She delivered a deep sigh and a smile of her own. "More than e'er."

"Ye always say that."

"And it be true every time." She looked up at him with a smile. "And it be 'cause of ye."

Warmth filled him once more, and he placed a kiss on her brow before he pulled her closer with his arm around her shoulders. Together, they watched the last of the Cornish sunset fade across the sea and into the land before them.

How relieved he was that she was happy, for she deserved it. She'd stood tall despite the winds and harsh weather that threatened to tear her down. Despite her hardships, she'd kept her dignity and kindness intact. And now, because of her weathering those storms, she was where she belonged. On the Mount, surrounded by the sea and by those who loved her for the beautiful flower that she was.

How he loved to see her living—to see her *thriving*. For thriving was what sea pinks were born to do.

THE END

Read the next book in the series!
A Heart to Keep, by Ashtyn Newbold

AUTHOR'S NOTE

If you haven't read one of my Author's Notes before, boy, are you in for a treat! Just kidding. It's really nothing special. I usually just take a few pages to share with you behind-the-scenes information about writing the book, fun stories and such, as well as any facts I discovered during my research. If that's not your thing...why is that not your thing?? Are you not as nerdy as the rest of us?? Tell me your secrets!

If that is your thing, welcome! And buckle up. You're in for a long ride. Lucky for you, I was super nice and created headings to make it easy for you skip boring bits.

If there's one thing you *should* read, though, it's the part labeled "AUGUST'S RESCUE OF THE SHOE—FOR REAL LIFE!" I think you'll like that story!

Okay. Moving on.

AUGUST AND LIVVY

In the beginning of the story, I intentionally had metaphors from Livvy's point of view be more about books, while August thought more in terms of plants. By the end of the story, however, Livvy had shifted to explain matters with plants, while August had shifted to books.

What's even more fun about this? I didn't even realize I had done it until later on in my final edits! It just spoke to me of how Livvy and August had become one as the story progressed —and how they influenced each other because of their sheer respect and trust for one another. It's a good example to us all!

LIVVY'S DECISION TO LEAVE

I knew there would be mixed responses and feelings about Livvy's decision to leave the Mount, even after August proposed and expressed his love to her. I wrestled with my own decision back and forth on the matter for months. I wanted it to be believable, realistic, and moving. But more than anything, I wanted to be true to Livvy's character.

I wrote the ending in two different ways, one where she chose to stay, and one where she chose to leave—and then stay. The first fell flat. There was no build-up, no monumental decision, no growth. More than anything, it didn't feel true to Livvy's character.

The second, however, the one I settled with, felt far more authentic to Livvy May. After all, she had spent her entire life feeling terrible about her father being disappointed in her and being embarrassed by her, that when she finally discovered the lengths he'd taken to be rid of her, she was crushed, even heartbroken.

With her distorted thoughts, in her muddled mind, and with a parent who put himself before his daughter, she felt she had no other choice than to leave—if only to remove herself from the constant reminder that she was an embarrassment to him.

In order for her to make that final decision to stay with August, she needed to walk away, to see what her life would be like away from the Mount, and she needed to see her father's true thoughts behind his actions. Only then could she finally make the decision for herself—instead of for her father—to stay.

QUOTATIONS

Before I get into the backdrop of the story and share more of what I learned about the beautiful St. Michael's Mount, I wanted to take a moment to share how unbelievably difficult it was to find fifty-eight quotes from obscure titles that matched up with every single one of my chapters. *Insert blank stare here.*

Why I thought it was a good idea to add quotes to each chapter was beyond me. I really thought it'd be fun. A great addition since, you know, Livvy loved to read and all. But what a pig it turned out to be. Don't get me wrong. I'm glad I did it. But the work it took...Seriously. Such a joke.

Also, I need to confess, that while I did my best to ensure that each book quote was taken from a book that would have been one that Livvy could have read herself...I did fudge the lines a bit. *To Know Miss May* takes place in 1815, and...*Persuasion* and *Northanger Abbey* weren't released until 1817. *Insert me hanging my head in shame.* But, like, she could have read them during the time the epilogue was set, so don't even worry about it. I know I won't. *Insert shifty eyes.*

Also, I'm certain there were other books she might have had difficulty getting her hands on—like the translations of rare novels. But where there's a will, there's a way, right?

Going along with those quotes, I was able to use some from *Don Quixote*, which was a fun nod, since Livvy asked August to read the book.

I did learn, however, that the novel was published in two parts, so the large, thick book August had in his hands might have been two. I did find one source, however, that said they had published the two parts as a whole before the Regency Era, so I wouldn't doubt that, with Mrs. Moon's passion for books, she would have made it a point to find an English translation in one bound book.

Okay. Finished with that. I just wanted to dedicate an entire section on how much effort I put into my stupid decision to include those quotes. Honestly, though. I kinda love every single one of them, so I don't regret it one bit.

OSLO WALTZ

Once upon a time, I went to three regency retreats, too afraid to join in with the dancing until the last retreat I attended. During the very last dance of the evening—the Oslo Waltz— my wonderful friends gently urged me to join in on the fun, and I finally caved. And do you know what? It. Was. The. Best.

As such, I had to add it into this story. Funnily enough, I included it first so August and Livvy would dance together, but in the end, August needed to put in a little more effort to dance with Livvy. Instead of waiting for her to come to him in the circle, he strode to her across the dance floor. Far more satisfying! At least, as far as I'm concerned.

MY VISIT TO ST. MICHAEL'S MOUNT

In the Fall of 2022, I was fortunate enough to be able to go back to England after a long, five-year hiatus. But oh, was it worth the wait! We got to see and experience so many new places, and we loved every second of our time there—especially the day we got to spend exploring St. Michael's Mount.

Things were made even more special as we were joined by my brother and sister-in-law (those whom I dedicated this very book to)! They were the best travel companions we could have asked for, helping with the kids and being chill with everything. It was a phenomenal time, and being able to share my love of all things Cornish with them was an utter dream come true—especially when they fell in love with it, too.

I had never heard of the tidal island until my first time in Cornwall when we drove past the Mount and my husband told me about the disappearing causeway. I was utterly enchanted, but we couldn't fit it into our schedule that time, so we had to wait, and wait, and wait until we could see it for ourselves the next trip.

Just as I had hoped, the place was magical. Walking across the causeway was so special—staring at the beautiful stones, having the Mount appear closer and closer with each step. We loved exploring the grounds, walking in the same places that Queen Victoria and Queen Elizabeth II walked, finding the Giant's Heart—more on that later—and eventually touring around the castle, where I was able to get a better idea of where the scenes could take place in my book.

Afterward, we walked back to Marazion and ate incomparable Cornish ice cream while viewing the Mount—just like Livvy would have seen it.

I highly recommend a visit to the Mount if ever you find yourself down in Cornwall. It is the most wonderful of places, and I hope I was able to help convince you of that through this book. There really was such a special feeling there. A love and respect you don't find many places. I so admire those who live there now, keeping the Mount a beautiful place to visit—and that they allow us to enjoy their home, as well.

While there, I was able to learn so many things about the incredible work happening on the Mount, as well as the rich history of the tidal island as a whole. I won't share everything with you. That would be insane. And even though I want to, because I'm a little insane, I'll just share the things I found most interesting, taking you on a little tour around the Mount. Ready??

THE CAUSEWAY

Marazion and the Mount have been connected for hundreds of years, though the current causeway today was created in the 20th century. It is under water for fifteen hours out of every twenty-four, if not more, so those living on the Mount have to take the boat to and from at high tides.

The causeway has to be maintained continuously, and during the last major storm there, it was destroyed in large parts. The workers found pieces of granite washed up on the shore and used them to patch the causeway back up after years of work.

It takes only about fifteen minutes to walk across the causeway, but the views are unmatched from it!

THE HARBOR

For the record, fishing is not allowed off the harbor wall at the Mount, so don't try to do what August and Nicholas were doing. Heh. One of my favorite things I learned about the harbor, however, was that it was said that kids could jump from boat to boat when the Mount was thriving.

AUGUST'S RESCUE OF THE SHOE—FOR REAL LIFE!

This is my favorite story ever—because it happened in real life! This was actually the very first scene I knew I would add into this story, so I was dying when I finally got to write it!

The true story goes...I was at Charlestown with my husband and kids, standing on the harbor, the wall jutting out into the sea. My daughter was dancing around, ran to my husband, then ran back to me, ultimately tripping on one of the pieces of stone sticking out.

Her brand-new shoe that lit up when she walked somehow shot off her foot, then tumbled toward the edge of the harbor until it plopped right down into the water. My daughter just stared, shocked it even happened.

I, however, was absolutely mortified. Naturally. I was ready to just get the heck out of there to escape the attention it had just caused. But a kind man stopped us, pointed to the fishermen behind us, then asked them for their help, suggesting they use their poles to fish the shoe out.

One fisherman walked forward, stared down into the water, then said, "It's too nice a day to stay out of the water." He stripped off his shirt, then jumped straight down into the harbor, to everyone's delight and surprise. He swam to the shoe, then delivered it promptly to my daughter who was beaming. We all were! The gathered crowd around us cheered, and the man said, "you might want to dry that first," before walking away with a laugh.

One of my favorite memories ever—and one we were able to record, as well!

SUGAR LOAF INN

The Mount used to be a very busy place, especially during the early 1800s, when it thrived with three hundred people living there—as opposed to around thirty now. They had three schools, a chapel, three public houses used by visiting sailors, a pilchard press, and, yes, three pubs! The Sugar Loaf Inn—a gentleman's only pub—was the actual name of one of the pubs on the Mount. It is now the change house, however, but can still be seen during visits.

THE GIANT'S WELL & THE GIANT'S HEART

Walking up the Mount on the tree-covered pathway, you happen swiftly upon the Giant's Well & the Giant's Heart, holding one of my favorite legends in all of Cornwall—Cormoran the Giant and Jack the Giant Killer.

Just like Livvy said, the legend tells of Cormoran the Giant terrorizing the mainland by eating and stealing animals and (in some stories) even children. Jack the Giant Killer was the only one brave enough to fight against the giant's tyranny. He snuck on the Mount one night and worked to dig a deep hole in the ground, then he lured the giant toward it with a loud blast of his horn. Cormoran fell into the hole, and his reign was ended. However, a small part of him remained—his small, dark heart, too strong to destroy.

Isn't that amazing? Now you can decide for yourself which version to believe—Livvy's or the original tale!

Also, the well on the Mount was rumored to be the hole that Jack had dug, though in reality, it was the main source of water for the castle and the rest of the Mount—along with a number of other natural springs on the island—until only about a hundred years ago.

COW-KEEPERS

There really were a herd of Jersey cows on the Mount that provided the St. Aubyn family and others with milk, butter, and cheese. There were cow-keepers, as well, but the Otterhams were obviously my own invention. Despite my best efforts, I could never find the names of any of the real cow-keepers on the Mount!

GARDEN ON ST. MICHAEL'S MOUNT

On our visit to St. Michael's Mount, I didn't get the chance to see the gardens, ironically enough, since they were closed for the season, but at the top of the balcony—the balcony August and Livvy, you know...kiss—we were able to spot the gardens from above, and they were stunning.

During the Regency Era, only the three-tiered walled gardens were there, the terraces built later on, so I did the best I could to show what the gardens might have looked like at that time. Unfortunately, there wasn't a lot of information on the flowers planted during that time, so every plant and flower I included is either in the gardens now or has been planted around Cornwall at some time or another.

And this probably goes without saying, but just to be clear, Mr. Caddy, Mr. May, and August were not real head gardeners.

SIR JOHN

Sir John was a real person! It was difficult to find which Sir John was during the Regency Era, as I believe there were four or five of them, but once I found him, I knew I wanted to include him in the story because he was quite an eccentric person. He fathered fifteen illegitimate children, eventually wedding the mother of the last nine, was friends with the painter Opie, collected cacti, and restored the church. And, just like August said, he was well-respected and well-loved by others.

SILVER RIBBON ON THE SEA

The current Lord and Lady St. Levan, those who live in the castle now, shared what it looks like when the moon shimmers on the sea, saying the causeway appeared like a "silver foot-path across the water."

I loved that detail, and though it's only visible from the castle inside, I fudged the lines a bit and had it visible in the gardens instead.

THE CHURCH

The church was restored in 1811, just like August said, and it really is spectacular with its stone pillars. The bronze statue of St. Michael is a modern-day addition, though I chose to include it to help August on his journey of finding courage to stand up to Mr. May. The stained-glass panels were installed in 1811, though, so that was accurate!

CHEVY CHASE ROOM

Honestly, when I first toured around this room, I was so confused by the name. Why would they name a historical room after the guy in National Lampoon's Christmas Vacation? However, I soon learned that Chevy Chase refers to the medieval ballad of that name, and the hunting scene in the frieze that runs around the room references to the ballad, not the man. (Of course.)

The hunting scene around the room has been beautifully restored and even shows someone riding an ostrich into battle. It's amazing!

CONCLUSION

It was phenomenal learning so much about St. Michael's Mount, visiting the stunning location, then writing a story to hopefully show my respect and love for the culture found there. I loved every second of it, and I hope you did, too.

If you haven't already, join me on Instagram and Facebook, then sign up for my newsletter to never miss a new release. I always share photos and videos from my recent trips to the UK —and Cornwall!—as well as giveaways and the latest news about my books. I'd love to have you join me!

Also, if you enjoyed this book, please consider leaving a review here. Reviews help authors out so much because that is how people hear about our books.

Until next time!
Deborah

ACKNOWLEDGMENTS

I am so grateful to all the people who helped me finish this book. First, Kasey Stockton, Jess Heileman, and Martha Keyes. Thank you for reading the first chapters and giving me the encouragement I needed to keep going on!

Next, I need to express my profound gratitude for Joanna Barker for reading the final draft of this story at the last minute and with a ridiculous time crunch. You always drop everything for my books, and I can't thank you enough for doing that again for this story!

Thank you to all of my readers and all of the bookstagrammers who encouraged me to keep going with this book. Ashley, Mandy, Kristin, Tasha, Marilee, and so many others—your timely messages always gave me the boosts I needed to finish on time!

Thank you to Arlem Hawks who is always there to chat, commiserate, and share her wisdom when I so desperately need it.

Thank you to the other authors in the Castles and Courtship series, Jennie Goutet, Ashtyn Newbold, Kasey Stockton, Rebecca Connolly, Martha Keyes, Sally Britton, and Mindy

Burbidge Strunk! (Plus Jess Heileman, our hype girl!) You ladies are always such a pleasure to work with!

Christian, my best friend. I'm so grateful I get to walk through life with you. Thank you for always being there for me, and thank you for your encouragement. How I love you!

The last few years—and the last few months—have brought one storm after another into my life and the lives of those I love. I'm grateful for Heavenly Father and my Savior, Jesus Christ, for Their ever-present guidance and help, and for the peace and courage I find in Them. I will forever be grateful for the calling from Them to bring light into this world through my writing.

OTHER BOOKS IN THE CASTLES & COURTSHIP SERIES

An Amiable Foe by Jennie Goutet

To Know Miss May by Deborah M. Hathaway

A Heart to Keep by Ashtyn Newbold

A Noble Inheritance by Kasey Stockton

The Rules of Matchmaking by Rebecca Connolly

A Suitable Arrangement by Martha Keyes

An Engagement with the Enemy by Sally Britton

Charming the Recluse by Mindy Burbidge Strunk

ABOUT THE AUTHOR

Deborah M. Hathaway graduated from Utah State University with a BA in Creative Writing. As a young girl, she devoured Jane Austen's novels while watching and re-watching every adaptation of Pride & Prejudice she could, entirely captured by all things Regency and romance.

Throughout her early life, she wrote many short stories, poems, and essays, but it was not until after her marriage that she was finally able to complete her first romance novel, attributing the completion to her courtship with, and love of, her charming, English husband. Deborah finds her inspiration for her novels in her everyday experiences with her husband and children and during her travels to the United Kingdom, where she draws on the beauty of the country in such places as England, Scotland, and her beloved Cornwall.

Made in the USA
Las Vegas, NV
04 September 2024